Searching for Eleanor

Book one

By
Lilly Adam

ISBN: 9798712627028

Dedicated to my wonderful readers; I hope you enjoy reading this book as much as I enjoyed writing it.

One day you will ask me
Which is more important?
My life or yours?
I will say mine
And you will walk away
Not knowing
That you are my life.
Khalil Gibran

Also written by Lilly Adam:

May of Ashley Green
Stella
Poppy Woods
The Whipple Girl
Rose
Whitechapel Lass
Daisy Grey
Beneath the Apple Blossom Tree
Faye
Secrets of the Gatehouse

CHAPTER ONE
July 1875

"Be sure to spend at least an hour practising your piano scales whilst I'm away, Eleanor, all ears and eyes will be on you come Saturday *and* your father will be home, eager to witness you receiving your award!" As usual, Beatrice Jackson was elegantly dressed and in a hurry to impress the ladies at yet another one of the afternoon tea parties to which she'd been invited to.

"Mamma, it's not guaranteed that I will win, you know; in fact, it's more likely that I will come last! There will be far more talented girls entering the recital competition!" stressed Eleanor, sensing that her mother was not listening to a word of her continuous objections. "When will you be home?" she added.

Beatrice stood in front of the ornate hall mirror, her blue eyes fully focussed on her reflection as she gently lowered the wide-brimmed, afternoon hat onto her head, tilting it to a slight angle before securing it with a lengthy hatpin. Eleanor watched with intrigue as her mother held out her hands as far from her sight as was possible, appearing to examine them before slipping on her lace gloves.

"It's a terrifying ordeal when a woman ages and begins to notice her beauty deteriorating!" she declared, taking a step closer to the mirror to study her face.

"*Mamma*! You are one of the finest looking women in Oxford and you are definitely not ageing. You're forty-three, not sixty!"

Beatrice shuddered at the sound of her age.

"My sweet, Eleanor, what would I do without your encouragement...you are a treasure!"

Blowing a kiss in the air, Beatrice Jackson quickly left the modest townhouse, without answering the question of when she'd return, leaving Eleanor to the boring task of practising her scales.

The pleasant odour of vanilla alerted Eleanor that Peggy was baking and instantly led her towards the kitchen in search of a treat. Peggy had been with the Jackson family since Eleanor was a baby, initially employed by Edward Jackson to help out around the house during Beatrice's confinement; nearly fifteen years later, she had become like one of the family and was indispensable. Peggy was a woman of many talents, taking care of the housework, cooking and the general running of the house. A wholesome woman in her early sixties, she had never married and no longer had any living family, but seemed to relish in living and working in the Jackson's home.

"How on earth did I guess that you'd soon be down here, Ellie?" Peggy teased.

Eleanor looked around the kitchen, immediately feeling sorry for Peggy having to wash so many dishes and clean the dreadful mess which surrounded her; there wasn't a surface spared from a heavy dusting of flour.

"Golly! Did the sack of flour explode, Peggy?"

"I don't want to hear any of your cheek, young lady; I told that delivery lad to put the sack of flour in the cupboard, but the foolish pup went and put it on the blooming top shelf...Perhaps he thinks that I grow a foot taller when I'm standing in my kitchen. Well, to cut a long story short, Ellie, I pulled it down with the washing pole, the sack split open, fell to the ground and for a fearful second there was such a dense cloud of flour, that I thought I'd never be seen again!"

Eleanor giggled, "Don't worry, Peggy; I'll help you clean up the mess!"

With her hands on her wide hips, Peggy shook her head, "Oh no, *Miss Jackson*, I've had strict instructions from your mamma that you have to practice... "

"I know!" interrupted Eleanor. "Practice my scales so that I make Pappa proud when he attends the stupid recital on Saturday. I don't know why it's so important; my father only comes home once in a blue moon, it's obvious he doesn't care too much about us!"

"That's a wicked thing to say, Eleanor! I'll pretend I've got flour in my ears and didn't hear it. By all accounts, your father works long hard hours in London so that you and your dear mamma don't go without! He's a kind and thoughtful man, if ever I've known one, and I'll not hear a bad word said against him!"

"Well, *I'd* prefer to *know* my father and see him every day rather than get myself into a nervous pickle on the rare occasions that he does come home! I suppose *that* mouth-watering cake is in his honour too!"

"Indeed it is; he has a sweet tooth, does your pappa and he always compliments my baking; it would be a crying shame not to spoil him a little when he comes to visit!"

"Well, I think you make far too much fuss of my father, Peggy, but I guess you feel a little obliged since it was he who gave you the position in our house!"

Peggy's smiling face changed to one of raging thunder all of a sudden, she turned her back on Eleanor and grabbed hold of the broom as she mumbled under her breath.

"Let me sweep the floor, Peggy while you finish your masterpiece!" stressed Eleanor, sensing that she'd spoken out of turn and upset Peggy.

"Maybe I'll have a word with your pappa on Saturday and tell him how your manners seem to be slipping! Go to your piano Eleanor and let me get on with my chores! You have no idea, my girl!"

Eleanor marched out of the kitchen, annoyed with Peggy and even more annoyed that she'd not managed to claim one of Peggy's delicious sweet buns, which she'd noticed on the cooling rack. She pondered on Peggy's words, wondering what she meant. Putting off her mundane assignment, Eleanor wandered through the finely furnished house, brushing her hands across every gleaming surface and stopping every few seconds to study the ornaments and pretty vases which were placed throughout and which had been a part of her life for as long as she could remember. She eyed the piano, crossly, thinking of how she'd much rather spend her time painting or sketching and already felt quite sure that she'd fail to perform well during Saturday's recital. She simply wasn't passionate about music and with her father sat in the audience, causing her to be a nervous wreck, she would be sure to play all the wrong notes.

Feeling lonely and bored and in defiance that she'd not be playing a single note, while her mother was out, Eleanor threw herself onto the couch where she contemplated many aspects of her life. Her mother was seldom at home, her father was like a stranger to her and she had no siblings. Peggy was nice enough, she considered, but even *she* had a tendency to switch moods in the blinking of an eye and she was too old and out of touch with the modern days of 1875. Overwhelmed with misery, Eleanor flung open the piano and channelled all of her anger into the ivory keys, bashing them loudly and carelessly, in tune only with her tears as they trickled down her cheeks.

Saturday soon arrived and filled Eleanor with such a panicky disposition that she could barely string a sentence together. The reality of the recital, which was to be held in the university's huge Holywell Music Room, had at last registered with her and she could no longer remain in denial about the dreaded day. Edward Jackson had arrived from London on the previous evening and had spent some private time with Beatrice before chatting for over an hour in the kitchen with Peggy. He had nervously placed a small package into Eleanor's hands on his arrival. She couldn't help but wonder if he felt as uncomfortable around her as she felt in his company. A dainty silver bracelet with dangling black jet gemstones fitted Eleanor's wrist perfectly. She thanked her pappa but felt shy to kiss him as she'd done on previous occasions.

 "Don't you have a cuddle for you darling pappa, Eleanor?" voiced Beatrice.

Red-faced, Edward was quick to reply, "Beatrice my darling, our daughter is a young woman now and is saving all her kisses for her future husband!"

Eleanor felt her entire body turn a shade of puce; of all the things to say, why had he said that she thought, feeling embarrassed and wishing she could simply vanish from sight.

"I'm going to help Peggy in the kitchen!" she blurted out before dashing off.

There were thirty young women taking part in the competition, Eleanor recognized only a handful of them as she took her nominated seat. It appeared that every one of the pianists had chosen to wear gowns in cream or subtle shades of pale pink and blue, causing Eleanor to look completely out of place in her midnight blue gown. Her mother had insisted the deep shade would show off her beautiful golden hair, emphasis her mesmerizing, lagoon blue eyes and not fail in catching the eye of the judges, even though Eleanor had reminded her that it was their ears which needed to be caught. Eleanor was to be the eighth to play her piece and as she sat nervously, with her hands sweating profusely, she could feel the eyes of the surrounding young women repeatedly glancing at her and smirking. She stood out like a beetle in a blossom tree and felt what little confidence she had, slowly ebb away.

The sixth pianist had just been called to take her place behind the impressive grand piano and had begun to play Beethoven's Moonlight Sonata when there was a sudden and loud thump in the audience which was quickly followed by a loud chorus of women's cries and gasps.

Presuming that one of the ladies had swooned in the stuffy hall, Eleanor was more concerned as to how the distraction might affect the performance of the strikingly attractive, Elizabeth Van der Meer, but within minutes her recital was forced to a halt and all eyes were now focussed on the audience. Suddenly catching sight of her mother standing out of her seat and in a state of distress, whispers soon travelled throughout the hall that a man in the audience had collapsed and might even have died. It was the perfect opportunity for Eleanor to rush from her place and hopefully, not have to return. She was met with the most distressing sight she'd ever seen in her life; her mother was now sobbing loudly as she cradled Edward Jackson's head in her arms. Eleanor looked on in disbelief, having never witnessed her mother so upset and so careless of her appearance in front of so many people. Eleanor almost felt embarrassed for her. Her father's face was hidden beneath the voluminous sleeves of her mother's gown and although Eleanor knew that she should have joined her mother in similar hysterics, she could only watch in wonder. A doctor had been sent for, but with a young scholar of medicine, who happened to be in the audience, already having quietly uttered that he couldn't find a beating pulse anywhere in Edward Jackson's lifeless body, it was merely a formality.

The entire competition had to be adjourned for an hour and with a sigh of relief, Eleanor already had a strong sense that she would not be taking place in the dreaded presentation.

CHAPTER TWO

Over the next few days, Eleanor was witness to
many peculiar events. As was expected, Beatrice
Jackson was in a continuous state of emotional
distress, which caused Eleanor to feel a little
guilty that she was not finding the sudden death
of her father anywhere near as heartbreaking.
She did love her father, as any daughter was
dutifully expected to, but a strong and adhering
bond was missing between them and she could
hardly miss a man who'd barely been a part of
her life. Eleanor often found herself wondering
why her mother was so overly upset since she
too had spent little time at her husband's side
and enjoyed a full and invigorating life,
mingling with Oxford's high society ladies. She
concluded that the close and very personal
relationship which her parents had initially
shared was the reason behind her excessive
floods of tears and hysterical outbursts. When
her mother was approachable, Eleanor persisted
in questioning her as to why her father's body
had been sent to London. Her mother gave no
answers but repeatedly said that she would
explain when she knew more, before bursting
into tears. Eleanor was baffled, but daren't bring
up the question of her father's funeral.
Peggy had been another mystery to Eleanor; she
appeared so shocked by the event that her tears

were never far from trickling out of her permanently watery eyes. With the constant look of worry etched upon her round face, Eleanor suspected that she was worried about losing her position with the family, should their finances be drastically changed by her father's untimely demise.

It was two days after Edward Jackson's death that Eleanor made another alarming discovery; the sudden disappearance of Peggy. Expecting her to be preparing a light breakfast, there was no sign of her in the kitchen. Eleanor checked in the garden and the cellar before assuming that she'd made a quick dash to the grocery, a couple of streets away, but as the morning dragged on, still with no sign of her, Eleanor concluded that even Peggy couldn't be chatting to the locals for such an extended period. Thinking that perhaps Peggy might have overslept, even though it had never happened before, she decided to check in her room and was thoroughly shocked at what she discovered; her bed had been stripped back to the bare mattress, Peggy was nowhere to be seen and neither were any of her belongings. After fourteen years, she had packed up and left without even saying goodbye to her. Eleanor hurried to her mamma's room, desperate to disclose her discovery but, once again, was left in total astonishment when her mother failed to show a single sign of shock.

"Why would she just leave, so suddenly?"

questioned Eleanor. "She didn't even tell me or say goodbye!"

"My darling; Peggy has gone and we will simply have to make do without her!"

Eleanor was not at all happy with her mother's response and could only put it down to the fact that she was in mourning and seemed to have lost all concern for worldly affairs.

Eleanor had limited cooking skills, and having never seen her mother set foot into the kitchen, she presumed that she too would possess no expertise and she was right. Beatrice Jackson seemed to be under the illusion that Peggy had taught Eleanor how to cook and was thrown into more dismay when she discovered the truth.

"All those hours I've spent socialising with *my ladies* and you didn't learn *anything* from Peggy!" she expressed after hunger had eventually dragged her from her bedroom, where she'd remained since the day of Edward's death. Eleanor searched through every cupboard in the kitchen; having finished off the last of the stale bread she was irritated by her mother's comments.

"Mamma, you never *once* told me to learn how to cook...practice that blessed piano until my fingers ached and improve on my sketching and painting skills...those were your instructions. Why can't you simply employ another cook to come and work here?"

"I can't possibly discuss that now, Eleanor, I'm

far too famished and need some sustenance...there must be something in the larder that's edible, without too much cooking knowledge needed!"

"I found a few eggs which I could boil, I suppose?" suggested Eleanor.

"It will *have* to do, bring the breakfast into the dining room, my darling. Will it take long?"

"I don't think so," sighed Eleanor, miserably, feeling more like her mother's maid than her daughter.

The eggs were boiled until the water had completely evaporated; she'd found a packet of plain, dry biscuits in the pantry and had also managed to make a pot of tea, all after burning her fingers on the stove which took over an hour to kindle. With painful fingers, Eleanor carried the heavy tray into the dining room only to find that Beatrice had dozed off to sleep again in the armchair.

"*I've burnt my fingers,* **Mamma** *and they hurt so much!*" she announced, loudly, as she slammed the tray down onto the polished table. Beatrice woke up immediately, eyeing the food in front of her and appearing quite disappointed.

"What did you say my darling?"

"I said that I burnt my fingers on the stove!" Beatrice had already bit into one of the solid eggs, giving Eleanor only the briefest of attention.

"Eat some food, my darling; it will soon make

you feel better!"

Becoming even more annoyed by her mother's careless attitude, Eleanor proceeded to pour the weak tea. It was hot and washed down the eggs and dry biscuits, but it didn't taste like Peggy's tea.

"I hope you're not expecting me to do the cooking every day, Mamma, because I really don't know how! Do you think that Peggy will ever return to us or let us know where she is?" Beatrice finished her tea and stared hard at Eleanor,

"What is it, Mamma? Have I done something wrong?"

"Don't be foolish, my sweet girl. It is me who has done something wrong; something so terribly wrong that I fear you might never forgive me!"

Eleanor felt the sudden invasion of butterflies in her stomach, her mother's face was sombre and Eleanor had a bad feeling about what her mother was about to disclose.

"Oh Mamma, how could you even think such a thought...there couldn't possibly be anything on earth that you could do that I'd not forgive you for! I completely understand if we can no longer afford to pay for a cook or a housemaid; it might even be fun learning how to cook...we could take it in turns, but perhaps you could spend less time with your associates though when you come out of mourning."

Beatrice's glum look remained on her face, she'd neglected her appearance since the death of Edward and hadn't bothered to dress or even put the brush through her blonde, wavy hair. Eleanor wished she could do or say something which would cheer her a little and she also wished her mother would be more open as to why there had been no talk of a funeral or why her father's body had been so swiftly taken to London.

"In four days, my darling, we will travel to London…"

"Is that when poor, Pappa is to be laid to rest? Why can't his funeral take place in Oxford? It will be such a journey every time we wish to visit his grave!"

"Your Pappa is being buried today, my sweetheart; I'm sorry, Eleanor, but you won't be able to attend. In four days we are to meet at the solicitor's office to witness the reading of his will."

"I don't understand…is he to be buried all alone, without us there to say our final goodbyes…"

"No more questions, for the time being, *Eleanor*, my head is splitting; I think I will return to my bed!"

With no time for Eleanor to voice her protests or ask any more questions, with her hand clutching her brow, her mother swiftly left the dining room.

During the following few days, Eleanor occupied her time by going through the pages of Mrs Beeton's Book of Household Management, optimistic of being able to present her mother with something tasty and appetizing, but without the basic knowledge of cookery, Eleanor found the terminology of the recipes incomprehensible. Being so famished and having consumed the last of the eggs, Eleanor left her home on Henley Road and walked into Oxford. With the meagre amount of money in her savings, she was able to purchase half a dozen eggs, three packets of biscuits, a large loaf and four jam tarts. Instead of putting a smile upon her mother's face, the treats only caused Beatrice to work herself up into a frenzy as she worried that any one of her acquaintances might have spotted Eleanor shopping for groceries. Eleanor was now of the opinion that her mother's, so-called, 'high society' friends were not friends at all; not one single caller had asked after her mother's well being since she'd disappeared from the social calendar all week and with Edward's untimely death taking place in such a public venue, where all of her cronies were in attendance, it was common knowledge of her fate. Beatrice insisted that it was only polite to leave oneself to grieve privately within the family circle and wouldn't hear a negative word spoken about her dear companions. Eleanor was under the impression that she and her mother were to visit her father's grave in London before attending the reading of his will. Fully dressed in their black mourning ensemble, they took the London bound stagecoach from nearby St Clements and after a dull and miserable journey, on a day when the sun had not yet revealed herself, they arrived at the busy London coaching inn and walked the remainder of the journey. Eleanor was a stranger to London; it had been ten years ago since her previous visit, which had left her with only vague memories of the day. Her mother, however, clearly knew her way around the bustling streets and marched with her head held high along the cobblestone pathways with Eleanor at her side, trying to keep up with her. She was in the most sombre of moods and Eleanor had almost given up all attempts of conversing with her.

"How far is it to the cemetery, Mamma?" she dared to ask when her feet began to ache.

"That is not our destination, Eleanor!" spoke her mother sternly, without even making eye contact with her daughter.

Suddenly turning off the main thoroughfare, Beatrice declared that they'd reached their destination as she led Eleanor down a narrow side street and through the glossy door of a house with a highly polished brass nameplate, *Thornberry &Son,* above the lintel. Eleanor looked around her as they waited in the smart and inviting lobby which was pleasantly bright with its white painted walls, black and white floor tiles and tall ornate brass plant stands, which held an interesting array of mature greenery. She could smell coffee and cigar smoke, a warming combination, which immediately reminded her of her pappa; it was the first time since his death that she'd felt like bursting into tears. She blinked rapidly, feeling her cheeks burning.

"Are you alright, Eleanor?"

It was the first time that her mother had taken any notice of her all week, mused Eleanor.

"Yes, mother. Why are we..."

Eleanor's intended question was interrupted as a young man, no older than fifteen and dressed in an uncomfortable-looking, oversized black suit, suddenly came out from one of the adjoining doors.

"Mrs Whitlock?"

Eleanor immediately felt like pulling the immature man up on his mistake; fancy using her mother's maiden name, she thought, but at the same time noticed how her mother had not even batted an eyelid at his mistake.

"Yes," she replied, formally, "I do apologise for my tardiness, I'm not local as I'm sure you are aware."

The man smiled politely, "That's perfectly alright, Ma'am, would you and your daughter like to follow me, Mr Thornberry is waiting for you."

Without further ado, they soon found themselves inside a spacious but overcrowded office. Eleanor felt uncomfortable; she didn't like crowds of strangers or being confined, it reminded her of her childhood and her mother's stuffy afternoon teas when she was forced to mingle with copious unfamiliar women who would stare hard at her and ask questions, which she inevitably was unable to answer, leaving her embarrassed and red-faced.

A group of strangers were all seated on straight back, wooden chairs to one side of the room. Eleanor and her mother were escorted to similar chairs, but for some bizarre reason, they were positioned on the opposite side, appearing detached and quite lonely. Mr Thornberry, A middle-aged and overweight gentleman sat behind a huge pedestal desk, as though protected from the band of invaders who'd descended upon his office. His large face conveyed a serious expression and he barely smiled as he greeted Beatrice with a polite 'good morning'. He briskly nodded his head to Eleanor before proceeding to open the large envelope in front of him as he muttered, somewhat annoyingly, under his breath, 'how time was getting on'.

As he began to talk in an official language which was quite incomprehensible to Eleanor, she furtively glanced from beneath her veiled hat, towards the huddle of strangers and taken by complete shock, gasped audibly as she noticed Peggy. She was sitting in the corner, almost hidden from view and wearing a concealing dark grey bonnet, tilted at such an angle to obscure as much of her face as was possible. Eleanor was suddenly overcome by the oddest of feelings and knew that she had been kept in the dark for many years about her family. She felt sorry for her mamma, who sat ashen-faced, appearing troubled and lonely and for the first time, Eleanor thought that her mother looked older than her forty-three years. She shuffled her chair closer to her, causing a loud scraping across the polished wooden floor. Mr Thornberry paused his reading for a brief moment and sipped his water. Eleanor now decided she should pay attention to what this man was reading out, with a strong and disturbing feeling that it was not going to be pleasing to her mother.

As the solicitor's voice droned on monotonously, Eleanor slowly began to realise that the young man had not made a mistake by referring to her mother as Mrs Whitlock, but had been kind in not referring to her as '*Miss*'. Eleanor's parents had not been married. Eleanor sat dumbstruck, coming to terms with the truth that she was, in fact, illegitimate. Her late father, it was slowly divulged, was married to one of the women who she dared not to glance at, on the opposite side of the office.

As the room became unbearably hot and stuffy, the words which seemed to echo off the walls were all concerned with large sums of money and legal jargon. Eleanor closed her ears to Mr Thornberry and concerned herself wholly with her mother who now looked completely grief-stricken.

The meeting came to an end and Mr Thornberry appeared in a sudden hurry to empty his office as he stood with his hand poised to shake the hands of each person. Beatrice was the first to leave, almost jumping off her seat as though it was scorching hot; Eleanor took a grip of her arm, feeling sure that her poor mamma required support.

"Thank you for attending, Miss Whitlock, you will be receiving further instructions regarding the tenancy of the property which you reside in, in due course."

Beatrice was unable to respond, leaving Eleanor to say a quick goodbye in a very small and shaky voice.

Outside, the strong July sun beat down onto the dusty pavement and the sudden brightness outside the solicitor's office caused them both to squint. Beatrice was also blinded by her tears. Eleanor glanced at her mother's miserable face and sensed that they were about to begin a new and harsh stage in their lives.

"Shall we find a tea room, Mamma; I think we would both benefit from a cup of tea and a slice of cake."

 "*No*, Eleanor, there is much to sort out in Oxford and I am desperate to leave these *awful* surroundings! Let's make haste to the coaching inn."

 "Very well, Mamma, as you wish."

 The journey home was one of near silence and although Beatrice closed her eyes for the entire duration, Eleanor knew her mother was not asleep but in a faraway place with her troubled mind. Thankfully there was only one other passenger in the carriage; a young woman who sat with her head in a book and only spoke to make polite greetings. Eleanor couldn't remove the image of Peggy from her mind; she was desperate to find out why she'd been present in the solicitor's office and why she pretended to be a stranger to them, after fourteen years of living under the same roof. It was quite unbelievable she deliberated.

CHAPTER THREE

As they stepped over the threshold into their modest townhouse in Henley Road, Eleanor was suddenly reminded of how there was very little food in the pantry. She felt her stomach rumbling, they hadn't eaten since breakfast and she was ravenous.

"I'm going to walk into Cowley Road Mamma; I believe there is a pie shop there and I'm too tired and hungry to stumble about in the kitchen trying to produce anything remotely edible."

Beatrice was clearly distressed by the announcement, "My darling, you can't do that, what if you're seen!"

"Does it really matter anymore, Mamma? Are we to starve to death now to add to our misery?"

"But we have our reputation to consider, Eleanor! Nobody can take that away from us!" she cried, distressingly.

"Mamma I'm going to buy two pies, I'm quite sure it won't bring any shame upon us!" Eleanor protested.

"But those places are frequented by the commoners, not people like us, my darling!"

"Well maybe we should become acquainted with the commoners then, Mamma, because from what I understood after today's adventure, we will soon be joining them!"

Eleanor hadn't meant to be so brutal in her reply

but, she was tired and hungry and fed up with her mother's insistence that they were part of Oxford's social elite. She had spent years mingling with the high society circles of Oxford and as far as Eleanor could see, it had got her nowhere; in her mother's hour of need, they were nowhere to be found. As Beatrice curled up in a ball on the couch and sobbed, Eleanor felt as though their roles had been switched. Ignoring her mother's childlike tantrum, she took some pennies from Beatrice's reticule and hurried out of the house, determined to feed them both and hopefully put them in a better frame of mind to discuss their plans for the future.

As she rushed along a narrow side street, leading to Cowley Road, Eleanor's mind was engrossed in the day's events. So much had happened since the day of the piano recital; she had lost her Pappa and although she knew she should be in mourning, it now seemed that he wasn't the man she'd thought he was and hadn't even been married to her mother. There had been too much to comprehend in so few days and then there was Peggy; she had behaved like a complete stranger in the solicitor's office. Why was she seated with the group of strangers and why had her mother hidden such a huge secret from her, throughout her life. Eleanor was so absorbed in her thoughts that she failed to notice the young man who stepped out from a nearby house, onto the pavement, a few feet in front of her; she collided straight into him.

"Oh gosh!" she exclaimed, feeling her cheeks blushing instantly, a most annoying tendency which having fair skin always caused. "I'm so sorry; I wasn't looking where I was going!"

The man bent down to pick up his bundle of books which had flown through the air during the collision.

"Don't be sorry, Miss, I'm a strong believer in fate and it's not every day that I get assaulted in broad daylight by such a pretty girl!"

Eleanor was lost for words, she wasn't sure if the man was joking; his tone was serious.

"I *did* apologise, you know!" she eventually said, indignantly.

"Allow me to escort you to your destination, Miss; I wouldn't be able to live with myself if the next person you walk into comes off worse than me!"

About to give the obnoxious man a piece of her mind, he suddenly broke into a loud and infectious chuckle,

"I'm sorry, but your face is a picture!"

"Well yours isn't!" voiced Eleanor as she continued crossly on her journey.

Thankfully, the pie shop was almost empty; the warming aroma of pastry caused Eleanor to lick her lips as she ordered four of the pies, having foresight for the following day. They were hastily wrapped in old newspaper leaving

Eleanor slightly embarrassed by the thought of having to carry such a parcel through the streets. She prayed that her mamma wouldn't catch sight of her. The man had followed her to the pie shop and was stood waiting outside,

"Don't think that I'm following you, Miss, but I just had to apologise sincerely for my rude outburst; I sensed that you didn't take my first apology seriously!"

For the first time, Eleanor glanced at the man's face; he had a strong angular jaw and was clean-shaven apart from a faint brown moustache which appeared soft, unlike her late pappa's coarse and prickly one, which had an unsightly tobacco stain to its centre.

"It doesn't matter at all, not after the terrible few days I've had, in fact, I'm quite glad that I've managed to put a smile on somebody's face"

The man stretched out his arms, "Let me carry your package, Miss, it's the least I can do," Eleanor's hesitation did not go unnoticed.

"Trust me, Miss, I simply want to make up for my earlier discourtesy, I'm a harmless soul!"

Eleanor liked him, he had an honest face and she liked the way he spoke. She noticed the ingrained ink stains on his fingers as she passed him the hot parcel,

"Very well, if it will make you sleep better tonight, I will gladly accept your offer!"

"Is your cook unwell tonight then?" he teased. "Has your home run out of soap and water?"

she replied.

"Certainly not, these ink marks are the sign of a hard-working pen pusher!"

"Don't you mean a pen smith?"

"I prefer pen pusher; sounds far more arduous, don't you agree? And what about your cook?"

"How do you know that I even *have* a cook?" quizzed Eleanor.

"By your awkward stance when you were purchasing your supper!"

"I hope you weren't studying my every move Mr...Pen Pusher!"

"I have to admit, that I'd love to laugh again but am fearful of repeating history!"

"A chance meeting in the street could hardly be construed as history! And yes, my cook *is* sick if you insist on delving into my family's staffing affairs!"

"As I said earlier, it was pure fate which enabled our paths to cross!"

"Then it will surely be pure fate that will see our paths uncrossing, Mr Pen Pusher; now if you'd kindly return my parcel, I assure you that you've earned my forgiveness."

The man immediately held the parcel above his head, knocking off his lofty hat as he did so,

"Walk out with me on Sunday afternoon, Miss...I don't believe we've yet been introduced!" he announced, cheekily.

Eleanor knew her mother would be horrified if she'd witnessed her conversing and walking the streets with a complete stranger, but there was something about him that she was growing quite fond of; he was light and funny and not overbearing, like the young men in her mother's social circles.

"I'm Eleanor."

"What an enchanting name, I will be sure to include that name in my next chapter!"

"Oh! And I suppose *your* name is *Charles Dickens* or *Thomas Hardy*!"

"No! Of course, it isn't; I'm far too young to be either of those fine gentlemen, but one day I *will* be a household name in the world of literacy!"

Eleanor giggled, more so at his animated face than his statement, "It is always good to have ambition, I suppose!"

"My name is August Miller! I want you to remember that just in case fate decides to separate our paths once more. One day you might find yourself reading my work!"

"I do declare, Mr Miller, you certainly are dramatic enough to have the makings of an author!"

"So, will you accept my invitation for a Sunday afternoon stroll, sweet Eleanor? May I call for you?"

"As much as I'd love to accept, Mr Miller, I will have to decline. You see, my family is in mourning...I am not dressed in black because I favour the gloom of it. My pappa was suddenly taken from us, last week!"

The expression upon August Miller's face instantly changed as he slowly lowered the parcel from above his head and handed it to Eleanor.

"Please accept my deepest condolences, Miss Eleanor...It is a harsh and cruel test in life to lose a parent. I will bid you a good evening and wish you well in your darkest of periods!"

As Eleanor walked the remaining few yards alone she felt her heart sink, she would have enjoyed a Sunday meeting with the amiable August Miller, he was like a ray of bright sunshine entering her miserable life. She wondered if their paths would ever cross again and found herself hopeful of another chance meeting with him.

Beatrice hadn't moved from the couch, she was snoring gently and looked to be in the most uncomfortable of positions. Still fully dressed and with her boots tightly laced, her wide-brimmed hat was now heavily creased against the side of the couch. Eleanor suddenly caught sight of the calendar on the mantlepiece, it had been six days since the day of the recital on the 26th day of July and six days since her father's death; with Peggy no longer around the calendar had not been adjusted and time in the Jackson's household had stood still. Eleanor clicked the tab six times on the brass instrument and was astonished to discover that it was the first day of August. Maybe it *had* been fate which had caused her to cross paths with Mr August Miller, she mused, with a tiny smile upon her face.

"Mamma, wake up, I've brought us a delicious supper!" she exclaimed, as she held the newspaper package under Beatrice's nose. Her mother's tired, blue eyes slowly opened, but there was no look of appreciation on her drawn face. Eleanor removed her mother's crooked hat and began to untie her boot laces.

"Are you as famished as I am Mamma? I purchased four pies so that we have a meal for tomorrow as well!" she declared, excitedly. Beatrice screwed up her nose,

"Don't be fooled by their tantalizing aroma, Eleanor, it will only turn out to be another disappointment in life, they will be full of chewy gristle with not the tiniest similarity to Peggy's mouth-watering steak pies!"

"Well, I'm sure they will taste better than the stale bread, which is all we have left in the pantry. By the way Mamma, why *was* Peggy at the solicitor's office today? And why did she completely ignore us?"

"Go and fetch some plates and a jug of water Eleanor, or are we to eat like commoners too!" Knowing that her mother was simply avoiding her questions, Eleanor did as she requested, determined to coax the truth from her mother before they retired for the night.

Her mother had been correct in her prediction of the meat pies, which were packed with chewy kidney pieces, thick gelatinous gravy and not a trace of steak. Eleanor filled up on all the pastry and was already considering discarding the two pies, which she'd left in the pantry. Beatrice refused to eat more than two bites of the pastry and filled up on cups of tea and jam tarts.

"I have some very serious news to tell you, Eleanor!" Beatrice suddenly stated.

It was the moment Eleanor had been waiting for; she felt nervous and had an unusual tight knot in her stomach, not sure if it had been bought on from the awful pies or in anticipation of what her mother was about to disclose. She faced her head on across the gleaming mahogany dining table.

"Is it about Peggy?" was the only reply which came into Eleanor's head.

"It is about *many* matters my darling and it is not news which any mother in the world wishes to tell her daughter."

Eleanor was becoming even more worried.

"I don't know how much information you managed to take in from our visit to Mr Thornberry's office but I'm quite sure it didn't escape your ears that I was referred to by my maiden name of Miss Whitlock, or Mrs Whitlock in the sympathetic words of the young office junior. The reason, of course, is that your father and I never married...not because he didn't wish to but because he was already married."

Her revelation didn't come as a shock to Eleanor;

it was the assumption she'd already worked out. She sat speechless, allowing her mother to continue. "I'm so *very* sorry that you had to find out in this harsh way, I did intend to tell you, of course, but didn't envisage your dear pappa leaving this world so prematurely. I was hoping to wait until you'd reached the mature age of twenty-one, at least. You are illegitimate, I'm sorry to say, but nobody in the world needs to know and it will not make any difference to your future, my darling. You are a bright and talented young woman who will, I'm certain, marry into a fine family and want for nothing in the future." For a brief second the image of August Miller clouded Eleanor's thoughts before her mother's voice continued.

"Your father was married to Peggy's daughter; that is why she was present at today's reading of his will and why she denied knowing us!"

Eleanor gasped loudly, taken by complete astonishment, she had always believed Peggy to be a confirmed spinster; she'd even felt sorry for the woman for never having married.

"Why did you allow Peggy to work in our house, knowing that, Mamma? She was nothing more than a fraud, how could you *Mamma*, when all the time she was Pappa's mother in law!"

Beatrice refilled her cup of tea; tears were already rolling off her flushed face.

"It wasn't as simple as that, Eleanor; do you

think I had any say in the matter? Why do you think that I made a separate life for myself by attending so many functions? I wished to be out of our home as much as I could!"

"Then why didn't we simply leave and make our own life somewhere else!"

"Because, *my darling girl,* I have *no* money to my name and everything which has ever surrounded us belonged to your father! When your father employed Peggy, I had absolutely no idea of the link between them, it wasn't until years later when you were nearly nine, that I discovered the truth and then, apart from it being a little too late to protest, your pappa threatened to stop all financial support if I made a fuss or attempted to dismiss Peggy. My hands were tied."

"Why did you even involve yourself with a married man in the first place, Mamma?" Feeling humiliated and ashamed of herself, Beatrice's answer was quick and unconvincing,

"These things happen in life my darling...It was not what I set out to do but it happened and there is no changing the past!"

"Did you know that Pappa was already married, when you began your assignations with him?" Mopping up the copious tears with her delicately, embroidered handkerchief, Beatrice suddenly appeared years older than her age, looking beaten and demoralized.

"Your father told me that he intended to leave

his wife, but when Peggy discovered this she threatened to disclose the truth about him to his many business associates; he would have been ruined and we all would have suffered irreparably."

"What about Peggy, wouldn't she have preferred to live near to her daughter? I understand now why she was always so attentive towards Pappa!"

"Peggy lost her husband years ago, when her daughter was only a baby and she was only a young woman, he died of some ghastly disease. It was a long time ago, when plagues were never far away, especially in the heart of London, where they resided. She became your late grandparent's housekeeper and her daughter was allowed to grow up in their modest mansion. She was no stranger to your father even though he was ten years older than her and when she was only sixteen and your father a young man of twenty-six, their relationship developed and I'm sure it doesn't take a genius to work out what happened next and when the young daughter was suddenly found to be expecting a child, your father was forced into a marriage against his will. His wife subsequently lost the child and never conceived again, leaving your father in a trapped marriage, where his wife was to benefit from a wealthy lifestyle, one which she would never have had if she'd not have become pregnant."

Eleanor sat motionless, hardly believing her ears,

"I can't believe that I've spent my entire life surrounded by so many lies. I wish I'd never said a kind word to Peggy, or my father; he was nothing more than a common rogue, like the ones you are always warning *me* about!"

"Your pappa adored you, my sweetheart, you are his only child. He detested Peggy and how she had so much control over his life, that's the reason why she wasn't permitted to live in his London home. Even Peggy's daughter believed that her mother had instigated the entire situation, right from the start when, instead of warning her daughter not to become too familiar with your father, she did the exact opposite and wholly encouraged her daughter's close encounters with him. She set out to secure a future for herself and her daughter, ungrateful of the fact that your late grandparents had been charitable and taken them into their service and provided for them both."

"Surely, if I am the only living child, I should have at least been bequeathed a small fortune, but I wasn't even mentioned in yesterday's reading!" expressed Eleanor in the hope that at least one scrap of good could be salvaged from the dire situation.

Beatrice hesitated; she took hold of her unruly hair with both hands, twisting it into a neat ponytail before setting it free again. Her eyes were sad, her face downcast and Eleanor already sensed that her one hope of light in this miserable chapter of her life was about to be extinguished.

"You are not a Jackson, my darling, but a Whitlock like me. But your pappa always intended to present you with a handsome gift on your twenty-first birthday. It would have been more than enough to keep you in a manner to which you have been accustomed to over the years and enough to provide for you until you marry."

Eleanor released a long sigh, knowing that she and her mother were now destitute and in the words of her mother, we're to become commoners, with no place in society.

CHAPTER FOUR

There remained a dark and miserable atmosphere beneath the Jackson's roof, with Eleanor struggling to come to terms with the many shocking revelations her mother had recently revealed and with Beatrice refusing to leave her bed, constantly complaining about a stomach ache, but refusing to put anything past her lips other than sweet tea, laced with honey. Reminding herself hourly that she was no longer a *Jackson*, but a *Whitlock*, Eleanor knew it would be a while until she was familiar with her new name. The little affection and small amount of love for her Pappa, which had once occupied a niche in her heart were now nowhere to be found. She now harboured an overwhelming sense of loathing for the man who had lied and in her opinion, been an absolute coward for most of his life.

Another long and drawn out week passed by, with Eleanor becoming more acquainted with lighting the kitchen stove and now an expert in boiling and scrambling eggs. She was about to take up a tray of breakfast to her mother's bedroom when the official-looking envelope in the letter basket made her stop in her tracks. Placing the tray on the hall table, Eleanor retrieved the letter; it was addressed to Mrs Whitlock. She paused to glance at her image in the looking glass, "I think *you* should open this letter, Eleanor Whitlock, your mamma is too poorly to read any more bad news!" she declared to her reflection, observing how she appeared to have matured since the death of her father. Was it the worry and heavy feeling of responsibility, which had suddenly been thrust upon her, she questioned, realising how she now found herself devoid of all childish thoughts.

The bad feelings she harboured towards her late father escalated when she read the lines of the letter; it was brief, cold and straight to the point, with a bitter tinge of politeness. She and her mother had been given less than a week in which to vacate their home in Henley Road. It was not a polite request, but a stark and threatening order. With her thoughts in total confusion, Eleanor found herself regretting not accepting August Miller's invitation to walk out with him and at the same time, she decided how she was no longer going to dress in her mourning ensemble. Why should she mourn a father who had not behaved like one or treated her like any father would treat a daughter; he had ruined her's and her mother's life, leaving Eleanor fearful of what the future was about to bring.

Surprisingly, Beatrice was not in her bed, but stood in front of her bedroom washstand splashing cool water upon her face; she turned to greet Eleanor, even managing a smile. As much as Eleanor had yearned to witness her mother's melancholy mood change, she secretly wished that it had not been on this day when she was about to hand her the dismal letter, which would undoubtedly set her back again.

"Good morning my dearest girl!" she greeted, enthusiastically, "I hope you are feeling as refreshed as I am on this beautiful sunlit morning?"

"Good morning, Mamma, you *are* looking well this morning, did you have a good night's sleep?"

Beatrice gently dabbed her wet face with the towel,

"Indeed I did, my darling and what's more, I've decided that from this day forth, you and I are going to put our miseries behind us and begin our new life as Mrs and Miss Whitlock...It is going to be a new beginning! Enough of this gloom, I say!"

Eleanor placed the heavy tray onto the dresser.

"And to start with," Beatrice continued, jubilantly, "we shall take breakfast together, in the dining room!"

Eleanor sighed under her breath and picked up the tray, "Very well, Mamma, I will keep your scrambled eggs warm while you finish your ablutions."

"Bless you, my darling, you are my *real* treasure!"

Knowing that her mother's buoyant mood would soon disappear, once she'd read the letter, Eleanor decided to keep it from her until after breakfast.

It was the first time in days that Beatrice had eaten with such enthusiasm, she finished the eggs and buttered bread and greengage jam and consumed two cups of tea in the time which Eleanor had barely made a start on her breakfast.

"I hope you're not sickening for something, my darling!" she said, concernedly, as she stretched her hand across the table, placing it on Eleanor's forehead.

"I'm fine, Mamma, but I do have some bad news to tell you."

"Whatever it might be, my sweet treasure, I assure you, I am decided that it will not change my positive mood. Since our little talk the other day, a huge weight has been lifted from me. I have at last revealed myself and no longer live in a life of pretence; I do believe it has done me the world of good and from now on, all bad news will be shared, as will news of a happier nature. Now tell me...did you break my favourite porcelain ornament?"

Eleanor swallowed hard as she took the envelope from her pocket.

"This arrived for you this morning, Mamma; I only opened it because I wanted to protect you from any more worries, but as you will soon read for yourself, this is news which has to be dealt with immediately."

The ticking of the grandfather clock was the only sound echoing around the dining room for the next few minutes. Eleanor could feel her heart pounding as she studied her mother who appeared to read the brief letter over and over again. There was a renewed look of woe etched upon her face and her smiling eyes suddenly looked vacant.

"Don't worry, Mamma, there must be somewhere we can go, we could move to a new area perhaps, or maybe one of your many friends might welcome us into their home, temporarily."

As Eleanor tried her best to cheer her mother, Beatrice calmly placed the letter onto the table before sobbing into her upturned palms.

"Please don't cry, Mamma!" begged Eleanor. "You awoke so optimistic about our future, this morning...something will turn up...we just have to be strong for each other!"

Beatrice took to her bed again, refusing to discuss the contents of the letter or to utter a single word, leaving Eleanor feeling completely alone. Her entire world had changed so much in the past few weeks and she'd never before experienced feeling so abandoned.

By midday, Beatrice was still beneath the covers and refusing to talk, she was not crying anymore nor sleeping, but staring at the ceiling with a blank expression on her drained face. Eleanor kissed her cheek as she placed a cup of tea on the bedside table. She whispered words of encouragement to her mother, knowing that she had already closed her ears to any outside intrusion.

Deciding to walk to the bakery in Cowley Road, Eleanor retraced her steps from when she'd walked to the pie shop in the hope of bumping into Mr Miller again. She deeply regretted not encouraging his friendship and realised that she must have appeared quite aloof. There was no sign of him and she couldn't even remember which house he'd been leaving on that day.

'August Miller', she muttered under her breath, *'Where have you gone?'*

Returning home with a loaf of fresh bread, Eleanor stepped over the threshold into the frosty atmosphere of her home. She missed the sound of her mother's joyful voice issuing her with instructions; she even missed the sight of her mother parading her beauty in front of the looking glass, dressed in her finery and in her usual euphoric mood about the afternoon tea she was to attend. Even though she now despised Peggy with every fibre of her being, she missed the sweet aroma and delicious taste of her baking. There were four days until she and her mother had to vacate their home and Eleanor hadn't a clue as to what she should do. As much as she felt that she'd suddenly grown up of late, finding a new home was completely beyond her abilities.

Two more days dragged by, with Eleanor repeatedly trying to coax her mother into eating and to rise from her bed, but with all attempts seeming to fail, Eleanor had a terrible feeling that if she didn't take matters into her own hands, come the day they were to vacate their home, they would be thrown out onto the streets and most probably end up in the dreaded workhouse.

Perched on the edge of her mother's bed, Eleanor spoke softly, "Mamma, we have to leave our home in two days; we must find somewhere to go!"

Beatrice made a throaty, moaning sound as she turned her face away from Eleanor.

"Do we own *anything* in this house, Mamma? Do you have any money? Maybe I could secure us some lodgings, perhaps?"

Beatrice was unmoved by Eleanor's words; she remained in the same position and Eleanor sat staring out of the window feeling utterly helpless.

"Drink your tea Mamma!" reminded Eleanor, "it will soon go cold!"

Beatrice obediently sat up and quickly drank the tepid tea.

"There is a little money in my jewellery box and you can sell all of my jewellery too," she said in a small deflated voice.

Eleanor dithered towards her mother's jewellery

box, unsure of opening it and removing its contents. She glanced at her mother before opening the lid; she had closed her eyes again and was clearly no longer bothered about her fine collection of jewellery, which she'd always worn so proudly. Eleanor felt a rush of sorrow flow through her veins as she wondered if her mother would ever be the same again. She counted four pounds, five shillings and eleven pennies and was quite sure it would be enough for them to live on for a few months if they were careful. She decided on taking the jewellery to a local jeweller's in the morning and would also try and find out how one went about renting lodgings in the City. Telling herself how she had to be strong and support her mother through these difficult times, she went to bed that night with her head full of hopes and plans for the following day, praying harder than she'd ever prayed in her life.

CHAPTER FIVE

Following a restless night, Eleanor left her mother sleeping and quietly crept out of the house with a couple of the jewellery pieces safely in her skirt pocket. It was eight-thirty and pleasantly warm. As she walked past the house of a friend, who she used to go to school with, she became annoyed by her mother's insistence that when she'd left school two years ago, she also cut all ties with her old friends. Her mother's obsession with those of a higher station had only left them alone and isolated; Eleanor wondered if those wealthy women ridiculed her mother behind her back and used her as nothing more than a focal point of amusement at all their afternoon teas and fancy soirees. Now understanding the reasons behind her mother's continuous endeavour to better her position in society, she worried that the sudden change in their circumstances was having a detrimental effect on her state of mind. Determined to secure a homely, modest place to live, Eleanor increased her pace. Her first port of call was the goldsmiths in the High Street and as she arrived at its glossy, black painted, exterior an elderly gentleman was unbolting the door and turning the '*open*' sign around. She continued past the shop, not wanting to appear too eager to cash in on her jewellery and also losing her nerve after noticing the stern look upon the aged jeweller's face.

After walking as far as St Martin's Tower and back again, she braced herself to enter into the gloomy inside of *H.W Hewlett*. The doorbell jingled loudly as she walked into the tiny shop and the old man, who she presumed was Mr Hewlett, appeared from behind a claret door curtain. He eyed her suspiciously before speaking.

"Good morning," he uttered, in an unwelcoming manner.

"Good morning, Sir," she replied sheepishly.

He took the lit lantern from off a nearby shelf, holding it up high as he stared hard at Eleanor.

"I've got some of my mother's jewellery, she is poorly and we have fallen upon hard times, so she has requested that I bring it to you. She assured me that you offer the best prices for precious gems and fine gold." Eleanor's unprompted statement sounded foolish and extremely childish. She could feel her cheeks burning and imagined they were emitting more light than the pathetic flame from the old man's lantern.

He opened out a piece of claret chenille, similar to the door curtain.

"If you'd place the items here, Miss, I'll be able to estimate their value," he voiced as he tapped the rectangular cloth with his gnarled fingers.

A huge emerald studded ring set in a wide gold

band, a diamond and black sapphire brooch in the shape of a bird and a pair of heavy, diamond ear ornaments were hurriedly taken from Eleanor's pocket and laid down in front of him. Noticing how his eyes widened, as he caught sight of the treasures, a wave of optimism flowed through her. He turned up the flame of the lantern, illuminating the entire shop. Eleanor took in the copious clocks which were displayed upon the surrounding walls, whilst the jeweller placed his magnifying glass in his right eye and began to examine each piece. His expression soon changed as he slowly shook his head and tutted under his breath.

"Who put you up to this prank, young lady?" he demanded crossly. "I might appear old, but I still have all my wits about me! I'm no fool and certainly not about to be robbed by some young girl, who's barely left her crib!" he continued, his brow displaying deep furrows.

Having little idea of what he was talking about, Eleanor stood in disbelief as he practically threw the items back to her.

"These are nothing but pure *paste*, Miss; you'd be better off trying to sell them to the theatre!"

Rushing out of the shop, speechless and with tears in her eyes, Eleanor couldn't help wondering if her mother was aware that her priceless jewels were nothing more than fake, just as their entire family had been. Surely she wouldn't have sent her to be humiliated if she'd known, she questioned. Had her father been such a cad as to trick her mother into believing they were genuine jewels, worth a fortune? All of a sudden she felt nauseous and since she'd intended to ask Mr Hewlett if he could give her some advice on how to go about finding lodgings in the City, all her hopes suddenly plummeted. Her legs continued to walk, leading her along the busy High Street, but her thoughts were far away; she was oblivious of her surroundings until a sudden and familiar voice broke into her reverie,

"And there was I thinking that nothing would go right for me for the rest of this day!"

Eleanor glanced up and there, standing as large as life in front of her was August Miller. He couldn't have appeared at a more appropriate time and Eleanor felt her heart dancing at the mere sound of his gentle voice.

"Mr Miller!" she cried out joyfully, as an instant smile wiped away her sorrowful face.

"And you even remembered my name!"

"I seldom forget names, Mr Miller."

"And I seldom forget a name which belongs to a pretty face, Miss Eleanor!"

"How are you, Mr Miller," she asked coyly.

"All the better for meeting you, Miss Eleanor, especially since I've just come straight from the publishers with yet another rejection to add to my ever-growing list."

Eleanor's eyes immediately glanced at the thick

bundle of papers in the crook of his arm.

"Well, my morning has been somewhat of a disaster too!" she admitted.

"Shall we unload our troubles over tea and toast, Miss Eleanor? I notice that you are no longer wearing your mourning ensemble!"

"That's very observant of you, Mr Miller, but it's not because an adequate period has elapsed since the death of my father!"

August appeared puzzled.

"Has fate once again brought us together, Miss Eleanor? I believe so!"

Eleanor couldn't help giggling at his animated face and for the briefest of moments her problems took a step backwards.

"To the tea room, Miss Eleanor?" he declared with his elbow poised outwards in the hope that Eleanor would take hold of his arm as they walked.

"Thank you, Mr Miller, that would be most acceptable!"

Gingerly placing her hand on the crook of his arm, Eleanor felt quite grown up as they proceeded along the High Street. Her nervousness, knowing how livid her mother would be, should she find out about her secret rendezvous, soon diminished as she remembered how shockingly her mother must have conducted herself years ago.

"We'll go to the 'Copper Kettle' if that's agreeable with you?" suggested August.

Eleanor was beginning to realise how sheltered her upbringing had been; she could count the times she'd been into Oxford on her fingers as she remembered frequenting the tea room with her mother on only three or four occasions. If it hadn't been for attending school every day and the occasional jaunts with her friends after school, the world beyond her home would have been almost a mystery to her.

"That sounds perfect, Mr Miller," she replied confidently.

The Copper Kettle was situated on the corner of Turl Street and Broad street and much to Eleanor's relief, only a couple of other customers were taking tea so early in the morning. August led the way to the small alcove next to the large stone fireplace. It was cosy and hidden from anyone who might be peering in from off the street. He pulled out the chair and Eleanor sat down gracefully, hoping to look sophisticated and at ease in her surroundings. His broad smile had a calming effect on Eleanor; she relaxed and wished that her time spent with August would pass by slowly. Dressed in a navy serge dress covered with a crisp white apron, the proficient looking waitress was soon stood at their table. August quickly ordered tea and toasted tea cakes, eager for the waitress to leave.

"Why don't you call me, August, I'd much prefer it, you know!"

Eleanor smiled, "What is your novel about,

August?" she questioned, shyly.

Walking side by side with August had been far more comfortable, but now, sitting opposite him she sensed his ogling eyes upon her, even though he diverted his glance every time she looked up at him, which she found herself wanting to do often. She wished to remember him properly, to have a crystal clear image of him in her mind.

"Oh, it's just a boring detective story, which every author in the country is writing these days!"

"I'm sure it's a jolly good detective story though!"

"Maybe I went wrong by not including a beautiful maiden named Eleanor in it!" he teased. "Now enough about my rejections, which I'm becoming quite used to, what about your problems…you certainly seemed miles away when I met you earlier."

Feeling as though August was the only person in the entire world to who she could voice her worries and problems, Eleanor sensed that she could trust him enough to speak freely and explain her predicament.

"Well, I had just stepped out of the jeweller's shop where I'd been trying to sell some of my mother's priceless jewels, which turned out to be no more than worthless fakes! A bit like my life really; you see, after my pappa died a few weeks ago, I discovered that he wasn't even married to my mother and that he had a wife in London, where he spent most of his time throughout my fourteen years."

Eleanor suddenly realised that by talking so frankly, she'd probably said enough to make August never want to see her again.

"I would understand if you should wish to leave this very minute, Mr Miller. I'm sure you don't wish to associate your good name with an illegitimate girl who is about to become a penniless pauper!"

"Hey, steady on now, *sweet Eleanor*...and by the way, I thought we'd agreed that you are to call me August! It's not your fault that your parents weren't married nor that you are penniless, which I find hard to believe for someone living in such a wealthy-looking townhouse in Henley Road!"

"How do you know where I live?" she declared, aghast.

"Well, I suppose I'll have to admit it now that I followed you home *and* I have also walked up Henley Road nearly every day in the hope of seeing you!"

Eleanor was lost for words. The waitress arrived in perfect timing, placing the order onto the table.

"Will there be anything else, Sir?" she dutifully enquired.

The very fact that Eleanor was now aware of August's genuine feelings infused her with a sense of security. She was inwardly thrilled that he'd taken the trouble to follow her home and that he'd been searching her out ever since.

"The wealthy-looking home where I reside will no longer be mine come tomorrow. My mother and I will be without a roof over our heads if I don't manage to find some kind of lodgings soon. Throughout my entire life, I've believed that my home in Henley Road was owned by my father, but it turned out to be merely rented. Maybe you should write a novel about my unscrupulous father...you never know, it might be a best seller!"

August was clearly concerned about Eleanor and her mother's plight as he listened intently.

"There is also the mysterious case of our cook; good old dependable Peggy, who actually turned out to be *far* from that. She disappeared shortly after Pappa's death, only to reappear in London for the reading of his will...would you believe it, but Peggy is no other than my late father's mother in law!"

August was now sat with a knitted brow, a look of complete confusion upon his face.

"I'm sorry, Eleanor, but you've lost me now, maybe you're right though, I think this has the makings for an intriguing novel, but honestly, as much as I don't wish to sound cold-hearted, it sounds to me as though you and your mother are better off without him and your devious cook!"

"I couldn't agree more, but that is not the opinion of my poor mamma. She is not handling her fall in society at all well and that's without the knowledge that her jewellery collection is worthless. I think she was putting all her last hopes on them being the answer to our deflated financial situation. So you see, August, I have the sum of nearly five pounds and desperately need to find relatively decent lodgings, which will not distress my poor mamma too much, before Friday!" Pausing to detect August's reaction, Eleanor worried that she'd said too much. "Now I'm quite confident that I could wager my five pounds on you regretting that I ever bumped into you on that fateful day!" August's stared hard at Eleanor, his penetrating, ocean green eyes seeming to gaze into the depth of her thoughts.

"You're right of course, it's more than I can handle!" he announced, as he stood up as if to leave. Eleanor was flabbergasted; this wasn't the reaction she'd been expecting.

August suddenly sat back down again, taking hold of Eleanor's slender hand in his; he smiled slightly, before gently kissing the back of it.

"I'm joking, sweet Eleanor, I would never abandon you in your hour of need; I'm here to help you, all the way; consider me, your rock!"

Eleanor pulled her hand from his, "That was a cruel trick to play, Mr Miller; I thought authors were renowned for their sensitivity!"

"And their eccentric sense of humour! And I hope you don't intend to revert to calling me, Mr Miller whenever you become annoyed with me!" Eleanor giggled; she was growing fonder of the charming, August Miller by the minute.

"Let's finish our tea and go in search of a new home for you and your mother, Eleanor...what is your surname, by the way?"

She sighed heavily, "Up until a few days ago it was Jackson, but now it is Whitlock!"

"*The girl with two names!* How does that sound for a title?" he teased.

"Don't you ever think to disclose my scandalous business on the pages of a book, Mr Miller!"

"Very well, *Miss Whitlock!*"

They left the Copper kettle in a mood of optimism, August was now convinced that he'd found the girl of his dreams and was determined to do everything in his power to hold on to her. Delighted that her feelings towards August weren't one-sided, Eleanor felt confident that with his help, life would now, perhaps, become more bearable.

CHAPTER SIX

Although only six years older than Eleanor, August seemed wise and well educated in the goings-on in and around Oxford's City, he also had many acquaintances and contacts which proved invaluable in securing a place for Eleanor and Beatrice to move into. It was by far anything slightly resembling their residence in Henley Road, but Eleanor knew that she had to be realistic and make the small sum of money last long enough until she'd secured a way of earning. The very idea of her trying to find employment seemed totally bizarre and a scenario which she'd never imagined finding herself in.

The one-room on the first floor was, according to August, considerably large for a lodging room; it was sparsely furnished with only one bed, a tiny battered-looking wardrobe and a heavily stained chest of drawers. The floorboards were still all intact, which August assured her was always a bonus, since many a time they would be used to keep the fire burning during the winter months. Two small and grubby rag rugs were randomly scattered on the floor, which Eleanor had already decided to discard at the first opportunity, convinced that the unpleasant aroma was coming from them. There was a communal kitchen on the ground floor and a privy in the alleyway which ran along the rear of the entire road and was shared by six houses in total. The smug housing agent boasted about the luxury of having so few people sharing one privy and also how only four other families were living in the house. Eleanor was horrified and already felt a tight knot gripping her stomach at the very thought of telling her mother about their new home.

The housing agent had presumed that the room on Bullingdon Road was to be August's and Eleanor's first marital home, turning Eleanor's cheeks aglow when he enquired if they'd only recently married. August was quick to explain how the room was for Eleanor and her mother, but even beneath his thick overgrown sideburns, there was no hiding the middle-aged housing agent's crimson glow. The deal was made and at two shillings a week, August proudly expressed that they'd struck a bargain, convinced that the house agent had made a slight reduction due to his embarrassing assumption.

Eleanor paid the first week's rent and was given a small, black rent book and a set of keys; it was all a new and quite unpleasant experience to her and as her mind strangely wandered off to the day of the piano recital, she wondered what all those obnoxious, stuck up girls would think if they could see her now.

"May I escort you home, Eleanor?" voiced August, invading her far off thoughts.

"Well, only as far as to where we won't be seen if my mother happens to be peering out of the window, which I very much doubt, but she's had enough shocks lately and I already dread informing her of our soon to be 'home'. She is not going to take it at all well, August."

"You might be pleasantly surprised, Eleanor; folk have an innate way at adapting to new circumstances no matter how difficult they might initially seem," reassured August.

"You haven't met my mother!"

Eleanor was suddenly reminded that she also had to break the news about her mother's so-called, priceless jewellery; no doubt she was expecting Eleanor to have sold them for more than enough funds to secure the rent on a similar home to theirs. All of a sudden, she felt her entire body break out into a nervous sweat.

"Are you alright?" asked August urgently, alarmed by Eleanor's sudden quietness.

"No, I'm not really, August, I've just remembered about my mother's paste jewels!"

August for once didn't have an answer; he felt so sorry for Eleanor and wished he could be at her side when she broke the news to her mother.

As they approached their place of parting, Eleanor realised that she had disclosed too much of her private business to August and allowed him into her life, but she knew so little about him. It was too late now, she mused, regretting not having asked about his family.

"Do you live nearby, August? Was that your home you were leaving on the day we first met?" August thought for a second, "Oh no, I was merely making a delivery!"

It was too late for any more questions,

"Be brave, my sweet Eleanor, my thoughts will be with you and my heart resting on yours until our next meeting, take care of yourself." August blew a kiss into the air as he turned around to head back in the opposite direction. A ripple of sadness engulfed Eleanor as she continued the short distance alone, but she sensed it wouldn't be too long before she was once again in the company of the charming, August Miller. Having become used to the new deathly silence of her home, Eleanor went straight to the kitchen and filled the kettle. Quite sure that her mother wouldn't have left her bed and was likely in need of some refreshments, Eleanor placed the fresh jam tarts, which she'd purchased, onto a fancy lace doily and proceeded to brew the tea. She refreshed her face with cool water and rinsed her lace gloves beneath the pump. Continuing to go over in her head how she would break the news to her mother, she already knew that however kindly she tried to phrase the grim news, it would fall like a cruel and heavy blow upon her mother's already frail state of mind. If only they were permitted to reside in Henley Road until the end of the year, she mused, once again becoming angry with her father and his secret London family who were obviously all equally as merciless as he had been. It was far too soon to subject a grieving family to the extra hardships which were about to fall upon them.

Taking in a deep breath as she carried the tray up the stairs to her mother's room, the dreadful sight which filled her eyes caused the load to spontaneously slip from her hands. As the elegant, bone china tea set crashed noisily to the ground, splashing scalding tea onto Eleanor's skirt, she felt nothing as she stared in horror and disbelief at her mother's pitiful body, hanging from the wooden ceiling beam. Her bare feet dangled at Eleanor's eye level and she couldn't help thinking how pure and lovely her silky, white skin appeared. The starched sheet was wrapped tightly around her neck causing her head to tilt to one side, leaving her long golden hair draped over her half-naked shoulder to the other side, like a sheaf of freshly harvested wheat. Time stood still as Eleanor could do nothing, but stare in horrified disbelief, before the sudden thought that her mother might still be alive engulfed her thoughts. She hurried down to the kitchen to retrieve the sharp carving knife. Climbing onto the dressing table, she was able to stretch up and cut through the twisted sheet; her mother crashed to the floor with a thump, but there was no movement in her body, no sign of life and Eleanor knew it was final when she felt the coldness of her poor mother's body. In the space of a few weeks, she had lost both her parents and was now alone in the world, but as much as she loved her mother, Eleanor couldn't help feeling angry with her for abandoning her and allowing her to become an orphan. Pulling the blanket from off the bed, Eleanor covered her mother in a drastic bid to warm her icy body, then she dashed back down the stairs, took the nearest bonnet from the hat stand and whilst securing it beneath her chin, ran along the street towards the Doctor's house. Reaching it in record time, she spluttered in an unladylike manner as she puffed out of breath, leaving the Doctor's wife immediately sensing that something was terribly wrong,

"Heavens above, Miss Jackson, what on earth has happened...is it your mother...is she poorly? I was so sorry to hear the sad news about your father's passing."

"It *is* my mother, Mrs Thompson...I believe she is dead!"

"*No!*" exclaimed Mrs Thompson...I pray to God that you're mistaken, my Petal!"

"As do I, Mrs Thompson...is the Doctor busy?"

"Oh, sweet Petal, I'm afraid Dr Thompson has been called away, but I'm sure he'll be home within the hour...I'll send him along...your mother *is* at your home I take it?"

"Yes, yes...please, ask him to call as soon as he can, but Mamma's body is ice cold..." The lump which lodged uncomfortably in Eleanor's throat made it impossible for her to voice another word; the tears poured down her face and although Mrs Thompson preferred not to make a medical prognosis whilst her husband wasn't present, she doubted there would be anything he could do for poor, Mrs Jackson.

"Shall I come with you, my Petal? I could leave a note for the Doctor?"

Eleanor shook her head, preferring to be alone than with Mrs Thompson, who as sweet as she was, would no doubt make a lot of fuss and continue to refer to her as *'petal'*, which she'd already heard enough of.

"Very well then, Petal, but you know where I am if you feel the need!"

What a ridiculous statement, thought Eleanor as she walked back down the garden path.

Still in the exact position and with no sign of warmth having returned to her body, even with the blanket over her, Eleanor now knew for certain that there was no hope at all for her mother and she had departed from the world. Not wanting to leave her mother alone, she rested on her bed, breathing in the familiar odour of her dear mamma. The brooch in her pocket was digging into her leg and Eleanor decided to return the worthless items to her mother's jewellery box, although she had decided to keep them all as a reminder of her mother and a warning to herself to tread carefully where men were concerned; by all accounts, they were not to be trusted, too easily. Her attention was suddenly drawn to the envelope beneath the box; it was addressed to her and since it hadn't been there that morning, Eleanor was certain it was her mother's last ever letter. She opened it immediately, noticing how unlike her mother's usually neat and precise handwriting it was written in. It was the briefest of letters, barely half a page.

My darling Eleanor,

Please forgive me, but I have done this for you. I would only have been a burden to you and ruined your chances of a good and decent life. I can no longer hide from the truth of my immorality; I have hurt and upset my dearest of loved ones throughout my life because of my sinful ways. I can no longer harm a living soul. Try to be happy, my darling girl and don't follow in your mother's footsteps. Sell the remainder of my jewellery; I'm sure it will provide you with a tidy sum. You have a grandmother, seek her out; I'm sure she will be sympathetic towards you, now that I have left this world; I have not seen her for more than fifteen years, but I believe her to be living in the county, some six miles east of here. Should you locate her, please beg her to forgive me and tell her how I have always loved her and regret, more than she will ever know, the hurt and shame which I caused her in the past.
I wish you a good, successful and happy life, my beautiful daughter; I am so proud of you, my darling.
Please take my love with you always. Forgive me.

As Eleanor read the letter for the third time, each time with a fresh flow of tears, there was a loud rapping on the front door. She jumped, startled by the intrusion as she quickly put the letter into her pocket and fled downstairs to let the Doctor in.

After his initial examination of Beatrice, his sombre look told Eleanor what she already knew.

"I'm afraid there is nothing I can do for your dear mamma, Miss Jackson, even if I'd have arrived an hour ago. The poor woman was obviously so grief-stricken by the death of your father that she became too depressed to cope with her raw emotions. At least she can be laid alongside him now and you must take comfort in that, Miss Jackson; that once again she is where she was most content, at the side of your father."

His words flew over the top of Eleanor's head; he knew nothing of their circumstances and was jumping to all the wrong conclusions.

"What should I do, Doctor? I have nobody to help me and I don't know how to arrange a funeral."

"You must visit the reverend, who attended your father's funeral, I'm sure he will be most helpful!"

"Pappa was buried somewhere in London, Doctor Thompson; neither I nor my mother attended and I don't have a clue as to where his grave is!"

Trying to hide his feelings of shock and surprise,

Doctor Thompson was intrigued by Eleanor's announcement.

"What about your cook? Peggy, isn't it? I'm sure she will be a huge help at a time like this!"

"She left after Pappa died and come tomorrow, Dr Thompson, this house will no longer be my home...you see, it was only ever rented by my father."

"Oh dear, Oh dear!" he uttered, his brow creasing as he thought deeply for a few minutes. "I will arrange for your mother's body to be taken to the local morgue, where she can rest until the necessary arrangements have been made. Is there anyone who can take you in, a close friend or distant relative, perhaps?" Terrified that if she spoke the truth, she might end up being taken to the workhouse, Eleanor assured the Doctor that she would stay with a family friend in Bullingdon Road.

CHAPTER SEVEN

Doctor Thompson had left the Jackson's home with a troubled mind. He'd known Beatrice Jackson since she'd moved to Henley Road, some fifteen years ago and he'd assisted in the delivery of young Eleanor. Beatrice had always struck him as a natural, vivacious and independent woman, one who didn't depend on a man being at her side constantly and according to Mrs Thompson, Beatrice Jackson spent most of her leisure time mingling amongst the wealthy ladies of Oxford. He had met Edward Jackson on the odd occasion and had always presumed that he and Mrs Jackson shared a long-distance relationship which appeared to work extremely well. Edward Jackson by all accounts worked harder than many men at his London based business and he found it difficult to believe that he'd left his wife and daughter so destitute. He'd always assumed that Edward Jackson worked so hard because he intended to take an early retirement which would enable him to spend his later years with his family in Oxford.

Making his way directly to St Mary and St John Church in the nearby Cowley Road, Doctor Thompson sensed that Eleanor had been lying to him and that she had nowhere to go come the following day. He glanced across the road at the workhouse on his way and prayed that Eleanor wouldn't end up in such a formidable abode. Feeling a strong desire and sense of duty to delve to the bottom of the plight of the Jackson family, he decided to make it his business to investigate further. Why shouldn't Beatrice Jackson be buried alongside her husband, he pondered, thinking that perhaps he had been buried in an already established family grave alongside his parents or siblings; he already knew that he was a Londoner, born and bred. After speaking to the vicar, it was arranged for Beatrice Jackson's body to be taken to the morgue for a couple of days, while he investigated the whereabouts of her husband's burial place.

Left feeling desolate and abandoned, Eleanor collapsed upon the couch in floods of tears, her mother had been taken away by two of the grimmest and unpleasant looking men which she'd ever seen..."*Poor Mamma*", she sobbed, as the thought of her lying in a bleak, icy morgue plagued her mind. Her mother had gone forever and she was left alone; it was a thought which Eleanor still found difficult to believe.

Everything had happened so quickly. Just a few hours ago she had been in the most euphoric of moods in the company of August Miller, drinking cups of tea and enjoying the delicious buttered teacakes and then, as though somebody had suddenly slammed a heavy wooden door in her face, she'd found her mother, hanging from her bedroom ceiling; it was an image which would haunt her forever. If only she knew where August lived, she needed him more than ever and yearned to be close to him, where she felt a sense of security. He was now the only person in her world who she trusted, even though she'd known him for such a short period. Not wanting to venture upstairs as the dark hours of evening fell, Eleanor spent the night on the couch. She fell asleep just as the dawn was breaking only to be woken, three hours later, by what sounded like a dozen or more heavy hands knocking on the front door and the downstairs windows. Bolting upright, Eleanor felt her head spinning; a sharp stabbing pain seemed to penetrate through her temple, made worse by the continuous beating upon the windows and door, which was now accompanied by the sound of men's voices.

Having slept fully dressed, within minutes, Eleanor had straightened out her crumpled attire and hurriedly tied back her long hair, bracing herself to confront the perpetrators causing the ruckus. Three rough-looking commoners filled her eyes, heavily built men who appeared threatening and completely insensitive to the tragedy which had befallen the occupants of the property, which presumably, they'd come to claim back for whoever paid their wages. Eleanor could only stare, reluctant to even offer the briefest of polite greetings to the scruffy mob.

All three of them suddenly turned around to a fourth man, who was waiting on the pavement side of the front gate.

"She's opened the door, Gov!" they all declared, as though it had been achieved by some magical power which they possessed.

"What do you *all* want so early in the morning?" exclaimed Eleanor, suddenly finding her voice. The gang's employer approached slowly and Eleanor gasped as she recognised him as being the house agent who had shown her the room in Bullingdon Road on the previous day.

He appeared as surprised as Eleanor,

"Is your mother available?"

"She is still sleeping," replied Eleanor, abruptly. He paused for a few silent minutes before reading out the official warning from his notebook which instructed Eleanor that she and her mother must vacate the premises by eighteen hundred hours or face the City's Sheriff, who would then proceed to evict them by force and possibly fine them or even imprison them.

"It's Miss Whitlock isn't it?" he then stated in the same breath.

"Yes," she replied in a shaky voice, already knowing what was going through his thoughts.

"Strange that, because I have your name written down on my official papers as, Miss Jackson! I'm presuming you *are*, Miss Jackson...not, Mrs

Jackson!" he said smugly, causing the three commoners to snigger.

"Mrs Jackson is obviously my mother!"

"So why do you go around calling yourself Miss Whitlock? There's something a bit fishy going on if you ask me and I dare say, that young man who accompanied you yesterday is behind it! Should I perhaps inform your mother? I doubt *she'd* be best pleased!"

"That won't be necessary," replied Eleanor, determined not to disclose the terrible fate of her mamma in front of a bunch of heartless strangers. Imagining that her mother was still alive also made her feel stronger; she knew that the moment she mentioned the truth about her mother, she would break down and that was the last scenario she wished for.

"I'm afraid I will no longer be able to rent the respectable lodgings in Bullingdon Road to you, Miss Jackson! Please return the keys to me forthwith." The keys were still in Eleanor's pocket, she took them out and shoved them into the man's outstretched hand,

"As you can see, Sir, I am more accustomed to a far superior abode than that dingy, flea-ridden room in Bullingdon Road!"

"I would control your tongue if I were you, Miss; come six o'clock, I will be back on this doorstep and I might find it difficult not to inform your mother of your shenanigans, which I'm sure she knows nothing about!"

"Are you threatening me now, Sir? Is that all part of the service you provide?"

The burly men were all laughing under their breath, their rough-looking faces aglow with amusement.

"Come along now chaps, let us leave Miss Jackson to her packing, I'm sure she has much to do."

Quickly closing the door, before the last of the men had reached the front gate; Eleanor flopped down onto the cool, tiled floor of the hallway and cried. *What should she do now*, were the thoughts which swam around inside of her confused mind? With nowhere to go, what would become of her by nightfall? She had no idea where August lived, which only added to her frustrations; why had she not asked him that question? Why had she not asked anything about his background? She realised, at that moment that perhaps she was following in her mother's footsteps. Had *she* known anything about her pappa before she'd willingly given herself to him? It was a warning to Eleanor, a warning that no man was to be completely trusted, no matter how her heart yearned towards him. If there was to be any future relationship between her and August, she vowed to make sure that he wasn't concealing a huge secret first.

Since August was of the assumption that Eleanor would be living in Bullingdon Road by the end of the day, she presumed that he would eventually try to make contact with her. It was a comforting thought and Eleanor suddenly came up with an idea. Doubting that any new tenants would be immediately moving into her house, Eleanor came up with, what she considered to be, a brilliant and infallible plan. She would camp out in the garden shed; it had its own key and if new tenants or the housing agent should try to gain access, they would most likely presume that over the years, the key had been lost and the shed not used by the previous tenants.

The day had barely begun, which gave her plenty of time to make all the necessary preparations. But first thing was first, she had the heartbreaking task of sifting through her mother's belongings. Having already decided that she would sell most of her expensive gowns, she quickly packed them into a wooden chest; to be kept in the shed for the time being. With the urgency and limited time to complete the copious jobs, before the return of the ghastly housing agent at six O'clock, Eleanor had little time to dwell on her mother's belongings and be overtaken by sentimentality. Tears were never far from her eyes and her heart was heavy with grief, but she worked meticulously through every drawer and cubby hole, then finally her mother's jam-packed wardrobe. The wooden chest was so full that Eleanor had to sit on it to secure the metal clasp. Finally, she took the jewellery box from off the dresser, pleased that her mother never had to find out the truth about her worthless collection.

Food, drink, lanterns, a couple of thick blankets and cushions were next on her list, which were soon collected and added to the growing stack by the back door. Next, she filled a carpet bag with her belongings; not too much though, just in case she had to make a speedy getaway. She also owned some items of jewellery, including the recent bracelet which her father had presented her with before the day of the piano recital. She wondered if she too had been fooled, but threw them into her bag anyway. As she searched through every cupboard and drawer in the kitchen, Eleanor came across a bundle of keys; they'd been pushed to the far, back corner of a shelf in the larder, concealed in a rusty, old cocoa tin. In an instant, Eleanor realised that they were all duplicate keys; it was as though she'd struck pure gold and it meant that until new occupants moved into the house, she would be able to sneak in and out at her leisure. She prayed that nobody would move in for months to come as she took the broom and a bucket of water out to the shed.

Much to her relief, the shed was not in as bad a state as she'd anticipated and was almost empty. A few garden tools and a small pile of terra cotta flower pots were abandoned in the far corner along with some old and worn out gardening boots, a pile of old newspapers and a jar of rusty nuts and bolts.

The shed was more spacious than Eleanor had predicted, but was in need of a thorough clean. An accumulation of cobwebs, complete with copious dead and shrivelled insects, now formed a thick curtain across the width of the shed and up into its slanting roof. Eleanor tied a cloth around her mouth before venturing inside and wondered how she'd ever muster up enough bravery to sleep in such a spine-chilling place. It had been at least five years since Eleanor had played out or spent time in the garden, time in which the surrounding conifers had grown substantially, concealing the entire garden from view of the neighbouring houses; it would make coming and going relatively safe she deduced, pleasingly.

By midday, the shed was spotlessly clean and Eleanor had covered its floor with a rug, from her bedroom, which proved to be a perfect fit. Her mother's wooden chest made a suitable tabletop, where three full lanterns and a box of matches rested together with a couple of candles. She'd filled a biscuit tin with the remains of a loaf of bread, cheese and a couple of jam tarts and filled the largest teapot with water. Finally, she added a few items of crockery and cutlery to be taken to the shed. After securing an empty coal sack to the tiny, shed window and transporting the rest of the items to the shed, Eleanor admired her temporary dwelling place, proud of her brilliant idea.

With plenty of time before she was supposed to officially leave the property, Eleanor made herself a modest meal and put the spare front and back door keys safely into her pocket. With her hunger satisfied, she decided to do what would be impossible after six O'clock when she might be heard by the neighbours and arouse suspicions. She went to the piano, lifted its cover and proceeded to play her mother's favourite piece; Mozart's *'Alla Turca',* which conjured up the bold image of her, dear mamma bobbing her head and tapping her feet, as she would so often do.

It was a minute past six O'clock when the gentler rapping on the door set Eleanor's nerves on edge; she had already positioned her carpetbag in the hallway and as she slowly opened the door, the same familiar house agent doffed his bowler hat, as he offered an insipid smile.

"Good evening, Miss Jackson, I'm glad to see that you and Mrs Jackson have everything in order!"

He stretched his neck, peering over Eleanor's shoulder and into the hallway as he spoke.

"My mother has already left, but here are your keys," stated Eleanor, wishing to make a swift exit without having to converse with the house agent.

He looked disappointed, having furtively been hoping to meet Mrs Jackson to infuse some fear into her wayward daughter. He guessed that she'd been persuaded to leave first by Miss Jackson, to save her from his possible disclosure of the *'Bullingdon Road'* business. Had Miss Jackson intended to abandon her poor mother, he wondered, to take up with that, young scallywag? He took the keys and watched as Eleanor picked up her bag and marched down the short path, taking a right turn towards the City.

CHAPTER EIGHT

Winifred Miller sat huddled next to the last flickering candle; her eyes squinting as she focussed on her needle which she speedily thread in and out of the piece of silk in her grasp. It was the tenth pair of bloomers which she'd put together since waking at dawn and she had yet to wash the plates from supper. It was getting late and there had been no sign of August for two days, leaving her fearing the worst, as she was always inclined to; she'd saved him a plate of potatoes and green beans along with the last sausage, but she had strong doubts that he'd show up. Winifred never ceased worrying when he vanished for long periods, into the City; he was a country boy at heart and not, in her opinion, suited to the likes of those ruthless, City tricksters who she feared would take advantage of his kind and trusting nature. She had been holding her breath and holding her tongue for the last couple of years until his ambition to become an author dwindled and he woke up to the reality of life and found himself a proper man's job. In the past, August had taken on a variety of odd jobs, never wanting to see his mother go without. He was an angel, Winifred had to admit and cared about her with all his heart; she would be a lost and forlorn soul without him. August supplied her with the bolts of cotton cloth, calico and the occasional remnant of silk and after Winifred had expertly made the ladies underwear, he would then sell them in Oxford. A few were sold to the City's retailers and the remainder taken to market, where they went for a cheaper price. It was not suitable work for a young man, considered Winifred, but with his burning desire to write and make his fame and fortune as an author, it was a compromise which they'd arrived at in order to put food on the table. August would never see his mother go without, they shared a special bond and August was determined to live his own life to the full, to make up for the life of his twin brother who had not quite reached his fourth birthday when he was taken from them after suffering for almost three weeks from a fever and swelling of the throat. Having already lost her, beloved husband during the final year of the Crimean war when August and Gideon were babies, Winifred imagined that she would become separated from August and taken to the workhouse. There was nothing the doctor could do to save poor Gideon, but with Winifred's determination to remain in the hamlet of East Hanwell and bring August up by herself, she pulled all her limited resources together and managed to earn a pitiful living from her handicrafts. She would work long hours into the night, knitting and sewing and making straw bonnets, which she would take into Oxford once a week. Having no conventional market barrow, Winifred would sit on the ground with her work displayed proudly upon an old flour sack. Some weeks she would leave with barely a penny in her pocket, but over the years her skills improved and she attracted more customers, some of them even requesting orders for specific embroidered undergarments and knitted baby layettes. Selling her wears became far easier when August became older and less of a responsibility; he was a familiar face at Oxford's Wednesday market and with his outgoing nature, he soon became a proficient salesman, even though it was not the type of job which Winifred envisaged for her only son. When August turned sixteen, he took over the selling side of the business, insisting that Winifred spent more time resting her now, arthritic bones. Often taking trips into London, where he could purchase fine silks, cotton and embroidery threads in every hue, direct from the docks at a much cheaper rate, Winifred now had a mountainous pile of material to keep her busy for years to come and August's obsession to become a writer was born. His vivid imagination and ability to capture an audience with his tales had been evident since he was just a boy and many a time he could be found surrounded by the hamlet children, who barely blinked when sat listening to August's mesmerizing stories. Winifred was about to leave her rocking chair when the sound of the door latch caught her attention; she viewed August with a huge feeling of relief flowing through her tired body and a wide smile upon her face.

"Well aren't you a sight for sore and tired eyes!" she declared, already feeling her drowsiness disappear.

"There's a plate of supper for you in the cupboard, son!" she announced, as she eased her aching bones up from her chair.

"Sit down Ma, I'm quite capable of fetching it myself, you know! Would you like cocoa or tea?"

"Ah, you never fail to take away my tiredness, son, I'll have whatever you're having, August! Where've you been all week, anyway? You been to London again? I don't see any supplies in your fair hands!"

"I've been in Oxford, Ma, helping a...friend!"

"Down on his luck was he? Another one of your author friends, no doubt! Mrs Young told me, only yesterday, as it happens, that authors rarely make any money until they reach old bones and sometimes not even 'til they're resting in the graveyard!"

August smiled to himself, it was always a delight to hear his ma's amusing anecdotes; she could talk until the cows came home and had an opinion about every aspect of life.

"I'll just put the water on to boil, Ma and then I'll be all ears!"

"Having said that though, Mrs Young thinks she

knows how the entire world is run...gets on my nerves, does that 'know if all.' So, who's this friend then? Is he anyone I know? Is he a market lad or one of your toff acquaintances?" Winifred continued firing her questions at August as he stood in the tiny scullery, making the tea and chewing on a mouthful of cold sausage.

"How are your bones fairing Ma?" he enquired on returning to the only room in the small hamlet cottage.

"Oh, son I'm not long for this world, my bones are as squeaky as the parson's garden gate and my eyes are tired...it's a wonder I can still thread my needle, son! Might help if you could get wed; a pair of young and bright eyes to take over the business is what we need."

"That problem could be easily solved; I could buy you a pair of spectacles! I've told you before, Ma, I'm not ready to get wed yet, not until I've established myself as an author."

"Don't talk such nonsense son; we can't afford such luxuries as spectacles! Did that publisher gentleman show any interest in your work son?" August sensed that as usual, his ma was making fun of his ambition,

"Don't worry ma, I'm sure I can find a good second-hand pair for you...they will make sewing much easier, you know!"

"Enough about me come and tell me what *you've* been up to these past days. Where's your supper?"

"I ate the sausage Ma, I'll eat the rest tomorrow, but you didn't have to save me any supper, you know; I don't starve myself when I leave East Hanwell!"

"A mother doesn't stop caring for her son just because he's become a man, you know!"

"And a son never stops caring for his ma, so the next time I'm in Oxford or London, whichever comes first, I'm going to make sure to purchase a pair of fancy spectacles."

August eyed the pile of camisoles and bloomers as Winifred poured the tea,

"You made all those in two days!" he exclaimed. "You must be able to sew with your eyes closed!"

"If only, son, if only. They are all ready for selling and the sooner the better since there are only two pennies left in the pot now. So what friend were you helping then?"

"She's called Eleanor..."

"*She!* Well, there's a turn up for the books! Is she an author too, son? Where did you meet her? Have you known her long? Is she a hamlet girl?"

"Steady on Ma, I barely know her myself; she's had a run of bad fortune, since losing her father at a piano recital..."

"*Piano recital!*" repeated Winifred, unable to conceal her surprised look. "Then I doubt very much that she's the girl for you August! Far too fancy and wealthy and more than likely looking for a gentleman who can keep her in riches and finery..."

"Which I will be able to, just as soon as I find an honest publisher to put his trust in my work!"

"Oh, August, don't let the world slip by while you're so preoccupied trying to make your dream come true...maybe it's not the right time for you to write a book...maybe when you're a mature man with a family, then there will be opportunities to put pen to paper. One day lad, I'm sure you'll be a well-known author, but maybe not just yet, eh?"

"Well, Ma, whatever you say won't dampen my ambition and won't change the fact that I've fallen in love!"

"You'll end up with a broken heart, August, mark my words! What's wrong with little, Iris Fielding? She's the prettiest girl in the hamlet and I know she has an eye for you!"

Overshadowed by a feeling of gloom, August had been depending on his ma's support and understanding. He put the steaming cup of tea to his lips, already wishing he'd not spoken of Eleanor to his ma. He could picture her beautiful face, she was adorable and he yearned to protect her for the rest of her days. He wondered how her mother had taken the news about her jewellery and how she'd reacted when viewing the room in Bullingdon Road.

"How did you meet her then? Have you met her mother, does she have a large family?"

"*Ma*! I've not been spending every second of the day in her company, but long enough to know how I feel for her and before you say it, Ma, it's not just a passing infatuation. One day, she *will* be my wife!"

Winifred was stunned into silence for once, she'd never heard her son speak so passionately about a young girl before and she distinctly knew that he meant every word he said. She secretly hoped that the girl in question had more sense than her son.

"You mustn't rush these things son, especially since the girl has recently lost her father; grief can make the most sensible head lose all sense of propriety...give her time to get over her loss and then see how the situation looks!"

August decided to change the subject, his ma knew nothing of Eleanor's circumstances and he doubted very much that she would understand.

Eleanor had crept back into her garden through the narrow alleyway behind Henley Street. She breathed a sigh of relief when there appeared to be no sign of anyone in the house, but although shrouded in darkness, she felt too nervous to use the spare key and go inside. There could be somebody sleeping there, she mused, feeling the hairs on the back of her neck stand up at the mere thought. She turned the key in the shed door and sat down on her familiar bedroom rug, her legs ached from all the walking she'd done since leaving the house at six O'clock. Feeling as though she were in a coal bunker, her eyes had yet to adjust to the wall to wall blackness, the night sky had been cloudy as she'd returned from walking the streets, waiting for darkness to fall and there was not the slightest hint of the moon. She felt for the lantern and the box of matches, shielding the bright glow of the match with her body as she struck it, just in case someone was watching from a neighbouring upstairs window. The intense aroma of the burning sulphur in such a confined area made her choke. Quickly lighting the wick of the lantern, Eleanor turned it as low as was possible, just enough to emit the tiniest glow and take away her fears. She untied her boot laces and removed her bonnet, but that was as far as preparing for bed was going. After plumping up the cushions and covering her body with the blanket, she prayed that sleep would soon overtake her exhausted body and that the following day would bring August her way. She had so much to tell him and she needed him so desperately. Tears trickled down her face as thoughts of her poor mamma were never far from her mind, she had yet to be laid to rest and while she remained in the morgue, Eleanor's life was standing still. She would visit the vicar at St Mary and St John Church at first light and beg him, if necessary, to make the burial arrangements. With the familiar scent of her blanket reminding her of home, Eleanor closed her eyes and imagined she was in her own bed and that her mother was in the adjacent room sleeping soundly and all was just how it had been, back in July.

CHAPTER NINE

Ignoring his wife's protests, Doctor Thompson had assured her that he only intended to spend one night in London in his search for Mr Jackson's resting place and in his quest to get to the bottom of why young Eleanor had not been financially provided for by her late and wealthy father. He knew little of Mr Jackson's business, only that he traded mostly in silk, plus a variety of other merchandise. He, therefore, presumed that his office would be located in the vicinity of the London docks and intended that to be his first port of call.

As the colossal locomotive, hurtled noisily along the railway line towards Paddington station, Albert Thompson found it impossible to remove the image of Beatrice Jackson from his mind. It had left a deep scar upon his heart to witness the devastating sight of the beautiful woman, who he'd always held a clandestine torch for, end her own life in such a distressing way. He had a positive inclination that she too harboured a fondness towards him, which was stronger than how a patient should feel towards her physician. He adored Cynthia, she was everything a man could wish for in a wife, especially a doctor's wife, but Cynthia lacked the tantalizing charisma like that which seemed to radiate from Beatrice Jackson. She was always turned out in the finest and most attractive ensembles. Even when she was feeling under the weather, she had a certain glamour about her which acted as a magnet whenever he was summoned to attend her, or when she'd visited his surgery. Over the years, Beatrice had not been coy during their meetings and he had conducted himself in quite an unprofessional manner, enjoying the flirtatious banter which was exchanged. But that was as far as it had gone, a little harmless fun, he had assured his guilty conscience after each of her appointments, but now as he viewed the rolling, lush green landscape as it passed by, he felt tears of sadness stinging his eyes as he remembered the pitiful sight of Beatrice's cold body, knowing that she had taken with her a certain sparkle within him which only came to life when he was in her company. In her memory, he prayed that he would be able to return with some kind of good news for Eleanor Jackson, perhaps enough to give *her* a glimmer of hope in the desolate world which had so suddenly encompassed her. Emerging from the blinding plumes of steam as he made his way along the platform of Paddington station, Albert hurried to the nearby, Great Western Hotel on Praed Street, stopping for a moment to admire the impressive French Chateau design of the huge building. After booking one of the hundred and three rooms for one night only and leaving his travelling case in his room, he was soon back out onto the bustling streets of London and hailing himself a Hanson cab.

"Whitechapel please, my good man," he instructed the driver, as he climbed into the small carriage and closed the door.

"Any particula' spot in Whitechapel, Gov?" shouted the driver from his elevated seat.

"The main thoroughfare please, I'm taking somewhat of a mystery tour!"

The bumpy journey took more than half an hour, leaving Albert feeling bruised and battered and with a huge loathing of the East End's copious cobbled streets. Coming to a halt, at last, Albert alighted from the stuffy carriage and as he was about to pay the driver, a large crowd which had gathered close by was suddenly brought to his attention.

"Any idea what's going on over there, my good man?" Albert inquired, as he pulled out a handful of coins from his pocket.

"Reckon yer chose the wrong day ter visit the East End, gov, there's gonna be a riot outside ov Jackson's ware'ouse, that's fer sure! Take me advice, Gov an' stay clear ov it!"

"*Jackson*? Did you say?" his eyes lighting up.

"That's right Gov, none uvver than Edward Jackson 'imself, the bleedin' *big shot* who popped 'is clogs afore payin' off all them there folk, who don't look none too 'appy!"

"You're certainly not mistaken there," agreed

Albert, without diverting his glare from the rowdy crowd. "But on the contrary, my good fellow, I do believe I chose the perfect day to visit the East End!"

"So was yer after puttin' in a bid fer Jackson's ware'ouse, yerself, Gov, if yer don't mind me asking...'ope the scheming blighter didn't owe *you* an' all?"

Albert's ears became deaf to the chatter of the cab driver as he stared hard beyond the crowd, to where the small group of officials had gathered. An auctioneer stood head to head with another smartly attired gentleman and there was no mistaking that a few feet to the left of them stood Peggy, with two unfamiliar, younger-looking women. Albert had spoken to Peggy on countless occasions when calling on Beatrice or her daughter and he'd also treated her a few times too. It was indeed a huge shock to witness her and he hadn't the slightest of ideas as to why she was here. Albert placed the handful of coins into the cab driver's hand, not even bothering to count it, but delighting the driver with his generosity.

"That's right generous ov yer Gov! Yer a real gent, there's no mistakin'!"

"Yes, good day to you too!" replied Albert, still in a state of disbelief as he began to meander towards the riotous crowd. Within seconds, half a dozen peelers appeared from the far side of the gathering, waving their billy clubs high above their lofty stovepipe hats, in a threatening manner. Albert kept his eyes sharply focussed on Peggy, fearful that she might suddenly vanish into the crowd, especially with the arrival of the peelers. The cacophony of the bellowing law enforcers and the demonstrators all shouting out simultaneously seemed to echo through the entire area of Whitechapel until suddenly, the auctioneer yelled from the top of his voice and repeatedly thrust his mallet down hard upon the wooden table before him.

"Silence if you please gentlemen...I cannot proceed with this auction until some kind of organised calm is brought about. I assure you gentlemen that I will do everything in my power to see you all right by the end of the day!"

With the eerie silence immediately descending upon the hundred or more strong crowd, Albert Thompson stood motionless at the auctioneer's request, finding himself on the side where the bidders had gathered. He had a feeling that he was in for a long, but intriguing day. One by one, auction lots were brought out from the warehouse behind the auctioneer. There was an assortment of the most extraordinary merchandise, varying from what was expected of a silk merchant to the very bizarre. The copious bolts of fine and brightly dyed silks were first to be auctioned, followed by a huge quantity of imported French, Chantilly lace and ladies' corsets, causing jeers, laughter and some lewd remarks from the crowds. Next, were the dozens of crates of, Portuguese port and Scottish whiskey and an entire shipment of cigars from Florida. Small, expertly crafted items of furniture and canteens of silver cutlery were also amongst Edward Jackson's hoard and there was also a mammoth collection of exceptionally realistic looking, paste jewellery which Jackson had apparently been slyly selling throughout the East End, causing many hopeful folk to sell every one of their possessions in order to buy the cut-price jewellery, thinking that they were about to make their fortune.

Every single lot was auctioned off quickly and successfully, leaving the final and largest lot of the, now empty, warehouse to be auctioned. There were at least ten interested bidders, as far as Albert could make out and as the light of day slowly faded and the lamplighters began their evening shift along Whitechapel Street, the warehouse was finally sold off and the much-reduced crowd began to disperse. With all debts being paid by the busy bank manager who had stood alongside the auctioneer throughout the entire day, it soon became evident to Albert that Peggy and the two women in her company were in a distraught state as he watched their gasps of disbelief and tears of frustration. Suddenly, one of the women keeled over in a most undignified way; her huge outdated crinoline upturned, creating a full display of her stockings and silk bloomers. As quick as they could, two other women shielded her modesty, whilst, Albert hurried towards the scene.

"I'm a Doctor, let me through please!" he masterfully ordered.

Peggy quickly covered most of her face with a handkerchief, not realising that Doctor Thompson was already aware of her presence. Albert felt the woman's pulse and loosened the ribbon on her bonnet,

"Could you fetch some water, *Peggy*!" he requested, shocking the younger girl who was at her side.

The woman soon came around, looking pale-faced and feeling quite embarrassed by her unladylike position.

"How fortunate I am that there was a kind physician nearby in my time of need," she declared, gratefully. "I'm Mrs Elizabeth Jackson, and this is my daughter Rayne and my dear mother...

"We are already quite well acquainted, Elizabeth!" interrupted Peggy, her cheeks rosier than Albert had ever seen them, even when she'd emerged from the stifling kitchen in Beatrice's home. "He just happens to be none other than the Oxford Doctor."

"I'm awfully sorry, Doctor, but I'm afraid I will be unable to foot your bill at the moment; as you have probably just witnessed, my late scoundrel of a husband has not only left me penniless but with a mountain of debts, to boot!"

"I'm so sorry to hear your sad news, Mrs Jackson, I did, in fact, meet your late husband a few times and I was also the physician who attended him at his untimely and unfortunate death."

"Then I presume you are here with all the other's he owes money to! This is so embarrassing; I'm feeling quite light-headed again!"

"Not at all, Mrs Jackson, I'm here in search of information. Is there somewhere private we can talk, perhaps?"

"There are no secrets anymore, Doctor Thompson!" expressed Peggy, urgently, "My daughter knows everything there is to know about the goings-on in Oxford and about that brazen hussy, Beatrice Whitlock!"

"Yes, it was that woman who caused Pappa's death....poor Pappa...if he'd have lived longer, he would have put his finances in order and we wouldn't be reduced to living like peasants!" cried Rayne Jackson, hysterically.

Albert rubbed his brow, it had been a long day and he was now left totally confused by the ever-growing, Jackson family; he hadn't a clue as to who the genuine, Mrs Jackson was, but concluded that Edward Jackson had been somewhat of a scoundrel and a bigamist.

CHAPTER TEN

Peggy had led Doctor Thompson to a few feet
away from her daughter and granddaughter,
 "We still have some unfinished business with
the bank manager and the auctioneer, Doctor
Thompson, but if you return in an hour, I will
endeavour to explain our bizarre family to you
and disclose the truth about *that* woman in
Oxford!"
 "There is something I think you should know,
Peggy," stressed Albert, seriously and with some
annoyance at the disrespectful way in which
Peggy and her family repeatedly referred to
Beatrice.
 "If you've turned up here today, Doctor, at the
request of Beatrice Whitlock, hoping to lay claim
on any of Edward's money, then you are not the
intelligent man who I have always credited you
to be. She has no claim, whatsoever, legally or in
any other capacity and as fond as I am of that,
sweet Eleanor, who is entirely innocent in all of
this, I'm afraid there is barely enough money to
clothe and feed us, so she and her mother will
have to look elsewhere for their financial
support! Oh, and you might as well know that
neither Beatrice nor Eleanor know nothing of
Edward's legitimate daughter, they know only
that Elizabeth lost her firstborn. It was Edward's
wish, which he believed would prevent any

unnecessary jealousy from Eleanor, so I'd appreciate it if you would respect the wishes of a deceased man and not breathe a word of what you have discovered today to Beatrice!"

It appeared that once Peggy had begun her declaration, there was no stopping her; Albert stood listening to the cook as thoughts of poor Beatrice floated through his mind. He was finding the situation difficult to believe; this woman's station in life had changed so dramatically in just a few weeks and here she was talking down to him as though he were a naughty schoolboy and he wasn't going to stand for it,

"*Peggy*!" he stressed, wishing that he knew the cook's surname, in order to sound less informal, "Beatrice Jackson, is sadly no longer with us! I had the grim task of recording her untimely death a couple of days ago. The distraught woman took her own life and was discovered by poor Eleanor!"

Dumbstruck, for the briefest of moments, Peggy puckered her thin lips and took in a deep nasal breath, "Well, I can't say I'm sorry to see the back of her, because it would be a lie, but I do sympathize with young Ellie...poor child!"

"Mrs Jackson took you into her home years ago and has treated you with nothing more than kindness over the years, Peggy, how can you stand before me without the slightest sign of compassion! Beatrice was a fine woman and I for one know that she cared a great deal for you *and* your welfare!"

"Do you indeed, Doctor Thompson! Well, perhaps you've just been seeing the fine theatrical show which Beatrice Whitlock seemed to have fooled many people with, including her daughter and my late rascal of a son in law!"

"I don't know what you're talking about and I refuse to speak ill of Beatrice Jackson..."

"*Beatrice Whitlock*...Doctor...you see, even her name was a charade!" interrupted Peggy.

"By the look of how everything has turned out, it looks more like the fault lies solely with that cad, Edward Jackson! He seemed to have led everyone in his path, a merry dance of lies and deceit!"

An anxious-looking, Rayne Jackson suddenly appeared at Peggy's side,

"Mamma needs you, Grandmamma, please hurry!"

"Please return shortly, Doctor Thompson, the news which you have disclosed shines a different light on the situation now and I *would* like to help young Eleanor if I can; she's a good-hearted girl."

Albert took himself to a nearby coffee house in Whitechapel Street, a gloomy den where he got the distinct feeling that there was more than just coffee being sold as he took note of random patrons being ushered through to a concealed area, behind a heavy brown, stained curtain. The olive-skinned waiter returned frequently to where Albert was sitting, armed with a silver coffee pot, he topped up Albert's small china cup for the third time. He had a welcoming smile and Albert couldn't help noticing how white and perfectly aligned his teeth were and also how he spoke no English, apart from '*thank you*', which he repeated too many times. The pungent coffee was thick and intensely strong, but Albert enjoyed every sip and felt as though he had stepped into another world, far away from the streets of Oxford. If Cynthia could see him now, he mused, with a slight lifting of his lip, he would never hear the end of it. The waiter topped up his cup once more, but this time he also placed a glass of cool water next to the cup, perfect to wash down the coffee. After paying his bill, Albert left the coffee house with his eyes open wide and with a feeling of renewed energy, the tiredness of the long day seeming to have vanished all of a sudden.

Forty-five minutes later, Albert found himself outside the now, practically deserted Jackson's warehouse; it was a stark contrast to the sight which had met him on his earlier arrival. The door to Edward Jackson's crooked empire was still open and Albert could only presume that the new owner was inside, gloating over his recent purchase. Elizabeth Jackson emerged, followed by her daughter and mother. They had already spotted Albert and were making their way towards him. Their strained faces and teary eyes became apparent to Albert as they approached.

"Doctor Thompson!" exclaimed Elizabeth, in a forced, jubilant tone, "I don't feel that I've thanked you enough for coming to my rescue when I swooned earlier...I really must insist that my maid refrains from lacing my corset so tightly in future!" If her comment was meant to embarrass Albert, then it failed to work; being a physician, there was not much that he hadn't witnessed or heard and it would take far more than the mention of a lady's undergarment to turn his cheeks scarlet.

"That would indeed be wise, Mrs Jackson," he agreed, calmly.

"Did my poor Edward suffer too much in his final minutes, Doctor?" she suddenly questioned, with her tears on the brink of flowing from her watery, honey eyes.

"His death was sudden, Mrs Jackson, I very much doubt he suffered too much pain."

"*Poor Pappa!*" cried out Rayne, with genuine tears streaming down her face.

"Now, now, the good Doctor doesn't want to be a spectator to your displays of hysterical mourning; control yourselves girls!" ordered Peggy.

In light of what he had discovered, about the unconventional Jackson family, Albert considered it would be quite inappropriate to request that Beatrice should be laid to rest alongside her husband, but he did wish to know where Edward Jackson was buried, it might be a comfort to poor Eleanor.

"Eleanor wishes to visit her father's grave, Peggy; might she be permitted? Could you disclose its whereabouts to me, in the strictest of confidence, I assure you."

"That little minx isn't going anywhere near my father's grave!" exclaimed Rayne, overhearing the furtive whispers. "It was all her fault that Pappa didn't die in his bed, with his loving family by his side to comfort him. He should never have been in Oxford on that day and if I ever see her, I will scratch her eyes out...*I swear I will!*"

"*Rayne! Control yourself!*" screamed Elizabeth Jackson. "You have not been raised and taught to conduct yourself in such an appalling manner!" Elizabeth's face was flushed with embarrassment and Albert couldn't help thinking how sweet-natured Eleanor was, compared to her vicious sounding half-sister.

"It is not *the girl's* fault, Rayne...but her mother's; she bewitched your father and when the strongest of gentlemen is seduced by such a loose woman, as Beatrice Whitlock was, he can find no power in him to resist; it's the very nature of men!"

"I still hate her, though, with all my heart and

soul!"

"Do please excuse my young and childish daughter, Doctor Thompson, she is only thirteen and feeling the sudden loss of her Pappa *too, too* painful."

"And I'm sure young Eleanor is too!" he replied annoyingly.

"She must come and live with us, we are her family now and we will take good care of her, won't we, Elizabeth?" declared Peggy, her once full cheeks now looking quite flabby from her sudden loss of weight over the recent weeks.

"But we have nowhere to live!" interrupted Rayne, "and we are now, *poor* people!"

"Hush yourself, child, haven't you said enough already!" ordered Peggy.

"She should come and live with us in our lodging house; it's only a temporary measure until my late husband's finances have been properly assessed after today's auction. I'm sure we will soon be standing on our feet again and it might be a step in the right direction for Rayne to become acquainted with her half-sister."

Rayne stood silently, trying to hide her obvious disapproval of her mother's invitation. She pouted her mouth and crossed her arms, distancing herself from her mother and grandmother.

"And by the way, Doctor Thompson, it would be completely out of the question for the girl to visit her father's grave. Edward, God rest his soul, is buried in a private graveyard, which once belonged to his family. Unfortunately, my husband was forced to sell the property when his business took a downward tumble, but he sold it on the condition, that only immediate members of the Jackson family could be buried in the Estate's resting garden."

Albert took out his pocket watch, it was getting late and the effects of the coffee were wearing off, leaving him feeling starving hungry and in need of a decent night's sleep.

"Where exactly are you lodging, Mrs Jackson? I will, of course, put your kind suggestion to Eleanor on my return, but she *is* an Oxford girl and might prefer to remain in her hometown, amongst familiar faces!"

"Well, if you must know, Doctor Thompson, Beatrice never had any proper friends. She was just a flirt and a gold digger, with her heart set on finding a suitable replacement for Edward, but the wealthy folk of Oxford could see through her conniving ways and I dare say they won't want anything to do with her daughter! Eleanor is destined for a sad and lonely life, thanks to the selfishness of her so-called mother!" exclaimed Peggy, bitterly.

Albert didn't like what he was hearing; these women were painting an atrocious picture of Beatrice and he knew she was not at all like they wished him to imagine her.

"I must take my leave of you now, ladies, but I

will be sure to inform Eleanor of your *most* generous offer. Where exactly *is* your lodging-house?"

"Twenty-seven Whitechapel Street; it's the finest looking building in the entire thoroughfare!" boasted Elizabeth Jackson.

The events of the day had left Albert with plenty on his mind, he was still shocked by the double life which Beatrice seemed to have lived and he wondered how much Eleanor knew of her mother's shady past. But no matter how any member of the Jackson family endeavoured to paint an unpleasant picture of Beatrice, nothing would sway his mind to think of her as anything other than a loving and beautiful-hearted woman.

CHAPTER ELEVEN

As September merged into October and Eleanor
celebrated her fifteenth birthday, alone in the
dismal shed, she was beginning to think that
she'd never again lay her eyes on August Miller.
It was becoming part of her routine to walk the
entire length, up and down Bullingdon Road, at
least twice a day. August seemed to have
vanished, leaving her completely alone and
sensing, with trepidation, that it wouldn't be
long before new occupants moved into her old
house and she would be forced to vacate her
makeshift home. Her daily walk also included a
visit to her mother's graveside; Beatrice had been
buried in St Mary and St John Church, with only
a handful of mourners from the Sunday
congregation in attendance. None of her
mother's high class and wealthy friends had
even bothered to find out what had happened to
Beatrice Jackson, leaving Eleanor with the
impression that her mother had, in fact, led a
lonely life, having had many acquaintances, but
without a single caring friend amongst them.
Doctor Thompson had given up on his search for
Eleanor. When he discovered that she was not
living in Bullingdon Road, as she'd previously
informed him, he merely concluded that she had
perhaps gone to live with one of Beatrice's many
friends. He did, however, keep an eye open for

her whenever he was out and about on his daily rounds, never giving up hope of being able to disclose the good news to her that she wasn't as alone in the world as she might think and that she had a half-sister in London, although, he thought it now quite impossible to find her. The Jackson family would surely have left the lodging- house by now; he speculated and probably resided in a less dilapidated area of the City.

August leaned against the wall as he stood in Oxford's market, behind a pile of ladies undergarments; not amused from the usual gags and comical banter which he always received from his fellow costermongers, as they joked about his merchandise, August had a deep and disturbing feeling of gloom about him which had taken away his smile and usual, jovial disposition. He had at last caught up with the housing agent who it would seem had taken a sudden dislike to him. Mr Fletcher had been quite hostile in his explanation about how he didn't take kindly to being lied to and tricked, by youngsters, but when August lost his temper and grabbed him by the throat, he eventually admitted that he'd terminated the agreement and taken the keys away from Miss Whitlock, with a strong emphasis when mentioning her surname. He also had no clue as to where she and her mother had fled.

The strong autumn winds whistled through the open market, the weather had suddenly turned and temperatures had dropped considerably. August wrapped the woollen scarf, which his ma had knitted for him, tightly around his neck and put another stone on top of his goods; it would make the costermonger's day if he had to start chasing bloomers around the market, should a strong gust send them soaring off into the sky like flying kites. His mind was focussed only on Eleanor, his beautiful Eleanor. He had to find her; she had become his sole purpose for living and the very thought of a life without her brought an immediate black cloud hovering above him. But where could she have gone to, he mused, over and over again as he rattled his brain, in a bid to remember every single word which she'd ever spoken to him, hoping to find a hidden clue or a lead to follow, but her words seemed to have floated away like puffs of smoke and he could only remember her beauty. He could picture her rosy lips and soft features and the way her striking blue eyes lit up when she spoke so excitedly and the sadness of her entire face when she had explained to him her heartbreaking story.

 'Come on August, use your head; call yourself an author? Then you should have the imagination to know where your true love has gone!' he scolded himself, unaware of how audible his voice had become. A couple of young girls giggled at him

as their mothers picked out four pairs of bloomers and matching camisoles. They handed their coins to August, as they simultaneously ordered their children to stop being so rude, leaving August red-faced.

Eleanor seldom entered her old house anymore; it brought back too many sad memories. It was also colder inside the house than in the shed, which took little time to warm up once she'd lit the lantern. She was also terrified of falling asleep and being discovered, should a new tenant arrive out of the blue. Eleanor would either remain in the shed for the entire day or leave early in the morning, returning in the obscure light of sunset. Her fear of being discovered seemed to increase with every passing day and her money which paid for candles and food was quickly diminishing. She knew, in her heart, that she would soon have to face the world and find employment. She'd read her mother's letter over and over again, finding herself becoming increasingly curious about her grandmother. She was, after all, the only family she had but was unsure as to whether her grandmother would welcome her...if she cared anything for her, why had she never been a part of her life, she pondered. It wasn't her fault that her parents weren't married and that she was illegitimate.

The strengthening October winds howled and whistled through every crevice of the tiny shed, causing Eleanor to shiver uncontrollably. Dressed in her warmest wool dress with her velvet, winter mantle and thickest bonnet tightly secured, Eleanor squeezed her eyes shut and prayed for sleep. Her empty belly rumbled but there was nothing but mouldy cheese left in her food tin, making her determined that in the morning she would pluck up enough courage and attempt to sell her mother's fine gowns to the local pawnbroker. The high winds caused a shower of pine cones to continuously crash down noisily upon the roof, startling her with every hit. The candle flame danced erratically in the draught, threatening to extinguish at any minute. Pulling the blanket over her head, Eleanor sobbed into her pillow, angry at how her parents had been so irresponsible and left her in such a dire situation. *"Why, Mamma, why didn't you stay here for me...I thought you loved me! How will I ever survive my life...oh Mamma...I miss you so much!"* After sobbing herself to sleep, Eleanor soon drifted into the most bizarre of dreams; August's handsome face became as clear as daylight, he was beckoning her towards him, even though she kept insisting that she couldn't leave the warmth of her cosy home; it was the warmest she'd felt for weeks and she relished in the luxurious heat and the comforting sound of the crackling firewood. Suddenly awaking to the stark reality that she wasn't dreaming at all, but surrounded by out of control, towering flames, Eleanor choked and coughed on the thick smoke which overwhelmed the tiny shed. In-between bouts of screaming and choking she cried out for her mamma as she viewed the surrounding inferno.

"Please help me!" she hollered, knowing that nobody could hear her cries for help.

The unforgiving, bright orange flames surrounded her as they climbed up the wooden walls, quickly devouring them on their journey. Eleanor frantically looked about her; her face was burning hot and through the black smoke she suddenly caught sight of the hem of her layered skirts and petticoat; they were alight and she knew that if she didn't venture through the curtain of soaring flames, she would soon be roasted alive. In vain, she attempted to open the wooden chest in a desperate bid of retrieving the box of jewellery, a keepsake to remind her of her dear mamma, but the red hot clasp only burnt her fingers, causing her to scream out.

Everything inside the shed was now burning as she held her breath, closed her eyes and crawled out like a maimed animal, scurrying away to lick its wounds.

The cold wind had never felt so refreshing upon her skin. She rolled over in the overgrown grass, relishing in its dampness. Within minutes of her escape, all four sides of the shed caved in, bringing the roof crashing down, noisily. Eleanor sat in shock, watching the huge bonfire as she hid her body beneath the concealing umbrella of the conifer trees. The neighbouring window suddenly opened and the grumpy faced, Mr Salmon, dressed in his nightshirt and cap, held out a candle as he viewed the shed. "Its only next doors shed, my love...probably some old paint and turpentine self-igniting... nothing to worry about! It will soon put itself out if the rain doesn't claim victory first!"

He closed the window and drew the curtain.

"Foolish old man!" whispered Eleanor, under her breath. *"How could paint and turpentine self ignite?"*

By the light of the flames, Eleanor inspected the hem of her dress; it was ruined and the strong, choking odour of smoke had overpowered her entire body, but she had a plan; she would wait for the fire to die down and search for the spare keys, sure that they wouldn't have been damaged by the fire. At least she could return to the house, wash away the stench and use the scissors to neaten the hem of her dress. In misery, Eleanor sat praying for a heavy downpour to arrive before the morning light and miraculously, as though the angels had been sent to her aid, the heavens opened and the heaviest downpour of rain was soon falling, like stair rods from the dark sky. Never before had

Eleanor enjoyed such an experience of becoming soaked to the skin; she could hear Peggy's voice in her head, warning her that she'd catch a chill and be left snivelling and sneezing for a week, but she was just too elated to be alive and to feel the cool rain soothing her burning face and hands and washing off the smoky odour from her clothes. She was homeless and penniless, with only the damaged dress upon her back, but after her near-death experience, Eleanor was grateful for such huge mercies.

Even after the heavy downpour, the shed continued to smoulder and with the arrival of daylight, Eleanor's worst nightmare became true; new tenants were finally moving into her old house and the disturbing sight of the familiar housing agent striding up the back garden pathway, to inspect the burning shed, sent her into a state of panic. Eleanor squeezed her body, as far as she could, beneath the overhanging conifers, barely breathing as she prayed that she'd not be noticed.

The housing agent looked on grimly at the smoking ruin of the shed as he moved bits of debris with the toe of his shoe. A middle-aged man soon joined him,

"Who would have committed such a dreadful act of arson?" he questioned, in a sorrowful tone. "I hope this is a safe area, Mr Fletcher...my wife is expecting our first child come the Spring and I don't want her living anywhere where there poses the slightest threat to her welfare!"

"Come now Mr Winterbottom, this place is as safe as houses if you'd pardon my pun! We've had the most vicious of storms overnight and I dare say the shed was hit by lightning and with the previous tenant probably leaving some highly combustible concoctions behind, my conclusion is that it caused it to go up like a box of matches!"

"Did you not think to empty the shed, Mr Fletcher, wouldn't that have been the wise approach when leaving a property empty for a long period!"

Eleanor grinned to herself, thoroughly enjoying the sight of the mean housing agent being talked down to and looking positively sheepish.

"My young clerk couldn't find the key to the outbuilding, Mr Winterbottom, but I assure you it was definitely recorded and ironically, I had intended to look into the matter this very week!"

Eleanor sensed that the housing agent was lying through his teeth.

Mr Winterbottom shook his head in a sign of disapproval,

"If I conducted my London business in such a shoddy manner, Mr Fletcher, I would not be the successful businessman that you see before you...let this be a lesson to you...it's all in the details, Mr Fletcher...it's the smallest and most vital actions which bring about achievement and wealth. That fire could easily have spread to the house and consequently the entire street! Think about that, Mr Fletcher. Now, shall we return to the house? And, by the way, I expect this to be dealt with and replaced by the end of the week!"

"You can rest assured that before the end of *tomorrow*, you will look out from the dining room window and see a smart new shed in position!"

"Hmmm, well in that case, perhaps you could instruct your workmen to position it on the other side of the garden!"

"Anything you wish for, Mr Winterbottom!" stressed the housing agent, "anything at all, we aim to please!"

Eleanor listened for the sound of the back door closing before daring to relax a little and breathe normally. She went over the conversation again in her head, wanting to remember every word so that if she ever did run into August Miller again, she could share the story with him. More urgently though, she knew that her days in Henley Road were now at an end and if she didn't make a quick exit from the garden she risked being discovered.

CHAPTER TWELVE

After spending a day in London, August had unwittingly purchased new supplies of fine silk from Jackson's warehouse auction, having no clue of the connection between the warehouse and his sweet Eleanor, who now haunted his dreams every night. Winifred was delighted with the exceptionally, fine quality bolts of material and euphoric at the low price which August had paid for them, but her joy soon diminished on witnessing the sadness which August was trying his best to hide.

"What is it son, have you realised that the young lass in Oxford is not for you? Has something happened? Look closer to home for love, my darling and if you care to take an old and wise woman's advice, young Iris Fielding would make a fine bride!"

"Ma, I'm not looking for any female to take for a bride...I only have eyes for Eleanor!"

"Well, with a fancy name like that, it's no wonder she's breaking your heart son!"

August let out a long sigh, wishing his mother would quit insisting that Eleanor was out of his reach when she knew nothing at all about her.

"She's vanished, Ma, and I'm really worried about her. She and her mother have been left destitute since the passing of her father...she also recently discovered that her parents weren't even married!"

"Well then, son, maybe it's a blessing that she's vanished! She sounds like bad news to me, with no mistaking. Now, come and tell me all about your trip to London. How on earth did you manage to purchase such fine silks and still put two shillings in the pot?"

August was not in the right frame of mind to chat to his ma, he was preoccupied with thoughts of finding Eleanor and he'd already planned to leave East Hanwell at first light in search of her. Suddenly remembering the spectacles he'd bought from Spitalfield market, he took them from his pocket,

"Close your eyes ma!" he instructed.

"Oh don't be so daft, August; I'm far too long in the tooth for children's games!" Her cheeks had tinged pink all of a sudden.

"Come on Ma, don't be shy now!"

"*Me! Shy*...that will be the day!"

"Then close your eyes...I've got a surprise for you!"

Reluctantly, Winifred went along with August's request and he gently placed the wire-rimmed spectacles in position on her face,

"Now take a look at how well you can see your needlework!" he declared, handing her the half-finished camisole she'd been working on. Her broad smile was instant as she blinked and examined the spectacles with her fingertips.

"It's like a blooming miracle...everything looks

so clear...*Oh, my dear Lord*, I never realised that table cloth had so many stains on it...that will have to come off on washday. Come and sit in front of me August, let me take a good look at my handsome son...see what I've been missing for so long!"

August laughed out loud at his ma's hilarious antics.

"God bless you August, you've given me back my eyes. I feel like a young woman again and I do believe I will be able to make two pairs of bloomers in the time it took me to make one!"

"Well in your own words Ma, tomorrow is another day and I reckon it's about time for a mug of cocoa and a good night's kip. I will be leaving early in the morning to Oxford, by the way!"

"What for, son! You've already sold everything I've made, or are you off to see another publisher?"

"*No Ma*, I'm off to search for Eleanor and her mother!"

Winifred's happiness had been immediately marred, she frowned and looked away holding her tongue from what she really wished to say.

Still in hiding beneath the conifers, the dreary, damp day had failed to infuse Eleanor with the energy to make her urgent and final exit from the garden. As she curled up in a bid to keep warm, she reflected on the traumatic night which she'd experienced and pondered on the discovery that after all the years, her home was about to have new tenants. She was left exhausted and as her thoughts drifted off, she failed to hear the approaching chorus of men's voices until they were practically treading on her fingers, with their huge boots. Horrified at the sight of the two constables, clad in their navy twill uniforms, Eleanor already knew that she'd been spotted.

"Come along, young Miss, you can't go living on private property! You should consider yourself most fortunate to be alive!"

Bolting upright, Eleanor felt the constable's boring eyes upon her as they stared down, from what seemed like a great height. Quickly jumping to her feet, she was overcome by the aching pains in her body and the burning of her hands.

"Eleanor isn't it?" stated one of the constables, with a friendly smile.

"Eleanor Jackson!" added the other. "Your neighbour has told us all about you; it would appear you've not had a happy few months too!"

"But that doesn't give you the right to take up residence in the garden shed, young lady!" stated the stern-faced constable, his smile replaced by a scowl.

"But I wasn't doing any harm!" protested Eleanor.

"I beg to differ, Miss Jackson; you have completely sabotaged property, which doesn't belong to you, not to mention the fact that you were trespassing, or that you could have killed yourself, or that you put the lives of the entire residents of Henley Road at risk, along with their homes!"

Eleanor burst into tears and at last, gained a little sympathy from the pair of law enforcers.

"What else was I to do?" she sobbed. "I have no one or nowhere to turn to and I've lost *both* my parents!"

"You could have brought yourself along to the police station; we are always ready to help such unfortunate cases."

"With your safety being our paramount concern, Miss Jackson, I have no choice other than to admit you into the workhouse, unless you can inform me of any relative who would be willing to take you in?"

"I have a grandmother; she lives somewhere east of Oxford!" stressed Eleanor.

"Can you take us to her?"

"No, I haven't met her before and I'm not *exactly* sure of where she lives."

"What's her name?" ordered the impatient sounding constable.

"I'm not a hundred per cent sure...it could be Mrs Whitlock...unless, of course, she has married again."

"It all sounds *rather* vague to me and we haven't

got time to waste chasing shadows!"

"At least in the workhouse, you'll be warm and have a roof over your head and three meals a day...it's not *all* that bad you know and there is always the prospect that they will find a suitable position for you, Miss Jackson!"

"My name is Miss *Whitlock*, not *Jackson*!" declared Eleanor with tears rolling down her bright, red cheeks.

The constables shared a furtive glance, choosing to ignore her statement.

"Come along now Miss, let's be on our way shall we?"

Escorted on either side of her, as though she were a common criminal, the walk to Cowley Road workhouse took them through Bullingdon Road, where Eleanor prayed, that by some small miracle, August might be in the vicinity.

"I have a close friend!" she blurted out in desperation. "He's called August Miller! Have you heard of him? He's going to be a famous author one day; I'm sure *he* would take care of me!"

The constables exchanged yet another wary glance, "Well, Miss Jackson, I'm sure that once you've got yourself settled in the workhouse and earned a penny or two you'll be able to post him a letter, telling him of your whereabouts!"

"I'm *Miss Whitlock!* I think I've already told you that!" stated Eleanor, crossly.

The workhouse was set back from the main thoroughfare, with a long, gated pathway leading up to its entrance. A few of its inhabitants wandered the grounds and Eleanor couldn't help but notice their drab and miserable expressions. A chilling wind suddenly whipped around her ankles, reminding her of how the hemline of her dress was now a few inches shorter, extremely scruffy and on the borderline of being deemed indecent. She was glad of the thick stockings which, although now full of burn holes, at least covered most of her flesh. She had no right to look down at the state of her prospective living companions when she was in a frightful state, she considered, as she took in every inch of the ominous-looking building which loomed in front of her. The constables led her around to a side door where they were all then escorted by an elderly man, whose serious expression seemed to be set in stone. The constable's heavy footsteps echoed off the stone walls as they followed the man to a small office. He knocked loudly upon its door and was greeted by a man's voice, telling them to enter.

"Thank you, Wolf, you may leave us now," said the constable, in a kindly tone.

The warmth of the office was immediately apparent, as the constables led Eleanor into the cosy room where a plump couple sat side by side behind a desk. A roaring fire crackled in the huge stone fireplace and the sweet odour of toasted muffins filled the well-furnished room.

"Good morning, Constables!" they declared in unison, with their eyes fixed firmly on Eleanor.

"Good day to you, Mr and Mrs Killigrew and I trust the day finds you both in the best of health!"

"And who do we have here then, constable?" questioned Mrs Killigrew, as she eyed Eleanor from head to toe.

"A young lass, who needs a new dress I'd say!" chuckled Mr Killigrew, displaying the half-chewed muffin in his gaping mouth.

Eleanor felt her cheeks burning even more.

"What's your name, girl and how old are you?" demanded Mrs Killigrew, her hooded eyes sending a chill through Eleanor's body.

"I'm Eleanor Whitlock and I'm fifteen!" she declared, with her head held high.

One of the constables coughed loudly to gain Mrs Killigrew's attention, "Her name is, Eleanor Jackson, but she seems to insist on calling herself, *Whitlock,* for some reason!"

Mrs Killigrew took in a deep breath and stared hard at Eleanor, "Well, well, well, young lady...think you're something else by the look of things...well, let me tell you this...you can call yourself whatever you like; *Jackson, Whitlock, Fisher, Smith, Walker* or even *Killigrew,* if it pleases you, but when you go to your allotted dormitory and your place of work and for as long as you are under our care, you will be on record as, Eleanor Jackson, as the good constable, has informed us, but since Eleanor is a blooming mouthful of a name, from this day forth, you will be known as, *Ellie*! Short and sweet and with no blooming fancy airs and graces about it. Is that clear, *Ellie*?"

Already taking a strong dislike to Mrs Killigrew, Eleanor felt too weary to put up a fight and simply nodded in agreement.

"Right, well, we will be leaving now then!" announced one of the constables, as he glanced at Eleanor. "Make sure you behave yourself, Ellie!" he added, with a hint of sarcasm.

"Oh don't you worry none, constable, we'll soon have her settled, in good '*Killigrew*' fashion!" Mrs Killigrew boldly expressed.

CHAPTER THIRTEEN

The constables had barely left Mr and Mrs
Killigrew's office, before there was a light rap on
the door and a painfully thin and haggard
woman was ushered in. Eleanor had been
planning to put her case to them, hoping to be
allowed to go in search of her grandmother, but
it was soon apparent that the workhouse was
run militarily and was more like a prison,
leaving no windows for informal conversations.
"This is Mrs Wolf," announced Mrs Killigrew.
"She will sort you out with your clothing and
other sundry matters and show you where you
will be sleeping, that being of course, that you
keep your nose clean and don't stir up any
trouble amongst the rest of the inmates!"
 Mr Killigrew, who was still stuffing muffins
into his overfull mouth, burst out into a fit of
laughter, spraying morsels of soggy dough
across the desk. "Don't talk daft, Mrs Killigrew, a
fine-looking lass like Ellie, knows better than
that; she comes from good stock, does *our Ellie*;
she will go far!"
Mrs Killigrew issued a thunderous look to her
husband before continuing,
 "As I was saying, Mrs Wolf will show you
where you will be working and anything else
which she thinks you need to know! Just make
sure you remember where you are now, Ellie; *is*

that clear?" Eleanor reluctantly nodded her head in agreement to the vile, Mrs Killigrew, already fearful of her new guardians and praying that all the stories she'd heard, over the years, about these unforgiving establishments had been exaggerated.

Mrs Wolf led Eleanor back along the same corridor, greeting Mr Wolf as they passed by him, on the way to the female wing of the workhouse. Eleanor had presumed that they were married, but when she gingerly asked if he was her husband, Mrs Wolf announced that they were, in fact, brother and sister; she'd given herself the title of 'Mrs' after being promoted from the sewing room to her current position, of being in charge of the storeroom. Eleanor was even more shocked when Mrs Wolf disclosed how she and her brother had been in the workhouse since being orphaned when they were both under the age of three. Eleanor felt an immediate sorrow for her, having lived such a dreary life, but Mrs Wolf seemed to be quite satisfied that she'd been rescued from a potential life of poverty and hardship. She declared that she and her brother knew no other life and were grateful for having been taken care of and more than happy to live out the remainder of their days in the workhouse. A sudden thought struck Eleanor; what if she became an old woman, never living a normal life in the outside world again? It was a thought which filled her with the greatest of fear, making her determined that no matter how long it took, she *would* escape; there surely must be a way, she mused.

Mrs Wolf's office was no bigger than a large broom cupboard. Having already prepared a bowl of warm water and a bar of overpowering carbolic soap, she ordered Eleanor to strip down to her undergarments and wash.

"Take my advice, Ellie and enjoy your last wash in warm water; from tomorrow morning it will be ice cold, direct from the outside pump, a most bracing start to the day!"

Eleanor watched from the corner of her eye as Mrs Wolf rolled up her fire-damaged dress into a ball and tucked it neatly under her arm.

"Right, young Ellie, I'm going to leave you for a few minutes...make sure you wash in all those hidden places, while I'm away!" she said, amusingly, smiling for the first time and displaying a mouth void of a single tooth.

Locking the door behind her, Eleanor listened to her footsteps as they faded away in the distance. She wondered where she was taking her dress and what she would be given to wear as a replacement. Eleanor proceeded to wash her feet and ankles, considering them the only part of her body in need of a wash, after becoming soiled from her night in the garden. She sat down on the wooden chair, still in a state of disbelief that this was really happening to her, as burning tears rolled down her face. How would she ever find August, she pondered...if only she'd asked him where he lived. Now he would find someone else, they would never be together and all her romantic imaginings would remain nothing more than dreams, for eternity. Her reverie was soon broken by the clanging of keys against the door and she quickly wiped away her tears, not wanting Mrs Wolf to witness her sorrow. The door suddenly flew open and a disturbing instinct told Eleanor that it was not the frail, Mrs Wolf.

"Now, don't you look a pretty picture, young Ellie...you've made my flesh tingle! I could quite easily *ravish* you, *you little beauty!*"

Eleanor quickly crossed her arms over her semi bare chest and tried to hide her legs beneath the tiny table, which was only slightly bigger than the washbasin upon it.

"Has Mrs Wolf left you alone, then?" he questioned, as his bloodshot eyes devoured Eleanor's body from top to toe.

She felt her insides contract with fear.

"She will be back in a minute, *she assured me!*" Eleanor was aware of how shaky her voice sounded; she lowered her eyes, praying that Mr Killigrew would leave. His breathing was heavy and his putrid breath soon filled the small space.

"I'm so glad that you've joined the workhouse, Ellie, it's been quite a while since I've laid my eyes on such young and unspoiled loveliness. Play your cards right, my girl and I'll make sure you don't go without!"

He suddenly stretched out his arm, lifting Eleanor's chin with his fat, grubby fingers; his grimy hand reeked of dripping. Eleanor was trapped between the table and his overweight body as he tried to squeeze the rest of his bulky weight through the tiny door. Just managing to bend enough, his face came close to hers. Eleanor swiftly backed away as his slobbering lips planted themselves upon her cheek, just missing her lips. He made a satisfying sound, as though he'd just filled his mouth with a tasty pie.

"*Mr Killigrew*! *What in Heaven's name are you doing in here? Shame on you!* Just you wait 'til I tell Mrs Killigrew; she will starve you for a week!"

Eleanor was euphoric to hear the sound of Mrs Wolf and watched in delight as Mr Killigrew begged her to keep quiet about his shenanigans.

"Be gone from here and leave this poor lass alone, d'you understand and I might just forget about what my eyes witnessed!"

Mr Killigrew did not leave without slyly winking at Eleanor; she turned the other way feeling quite nauseous from her experience and from the obnoxious odour which he'd left behind.

"*Filthy rotten scoundrel*!" declared Mrs Wolf, under her breath as she locked the door and took out an enormous pair of scissors from her apron pocket. Eleanor viewed them in horror.

"Don't look so worried girl; I'm not going to hurt you, just chop off your hair."

"*No! Please don't do that!*"

"They're the rules...*no long hair*...it spreads fleas and it's not practical to keep it clean. Now don't make my job difficult, Ellie or I might end up cutting your pretty face...my eyes are as old as my bones, you know!"

Eleanor wasn't sure if Mrs Wolf's display of gums was a warning sign or if she was merely smiling at her, in the hope of calming her down. She suddenly remembered her mamma and how she would brush her hair a hundred times every night before bedtime; she would never fail to tell her how beautiful her golden locks were and how they were her crowning glory, like a princess's coronet.

"May *I* be permitted to cut my hair then, if there's no choice in the matter?" requested Eleanor.

Mrs Wolf chuckled and shook her head as though Eleanor had requested something outrageous.

"I wasn't born yesterday...I knows all the tricks in the book and I don't trust nobody, but myself with these here scissors...who's to say that you don't plan on stabbing me before you steal my keys and make your hasty escape?"

Eleanor couldn't believe what she was hearing, "I wouldn't even dream of doing such a terrible thing, Mrs Wolf! What sort of girl do you take me for?"

"Well I'm not about to change the rules, so just keep still and let me do what I have to do!"

Mrs Wolf handed Eleanor a dark grey cotton work bonnet to cover her hacked off, ear length, hair, it matched the grey, serge working dress she'd been given along with a black shawl and thick dark grey stockings.

"Look after these clothes, Ellie, because you'll have to pay for any future replacements from your earnings and it will be a good few months before you get to hold a penny in your fair hands!"

Feeling like a proper workhouse girl and as though her life had drawn to its end, Eleanor followed Mrs Wolf through another seemingly endless corridor, before they reached the sleeping dormitory. A row of rudimentary wooden beds, each topped with a palliasse and a grey blanket, filled the depressing room. Consumed with sorrow, Eleanor could only stare, speechless at the sight.

"I can't tell you which bed you'll be sleeping in tonight, but I can tell you that there are more women than beds, so you might find yourself sharing...which is sometimes a blessing on a cold winter's night!"

Completely disheartened, the sight of a large tin pail caught Eleanor's attention.

"The warden always locks the door, so if you get desperate, that's where you can relieve yourself!" stated Mrs Wolf, as though she was reading Eleanor's thoughts.

"Come along, Ellie, let me take you to Mrs Wishbone, she's in charge of all the females who work in the sewing room, which is where you have been allocated to work for the time being."

Feeling as though she was in the midst of a nightmare, Eleanor followed behind Mrs Wolf like a dutiful puppy.

CHAPTER FOURTEEN

The sewing room was not how Eleanor had
envisaged it; the gentle hum of chatter
immediately silenced as the countless groups of
women all ceased sewing to fix their eyes on the
new inmate. Eleanor felt her cheeks burning.
There were countless women crammed into the
spacious room, all seated on low benches or
stools and stooped over the pieces of fawn
sacking, which they were busily working on.
Some of them called out their greetings to
Eleanor, while others merely stared, their gaunt
faces showing no sign of emotion. Eleanor
couldn't help but notice how frail and
undernourished they all looked as she glanced at
the sea of grey faces, devoid of all colour.
Expecting to be met by a more colourful sight in
the sewing room, Eleanor had been hoping that
she might be stitching beautiful dresses to be
sold outside of the workhouse, the depressing
news that the work consisted entirely of sewing
mail sacks and flour sacks from morning until
night only added to her disappointment.
"And *who* do we have here, *Mrs Wolf?*"
Eleanor's immediate thoughts were that her
voice was far too loud for her short stature. She
looked down at the short, spherical woman who
stood at their side.
"This is Ellie; she's only just arrived, this very

morn; recently lost her parents, so I've been informed. She's fifteen, Mrs Wishbone!" Eleanor was becoming quite tired of being studied by every new pair of eyes which caught sight of her. She stared directly into Mrs Wishbone's eyes as they met hers and boldly poked her tongue out at her, aiming to show a bit of defiance and bravery for a change. Mrs Wishbone squinted her eyes and yelled out to one of the women, who was bent over her work, sewing as though her life depended upon it, "*Suzy,* pass me '*Frederick*' and make haste girl!" No sooner had Mrs Wishbone spoken, than the pitiful waif-like girl hurried to the corner of the workroom and retrieved a length of knotted, tree branch, which had been stripped of its bark; she handed it to Mrs Wishbone; it was the same height as her and Eleanor watched as her fascination suddenly transformed to fear when realising what Mrs Wishbone intended to do with her weapon. Grabbing one end of it with both of her podgy hands, the tense faced woman swung the branch around in the air before striking the side of Eleanor's body with it. Releasing a loud cry, Eleanor spontaneously grabbed the end of the branch. The room was suddenly filled with loud gasps from every woman in the room as they witnessed Eleanor's rebellious actions.

"*How dare you touch Frederick!*" roared the mad looking, Mrs Wishbone. "You have a lot to learn,

Ellie! And you've started your days at the workhouse on the wrong foot!"

"Mrs Wishbone is there *really* a need for such an unfriendly welcome!" intervened Mrs Wolf, as she nervously took the branch from Ellie's hold.

"Start as you mean to go on, that's always been my way and it hasn't failed me yet, Wolf...and I'd thank you to keep your interfering nose out of my business! Now if you've said your piece, I'd also thank you to leave my sewing room before *all* my women find themselves missing luncheon, on account that they are a sack behind, come midday!"

Mrs Wishbone's threat caused all the women to instantly return to their sewing as silence befell the spacious room once more, she was a vicious tyrant, considered Eleanor as she rubbed the side of her thigh and observed Mrs Wolf leaving the sewing room.

Mrs Wishbone held her branch like a staff, occasionally banging it upon the stone floor as she surveyed her workers, with her lips tightly pursed.

"*Tilly!*" she suddenly screamed out, like a madwoman, her sharp voice causing Eleanor to flinch. "Get your lazy bones over here!"

Eleanor watched as a younger-looking girl hurried towards them; she had a pretty face, small features and huge brown eyes, but like everyone else in the workhouse she was painfully thin.

"Yes, Mrs Wishbone?"

"I want *you* to take Ellie under your knowledgeable wing and teach her all that she needs to know about her new life here in the workhouse...is that clear Tilly? And I mean everything because if she puts one step out of line, it will be *you*, young Tilly, who feels the anger of Frederick upon your miserable hide! Have I made myself clear?"

"Yes, Mrs Wishbone!"

Mrs Wishbone diverted her stern glare back to Eleanor, "Well, Ellie! Have I made myself clear?" she hollered.

"Yes, Mrs Wishbone," repeated Eleanor, in parrot-fashion.

Tilly took hold of Eleanor's hand as she meandered back through the sea of grey-clad workers. She picked up her stool from where she'd been sitting before and pointed to the row of spare stools beneath the long table, which stretched the length of the room and was covered with completed sacks and piles of sacks waiting to be sewn. Eleanor quickly retrieved a stool for herself.

"We'll sit in the corner so as we don't disturb anyone. I hope you know how to sew, Ellie, it will make my job a lot easier if you do!" She smiled at Ellie and, for the first time, made her feel as though she wasn't quite so alone in the world.

"I've done embroidery before, so yes, I think I

can safely say that I know how to sew!"

"Well, you won't be needing any fancy embroidery stitches for these rough bits of sacking, it's just tiny, neat, running stitches all around the edges, apart from the top...you can't go wrong...although, there once was an old woman who sewed all four sides of forty sacks in one day! I think she might have been half-blind though, poor old dear!"

"Don't tell me that Mrs Wishbone took her branch to the old woman!" exclaimed Eleanor in horror!

"Of course she did, nobody is spared from *Frederick*!"

"*She's mad*!"

"Yes she certainly is, but don't whatever you do, let her hear you say such a thing! Come on we'd better start doing some work before old Wishbone comes over to inspect us. I'll fill you in on everything you need to know as we stitch; don't expect to keep those soft hands for much longer, Ellie, with these sacks rubbing against them all day long, they'll soon be as rough as sandpaper!"

"Well, since I've already had my long hair hacked off in the ugliest of hair fashions; I don't suppose sandpaper hands will prove too heartbreaking!"

Tilly giggled, "I can see you are going to be good for me, that's the first time I've laughed in months!"

"How old are you Tilly?"

"Seventeen...how about you?"

"Fifteen, only just though, it was my birthday a few weeks ago. How long have you been in here?"

"I came in here with my ma, about ten years ago. She was sick and my pa had recently died, so we didn't have any choice. It was either here or a life of begging on the streets. We were separated on arrival, my ma's health deteriorated and she only lived for a few months. I was put with all the children and Ma was in here, sewing these damned sacks. They only let us spend time together on Sunday afternoons and when she got too ill to sew, I wasn't even allowed to visit her!" Tilly's sad eyes and her tragic story reminded Eleanor of her own sorrow and she felt an instant bond with Tilly.

"Did you come in here alone, Ellie?"

Eleanor had already threaded her needle and had begun sewing down one side of the rigid sacking material.

"Yes, my mother died a few weeks ago and I have been living in a garden shed since, but it caught on fire and the police brought me here." Tilly's jaw dropped, "That's terrible, you must have felt so lonely and scared! Do you not have any other family?"

Not wanting to divulge too many secrets until she knew Tilly better, Eleanor answered cautiously,

"No, I have nobody else."

"I trust you're not just gossiping and time-wasting, over in that corner, Tilly Vine!" sounded the screaming voice of, Mrs Wishbone as she brandished the formidable '*Frederick*', high above her round head. "Remember, you have a task to complete if you don't want to be nursing a pair of black and blue legs, come nightfall!"

"Don't look at her," warned Tilly, "just keep sewing and whatever you do, don't ever let that old dragon catch you smiling or laughing; it's forbidden to be happy in this place!"

Not believing what she was hearing, Eleanor considered that she'd rather be laying alongside her mother than living a life in such a detestable environment, with the likes of Mr Killigrew and Mrs Wishbone breathing down her neck. She had to find a way of escaping, she mused and that would be her only plan for the foreseeable future.

"I considered myself fortunate that the police constable didn't arrest me for trespassing, but I think prison might have been a far better place to be sent to!"

Tilly smiled discreetly, "I doubt that and either way when you'd served your time in jail, you'd still have found yourself in here at the end of it!"

"I suppose so."

"You need to watch out for, old Killigrew...he's a filthy, perverted beast and I bet my month's earnings that he's already marked you as his next conquest! Just make sure you're never alone anywhere in the workhouse, he's got his spies who will do anything for an extra helping of grub!"

Eleanor shuddered as she remembered her recent encounter with the repulsive, Mr Killigrew,

"I had a close escape in Mrs Wolf's storeroom; if her room wasn't so tiny, I daren't think what might have happened! He managed to slobber his disgusting lips over my cheek though and have a good eyeful of me in my undergarments!"

 "Oh, that's awful...poor you! You can guarantee, that won't be the end of it, you'll be playing on his mucky mind from now on...*be extra careful, Ellie!*"

As they continued sewing in silence, Eleanor imagined August's handsome face, knowing that it was the only way she would get through the miserable days ahead, before finding a way to escape.

CHAPTER FIFTEEN

Twelve O'clock soon arrived and with the noisy clanging of the dinner gong sounding out throughout the workhouse, every woman in the sewing room immediately downed their work and waited nervously while Mrs Wishbone conducted a quick tally of the completed sacks. Put into neat piles of twenty, it took only a couple of minutes before she declared that they could all proceed to the dining hall. In single file, the women silently hastened through the long corridor towards the ever-increasing odour of food. Eleanor followed behind Tilly; she was starving and eager to satisfy her hunger. She copied everything that Tilly did, first taking a wooden bowl from one of the lofty stacks by the entrance and marching behind her to where three women stood, dishing out ladles of stew, at the far end of the hall. Eleanor watched as the two extended rows of tables and benches soon became occupied by the hungry women. With her bowl filled with the watery, turnip stew and a small chive of bread in her hand, which Tilly instructed she put securely into her dress pocket, they sat at the next vacant space on the bench where they hurriedly picked up a spoon and began their meagre meal.

"Always put your bread or anything that can be snatched into your pocket, Ellie!" whispered

Tilly. "Trust nobody in this place...there are some mean and nasty characters in here who wouldn't think twice before nicking your share!"
Grateful for Tilly's advice, Eleanor soon came to realise why everyone in the workhouse was so thin and sensed she would soon become a replica of them; the food was barely edible and if she hadn't been so unbearably starving, the doughy bread and the unappetizing, peculiar tasting stew would never have passed her lips. She clandestinely viewed the surrounding women as they gulped down their food.
"You'll be starving later if you don't finish that!" expressed Tilly. "You'll soon get used to the grub in here and strangely enough, even come to look forward to it!"
Eleanor *was* starving, but in her opinion, the meal in front of her wasn't fit for a dog and the dismal thought of being in the workhouse for so long that she would come to look forward to such foul tasting meals, infused her with a sense of despairing gloom. She lifted her mug of water, washing down each mouthful as she tried to stretch her imagination and convince her taste buds that she was eating one of Peggy's deliciously rich, meaty stews. A few of the other women kept glancing at her, all hoping that they might get the chance to finish any leftovers. Luncheon was over in a flash and they were all herded out of the dining hall and back to the sewing room, to toil for another gruelling six

hours, before supper time; Eleanor prayed that supper might prove to be more appealing.

It took little time for Eleanor to become familiar with the sewing room routine and even though her hands were fast becoming sore from the coarse sacking material, as Tilly had warned her, stitching the sacks was quite a simple task compared to the elaborate embroidery work which she'd been used to; it was, however, extremely boring work and made a hundred times worse by having Mrs Wishbone's sharp eyes never seeming to miss anything untoward which took place. During that first long day, Eleanor witnessed seven other women suffering from the heavy blow of her sinister weapon. She wondered why these women didn't simply defend themselves and unite in teaching Mrs Wishbone a lesson. It was a question which was soon answered when Megan, a woman in her late twenties, refused to allow Frederick to touch her body. She had been distracting the women she was sat with by chatting too much and when Mrs Wishbone called her out from her corner of the room to take her punishment, Megan grabbed the lethal branch before it had the chance to inflict any more bruises upon her body; In her anger, she thrust it down and reeled out a mouthful of abuse to Mrs Wishbone, who surprisingly remained quite calm. Ten minutes later, one of the elderly women was seen being sent out of the sewing room, only to return accompanied by none other than the repulsive, Mr Killigrew. Grabbing Megan roughly by her arm, he dragged her away with him. Eleanor watched in horror, feeling quite nauseous at the cruel treatment which poor Megan was subjected to.

"Does he have to be so rough in his handling?" she stressed to Tilly.

"That's nothing to what she's got coming to her!"

"Surely he's not going to torture her, is he?" declared Eleanor, innocently.

"He's going to torture her by satisfying his own monstrous desires if you know what I mean," explained Tilly, speaking as her hands continued to sew at speed. Eleanor gasped.

"Keep sewing Ellie, old Wishbone will be in a foul mood for the rest of the afternoon and eager to give someone a good thrashing!"

Eleanor took Tilly's advice. "Do you mean that he's going to be intimate with her? Like married men and women?"

"Sounds as though you've led a sheltered life, but yes, that's the gist of it, though I doubt he will be so loving and compassionate, as most husbands would be to their wives! He'll take her up to the empty dorm and most likely leave poor Megan with far more bruises than she'd have got from Wishbone's bloody stick!"

Feeling ill at the thought of the terrible goings-on in the workhouse, Eleanor came to realise that the stories she'd heard were tame, compared to the truthful reality. She already feared Mr Killigrew, more than she'd feared anyone in her life and remembered Tilly's words, with great trepidation, about how he would be after her. The very thought of him made her shudder. Supper proved to be even more of a disappointment, consisting of more under baked bread, but this time covered with a thin spread of dripping. Eleanor was so exhausted that her hunger pangs had been overtaken by sheer tiredness and the need to close her eyes and sleep, in the hope of blocking out the dreadful reality of where she was. In charge of the dormitory was, Mrs Blake, a dowdy woman in her fifties and a distant relative of Mrs Killigrew, although there was not the slightest resemblance in their appearance. Mrs Blake was of a lean stature with a permanent cross looking face. She spoke very little and used her long boney fingers to gesture her instructions rather than speak them. Eleanor was given an off white, nightgown to wear, made of the thinnest, almost threadbare material, giving little protection from the ever-decreasing temperatures; even Tilly tried in vain to persuade Mrs Blake to replace it, but she simply shook her head and turned her back on Tilly. Many of the elderly women chose to share beds; they had formed strong bonds over the years and took comfort and warmth in this close contact. Tilly slept alone and had persuaded the woman in the bed next to her to move along the row, allowing Eleanor to take her bed. On a table in the centre of the dormitory stood the only source of light; a dimly lit lantern which gave off a pathetic glow, leaving most of the room in total darkness. Some of the women knelt in prayer, others who had no energy, prayed as they laid on their beds and a few, who had seemingly lost all faith, looked on at those in prayer with a curious and questioning expression. Mrs Blake gave them no more than five minutes to settle before snatching away the lantern and locking them in for the night. Eleanor closed her eyes, she had never in her entire life felt so drained or so demoralized. She slept with thoughts of her mother, knowing that if her mother had not taken her own life and they'd moved into the lodgings in Bullingdon Road, life would be so much better and she might also be in the midst of a blossoming romance, with August Miller.

No sooner had Eleanor drifted off to sleep, than the strange and distressing sounds of wailing woke her; coming from every direction of the workhouse and echoing throughout the cold building, some so distant that at first, she thought she was imagining the helpless cries; children calling out for their mothers, mother's heartrending sobs of despair and guilt at not being able to comfort their beloved babies; older women breaking down as they reminisced on happier times, but the most disturbing of all were the far-away howls of the men, missing their wives and haunted by the fact that they had been unable to provide for their families, consequently bringing them to a life, barely worth living. Eleanor covered her face and sobbed into her hands, sensing that the chorus of misery would be a regular occurrence during the lonely dark hours.

As the disturbing thoughts, that his beautiful Eleanor had left Oxford, it was becoming more and more difficult for August to concentrate on his day to day life; her clear image was never out of his mind and occupied his thoughts from the moment he opened his eyes until he closed them, at the end of each day. When he was supposed to be writing, he found he'd completely gone off the plot and theme of his original story and it had changed from a mysterious detective tale to a story of love, with Eleanor becoming the beautiful damson, waiting to be rescued. His raw emotions jumped out from every chapter he wrote and for the first time, he felt as though his pen was directed implicitly by his aching heart.
It had been weeks since he'd travelled into Oxford and as much as Winifred loved having him around, she knew that his heart was many miles away, even though he was putting on as

normal a face as he could. Her new spectacles had enabled her to increase the speed of her needlework so that she was now turning out twice as many bloomers and camisoles in a day and a stack of the undergarments had now accumulated, taking up much of the space in the small cottage.

"When will you next be selling at Oxford market, August?" she casually asked, over breakfast.

Oxford seemed to have lost its appeal since his failure in finding Eleanor, but he knew that their funds were nearly depleted and with winter looming, food, fuel and candle supplies were desperately needed. He drank his mug of tea, deep in thought, contemplating whether he should sell the stock somewhere else instead.

"I reckon that you might find a lead to your sweetheart if you ask in her local church; you'd be surprised at how much a local vicar knows, August! And if she *is* still living in Oxford, she will surely be attending church, of a Sunday."

For the first time in weeks, August felt his spirits lift...why had *he* not thought of that? It was obvious, the vicar would be sure to know the whereabouts of his flock. August leapt up from his chair, spontaneously hugging his ma as he kissed her round cheeks.

"Ma! You are a genius...Sherlock Holmes has nothing on you...you have the mindset of a brilliant detective!"

Winifred threw back her head in laughter, delighted to see August's dreary mood change at long last.

"God bless you son...and while you're away in Oxford, maybe you could see your way to selling a few items and purchasing some provisions for our near-empty pantry and those two candles in the drawer, our the last..."

"Don't you worry Ma, consider it done...I'll be on my way before you've finished your breakfast!"

"Oh, and while you're about buying our victuals, see if you can stretch the budget to buy a few extra bits for poor old Prudence, with it fast approaching the festive season...she's been even more melancholy of late...poor old soul. She must get so lonely, all by herself."

"It's not as though nobody in the hamlet hasn't tried to bring her out of her dwelling Ma, she's a recluse and has been a miserable faced old crow since as long as I can remember...even when I was a boy, I remember how all of us used to be terrified of her...reckon the earth would split open if she were to smile!"

"Even so, August, it's our neighbourly responsibility to look out for her...poor woman must have suffered something dreadful to make her like she is. She must be *so* lonely. We have no idea what it's like to be in her boots, or what she's been through during her lifetime. She must be well into her seventh decade by now!"

"Don't fret Ma, I'll make sure I return bearing gifts for our mysterious neighbour; maybe you should try your detective skills on her!"

"Oh be gone with you, you daft lad...it cheers me to see you with a happier face though...you of all folk shouldn't be critical of, old Prudence when *you've* not shown me your handsome smile for weeks!"

August felt guilty all of a sudden, he *had* been wearing a stony face and it wasn't what his dear ma deserved to be stuck with. "I'm truly sorry Ma, can you forgive me?"

Winifred could always forgive him; he was, after all, her pride and joy.

"Of course I forgive you, son...and I'll be praying for you whilst you're away in Oxford. Now make haste, the days are becoming shorter and shorter; it will be nightfall before you know it!"

After having sold all of his ma's work, in a few of the local ladies fashion shops, August already had a feeling that his day would continue along a successful line; his ma's work had improved since she'd been wearing the spectacles, her stitches were now so neat, that they could easily be mistaken for being worked on a machine. She'd also found time to add a touch of embroidery to the garments and trim them with French lace. With a pocket full of change, August couldn't wait to tell his ma how much he'd raised, but first, his mission to find out any information he could, about Eleanor, was his priority and he began the walk out of Oxford towards Cowley Road, where he hoped the vicar would be able to throw some light on his inquiry.

It was the vicar's wife who met August; a trim figured woman with a warm and welcoming face, she was busy polishing the brass candle holders and had been miles away in her thoughts until August's footsteps echoed throughout the empty church. She stared curiously at him, not recognising him as one of the regular flock who attended St Mary and St John Church.

"Good morning, young man,"

August fiddled nervously with his cap; feeling a little ashamed that it had been such a long time since he'd attended church.

"Good morning, Ma'am, I'm sorry to disturb you, but I just wondered if I might talk to the vicar for a moment."

The vicar's wife put down her polishing cloth, "I'm afraid that my husband is out, but if there is anything I could help you with...are you wishing to arrange a wedding or a christening, perhaps?"

August smiled broadly, "Oh no, Ma'am, nothing so grand as that, I'm just looking for someone who seems to have vanished and I was hoping that you might know of her whereabouts; you see, she used to live quite nearby, so I'm assuming she attended this church."

"Well, I can tell that she must be a dear friend of yours, Mr..."

"My name is, August Miller."

"Well, Mr Miller, I will do all I can to help solve your mystery!"

August had taken an immediate liking to the vicar's amiable wife and was feeling even more optimistic that the day was going to be a success.

"Thank you, Ma'am!"

"Call me Mrs Doyle, I'm only a vicar's wife!" she insisted, with a smile. "Now, what's your friend's name? Is she your sweetheart, Mr Miller?"

"I know you're going to think this sounds rather vague, but when I last spoke to her, Eleanor said that she'd been called Eleanor Jackson all of her life but, that she'd just discovered she was actually, Eleanor Whitlock on account of her parents never having married and yes, she is my sweetheart." August was glad of the darkness inside the church as he felt his cheeks redden, he noticed a look of recognition on Mrs Doyle's face, but she looked tense all of a sudden and had lost her smile.

"You know something don't you, Mrs Doyle...please tell me!" urged August, feeling his heart suddenly beating out of control.

"Follow me, Mr Miller; I have something to show you."

She proceeded down the aisle and out through

the arched doorway, with August following behind. She didn't utter a word, causing August to be weighed down by a feeling of woe. She led him through the graveyard, to the back of the church where she stopped by a tiny headstone, barely noticeable compared to the rest of the huge and elaborately worded headstones.

"She shouldn't rightfully be buried here at all, you know." She spoke with a strained voice and watery eyes. "I don't know the full story of what happened, but it was all too much for Beatrice Jackson. Your friend, Eleanor, *poor girl*, discovered her mother's body...she'd hung herself...*poor woman*..."

Mrs Doyle was unable to utter another word. In a state of shock, August's need to find Eleanor suddenly became even more urgent, he couldn't begin to imagine what she'd been through and he hadn't been there for her. His heart dropped like a heavy stone beneath his ribs, as he stood staring down at Beatrice Jackson's resting place.

CHAPTER SIXTEEN

The look of shock was etched upon August's face; Mrs Doyle felt sorry for him, sensing that his feelings for Eleanor Jackson were stronger than he was letting on.

"Mr Doyle will be back shortly, perhaps he knows where Miss Jackson is staying. Would you like to join me for afternoon tea, Mr Miller?"

The sudden news about Eleanor's mother had thrown August into darkness; his mind was going over how terrible it must have been for Eleanor to discover her mother as she had. His need to be with her, comfort and protect her had increased tenfold in the last few moments, making him more determined that he would do everything in his power to track her down.

"I have to meet a friend, Mrs Doyle but thank you for your kindness. May I return a little later to speak with the vicar!"

"Of course you can, Mr Miller, I'll tell him to expect you."

As though in a trance, August left the church grounds and walked aimlessly through the streets of Oxford. He passed by the pie shop with clear images in his mind of that day when he'd first met, sweet Eleanor; he spontaneously wandered towards the lodging house, where she should have been residing with her mother if her plan had followed its course and then on to the home, where she'd lived all her life. He felt closer to her as he stood at the gate; how many times had her hands touched the gate; he held on to it, all of a sudden, as though it was his only lifeline. How many times had she walked the short garden path, he thought, tempting himself to retrace her footsteps. He looked up at the house, wondering which room she had slept in before becoming overwhelmed by the darker thoughts of the recent suicide which had taken place inside. He noticed the neighbour's curtains move slightly and released his hold on the wrought iron gate. His eyes stung and an uncomfortable tightness claimed his throat. A thousand words filled his head and he regretted not having a notebook and pencil in his pocket to capture the sorrowful song which cried out from between his ribs.

It was an hour later when August met with the vicar; declining his offer of refreshments, August was just hungry for information and reminding himself that he had yet to purchase the victuals before the shops closed, time was not on his side. The vicar knew little and had presumed that as he'd not seen anything of Eleanor since her mother's burial, she'd gone to live with relatives. He explained to August that Miss Jackson and her mother hadn't attended his church as often as he'd have liked to have seen them, they were a very private family, he had stressed and with Mr Jackson spending so much time in London, he had presumed that they fled to the City many a time to be with him. August was not hearing the news which he'd hoped for and with a downcast expression, he was just about to thank the vicar and bid him farewell when a sudden look of delight erased the vicar's serious face. "You should pay Doctor Thompson a call...as I recall, he said he was going to discover whereabouts in London, Mr Jackson had been buried. He might know of Eleanor Jackson's whereabouts too...perhaps she has relations in London and is now residing with them!" August was elated, finally a piece of positive information which might lead him to Eleanor. His heart pulsated with anticipation as he thanked the vicar and hurried back to Henley Road again, praying that the Doctor would provide the answer to his question.

Cynthia Thompson was polishing the brass wall plaque on August's arrival, she took a step back to admire the shine and check for smears. She was immensely proud of her husband and after thirty years of marriage, although they had not been blessed with children, she counted her blessings every day that Albert had chosen her to be his wife when there were a string of far prettier and wealthier young women who had all been hoping to become his wife.

"Ooh, you made me jump!" she declared, suddenly catching sight of August, as he waited at the gate. She gazed curiously at him,

"Forgive me if I'm speaking out of turn, but I can't say that I've ever seen you before, young man...are you new to the area?"

"I'm sorry, ma'am, I didn't mean to startle you...I'm August Miller, a friend of Eleanor Jackson."

His declaration immediately grabbed Cynthia's full attention; she knew how much this would mean to Albert.

"Then you must come in and refresh yourself. My husband will be thrilled that you've come. He'll soon be home! Come in, Mr Miller!"

Not expecting such an enthusiastic welcome, August coyly followed the Doctor's wife. The home was full of beautiful, highly polished pieces of furniture; everything was spotlessly clean and there was a warm and welcoming atmosphere radiating from within. This was just the sort of home that he would like for him and Eleanor, he mused. Mrs Thompson led him into the front parlour, a small, cosy room, bedecked in the deepest of red with gold trimmings. August rubbed his hands together, taking pleasure in the warmth emitting from the fireplace.

"Make yourself at home, while I make a brew, Mr Miller!"

He sat down gingerly in a red velvet armchair, feeling uncomfortably out of place.

A few minutes passed before he heard the sound of a man's voice; he quickly stood up, patting down his hair with the flat of his hand.

"Mr Miller, I presume!" declared the Doctor, as he marched into the room accompanied by an air of authority. They shook hands and the Doctor smiled cordially, causing August to immediately feel relaxed.

"My wife informs me that you are a friend of Miss Jackson...Eleanor Jackson!"

Albert's eyes were bright and questioning, he had been hoping for any lead to Eleanor's whereabouts for weeks, anxious to announce the good news to her about his discovery of her half-sister in Whitechapel.

Mrs Thompson soon returned to the room, pushing a tea trolley. She poured out the tea before the sound of rapping upon the door had her dashing off to answer it. Doctor Thompson stopped in mid-conversation, briefly listening to the voice of the caller; his concerned expression soon relaxed again, realising that no one was seeking his attention.

"I do beg your pardon, Mr Miller, please, take a seat and pray tell me how dear, Miss Jackson is fairing after the most unfortunate recent loss of her parents. Where *does* she reside now? I have some urgent news for her and I can't tell you how delighted I was when my wife informed me that you were here!"

He passed August a cup of tea from the trolley and placed the sugar bowl down onto the nearby gilt-edged table. August felt nothing but disappointment as the Doctor's words registered with him. He placed the delicate cup and saucer next to the sugar bowl, worried that it might slip from his trembling hands.

"Doctor Thompson, I came here to see you because I'm in search of Eleanor and the vicar at St Mary and St John Church suggested that *you* might be able to help *me*!"

Albert Thompson's mouth fell open in shock as he became even more troubled about what had happened to Eleanor. In that brief moment, when silence filled the parlour, Albert had a sudden flashback of Beatrice Jackson. It had not been the first time that her beautiful face had taken over his thoughts, since her death. If there was one thing Albert regretted in his mundane life, it was not taking his friendship with the flirtatious, Beatrice one step further; he could picture her now, her curvy body teasing him as she chatted so openly and freely with him; she would always compliment him and never failed to notice the slightest of changes he'd made to his facial growth, unlike Cynthia, who never really took the time to look at his face, let alone notice that he'd trimmed his moustache or sideburns.

August rubbed his forehead, once again feeling as though he'd just crashed into a brick wall; Eleanor clouded his thoughts and although his innate instincts told him that she was alive, he harboured the strongest sense that she was in some kind of trouble; he had to find her, he told himself angrily, his life would be like an unfinished book without her in it. He loved her with every fibre of his being and felt like a man torn in half without her.

Doctor Thompson and August were suddenly brought out of their thoughts as Cynthia Thompson breezed into the room,

"I do apologize, I got held up by one of our neighbours...*do* have some cake, Mr Miller!" She held the plate under his nose and as August glanced at the Doctor; his sad and watery eyes mirrored his own. August took a slice of sponge and bit into it, his thoughts still miles away.

"So have you at last discovered where young Eleanor is?" she asked, oblivious to the sorrowful atmosphere which hung in the air. Albert shook his head as he took a cake, "Mr Miller, it transpires was hoping that I would be able to tell *him* where she is!"

"Oh dear, Oh dear!" uttered Cynthia Thompson, shaking her head in dismay. "Where on earth could that girl have gone to!"

After hearing all about Doctor Thompson's journey to Whitechapel, over another cup of tea, the one hope which gave August a tiny window of optimism was that by some means, Eleanor had also discovered the existence of her half-sister and had gone in search of her one and only family tie. It made complete sense, he considered; it would have been exactly what he'd have done in her position. August left the Doctor's house assuring him that should he discover any news of Eleanor, he would let him know immediately. It was a bonus that he was not a stranger to Whitechapel and after hearing the Doctor's story, he now realised that he must have been in Whitechapel on the same day as him when he'd purchased the low-priced silk from the auction. It was a lucky omen, he mused, that his purchase had been from Eleanor's late father's warehouse.

August made a last-minute dash to the nearest grocery, remembering his ma's list and her request to buy some extra victuals for their lonely recluse of a neighbour.

CHAPTER SEVENTEEN

The winter snow had arrived early and as rumour spread throughout the hamlet of East Hanwell, that they were about to endure the coldest ever winter, August's heart sank as he viewed the thick layer of snow which had fallen overnight. The white sky appeared relentless as the huge snowflakes caused a complete whiteout and as much as he was glad that he'd bought a good stock of food and candles during his recent visit into Oxford, he was saddened that a journey to London would now be out of the question until there was a change in the weather. Winifred, however, was doubly delighted; she had a well-stocked pantry, plenty of fine material to keep her hands busy throughout winter and she had the company of August. He had already confided in her about his discovery whilst in Oxford and although Winifred said nothing to discourage him from continuing his search, she silently prayed that by the time the thaw had set in, August would have thought the situation through a little more and seen sense. She knew that his heart had overruled his head and was still in full charge of anything relating to the girl who had captured it; she was also quite positive that she didn't harbour the same feelings for August, and she couldn't bear the thought of him having his heart broken.

Time passed by slower then Eleanor had ever experienced. The boring monotonous work and the daily routine of the workhouse made for the most unbearable life and was made far worse by the plummeting temperatures, making sleeping almost impossible. Eleanor would drift in and out of sleep every night, constantly woken by the cold. The women now all slept in their work dresses with their nightgowns over the top and their woollen shawls wrapped tightly around their heads and shoulders. The regular night time wailing was now accompanied by the chattering of teeth and the haunting cries, induced from hunger and cold. Eleanor reminisced on the days she'd spent in her garden shed, wishing they'd not come to such a disastrous end. August Miller often filled her thoughts as she lay shivering every night, she wondered if he had forgotten her and if he'd been successful in having his book published; she hoped he would one day fulfil his ambition and become a famous author, at least she could say boastfully, '*I once knew August Miller!*' Eleanor had formed a close friendship with Tilly, who seemed like the only trustworthy person in the workhouse; they also harboured the same desire of one day escaping and becoming free from the life of slavery. Tilly looked out for her and they kept close company whenever possible, knowing that Killigrew was like a starving animal, desperate to satisfy his evil desires and have his wicked way with Eleanor. A couple of weeks after Eleanor had arrived at the workhouse, she'd been summoned to Mrs Killigrew's office on account that she was upsetting Mrs Wishbone, by not working hard enough. Fully aware of this scheduled meeting, Mr Killigrew waited patiently in a dark recess, halfway along the corridor. Suddenly grabbing her arm, as she passed by, Eleanor yelled out, as loud as she could. He was quick to cover her mouth with his unwashed, foul-smelling, hand as he roughly dragged her into the recess. He stood with glazed eyes, licking his lips, but just like a cat teases a mouse before putting it out of its misery, Killigrew wanted to bide his time until the opportunity arrived when he could savour every single second spent with her. He grabbed hold of her chin and proceeded to smother her face with his slobbering lips. Eleanor struggled, kicking out and twisting her head until she feared her neck might break, but Killigrew seemed to find her trauma amusing; he chuckled as his eyes lit up in delight.

"You've got spirit, young Ellie and there's nothing I admire more in a woman than a bit of a tussle before the final submission!"

"You will never have me, you filthy, disgusting beast! I would sooner die than let you touch my body!"

Killigrew laughed even louder, his sour breath turning Eleanor's stomach.

"I'm a patient man, Ellie and you aren't going anywhere, but just like a sweet plum, you're becoming riper with each passing day! I might just bide my time 'til I indulge in such a sweet and tasty meal, but in the meantime, I have this to sniff on and it's a hundred times better than Mrs Killigrew's old snuff!"

Still keeping a firm grip on Eleanor's arm, she looked in horror as he pulled out a thick lock of her hair from his pocket. She felt nauseous, as she watched Killigrew kiss her hair and run it under his repulsive, wart covered nose.

"You disgust me and I'm going to tell, Mrs Killigrew about your behaviour!"

"Be my guest, but I doubt she will believe a single word that comes out of your mouth!" As he tried to plant his drooling lips upon hers once more, Eleanor gave his shin a brutal kick; he immediately ceased and in that instant, she was able to free herself from his hold.

"You'll be sorry you did that, Ellie!" he hollered after her, as she ran towards Mrs Killigrew's office.

After receiving her punishment from Mrs Killigrew, which was to work through the luncheon break for five days, Mr Killigrew left her alone for a while, but it was a continuous nagging, always at the back of her mind that she was being stalked by him and Tilly had also confirmed that once he took a fancy to one of the women, he didn't give up easily.

Christmas had been a far cry from the usual way in which Eleanor had ever experienced the festive day; there had been no work on that day, but a long and drawn out sermon given by one of Oxford's most aged of vicars who, in return, had welcomed the invitation to join the Killigrews in their private, lavish Christmas feast. There had been no presents given or received, but the extra portion of vegetables on their dinner plate and the slice of dry sponge cake had been more than enough to satisfy many of the workhouse inmates. Eleanor had put in a request to visit her mother's graveside, but wasn't shocked when Mrs Wishbone informed her that it had been rejected; there had been no reason as to why, but over the months she had noticed how the older women were given more freedom to leave the workhouse on Sundays and seldom had their requests rejected. Escaping wasn't on their minds and for most of them, the workhouse had become their place of refuge where they felt secure in the knowledge that they wouldn't starve to death or sleep out in all weathers. Many of the women had husbands and older sons in the workhouse; they spent their days picking oakum and waiting patiently for each Sunday afternoon to arrive when they could unite as a family for a brief time and when parents were at last able to hug and comfort their young children. But better than any Christmas present which Eleanor could have

wished for was the news circulating throughout
the workhouse that, in a drunken state, Mr
Killigrew had taken a tumble, badly spraining
his ankle and due to his exceedingly heavy
build, the Doctor's orders were that he was to
put no weight on it for four weeks. His loud
hollers of frustration and pain could be
heard throughout the corridors, delighting
everyone, who felt that at last, he'd received his
comeuppance. Eleanor felt she could at last
lower her guard, it was a huge relief and made
life just the tiniest bit more bearable. However, it
had been less than two weeks, when Mr
Killigrew disobeyed the Doctor's orders and
arrived hobbling with the aid of a walking stick
to the sewing room. He stood in the doorway,
larger than life and looking as though he'd spent
his entire period of convalescence consuming ten
people's share of food. He coughed and
spluttered as he tried to catch his breath,
"Oh, bless my soul!" exclaimed Mrs Wishbone,
the moment she caught sight of him. "How
wonderful to see you up and about again, Mr
Killigrew...*dear Mr Killigrew*, we have all missed
your presence! Haven't we girls?" she voiced
loudly, expecting an eager response from
everyone. There was none, which only left Mrs
Wishbone fuming as she glared at the copious
pale faces before her, sending out messages with
her beady eyes, that they would all pay for their
insolence later.

"They're all a bit out of sorts this morning, Mr Killigrew...must be this prolonged spell of freezing weather which we've been having...reckon it has frozen their brains...if they've got any that is!" Mrs Wishbone roared into a fit of laughter at her witty statement and Mr Killigrew chuckled along with her, in between bouts of coughing.

"I don't think the cold weather is to blame Mrs Wishbone! I do believe that these women have all been overfed! Maybe they should forego luncheon today...I will, of course, leave the decision in your very capable and expert hands, Mrs Wishbone."

"Oh Mr Killigrew, you are *such* a gentleman!" declared Mrs Wishbone, her full cheeks turning pink as she straightened her flimsy bonnet and batted her sparse eyelashes, like a coy young maiden. Mr Killigrew beamed, satisfyingly, as his eyes scanned the rows of faces who were all watching the interaction between him and Mrs Wishbone, with a feeling of repulsion. As soon as he spotted Eleanor amongst the assembly he immediately froze, as though filling up on what his eyes had missed over the previous weeks. Tilly gently nudged her with the toe of her boot, as Eleanor lowered her gaze and continued sewing.

"I wonder, Mrs Wishbone if I might beg a favour of you?" he announced, in his booming voice. Eleanor felt her stomach tighten; she swallowed hard, convinced that, somehow, she would be part of this favour, which he was requesting so loudly.

"*Anything* for you, Mr Killigrew, you only have to say!"

With his eyes still firmly focussed on Eleanor, he stated his request, "Dear Mrs Killigrew has been so busy since my unfortunate accident and is rushed off her feet with no time to spare for my medical needs...I simply wish to borrow a young and able woman who can change my bandages every morning...It should only take half an hour, so she will still be able to fulfil her sewing duties properly." He paused for a while, hoping, in vain, that Mrs Wishbone might suggest Ellie for the task, but instead she stood with her lips pursed tightly. "Might I suggest young Ellie...Mrs Wishbone?" he said, shrewdly. There wasn't a woman in the entire sewing room, including Mrs Wishbone who wasn't aware of Mr Killigrew's real purpose for asking such a favour; it was common knowledge that Ellie was his latest infatuation, with most women now out to protect her from his abusive desires.

Agnes, a woman in her fifties, stood up, "I would gladly attend to your ankle, Mr Killigrew; I've had a lot of experience in such duties as I once cared for our brave soldiers after the Crimean war!"

Mrs Wishbone gave a sideways glance at Mr

Killigrew, taking note of his annoyed expression, "*Sit down Agnes*...it's up to Mr Killigrew, who he selects!"

"Thank you Mrs Wishbone... that's most understanding of you! May I suggest, young Ellie?"

"Ellie!" she cried. "You are to go to Mr Killigrew's private quarters and take good care of his injured ankle!"

Ellie stood up, noticing the immediate look of delight spread across Mr Killigrew's sickening face,

"If I am to be forced into such a duty, then I will change his bandages in the corner of the sewing room...*I refuse to go to his private room!*"

Everyone in the room was dumbstruck by Ellie's display of defiance. Mrs Wishbone seemed to be holding her breath, her face looking as though it might explode at any minute and Mr Killigrew frowned profusely as he instantly made up his mind that he would steal Ellie's virginity at the first opportunity; he'd had enough of her teasing ways and after this little show of ingratitude she didn't deserve the soft and gentle approach any longer.

"It's the sack for you! Ellie...and you've only yourself to blame!" screamed a humiliated, Mrs Wishbone.

She marched to her desk drawer and took out a specially made sack, it was double the size of the mail and flour sacks and attached to a length of thick rope, Ellie knew exactly what to expect, she'd witnessed this punishment already in the few months she'd been in the workhouse. It was another one of Mrs Wishbone's cruel ways of punishing the women by forcing them into a sack which was then hoisted up and left dangling from one of the wooden beams, she would usually only leave them inside for an hour or two, not out of compassion, but because she was obsessed with churning out the most completed sacks and whilst a woman was swinging inside of a sack, she was not producing. Mrs Wishbone would receive an annual bonus if Cowley Road workhouse produced more sacks than the other workhouses throughout Oxfordshire and over the past ten consecutive years she had been victorious and taken first place, priding herself on her strict disciplinary skills. In Eleanor's experience of witnessing other women's fate, they hadn't appeared too badly shaken after their ordeal and it was a far better punishment than being subjected to the wretched, Mr Killigrew and his lustful ways.

"Have you ever heard such rudeness, Mrs Wishbone? This young, ungrateful female doesn't deserve the luxury which she receives here in the workhouse and she will not receive her monthly sixpence until she fulfils my request! If you have no income Ellie, you will be unable to pay for your bread and board and will be indebted to the workhouse, perhaps never able to save enough to step foot outside again!" Mr Killigrew's harsh words meant little to Eleanor, she intended to escape at the first opportunity and already knew how impossible it was for anyone to save enough, to prove they could support themselves in the world outside the confines of the workhouse, or be allowed to work in service, unless, of course, you were prepared to please the beast inside of Killigrew, first. He was a brute of a man who abused his position and over the years had ruined the lives of many a lonely and destitute woman.

"She doesn't know how lucky she is, if you ask me, Mr Killigrew...and after all the kindness you've shown her!"

"String her up, Mrs Wishbone and have her brought to my office in four hours!"

Gasps of shock passed through the sewing room, four hours was longer than anyone had ever been left in the sack, but the women knew the reason behind Killigrew's ruthless punishment.

CHAPTER EIGHTEEN

Eleanor had not found her four hour ordeal inside the coarse, sack to be as bad as she'd imagined; feeling warm for the first time in ages, after a short while she had drifted off into the best sleep she'd experienced since the arrival of the inclement winter temperatures and awoke refreshed, even though, most startlingly, when Mrs Wishbone, without any warning, simply allowed the sack to drop freely to the floor. Making out that the punishment had been a terrible experience, as she stood before Mrs Wishbone, rubbing the arm which had taken the brunt of the undignified landing, Eleanor was infused with a renewed strength and felt confident that she would be able to fight off the amorous Mr Killigrew when she was frog-marched to his office.

"You know where you're going now, don't you, Ellie!" instructed Mrs Wishbone, with a satisfying gleam in her eye. "Don't go keeping the master waiting now and if you take my advice, you'll do as he asks and apologise for your earlier rudeness!"

Eleanor wanted to beat the confounded woman with her ridiculous 'Frederick', she loathed her as much as Killigrew and knew that her life was destined for a far better place than the workhouse.

"Yes, Mrs Wishbone, thank you, Mrs Wishbone,"
she said sarcastically.

Mrs Wolf caught up with her as she dawdled
along the bleak corridor,

"What are you doing out here, Ellie?"

"I have to go to Mr Killigrew's office," she
replied in a small voice.

"Not in trouble again, I hope!"

Eleanor shrugged her shoulders, "I'm not sure;
I've been in the sack all morning because I
refused to change his bandages!"

Mrs Wolf shook her head; she knew all too well
what Killigrew was up to and knew he'd been
giving Ellie a hard time since the moment he'd
set his shameless eyes upon her.

"Come into my storeroom for a minute, I can see
it's about time you had your rat's tails trimmed,
they're poking out of your bonnet and we don't
want to give Mr Killigrew any cause to find fault
now, do we?"

Eleanor reluctantly followed her to the tiny
storeroom, removed her bonnet and sat down.
Strangely though, Mrs Wolf only snipped two
short cuts with the scissors before placing them
down onto the table in front of Ellie. She looked
her straight in the eye and Eleanor sensed that
without committing herself to words, Mrs Wolf
was willing her to put the scissors into her
pocket.

"If things don't work out right, Ellie; remember,
I'm an aged and absentminded woman!" she

stated, with an exaggerated wink, as she watched Eleanor put the scissors into her pocket.

"Thank you for the haircut, Mrs Wolf!" declared Eleanor, smiling warmly at dear old Mrs Wolf, as she left her storeroom.

Mr Killigrew was already waiting outside his office door, leaning heavily on his walking stick and staring at his pocket watch.

"You're ten minutes late, Ellie!"

"I had to relieve myself, Mr Killigrew, Sir!" He smiled, delighted at the respect he was receiving. "I can see that your punishment has already proved most beneficial and taught you some sense, Ellie!"

"Yes Sir, I'm sure it has."

"Well, in that case, you'll be most pleased to know that I won't be asking you to change my bandages today since they have already been attended to. Now come and sit down next to me Ellie and *if* you behave yourself, I might just see my way to permitting you to visit your dear mother graveside on Sunday!"

Before sitting, Eleanor slyly pulled the chair away from Killigrew's chair, hoping he'd not notice; he let out a hearty chuckle, immediately dragging his chair closer to her. "I'm as gentle as a spring lamb, Ellie, so don't worry your pretty little head."

He pulled out the lock of her hair from his desk drawer and held it beneath his bulbous nose, taking in a deep breath as he glared at Eleanor.

She knew what he was trying to do and felt like laughing in his face.

"That lock of old hair must smell quite revolting after all these months!" she stated, boldly.

Killigrew suddenly placed his podgy hand on her thigh, squeezing it tightly. His piercing eyes appeared glazed as he breathed heavily, leaning his body toward Eleanor.

"Satisfy my desires, Ellie and I promise, by the summer you will be working in service in one of the finest Estates in Oxfordshire."

Eleanor could feel the rush of wind emanating from his nostrils and smell his rancid breath as his face closed in on her; she gagged and knew she had to act quickly before she was completely overpowered. Suddenly his entire body weight caused her to topple off the chair and land on the floor with Killigrew's overweight body following.

"I knew you'd see sense!" he muttered, as his hands frantically mauled every part of her body. Eleanor furtively pulled out the scissors from her pocket, holding them up high. Killigrew saw nothing, his head was buried between Eleanor's head and shoulder as he ran his slobbering lips over her neck. The strong beating of his heart could be felt through his thick layer of blubber, prompting Eleanor to take immediate action. With every ounce of strength she could muster, she stabbed the pointed scissors into the back of his fat thigh. He froze for a second before screaming out loud, deafening Eleanor as she lay trapped beneath his bulky weight. The scissors were stuck like a sword in his leg and as they both viewed the sight, Killigrew lashed out and slapped Eleanor around her face, before pulling the scissors from his leg.

"You're nothing more than an evil witch!" he cried out as he viewed the bright, red blood, soak through his trousers. *"I'm going to bleed to death!"* As quick as she could, Eleanor scrambled to her feet; Killigrew's fresh blood had already spread to her dress; she felt her heart beating rapidly as her head became foggy inside. Willing herself not to swoon, she remembered her mother's words and took deep breaths.

"Go and fetch help, you evil little bitch...You'll pay for this, by God, you just wait and see..." Killigrew was like an upturned beetle, rolling around on his back as he howled loudly. Eleanor could do nothing but stare at him. In her entire life, she had never so much as harmed a fly and was left in total shock by her violent action, blaming it on the gruesome workhouse and its appalling master and mistress, who treated their charges worse than cattle. The door suddenly swung open and the doorway was filled by the portly figure of Mrs Killigrew, with a timid looking, Mrs Wolf peeping over her shoulder.

"Is he dead?" questioned Mrs Wolf.

"Don't be ridiculous!" screamed Mrs Killigrew, as

she marched into the office, giving her wayward husband daggered looks. "Since when has a corpse made such a hullabaloo, Wolf?" Mrs Wolf stuck her fingers in both ears, loosening the hard wax.

"*She tried to kill me!* That ungrateful, stuck up bitch, tried to put an end to my life! Can you believe it, Mrs Killigrew!" cried Mr Killigrew, in a bid to gain a little sympathy from his angry faced wife.

"Get Mr Wolf to throw her into solitary, a month should cure her of her wild and aggressive ways," ordered Mrs Killigrew. "She's been overfed all her life and this is the result; a girl with the spirit of a feral *'she'* cat!"

"Yes, Mrs Killigrew," responded Mrs Wolf, obediently.

"And where did she acquire *these* from?" questioned Mrs Killigrew, her nose wrinkling in disgust as she held up the blood-covered scissors between her fingertips.

"I stole them!" stated Eleanor. "Your husband is a beast and has been trying to force himself on me since I arrived!" she screamed hysterically. In his pain, Mr Killigrew still managed to produce a loud throaty chuckle,

"Can you believe such twaddle!" he declared. Mrs Killigrew stared hard at him, knowing that Ellie was speaking the truth, but as she'd always done throughout her married life, continued to protect her husband's shortcomings. He was a weak man when it came to food, wine and a pretty young maiden, but he loved her and always saw to it that she had everything she wanted in life.

"I don't believe that for one second, husband dear and for telling such slanderous lies, I am going to increase her month's sentence in solitary to six weeks! She'll think twice before spreading any more malicious gossip and demeaning your good and honourable name, Mr Killigrew! Now let me attend to your wound, you poor soul...and to think that *you*, already suffering from an injured ankle and barely able to hobble around, could even be capable of such a sinful feat!"

"Quite right, Mrs Killigrew, quite right indeed! Now get her out of my sight, would you, she's causing me to feel quite queasy!"

Feeling guilty for having supplied Eleanor with the weapon, Mrs Wolf hurried off to fetch her brother without even glancing at Eleanor. She already regretted her foolish course of action, but had been hoping that Ellie had it in her to finish Killigrew off completely; she and her brother deserved to be Master and Mistress of the workhouse, they practically ran the place already, she mused, while the Killigrews did nothing other than to stuff their faces all day long, with rich and exotic victuals. Now, that poor young girl was going to visit Hell and there was nothing she could do to stop it. If she had her way, there would not be such a cruel punishment in the workhouse.

"Not a word of this to our dear, Reverend Doyle on his next visit, d'you understand, my precious?" uttered Mr Killigrew, as his wife bathed and bandaged his wound. "He'll think we are incapable of running the workhouse and report us to the Parish council...we risk being toppled from our thrones and we have worked so hard to reach the top!"

"We have indeed, Mr Killigrew, thanks to your ingenious ways of thinking!"

"Our dear vicar was asking after Ellie, only a few weeks ago. It seems she has gone missing from Oxford and nobody knows of her whereabouts!"

Mrs Killigrew looked puzzled, "Why didn't he simply check the admissions ledger then? He has access to it?"

"Don't be daft, *woman*! Unlike you, I can recognise a trouble maker from a mile away and as I just said, we don't want to risk upsetting our peaceful lives, now, do we? So as far as you and I are concerned, should he ask again, we've never even *heard* of any, *Eleanor Jackson*!"

Mrs Killigrew knew it was on account that her husband had taken a strong fancy to Ellie, the lustful gleam in his eye had not escaped her notice on the day of her arrival, but at least by the time six weeks had passed, she consoled herself, Ellie would have lost all her charm and sparkle, together with her sensual curves and even though she knew it was a terrible, sinful thought, part of her wished that Ellie wouldn't survive her punishment.

"Well, you'd best make sure you don't allow her to go and visit her mother's graveside because she's buried across the way, in Reverend Doyle's graveyard!"

"*Foolish woman!* Do you take me for an idiot! Ellie won't be stepping outside the workhouse for years to come...not until she is well and truly forgotten and has become dull and dreary like the rest of the women under our roof!"

Mrs Killigrew purposely pulled hard on the bandage causing Mr Killigrew to yell out "Not so damned tight, for God's sake! You make an appalling nurse! I'm fortunate to be alive, you know!"

CHAPTER NINETEEN

Elizabeth Jackson refused to leave the confines of what she referred to as her *'beggar's refuge'* and spent most of her day in a dream, trying to block out her embarrassing fall from society. Pondering on lucrative ways of how to make a quick fortune which would enable her and her daughter and mother to leave the festering squalor of Whitechapel's Castle Alley had been unsuccessful and so far, the only feasible route of escape was for her to accept the hand of a wealthy admirer, whom she couldn't abide. After Edward's copious debts had been paid off, together with the bill for their prolonged stay in the lodging house, they were left virtually penniless and could only afford the rent on a dilapidated, flea-ridden, upstairs room in one of the most deprived areas of Whitechapel. The run- down, narrow Castle Alley was barely wide enough to squeeze Elizabeth's fancy whalebone crinoline through and as a result, the structure had become a complete ruin. Comforted by Rayne, who was quite happy to see the end of her mother's outdated fashion accessory, the three women spent the evenings customising their flamboyant gowns into everyday dresses which would blend in with their new, pauper's surroundings. Peggy then took a trip to the pawnbroker's and managed to fetch a few shillings in exchange for the remainder of their fine clothing. Rayne was forbidden to leave the room in Castle Alley, given the terrible crimes and muggings which took place in the notorious area, not to mention the proximity of the *Three Crowns inn,* where drunkards and prostitutes frequented nightly.

"You can't keep me locked up like a prisoner, *Mamma*! Why don't we go out together? All three of us? There's safety in numbers, so you always tell me!" nagged Rayne, who felt she might die from the boredom of sitting all day long in the stuffy room with very little to keep her occupied.

"I can't bring myself to leave, Rayne, can't you understand that? I've been a respected and wealthy woman of society all my life and I simply can't find it within me to mingle with these common street hooligans. Just listen to them shouting out there in the street...have you ever heard such a ruckus in your life? Rayne, my darling, I do believe these people don't possess an ounce of decency or a good manner between the lot of them?"

"They are trying to sell their goods, Mamma and make a living! Unlike us, who will soon have nothing left to sell and then we will be homeless too! Then what will happen to us?... *The workhouse...that's what!*"

"*Homeless!* As far as I am concerned, we are already that...*this* is no home, I wouldn't even house a dog in such a dwelling!" cried Elizabeth, as she viewed the room with disdain.

"Can't an old woman take a nap around here without being woken by you two at each other's throats!" yelled Peggy, from the corner of the room.

"Grandmother didn't come from a wealthy family! *Did you, grandmamma*?" declared Rayne, unsympathetic that her grandmother had been woken. "Is that why *she's* the only one allowed out of this prison? And what about my half-sister? Why isn't she here, suffering like we are...I bet Pappa loved her more than he loved me and left her well provided for, with a healthy allowance...I expect she's living in absolute luxury, while we are forced to survive on those awful, grisly meat pies and undercooked mash *and* put up with the rotten stench from the washhouse, wafting in through the cracks in the windows. *I hate it here*...it's not fair...and tomorrow I'm going to walk the length of Whitechapel Street and see if I can't find work! One of us has to be realistic!"

"Don't you dare to raise your voice to your poor mother, *Rayne Jackson*!" ordered Peggy, as she hauled her stiff body up from her palliasse. "Your mother has been through a terrible ordeal and she is only protecting you, young lady. A pretty young and naive girl like you would be gobbled up by the thugs out there!"

"Well, I refuse to believe that! You can't scare me, you know; I'm not a child! There are hundreds of young women and children around here, why do you insist that they are all monsters; it's truly sinful the way you speak about them...aren't we all human beings? They can't possibly be as bad as you make out!"

"If your mamma is feeling strong enough, we will all attend church on Sunday," compromised Peggy, hoping to bring about some peace and harmony within the tiny dwelling place. "And you are completely wrong about young, Eleanor, you know...that poor young girl has suffered more than you...God alone, knows where she is now, after the passing of poor, Beatrice." Peggy wiped away her tears as her thoughts took her on a nostalgic journey to her days in Henley Road.

"Why don't you simply pay your dear acquaintance, Mrs English, a call, you know how her son would jump at the opportunity to marry you and then all of our problems would be solved; we could live in luxury again. I think it's a small price to pay to make two of your nearest and dearest relatives happy!"

Elizabeth's ears had listened to more than enough of her spoilt daughter's ridiculous suggestions over the passing months, but her latest one riled her, like no other, causing her pent up feelings to explode,

"How dare you even suggest such a vile idea, let alone allow it to cross your immature thoughts!" screamed Elizabeth, as she vacated her chair, unexpectedly pouncing on Rayne like a wild cat, mauling its prey. She grabbed a fist full of Rayne's shoulder-length hair, tugging on it with such a force and causing Rayne to shriek at the top of her voice, from the pain.

"Let go of me, Mamma! You're hurting me!"

"Well since I've got your undivided attention, *you spoilt, little madam*, let me make myself crystal clear; if Tristan English, was the last man on earth, I would not touch him with a barge pole! He is a vile, slimy, underhanded excuse of a man and at least a quarter of a century older than me! I would sooner die in this hovel! Do you understand, Rayne?"

"Leave the poor child alone for pity's sake, Beth! Hasn't she been through enough already, without her own mother turning on her!" voiced Peggy, as she prised Elizabeth's clenched fists open.

"I think we could all do with a cup of tea and a bit of cooling off time!"

"Oh, mother! Is that your solution to every problem in life, *a cup of tea!*" screamed Elizabeth, hysterically.

"Do you have a better idea then? Because I'd welcome it, to say the least!"

"I would love some tea, Grandmamma," sobbed Rayne as she nestled her body against her grandmother, refusing to look at her crazed mother.

"There, there, my little, darling, your mamma

didn't mean to hurt you so! And after our tea, you will accompany me to the pie shop...a hearty meal will make us all sleep well tonight!"

"I forbid you to parade Rayne out there amongst the peasants, Mother!" Elizabeth intervened. "Just supposing some hot-blooded young costermongers takes a fancy to her. The young men around here just take what they desire by force, you know...they live by the rules of the jungle...the ways of the beasts. They know nothing at all about social etiquette, mother!"

"Well, that's the silliest statement you've made all week, Elizabeth...there are some *good*, *decent*, *God-fearing* and *kind-hearted* folk in Whitechapel, who would give a starving man their last slice of bread! They're not all harlots and drunkards and the sooner you stop wallowing in self-pity, get off your backside and accept that you are in the same boat as them, the sooner you might start living again! So don't you dare try and stop me from taking Rayne out, you can't make her a prisoner for the rest of her days!"

"Oh do what you wish, *Mother*! You seem to be adjusting to the ways of these dregs of society, all too well, but after all, I'm forgetting that you did spend many years living with that cheap hussy and her wayward daughter, in Oxford, so I'm guessing you live by a different class of standards to those which we have been accustomed to. Just don't be getting any wild notions that you can marry Rayne off to a common butcher or a brawling street merchant!"

So began Rayne's initiation to freedom and independence, which over the following months, much to her Mother's annoyance, transformed her; she adapted quite easily to the ways and the people of Whitechapel and was soon a popular and well-liked young woman about the streets. She had observed and learned the skills of haggling and had managed to redeem a healthy sum for her mother's wedding ring, the only item of jewellery which was worth anything. As the months passed by, it was becoming more and more apparent how Edward had been supporting them by borrowed means and how so many of his expensive gifts, were either cheap fake replicas or stolen goods. As Peggy and Rayne put sentiment to one side and came to grips with the reality of their new way of life, Elizabeth's stubborn and spoilt nature, however, worked against her, as she refused to accept the dire situation which she and her family were now in. She had become antagonistic and moody, shutting herself off from the world as her spirits slipped slowly into a state of melancholy.

Crippled by the harsh winter, the Jacksons had no alternative than to spend most of their meagre funds on firewood; their staple diet consisted of potato soup with the odd vegetable added, on a fortunate day. With a trivet hanging over the open fire and hot water always available, copious cups of warming tea and cocoa helped keep out the bitter cold. Dressing and undressing, were now completely out of the question as the family huddled in front of the fire with every item of clothing they owned draped around their shoulders.

It was a bright, sunny January morning when Rayne finally persuaded Peggy to allow her to venture out onto the snow-covered streets; their supply of firewood was nearly burnt out and they had very few provisions left. Peggy had refused to put one foot onto the slippery surfaces again, since she'd slipped up during the first week of the big freeze, severely bruising her hip and causing it to turn a deep shade of purple, for three weeks, not to mention the pain she had endured. Rayne was nimble and very light on her feet, considered Peggy and they were in desperate need of stocks, so with her hand on her heart and with a mouthful of instructions, which Rayne paid little attention to, Rayne left Castle alley with her grandmamma's blessing. She had dutifully asked her mother if there was anything she needed but as was now the norm, she received a cold and sarcastic reply.

"A book, perhaps, Mamma?" she suggested, hoping that something light-hearted might bring her out of her depression.

"We can't afford such luxuries!" she snapped.

"Mr Levi has many books for a penny in his

shop!"

Elizabeth looked aghast, "If you think that I have stooped so low as to lay my hands upon a second-hand book from the pawnbroker's establishment, Rayne, then you are mistaken! The very thought of how many filthy, beggars have left their vile diseases on such an item makes my skin crawl! Do you wish your mother to catch cholera or typhoid and be buried in this slum!"

"Of course not, Mamma, I was simply trying to make your life a little more bearable!"

"Well, it will take a lot more than an infested book!"

As much as Rayne was tempted to bring up the subject of, Tristan English again, she hurriedly kissed her mother's cheek and made her way down the precarious staircase which had been stripped bare of most of its wood, leaving no banister to hold on to as she carefully placed her feet on the narrow remaining bits of each stair. The winter sun made a pleasant change upon her skin, from the intense flames of the open fire. The snow was firm beneath her feet and sparkled as it caught the sun's rays. The streets were surprisingly busy, as though everyone had been waiting patiently for this respite from the stinging winds and blinding snow. There were smiles and chatter as friends and neighbours united to discuss the severity of the weather; old folk talking with an air of expertise as they proudly recalled previous years when it had been just as bad. Women talked of the lack of provisions and some of how the local midwife had been unable to attend their latest delivery; Rayne's ears heard all the gory details and she was glad that her mother could not hear these street narratives. With only a shilling left, Rayne hoped that her smile and casual banter would be sufficient to push the costermonger's prices low enough so that she'd have a penny or two left to purchase a couple of books from Mr Levi's shop. If her mother didn't appreciate it, her grandmother certainly deserved a good book to keep her entertained during the drawn out evenings, which were as long as the face on her mother; a miserable sight which they were constantly subjected to.

Whitechapel Street was bustling with everyone either trying to find a bargain or make some money. Street entertainers gathered on every corner; magicians, dancers and singers and solitary artists playing their instruments. Rayne stopped for a moment to watch and listen and as she viewed the accumulating farthings, ha'pennies and pennies, which people had tossed into the artist's hats, upon the ground in front of them, she was suddenly struck by a brilliant idea. She could play the violin. Her mamma had forced the lessons upon her and employed one of Mayfair's finest music tutors. For two long years, she'd endured three hourly lessons every week and although she wasn't one to boast, she had become quite an accomplished player, but when her pappa had died and they were left destitute, her music lessons were immediately cancelled. Rayne was so engrossed in her idea that she walked past dozens of street sellers, forgetting that she needed firewood and groceries. If only she could get her hands on a violin, she mused, quite convinced that she'd soon make a fortune and put the smile back on her mamma's strained face.

"Lookin' fer firewood, Miss?" Rayne looked down at the two street urchins, who were selling sawn up floorboards and doors. Dressed in thin and filthy rags, their bare feet were red and sore from the cold and their huge pleading eyes called out from their gaunt faces. Rayne felt immediately sorry for the poor mites, even though she was warmly dressed, wearing thick stockings and solid boots, she still shivered when a sudden gust of wind blew through her and couldn't even imagine how cold these poor lads were feeling.

"Are you brothers?"

They nodded enthusiastically.

Rayne purchased four bundles of the firewood from the boys and bought them each a bag of roasted chestnuts, from the nearby street vendor. Their eyes lit up as they devoured the sweet-smelling nuts, thanking Rayne a dozen times in between each bite. She laughed at their excitement, wishing her mother could see how such a small gift made these poverty-stricken folk so happy.

After purchasing a modest amount of vegetables, some tea, cocoa and a box of candles, Rayne was left with only half a penny, but in the hope that Mr Levi might have some less presentable, but more affordable books tucked away under his counter, she hurried towards his shop. Her load was heavy, causing her to keep taking breaks after every few steps; walking on the slippery pavements proved a tiring task and had already given Rayne a backache, making her feel more like an old woman.

"Allow me ter carry yer load, Miss an' I won't even charge yer, it would be me pleasure!"

No sooner had Rayne heard the stranger's words, than he had quickly grabbed her entire shopping, with one large hand.

"Do you mind!" she exclaimed.

"Ah, come on now, Miss, I've bin walkin' be'ind yer watchin' yer struggling...I just wanna help a pretty lass, that's all!"

"So you've been following me!" cried Rayne, indignantly, as she viewed the tall young man, instantly taking notice of how the sleeves of his jacket were too short as were the length of his trousers and his cap was too big, leaving large gaps at each side of his head. He had a kind and trustworthy face though, considered Rayne and he was visibly strong.

"Well alright then, since they are causing my hands to sting a little and my back to tire, I would be most appreciative of your assistance!"

"So, does that mean yes then?"

Rayne was instantly annoyed by her hoity-toity attitude towards this helpful man, feeling more like she was in her mother's boots and not liking it at all.

"It does," she replied with a wide smile. "I'm going to Mr Levi's shop...are you familiar with it?"

"Now that's a bit like askin' a docker if 'e knows where the river is! Course I knows, Uncle Levi...who doesn't 'round 'ere!"

CHAPTER TWENTY

By the time they'd reached the pawnbroker's, Rayne had told Tommy Kettle a little about herself and discovered that he was nineteen and worked on the docks. He even vaguely knew her late father and was not at all shocked to hear of how he'd left his family penniless. It seemed that Edward Jackson had two completely different personalities and his most prominent one was kept well hidden from his loved ones. Rayne wondered if her mother really ever knew her husband or had simply turned a blind eye to the other side of him, so long as she was financially comfortable.

As usual, Rayne gave the shop display an inquisitive glance before stepping over the threshold; she always hoped to see some of hers or her mother's fancy gowns in the window, curious to know how much they were selling for, but today, something entirely different caught her eye which was a hundred times more appealing than her old clothes; a fine-looking violin. She felt her heart skip a beat as she hurriedly thanked, Tommy Kettle for his kindness and said goodbye to him. Mr Levi always had a beaming smile for Rayne, he had taken a liking to the young and spirited girl and had also noticed a change in her over the months since she'd been frequenting his shop; she had lowered her stuck up nose and adjusted well to ways of the East End.

"Miss Rayne!" he declared, his booming voice never failing to startle her. "We have had the most crippling of winters, have we not...I have been like the brown bear, hiding away in hibernation! How are your mamma and your lovely grandmamma...and how are you…what can I do for you on such a refreshing morning?"

"I am very well, Mr Levi, as is my family...how are you, Mr Levi?"

" *Miss Rayne...Miss Rayne*!" he implored, "Why you not call me *Uncle* Levi, as everyone else does...Mr Levi? It sounds too official! We are friends now, *yes*?"

"Yes, Mr Levi, we are indeed, but I will be in trouble with my grandmamma if I am not courteous!"

Mr Levi looked around him, emphasising his every move.

"I don't see no sign of, *grandmamma*...unless she has shrunk and you have her in your pocket!"

Mr Levi suddenly roared with laughter.

"She will not know, and I will not tell her, Miss Rayne and so you can lose that serious face!"

"Very well then, *Uncle Levi*, if it makes you happy!"

"Yes, yes, it makes me happier than you can imagine, because now you like my ever-growing family in Whitechapel...and I can call you Rayne? *Yes*?"

"Yes, Mr...Uncle Levi, please, call me Rayne!"
"And when you take Grandmamma from your pocket I will call you, *Miss Rayne* and you may call me *Mr Levi*!" Once again he threw his head back as he burst into a bout of infectious laughter.

"So what are you looking to pawn or buy today, *my special one*?"

"I have my eye on the violin in the window, but I only have half a penny left," declared Rayne, enthusiastically

"Oh, I see, now *you* are telling the jokes, *huh*!"

"How much *is* the violin, Uncle Levi?"

"It is the best violin I have ever had the pleasure of owning, young one. I am left with the broken heart that, alas, I know nothing about the art of playing such a magnificent instrument. It is, so I have been informed, the finest spruce wood violin from Bohemia and I want *at least* five shillings for it."

Rayne's look of disappointment did not go unnoticed by Mr Levi,

"Why you want it, anyway? Can you even play it?"

"Of course...I want to make some money by playing it on the streets!"

"What about your mamma and grandmamma....surely they will forbid it...to them, you will be nothing more than a common beggar!"

"I will be entertaining, not begging and besides,

they don't have to know. Anyway, it doesn't matter now because I will never have a spare sixpence, not to mention *five shillings*!"

Mr Levi left his counter and lifted the violin from the shop window.

"Entertain an old man, and maybe I will have a proposition for you."

Rayne swallowed hard, with no sheet music to play from she was left with a choice of three tunes which she was confident enough to play from memory. Placing the instrument beneath her chin, she gently tested the bow as she slowly ran it across the strings; it sounded in good tune as she began the uplifting and beautiful piece, which mesmerized Mr Levi as he stood motionless, enjoying every harmonious chord which filled his ears.

"Oh, Rayne! *That was superb*...you are a most talented musician...*bravo...bravo*!" He clapped his hands together, as Rayne felt her cheeks blushing.

"That violin is wasting away in my shop window, everyone should hear its magical sound! I have an idea...you will play in the streets and for every shilling you make you will give to me two pennies. When you have saved five shillings, that you can spare, you may purchase the instrument!"

Rayne didn't need to think about the proposition, her only worry was how to conceal the violin from her mamma and grandmamma and prevent them from finding out about her money-making scheme.

"That's a deal, Uncle Levi, but there is just one favour...could I keep the violin here?"

"Ah! you are keeping the secret from your family...I don't want any trouble, Rayne, an old man like myself can't cope with angry guardians and threats of violence and revenge!"

"Oh no, Uncle Levi, my mamma would never do anything like that! She might forbid me to ever leave our room again, but if I make enough money to feed us and buy the firewood and candles she might have a change of heart....she's not used to being so poor, you see."

Mr Levi nodded his head, as he remembered, Mr Jackson; a frequent customer, often after a cut-price bargain as a gift for one of his many lady friends. He always drove a hard bargain and was quite the expert in the art of haggling and an even better liar, but he didn't wish to disclose what he knew to young Rayne, so remained silent, even though he knew that if she lived in the East End for long enough, she would come to realise that there weren't many folk who didn't know of her father's escapades. He stretched out his hand to Rayne,

"Very well my young friend, we have a deal...let's shake on it as the proper business folk do!"

"Thank you, Uncle Levi, *thank you!*" cried Rayne in delight. "I promise you won't regret it...Oh, and just one more question, about my half a penny, could I perhaps purchase one of your, not so pristine, books with it? For my mamma or grandmamma to read during the long, cold evenings."

Mr Levi admired Rayne's fighting spirit and already sensed that she would go far in the East End. Concealing his smile from her, he declared in his booming voice,

"So you are wanting to skin your, Uncle Levi alive, *huh*? Haven't I already done enough for you? And what makes you think I keep anything, other than the *best* of books, in the top condition?"

"Well, it was worth a try, I'm sorry if I've offended you..."

Mr Levi held on to his skullcap as he doubled up in a bout of raucous laughter, spluttering as he tried to control himself. Rayne watched in fascination, wondering what he found so amusing.

"You are one of my *own* kind, Rayne...and I predict that the future holds much wealth for you...and for that reason, I intend to remain your humble friends...just don't forget old, Uncle Levi when you are sitting in the parlour counting your fortune!" He hurriedly pulled aside the curtain and dashed through to the back of his house, returning with a pile of books in his arms. "Here you are, seize the three which take your fancy...I wouldn't want your lovely family to squabble over who gets to read first!"

"Thank you, Uncle Levi!" Rayne exclaimed, gratefully, as she quickly picked three of the rather tatty books, suddenly realising that she'd been out for far too long.

"I will see you in the morning, Uncle Levi when I come to collect the violin!"

Rayne sped back to Castle Alley, her arms laden with the morning's heavy, but successful shopping in one arm and the books in the other, thankfully the sun had melted random patches of snow and she hopped from one safe clearing to another. She was thrilled with her accomplishments, but already feeling nervous at the thought of playing the violin on the street, the following day.

Three days had passed since Eleanor's release from her dark, damp prison and she could still do no more than lay upon her palliasse, in the dormitory, for hours on end. Her body severely undernourished and weakened, she had gone passed the point of fighting for her life; wishing for nothing more than to join her mother in the hereafter. She kept her eyes closed for most of the time, they still stung from the brightness of natural light and she wished not to glance at the weeping wounds on her body, which had come about from six weeks of lying upon the cold stone floor of her prison.

Tilly spent every spare moment at her bedside

and Mrs Blake and Mrs Wolf sacrificed their meagre portions of meat and chicken from their dinner plates in the hope that Eleanor's poor health would benefit from them, but with every mouthful seeming impossible to swallow, the tough meat only caused her to choke and so she was kept on a diet of porridge which Mrs Wolf fortified with the cream of the milk. Mr Killigrew's infatuation with Eleanor had temporarily diminished, she no longer claimed his flirtatious eye, in fact, she now repulsed him, but everyone knew it would only be a matter of time before Eleanor regained her health along with her beauty and the problem would once again rise to the surface.

"Please get better, Ellie!" prayed Tilly, aloud, as she snuggled alongside her, trying to keep her waif-like friend warm. "I've missed you so much, Ellie. Remember our escape plan? One day it *will* come true and we will see the back of this stinking abyss!"

Ellie could only offer Tilly the slightest of smiles, as she listened to her words.

Agnes, who was, somewhat of an expert in bandaging wounds and had gained much medical experience from her time nursing the casualties of the Crimean war, attended to Ellie's sores every morning before she went to breakfast. At her request, Mrs Wolf had managed to supply her with a small pot of animal fat from the kitchen, which was invaluable for soothing Eleanor's weeping sores. Mrs Wishbone and Mrs Killigrew, however, had not been so compassionate, insisting that Ellie was to return to a full day's work in the sewing room, before the end of the week.

It was early February, when the thaw set in and with the signs that the freezing temperatures were slowly picking up, August planned to make his journey into Whitechapel. Having completed his book during the drawn out, winter months, he felt optimistic that it might be the one to pave his way to a lifelong career as an accomplished author; it was the best he'd ever written; a cry from his heart which seemed to flow through the ink, as every sentence was formed. A swashbuckling adventure with a powerful story of love running through its core; Eleanor had jumped out at him on every page he'd written, melting his heart as he inked his emotions freely and without the need to concentrate, as he wrote each sentence. His only dilemma now, was whether he should take it to an Oxford publisher or one in the City. But his predicament was soon to take a backwards step when on the day of his planned journey, his ma had become ill. Winifred had taken to her bed earlier than usual the night before, complaining of a headache and not even finishing her cocoa. When August went to see why she'd not risen in the morning, he found her burning up with a high temperature; her chest was rattling noisily with every laboured breath and her face was void of all colour. As he froze in shock, August panicked as he realised that losing his mother had been a thought which, until this day, had never crossed his mind. He didn't know what to do to ease her suffering and felt utterly helpless as he watched her struggle with every short breath. Although reluctant to leave his ma alone for one second, he hurried down the narrow dirt track to where their neighbour, Prudence, lived. He pummelled hard upon the door.

"What in God's Blessed name is wrong, son!" declared the old woman, as she stared aghast at August's dishevelled appearance.

"It's Ma, she's been taken poorly...she's in a really bad way, Mrs Prudence...please, I beg of you, come and see her!"

"Well, I'm no doctor son, but I've seen my fair share of ailments in my lifetime, so I'll just wear my boots and be with you shortly...your cottage is the one with the hazel fence and brown door, is it not?"

Prudence had described half of the cottages in East Hanwell, but he simply nodded, not wanting to waste any more precious time.

"You go to your mother's side, August Miller, I will soon be with you. Don't you worry, now and make sure you put the water to boil...hurry lad!"

The gasping sounds of Winifred's laboured

breath could be heard as soon as he entered his home, following Prudence's instructions, he speedily placed the kettle onto the trivet over the fire. Prudence followed quickly and was soon stood in the snug cottage, with a handful of garden canes in her hand and a large bundle under her arm.

"Don't look so alarmed, son...we are going to make a steam tent, to ease your ma's breathing."

Prudence didn't wait for a response, but made her way up the narrow staircase, bashing her awkward canes noisily against every surface. She was a strange woman, thought August, she'd never appeared bothered about anything that went on in the hamlet and had lived as a recluse for so many years, that most folk seemed to have forgotten about her, apart from his ma, it seemed, but Prudence was proving to be a caring neighbour and August was suddenly of the opinion that at some point during her life, she'd had her heart broken.

"Bring me that boiling water and a bowl of cold water, son...as quick as you can!" she called down from the top stair.

The icy water from the well had never taken so long to boil; August took up the cold water while he waited and found that Prudence had swiftly secured four of her canes to each corner of his ma's bed and covered it with a huge white sheet, he couldn't see his ma or Prudence and wasn't sure if he should poke his head into the private construction.

"Don't be bashful, now August Miller, bring me the water around to the far side."

August was taken by surprise that Prudence even knew he was in the room; he was in his stocking feet and trod lightly.

"How is she, Mrs Prudence?"

"I need the boiling water, son...have you brought it?"

"Only cold water!"

"Pass it to me then, son."

Prudence was sat on the floor next to his ma surrounded by a pile of rags and half a dozen small wooden bowls.

Winifred looked the same as earlier, leaving August wondering if he'd been right in bringing old Prudence to her bedside; maybe he should have borrowed a horse and rode straight into Oxford for a Doctor, he mused, guiltily. She immediately set to work, soaking strips of rag and laying them upon his mother's bare skin.

"Go see if the water is boiling, son!"

August felt like a ten-year-old again, under the dominant instructions from Prudence, but he didn't mind in the least, it was worth being at her continuous beck and call if it was to make any improvement to his mother's health.

With the small, randomly placed wooden bowls soon filling the makeshift tent with their steamy vapours and August repeatedly boiling up kettle after kettle, within a few hours, Winifred's breathing had miraculously become much less of a chore and the wheezing could no longer be heard.

"She's not out of the woods yet!" warned Prudence, "but at least she's more comfortable, thank the Good Lord!"

CHAPTER TWENTY-ONE

The day for Eleanor to return to the sewing room had arrived far too quickly; she was but a mere shadow of her former self, gaunt in appearance and pitifully frail; her fighting spirits had been quashed, leaving her continuously tearful and in a state of hopelessness. Tilly was worried that the workhouse had claimed yet another victim, leaving her new friend like so many of the inmates, who monotonously trudged through the labours of each day, showing not a single emotion about anything in life.

"We'll soon have you back to your old self again, Ellie!" encouraged Tilly, as she clandestinely spooned half of her gruel into Eleanor's bowl at breakfast.

"Do you think they might allow me to visit my mother's grave now, Tilly...I have so much to tell her and I miss her more than I've ever done before..."

Tilly blinked away her tears; Ellie's sadness was heartbreaking and she couldn't bring herself to admit the stark truth to her suffering friend. All favours would be denied to Ellie from now on unless she submitted herself to Killigrew.

"Maybe, Ellie, but you must regain your strength first and get used to working again...I will help you, Ellie. I'm going to do everything in my power and then we can plan our escape.

This time I'm serious. We're both young maidens who deserve the right to live a full life, with a husband and our own babies...I'm going to make sure my husband has a few bob to his name too. Once I'm free from this stinking hell, there's no way I'm going to return, one day, especially if I become a mother. It must be so heartbreaking for those poor women, separated from their little ones for days on end!"

Eleanor's huge blue eyes stared at Tilly, as she listened to her words,

"I feel too weary to even think about the walk from here to the sewing room, Tilly, and I couldn't risk being put into solitude again. It was worse than being buried alive and the pain of hunger was crippling!"

"It's early days, Ellie, you'll soon feel different!"
Barely able to walk and with Mrs Wishbone not allowing Tilly to give Eleanor any support, by the time they reached the sewing room, Eleanor was breathless and exhausted. But true to her promise, Tilly sewed faster than she'd ever sewn before and managed to complete most of Eleanor's work, as well as her own.

It had taken another five days before Winifred's fever broke and she was, at last, able to enjoy the delicious chicken broth which Prudence had cooked. The heavy, metal pan hung above the fire from the tripod, filling the cottage with its appetizing aroma. During those five days,

Prudence had seldom left Winifred's bedside, even though August had given up his bed to her. August had also barely slept since his ma had become ill, only managing to catch the odd nap upon the wooden settle or forty winks in his ma's rocking chair. He thought of Eleanor often, especially when sleep was a stranger to him and the only sound which broke the deadly silence of the small hours was that of his ma and Prudence gently breathing. He would wonder where she was and how she was fairing and he harboured an uncanny sense that she wasn't in Whitechapel at all, but knew that was more likely to be his subliminal wish, rather than fact. He wondered about her half-sister; did she yet know of her, or perhaps she already knew but had not mentioned her to anyone...surely she had gone in search of her, he continuously mused, she was after all her only living family...but deep inside he was pricked by the painful thought as to why she hadn't tried to find him when she had come face to face with so many tragedies in her life. Did she not know how much he adored her; could she not sense it? Did she feel anything towards him, or had his romantic nature simply overtaken his rational train of thought? It now seemed like an age ago since their brief encounter and had left him feeling confused. He'd written about her every day and had created, what he could only imagine her true characters to be like...had his imagination overtaken the reality of Eleanor Jackson, or Whitlock as he'd brought her to life through the pages of his manuscript?

Some nights, August would become so frustrated and angry, that he'd be forced to leave the cottage; he would march with his head hanging, deep in thought until the frustration subsided and he had convinced himself to be more patient, reminding himself of his ma's words, *"all good things come to those who wait!"* She never failed to repeat, whenever she'd noticed August become impatient about anything.

His journey to Whitechapel would now have to be postponed until his ma was strong again and recovered from her sickbed, but no matter how long it took, he knew he would never give up searching for Eleanor.

Prudence sat at the small deal table, enjoying a bowl of her soup while August was upstairs tenderly spoon-feeding his ma. Prudence took pleasure in the comfort of being able to rest her tired bones and take a break from Winifred's bedside. She missed her own cosy cottage and her own company, but Winifred had always been kind and thoughtful towards her and she felt glad that it was a way in which to repay her for her many favours over the years, especially lately when she'd reached her twilight years. Her pantry and firewood supplies would be completely depleted by now, if not for Winifred's kind and generous donations. Her eyes caught sight of the large pile of papers in the deep window ledge, they were neatly secured by a length of string and having heard Winifred proudly talk of how her son was an author, curiosity couldn't prevent her from turning up the pages to gain a little insight into August Miller's writings. She scanned a few random pages nervously, with one eye fixed on the stairway in case August should reappear. Quickly reading a few random paragraphs, she liked what she read and knew that Winifred's son did indeed have talent. Coming across The name *Eleanor*, however, set her mind wandering off in a completely different direction, bringing back distressing memories which were never far away and which she knew would accompany her to the grave. She stared up at the rain-filled clouds, their gloomy shade mirroring her sudden mood.

"Eleanor...Eleanor...Eleanor..." she whispered under her breath as she closed her tired eyes, allowing her thoughts to drift back in time. She could see him now, as large as life sat up high on his enormous black stallion, looking down on her and Beatrice as he politely doffed his pristine hat. She remembered the look in Beatrice's eyes and instantly knew that it was not the first time they had crossed paths, even though she was making out that Edward Jackson was as much a stranger to her too. From the moment she set her glance on that scoundrel, she knew he was a

man not to be trusted, as too was her flirtatious daughter.

Beatrice had always been a handful, she'd inherited her beguiling manner from her father, who had found it impossible to control his roaming eye and his sweet-talking tongue, whenever a female was within a few feet of him. He had left home one day, claiming he was going into Oxford for provisions but had never returned. Two days had passed and as Prudence decided to venture into the City in search of him, she was saved the journey with the arrival of a letter. In the fewest of coldly, written words, he had told her that he would never return and that he'd found genuine love with another. Prudence had torn the letter into shreds and stamped it into the dirt floor of the cottage. Enraged and heartbroken, it marked the beginning of her detachment from her hamlet neighbours as she wished not to answer any of their prying questions, as to where her husband had gone and neither did she want to make excuses for his scandalous behaviour. Beatrice was not quite five years old when this had happened and seemed to be content with just knowing that her father had gone away in search of work. Prudence seemed to have spent her life trying to install a little self-respect into her only daughter, but by the time Beatrice was fifteen, she had come to realise that no matter how many punishments and scoldings she handed out, nothing was having the slightest effect on taming her daughter. Beatrice had grand ideas, she was not content to reside in the hamlet and hungered for the City life. She yearned to mix with the wealthy society of Oxford's elite and believed that her astounding beauty and her ability to attract men was the key to a new and adventurous life. After turning down every suitor in the hamlet, by the time Beatrice was in her early twenties, there was not a single suitable man left for her to marry and she used that as an excuse to look for a position in Oxford, assuring her mother, that with such choice and availability, before long she would find a potential husband in Oxford. As much as Prudence objected to this idea, living with Beatrice had become a nightmare, she'd become lazy and uncaring and spoke disrespectfully, always accusing Prudence of being old fashioned and out of touch with the real world and claiming that she was ruining her life. Beatrice eventually found work in Oxford as a companion to a wealthy octogenarian. The old woman spent most of the day napping, giving Beatrice the freedom to do as she pleased in the west wing of the mansion, which was exclusively hers. The rest of her family didn't bother her, apart from inviting Beatrice to their weekly dinner parties. It was during one of these gatherings when she'd been introduced to the tall and exceedingly handsome, Edward Jackson and had fallen instantly in love with him. Edward and Beatrice had secretly set up home together, claiming to be husband and wife. She had left her employment as the old lady's companion, without breathing a word to Prudence and on that day, when Beatrice had been visiting her and Edward Jackson strolled into the hamlet, claiming he'd taken a wrong turning and strayed from the main Oxford road, Prudence could see through him, sensing immediately that he was a liar and a fraud. It had all been part of Beatrice's sly plan to introduce Edward to her, but she was no fool even if Beatrice was of that opinion and she figured out their wicked scheme. To this very day, Prudence was convinced that every pair of ears in the hamlet could hear the heated argument between her and Beatrice; they screamed at each other for hours on end, resolving nothing. It was clear that Beatrice was so besotted by the already married, Edward Jackson, that nothing, Prudence could say would change her daughter's course of action. By sunrise, Beatrice had left the hamlet for the last time.

Feeling completely alone and with a strange sense of guilt eating away into her thoughts, Prudence spent days and nights going over her life, searching for reasons why she had been abandoned, first by her husband and then her daughter. A black cloud of gloom and despair seemed to hover above her, for months on end and she became a recluse, refusing to answer the door to anyone. Even when she had to leave her cottage, to buy essential provisions she became almost unrecognizable beneath the huge veil which she'd hide beneath, leaving only a tiny gap, through which she could see her way. As the weeks turned into months, the neighbours soon gave up trying to connect with her and as she sat in solitude, deep in contemplation, it was a year later that an alarming thought disturbed her, forcing her to take immediate action. Prudence's sudden and disturbing theory, that perhaps her daughter was trapped in a cruel and uncaring relationship, with the wicked, Edward Jackson holding her like a prisoner, had engaged her thoughts and she knew that it was her responsibility to rescue Beatrice from his evil hold. Without further ado, Prudence set off on the six-mile journey into the City, heading to where Beatrice had once worked. It was with ease that the stern-faced housekeeper disclosed Beatrice's new address, she was most likely ashamed in having to admit that she knew such a brazen young woman, concluded Prudence, who felt nothing but shame and dared not to hold her head up high as she thanked the housekeeper, before hastening away.

Thoroughly exhausted from her travels, when she finally reached the address in Henley Road, Prudence stood holding the wrought iron gate, gazing up at every immaculate, white laced window of the house, rather than making her way up the short path and knocking on the door. It appeared to be a peaceful, well cared for home; perhaps she'd been mistaken in her hasty judgement, she mused, or maybe her daughter no longer lived here...maybe she'd never lived here and the address was merely a decoy. As every possible scenario circled like a whirlwind inside her head, the front door opened and a well-dressed man, carrying a Gladstone bag, emerged, closing the door behind him.

"Excuse me, Sir," said Prudence in a timid voice. The man immediately smiled, appearing to be in a jovial spirit, as he waited for Prudence to continue.

"I'm looking for Beatrice..."

"Ah, how wonderful, you've come to see the new arrival...and a beautiful little infant she is too. As pretty as her dear mother, in fact!"

"A baby?" uttered Prudence, stunned, as she felt the ground beneath her feet spin around as the man's voice seemed to fade away into the distance.

Doctor Thompson dropped his bag and just managed to save Prudence from crashing to the ground.

When she next opened her eyes, Prudence found herself upon a red velvet couch, in Beatrice's well-appointed front parlour. Doctor Thompson was still smiling and chatting warmly to

Beatrice, as she stood straightening his cravat. As she viewed her daughter, with a babe in arms and still flirting outrageously, Prudence knew that there was little she could do, but face the truth; just like her father, Beatrice would never change her ways.

"I'll take my leave of you now, Mrs Jackson, your guest appears to be recovered, but you know where to find me should the need arise!" He gently stroked the baby's cheek and smiled at Beatrice as he left.

"*Mrs Jackson!*" voiced Prudence, coldly. "So you're married then and didn't even think to invite your own mother to your wedding! Ashamed of me, no doubt...not up to your hoity-toity Oxford lot, I presume!"

"I'm not married, mother, Edward already has a wife, but he only loves me!"

Prudence shook her head in disbelief. "You have much to learn, my girl, and you've already made the biggest mistake of your life! You are nothing more than a wealthy man's cheap mistress and they come along at two a penny!"

"You're wrong mother! Edward adores me and now we are a family!" Beatrice placed the three-week-old baby into Prudence's arms. "Meet Eleanor, your *granddaughter*."

Prudence reluctantly glanced down at the tiny bundle in her arms and with the heaviest of hearts, knew that this would be the one and only contact she would have with the child.

"You've made your bed, *Beatrice Whitlock* and now you have to reap the consequences and I want nothing to do with your shame! You've broken my heart more than once already and ruined my life!"

Prudence took a last look at baby Eleanor, before laying her onto the couch and making her way to the door.

"Please don't go, Ma...think about what you're going to miss by being so stubborn, nobody knows that Edward and I aren't married! We will be one day and besides, his wife lives miles away, in London."

"I don't care if she lives across the seas in a foreign land, it doesn't make what you are doing right! It is positively, *sinful!*"

Peggy suddenly appeared in the doorway, "I thought I heard voices! Sorry, Beatrice dear, I was out in the garden, cutting some beautiful roses; would you like me to bring you some refreshments?"

Beatrice smiled warmly at the middle-aged woman, while Prudence could do nothing but stare angrily.

"You see how caring Edward is, mother? He has even found this lovely woman to take care of me and help me run the house so that I have plenty of time for little Eleanor!"

Prudence uttered a word of greeting under her breath and hurried out of the house as quickly as her feet would carry her, with tears already rolling down her face.

The sound of August's footsteps on the stairs brought Prudence out not her reverie; she quickly wiped away her tears and tried to appear normal.

"Ma ate the entire bowl of broth, Mrs Prudence and she is asking for her needlework...thanks to your expert care, I'm sure she'll soon be back to her old self again!" August was so euphoric that he failed to notice Prudence's watery eyes.

"Mustn't rush these things, now August, a slow pace is always the best way to a sure recovery, but I have to agree, your ma *does* look as though she's over the worst, which means that I will be going back to my own cottage come sunset."

"Oh yes, of course, you must be missing your home comforts!"

August's innocence caused Prudence to smile; if only he knew how much she'd enjoyed spending time away from her lonely life.

"Well, I'm only a stone's throw away, should you need me, son!"

The story of the girl hiding in the garden shed had reached Mrs Thompson's ears, which she immediately reported to her husband, convinced that the said girl was Eleanor Jackson...It must be, she considered *and* it made perfect sense. Doctor Thompson agreed with his wife and began his private enquiries which in turn led him to believe that she'd been admitted to the workhouse, but when the vicar allowed him to search through his copy of the parish ledger, where the details of all the inmates were recorded, there was no recording of anyone called Eleanor Jackson, or even anyone with a similar name. Already having meticulously gone through all the newly recorded names, Reverend Doyle had gone a step further by visiting Mr Killigrew, thinking that perhaps he or his wife might have accidentally omitted recording Eleanor's details in the ledger. It was an incident which left Mr and Mrs Killigrew adamant that Eleanor would never be permitted to visit her mother's grave or attend a Sunday church service, at least not while Reverend Doyle was in attendance of St Mary and St John Church.

CHAPTER TWENTY-TWO

Stood beneath the scorching summer sun, on
Whitechapel Street, Rayne could feel the sweat
trickle down her back as she pushed her bow
back and forth across the strings of her violin. As
usual, a large attentive audience had gathered in
front of her, tapping their toes and moving their
heads to the merry little tunes which seemed to
please them more than the classical pieces,
which Rayne had been more accustomed to
playing. Now brimming with confidence as she
delighted the local folk, she had gained quite a
reputation and now known as the *'fiddle girl'*.
She disclosed her name to nobody, apart from
Tommy Kettle, warning him that he should not
breathe a word to a living soul or let it be known
that she was the daughter of Edward Jackson.
He had become like her devoted puppy over the
months, obeying her every word and assisting
her whenever he could. She sensed he was sweet
on her and took advantage of his eagerness to
please. Word of 'the fiddle girl' had not escaped
Peggy's ears either and although she'd yet to lay
eyes upon the elusive girl, whenever she'd been
out shopping, Rayne had assured her that she
wasn't as proficient as rumour foretold.
Considering herself lucky so far, whenever
Rayne did happen to catch sight of her
grandmother approaching down Whitechapel

Street, she would immediately quit her fiddling and dive into the nearest shop to hide. Another one of Tommy's uses was that of a lookout; once he'd come to recognise Peggy, he would often race ahead of her to warn Rayne. Mr Levi had agreed to go along with Rayne's story, that she was employed by him to tidy the shop, take stock and make deliveries. So on occasion, when Peggy popped into his shop, he was forced to lie, telling her that he'd sent Rayne out on a delivery. Although telling lies went completely against Mr Levi's principles, Rayne had managed to persuade him that it wasn't a complete lie since she did work for him, in a way, but not as she'd explained to her family. Witnessing how popular Rayne had become and knowing a good business deal when he came across one, Mr Levi put his principles to one side and enjoyed the extra income which Rayne was earning for him, every day.

Both Peggy and Elizabeth were proud of how Rayne was working so hard to support them, but they also felt disturbingly concerned that she was becoming too accustomed to the ways of the East End and as Elizabeth would so often phrase it, 'turning into one of the peasants.' Rayne had slipped up a few times with her pronunciation, causing Elizabeth to condemn her lazy and improper speech and making her repeat the word correctly, ten times, before being satisfied. Knowing that the longer they remained in the slums of Whitechapel, the harder it would be to keep Rayne inline, caused Elizabeth to rethink her only option of leaving the squalor by marrying the loathsome, Tristan English.

"I might endeavour to leave this God-forsaken hovel one day next week and travel into Mayfair to call on Mrs English!" declared Elizabeth, one evening, speaking from beneath the heavy veil she now insisted on wearing to keep the swarms of summer flies from landing on her face. "Sacrifices have to be made, I'm afraid. Can we afford the cab fare?"

Both Peggy and Rayne nearly choked on their tea on hearing Elizabeth's announcement.

"You can't!" cried Rayne, in horror. "You said yourself, how Tristan English is a nasty, repulsive man…and he's built like a haystack and *far* too old for you!"

"Don't be so cruel, Rayne!" warned Elizabeth. "You are picking up some very common habits and that's one of the reasons why I am going to make the ultimate sacrifice, in agreeing to become Tristan English's wife…at least I can rely on him treating me…I mean, *us*, well. He's been desperate to make me his wife for almost a year now and I feel that I've shown a decent period in mourning for Edward, not that he deserved any respect after the debts he left us with!"

Peggy and Rayne clandestinely, eyed each other, unsure if Elizabeth was watching their reactions from behind her shield of netting.

"Well, I for one won't be moving into their grand mansion, I doubt that Mrs English and I will ever see eye to eye! I'd rather stay here than have that obnoxious old crow looking down her pointed snout at me and thinking she can treat me just like any other servant!" stated an infuriated Peggy.

"You've certainly changed *your* tune, mother...you were fine with being...*and I do so loathe having to say her name*, Beatrice Whitlock's skivvy!"

"You might do well to look into your roots, Elizabeth...and remember that if Edward's generous parents, God rest their souls, hadn't taken me into their care when I was a young widow, with you in my arms and barely a few bob in my pocket, we might have grown up in this very area and you would have likely married some *common docker*!"

"What's wrong with *dockers*?" exclaimed Rayne, with Tommy Kettle immediately springing to her thoughts. "They always seem very polite and courteous."

With both her mother's and grandmother's glaring eyes upon her, Rayne knew she shouldn't have opened her mouth.

"What business do *you* have with dockers?" they cried, in unison.

"Nothing, nothing at all, I've just seen them heading off to the docks of a morning...I'm just voicing my opinion if that ain't a crime!"

"*Ain't....ain't!*" screamed Elizabeth, hysterically. "Did that slang word actually spring from my daughter's lips? *Oh dear God...what is to become of us?*"

Elizabeth threw her thick veil across the room and held her face in her hands, appearing to sob dramatically into them. Rayne, however, knew that this was simply one of her mother's little dramas, which she often took to performing when life wasn't going to her liking. It felt like a sudden turning point in Rayne's life. Witnessing her mother's refusal to credit any of their neighbours with a single positive attribute and seeing the snobbery which had taken a firm hold of her mother, causing her to look down on everyone less fortunate than what she'd been a year ago, made Rayne determined that she did not want to become a mirrored image of her mother.

"It was merely a slip of the tongue!" voiced Peggy, in defence of her granddaughter.

"*No it wasn't!*" insisted Rayne, defiantly.

"You are like two peas in a pod... and you deserve each other!" hollered Elizabeth. "What is your plan *this* time around, *Mother*? Are you trying the other end of society's scales and going to insist Rayne marries into poverty, instead of wealth. Are your next of kin merely experiments to amuse you? I suggest you go in search of Rayne's half-sister in Oxford...You'd surely make a superb trio! But thanks to you, *Mother*

dear, I've become more accustomed to the superior ways of life, so I will go after Tristan English, if only to live the rest of my life in the comfort to which I was *forced* to grow used to!"
Peggy couldn't take any more insults from her daughter, she was furious and marched out of the room, leaving Elizabeth and Rayne sat in shock, as they listened to her heavy footsteps upon the staircase, followed by the slamming of the main door.

"*Mamma*, we can't let Grandmamma wander these streets! Not at this time of the night! The drunks and harlots will be out in full by now and anything could happen to her!"

"Calm down, child, it's quite unladylike to show such displays of hysteria!"
Rayne felt her blood heating up as she viewed the cold and carefree way in which her mother showed no concern at all for her grandmother. Already stood on her feet, she wrapped the blade of the bread knife in her handkerchief and pushed it down the inside of her boot; it wasn't sharp, but at least it looked threatening and if the need should arise, it might prove to be a useful weapon.

"Don't even think of leaving this room!" warned Elizabeth, sternly.

"Oh, *do be quiet, mother*...haven't you caused enough trouble this evening...I'm going to find my grandmother and I *ain't* coming home without her!"

Purposely adding the word of slang to her sentence, merely to vex her mother, Rayne took great satisfaction in watching her flinch, as though the word had caused her physical pain. She hurried from the dilapidated building in Castle Alley, out into the overcrowded and disorderly Whitechapel Street, where she was met by a sea of folk, most of them so intoxicated that they were unable to walk in any orderly way. Provocatively attired *'night women'* hung on every street corner, some in pairs or groups fighting each other like wild cats, as to who would claim the next client. Rayne kept her head low as she began marching up Whitechapel Street, already feeling doubtful about finding her grandmother in the huge crowd. She silently prayed for her safety. The evening was almost as warm as the day had been, causing more folk to leave their homes, but as she caught wind of their amplified conversations she soon realised why it was so busy and why everyone seemed to be heading in the same direction, towards Aldgate. A dog fight had been organised for that evening, in Wentworth Street and with everyone eager to wager on the winning hound, the buzz of euphoria was contagious throughout the East End. Having little choice other than to remain in the flow of the mass gathering, the chances of spotting her grandmother were looking almost impossible. Dressed in her attractive, floral print summer dress and cotton bonnet, Rayne already stood out from the drably clad crowds; she prayed that in their enthusiasm to reach the dog fight and with the bonus that half of the street lamps had not been lit on this evening, nobody would take any notice of her.

All of a sudden, as she was about to turn into a densely populated side alley, which led into Wentworth Road, a gang of four, odious looking lads sprang out from nowhere and blocked Rayne's way with their bulky bodies. One of them took hold of the dangling ribbons from her bonnet. The stench from the Thames was bad enough during the heated months of summer, but the foul, choking odour which radiated from the gang's filthy clothes and unwashed bodies was nauseating. Rayne felt her legs turn to jelly as she suddenly recalled the tales, which Mr Levi had often told her about the unscrupulous thugs, who preyed on innocent maidens under the shadows of night.

"Well, if it ain't the pretty little, *fiddle girl!*" mocked the ruffian, as he yanked hard on Rayne's ribbons.

"Ain't it yer bedtime, then?"

The three other members of the gang fell into each other, jeering loudly at every word their leader uttered.

"Don't take no notice ov this drunken lot...they don't appreciate a sweet, young petticoat like I does!"

"Where's 'er bleedin' fiddle ternight then?"

drawled one of the gang.

"Per'aps little Miss Fiddle is gonna try 'er luck at the dog fight!" replied the leader, smugly.

"I'm actually on my way to meet my beau and if he happens to catch *you lot*, you'll regret ever laying a single finger on my ribbons! He has more muscle on his body than all of you, put together and is twice the size of any *one* of you!" This time, all four men fell about laughing as Rayne felt her cheeks burning.

"She's a proper little madam, ain't she lads? Finks she's a bleedin' little princess or some'it!"

"She ain't nothing but a bleedin' East End, bint, who 'appens ter play a fiddle!" drawled one of the drunkards.

"Come on lads, we ain't got time ter be entertaining the gals ternight, we'd best get a bleedin' move on, afore the fight starts wiv out us..."

Just as Rayne felt she could lower her guard and that the menacing gang were about to leave her alone, the leader suddenly scooped her up and threw her over his broad shoulder.

"If yer even squeaks, you'll regret it! *Understand*!"

"Please let me go, I'm really looking for my grandmother, who fled the house in a cross mood..."

"Ah, ain't that sweet...she's looking fer 'er little old granny! What 'appened ter mister bleedin' muscle man then, eh?"

As more mocking jeers spluttered from the gang's mouths, Rayne knew that her only hope of escaping their hold would be to outwit them.

"Maybe yer granny is already in Wentworth Street, puttin' 'er money on the winning mongrel!"

Rayne kept quiet, sensing that whatever she said would make little difference.

It was in a run-down, dead-end side road off Wentworth Street where they soon reached a huge, energized gathering. Cries of encouragement filled the area as a circle of spectators surrounded the vicious dogs, yet to be released from their handlers. The gang leader, at last, put Rayne back onto her feet but kept a tight and uncomfortable hold of her arm. His attention, though, was now solely on the two dogs and the fight, which was about to begin.

"Relax, *Miss Fiddle*, I promise ter give yer me full attention just as soon as this brawl is over!"

The bitter-tasting bile found its way to the back of Rayne's throat, as she felt her stomach contract. As soon as there was a moment of silence she would scream for help at the top of her voice, she decided, nervously.

The two hounds looked as rough and as starving as the people of Whitechapel, thought Rayne as she watched them snarling at each other as they tugged hard on their holder's rope, trying to break free before the fight was ready to commence and all the bets had been collected.

Suddenly the two dogs were in a frenzied attack, snarling and growling at each other as they revealed their lethal, pointed canines. The audience became silent at the onslaught but soon broke into a screaming ruckus in support of their chosen dog. By now, Rayne had deduced that the black pug was named, Boxer and the slightly smaller, feisty terrier was Tib. They were soon at each other's throats and the sight of blood, oozing from each dog made Rayne divert her gaze; she had been hoping that Tommy Kettle might be amongst the crowds, but typically, when she needed his assistance more than ever, he was nowhere in sight. Taken by complete shock, she suddenly caught sight of Mr Levi in the crowds, he wasn't at the front, but there was no mistaking his familiar face as he peered over another man's shoulder. He too was yelling out in support of Tib. Feeling a little more at ease, knowing that she had an ally in the crowd; when the man in front of Mr Levi bent down, Rayne was in for the biggest shock of the night; standing next to Mr Levi, with her hand unmistakably holding onto his arm was her grandmamma. Rayne blinked a few times before taking a hard stare, just in case her mind was playing tricks on her eyes in the dimly lit area, but there was no mistaking what she'd seen. The fight soon came to a cruel and bloody end, with poor Boxer being led off to the side of the street to lick his wounds. It appeared that more people had wagered on Tib, making the odds less than they'd bargained for and creating mixed feelings amongst the over-excited folk. With nobody going home any the richer from the evening's activities, most of the men made their way to the nearest alehouse to drink their pitiful winnings. Rayne screamed out to her grandmother as the crowds began to disperse, but it was Mr Levi who recognised her voice and hurried to her rescue. The gang seemed to shrink in their boots at the sight of the old man,

"It's bleedin' Levi! Might 'ave known he'd be 'ere, tryin' 'is luck!"

Mr Levi had a sobering effect on the gang, who weren't nifty enough to make a quick getaway. Still holding on to Rayne, the leader of the gang became meek in Mr Levi's presence.

"What will your dear Pappa say, when I tell him the reason why I will not let him pawn his Sunday best on Monday morning, huh? Your family will go hungry! How many times, I must tell you, *young Mattie...find some work*...be more responsible. You never find a pretty wife 'til you are good man, huh?"

Mattie released his hold, appearing quite humble all of a sudden.

"Now, you apologise to this young lass and maybe old Uncle Levi will forget. Huh? And don't think I didn't see your accomplices...I know each one's mother and father...you tell them that from me, huh?"

With a hurried apology forcing its way out of Mattie's mouth, he sloped off into the night, feeling quite humiliated and leaving Rayne much relieved.

CHAPTER TWENTY-THREE

"Not a word to your mamma, understand!"
Peggy repeated, for the tenth time since leaving
the company of Mr Levi.

"Of course not, Grandmamma, I think you and
Mr Levi make a lovely couple!" giggled Rayne,
as Peggy's cheeks turned bright scarlet once
more.

"Don't be so silly, Rayne, we are merely friends
and nothing more, do you understand, but your
mamma would have a fit if she knew that I was
friendly with the local pawnbroker, let alone if
she should find out about her daughter begging
on the streets every day!"

"It's not begging, Grandmamma, it's
performing! I am an artist and people pay to
hear my music...it's the same as being inside a
music hall, but better because everyone can
afford to hear and enjoy my music, as they go
about their business!"

They arrived at the narrow entrance to Castle
Alley just as the clock struck its eleventh chime.

"I'm proud of you, Rayne, proud of the way
you've adjusted to living here and being
resourceful enough to provide for us, but you
and I both know how your mother thinks, don't
we, so we must keep our business a secret from
her at all costs!"

"I couldn't agree more," whispered Rayne,

already sensing the strict presence of her mother becoming ever closer.

 "We will simply say that we ran into each other in Whitechapel Street and we took a leisurely evening stroll," suggested Rayne.

 "I doubt she will even bother to enquire, but fair enough, it sounds like a plausible story to me." Elizabeth was already fast asleep and snoring loudly on her palliasse when they crept into the room. The bright summer moon shone down from high, managing to find its way in through the filthy windows and bringing a gentle illumination to every corner of the compact room. Rayne and Peggy exchanged loving smiles as they quietly removed their boots and bonnets and took to their shared bed. Rayne lay thinking about the evening's events, she wondered if her grandmother had known about her violin playing for a long time or if she'd only found out tonight. She also felt a little betrayed by *Uncle Levi*, even though he'd saved her skin earlier, but he did promise not to breathe a word to her family. Grown-ups were not to be trusted, she concluded before she dozed off into a deep sleep.

The following morning began in an abrupt and most distressing way, with Elizabeth bolt upright on her mattress, screaming at the top of her voice as she threw her boots across the floor, aiming for a couple of rats which had somehow managed to gain access into the room, even though every single hole in the wall had been stuffed with lumps of firewood. Peggy and Rayne woke immediately, fearing the worst.

"That's it, I simply refuse to sleep another night in this filthy slum!" screamed Elizabeth. "We will all be eaten alive by the starving, flea-ridden vermin if we don't contract some deadly disease first!"

Peggy hurried out of bed to fetch the broom, but the rats quickly disappeared through a narrow gap, where the floorboards met the wall.

"I *hate* this place...*hate it, hate it hate it!*" continued Elizabeth, hysterically, as she closely inspected every tiny gap in the room. "Why oh why did I ever marry that selfish beast of a man? It's all *his* fault...he was an utterly *useless* husband and an even worse businessman!"

"Come on now Beth, you know that talk isn't going to change a thing and I doubt those rats will return in a hurry with all the commotion you made!"

Elizabeth glared at her mother in disgust, "Doesn't it bother you in the least, *mother*, that we now share our so-called *home* with starving, flea-infested rats!"

"You need to remember the sacrifices I've made for you, my girl! I've put up with your demands for as long as I can remember. You deprived me of spending barely any time with my granddaughter, just because you couldn't keep Edward interested in you after your wedding!

Sent me packing to Oxford and even then, Edward spent more time with, God knows how many other women in London, rather than put up with your sour face every night!"

Peggy stood in the middle of the room with one hand resting on her hip, while she waved the broom around with the other.

"Oh, *mother!* Don't become the proverbial Saint after all these years, you were quite content to spend your life in Edward's family mansion; you encouraged me to set my sights on Edward and were delighted when I found myself with child, snaring Edward at the same time; it was not the foundation to a successful marriage!"

Up until this point, Rayne had been sat quietly, taking in every word which was spoken, but the last statement caused her to immediately intervene,

"Are you saying that I was conceived outside of marriage! Am I illegitimate? How *could* you, Mamma!"

In the heat of the moment, both Peggy and Elizabeth glared at Rayne and shouted in unison, "*No*...you are not that child!"

Peggy proceeded to explain to Rayne, in a gentler tone, how her mamma's first child had died shortly after birth and Rayne was born the following year.

"I honestly thought that producing you to your father would bring his heart and attention back to me," sobbed Elizabeth, "but, by that time, your half-sister had already arrived into the world and even though your pappa spent very little time in Oxford, that dammed Beatrice woman seemed to attract men like bees to a honey pot and she had her claws firmly dug into him."

"I believe that he always loved her!" added Peggy, "She was a very charismatic woman, was Beatrice; turned the heads of every gentleman she came in contact with."

Elizabeth pursed her lips, not wishing to hear any talk about her old enemy.

"It's young Eleanor who I sympathise with..." continue Peggy, choosing to ignore her daughter's cold glares. "It must have been such a shock when Beatrice suddenly discovered that her home and almost everything in it were not going to be hers, after Edward's passing. She was a very glamorous woman, you know...not one to accept a fall in society easily; she was very highly strung and over-emotional, that's probably why she took her own life!"

"I actually feel quite sorry for my half-sister!" uttered Rayne, "I wonder where she is and what she's doing now?"

"If she's anything like her *trollop* of a mother, she's probably latched on to some poor wealthy man by now!" cried Elizabeth.

"No, no! Little Ellie isn't a bit like her mother...she's a lovely, gentle girl; she didn't inherit her mother's flighty and flirtatious nature!"

Elizabeth had heard enough, she jumped up from her palliasse and marched to the other side of the room to retrieve her boots.

"Why are we even having this conversation? It's ridiculous...but I can quite see how the sighting of a couple of filthy rats can bring such a topic to mind!"

"Shall I store your palliasse away, Mamma?" asked Rayne, timidly.

"Well I'm going to the street pump, I think we could all do with a cup of tea and with a little luck, I might run into the muffin man on my way; I'm sure I just heard his bell ring out!" Peggy pulled on her bonnet and grabbed hold of the kettle while speaking, but before she'd reached the door Elizabeth made a sudden announcement,

"I don't give a care as to what you do with that rotting palliasse, Rayne darling, because I will not be sleeping on it, *ever again!* I intend to leave this miserable pit by midday and appeal to the better nature of Mrs English, that's if she has one, beneath her crisp shell. But whatever happens, I don't think she will have the heart to throw me out into the street and should, Tristan English ask for my hand in marriage once more, I will gladly accept; anything is better than waking up to rats gnawing away at your body!"

"What about us?" cried Rayne, shocked by her mother's selfishness.

"I will send you an invitation to my wedding, of course, and after that, perhaps, just as that *Beatrice* woman did, all of her life, I can use my wily womanly ways in persuading Tristan and his mother to allow you both a place in their home!"

Peggy let out a cynical laugh, "Oh, yes...I can see it now....I'll be the cook's hand and young Rayne will end up as lady's maid to that obnoxious old, Mrs English!"

"I'm sure it won't come to that, mother!"

"Please change your mind, Mamma, I'm earning money now, working for Mr Levi and I'm sure we might soon have enough money to find a nicer room to rent, maybe nearer to Westminster...there are some quaint cottages there...you'd like that wouldn't you, Mamma?"

"A rural cottage with no modern facilities and surrounded by even more breeds of vermin...*certainly not, Rayne!* I have my sights set on Tristan's Mayfair mansion and I intend to live there, *come what may!*"

Mr Levi wondered if it was due to the events of the previous night, why Rayne hadn't shown up to collect her violin that morning. Continuously poking his head outside the front door and peering down Whitechapel Street, he prayed that she wasn't in trouble and that she'd forgive him for betraying her trust in keeping her activities a secret.

Rayne spent the entire day with Peggy, trying to persuade Elizabeth to change her mind. They both knew she would loath every second of her life, should she become, Mrs English. There was a reason why a wealthy man like Tristan was still a bachelor at his age, he was a repulsive man, to say the least. With Elizabeth only seeing the elegant home and its decent location though, both Peggy and Rayne had little influence over her and so, by the afternoon, they watched and waved her goodbye, as the Hansom cab took Elizabeth out of Whitechapel.

CHAPTER TWENTY-FOUR

With the summer months coming to an end, the population of Whitechapel was already dreading the crippling temperatures, which would soon be upon them. Many families had spent their Sundays out in the countryside collecting wood in preparation, but it was a meagre contribution to the amount they would need to keep themselves warm all winter long. Old women read the tea leaves and ominously predicted the impending winter to be one of the coldest in a decade, which seemed to be a yearly practice along with predicting the hottest summer too. Mothers took to purchasing old and worn out jumpers from the market stalls, which they would painstakingly unpick and re-knit, having to use two strands of the thin wool to make anything at all warming for their young children. The only advantage of the cold months was the disappearance of the copious swarms of flies and the vile stench from the Thames.

Rayne and Peggy were still living in the same squalid room in Castle Alley and Rayne continued her performing every day, quickly becoming one of Whitechapel's most popular street entertainers. Peggy had also found work in a grocery, which was conveniently just two doors away from Mr Levi's shop. They would leave Castle Alley together every morning and return together at the end of the day.

It had taken Elizabeth three weeks before she got in touch with them, but her news was not what Peggy and Rayne had anticipated. Tristan English had married another; a much younger and quite pretty woman, so Elizabeth wrote, but also probably an ignorant gold digger with little breeding, she added, bitterly. The news was a huge relief to them, but Elizabeth went on to explain how she had heard the news that one of her old acquaintances, who resided close to Regents Park had become a widow since they'd left the area and after hearing Elizabeth's tragic news, she'd invited her to share her spacious lodgings, which spread over the ground floor of the very desirable property, close to London Zoo. Elizabeth went on to explain how unfortunate it was that there wasn't enough room to accommodate Peggy and Rayne and even if there was, she couldn't possibly impose on her new and most congenial friend. She justified her actions, of practically abandoning them, by declaring how she considered herself to be making an *ultimate sacrifice* in her separation from Rayne but thought it an ideal way for Peggy to establish a strong bond with her granddaughter, who up until Edward's death had been almost absent from her life.

Peggy read the letter aloud and although no words were spoken on the subject, both Rayne and Peggy knew that Elizabeth's selfish and snobbish side had been the catalyst in her actions.

"We'll show her, Rayne! And prove that you don't need to sponge off the better folk to raise your standards in life!"

"Yes, we shall, *indeed*, Grandmamma, we will soon be living in our very own desirable property!"

"I might even have a maid one day," joked Peggy.

They both laughed, knowing deep down that their life was going to be a struggle.

"How much savings do we have in our pot now?" asked Rayne.

"Half a crown and a few coppers!" declared Peggy, jubilantly.

"Pennies?"

"Sadly, only farthings, but who knows what the day will bring, sweetheart, now let's be off to work and this evening we will endeavour to make plans for the future; *our* future and we'll prove to your mother that we are as clever as she is cunning!"

There was a noticeable freshness in the air as they hurried along Whitechapel Street, shivering.

"Maybe I'll pop into Mr Levi's shop at lunchtime and see if he's any decent warm winter clothes for sale, or at least ask him to put them aside should he come upon some!" mentioned Peggy.

"You mean to tell me that you don't already pop in every lunchtime?" teased Rayne.

"What nonsense has that man been filling your ears with?"

"Don't try and hide it Grandmamma, you two already look as though you've known each other for a lifetime! I'm not a child you know!"

"*That*, I do know! You've grown up older than your years over the last twelve months! Maybe I should be keeping my watchful eye on you!"

"Oh, Grandmamma, don't try and change the subject, your cheeks are positively glowing this morning!"

"That's on account of the cold air...and naught else!"

Winifred had never been more worried about her son. After she'd made a full recovery at the beginning of the year, she'd encouraged August to chase after his dream, of finding his beloved Eleanor. He had spent a few days in Whitechapel and its surrounding areas, but there was no sign of her and neither had anyone he'd asked, ever heard of her. Her name failed to put the slightest of glimmers in any one's eyes. He had also had his book rejected by two London publishers and one Oxford publisher, who strangely enough gave the same criticisms, telling August that the underlying love story was outstanding, but was weaved into the wrong genre. Female readers would buy up every copy of his book if it wasn't centred on the swashbuckling pirate theme and a male audience would be put off by so much romance. August was advised to rewrite his book as a pure love story, but whilst feeling so disheartened and with there seeming to be no happy ending to his experience of love, he didn't think it possible to write such a book and so, for the rest of the summer, he'd not even attempted to put pen to paper.

As much as Winifred had always hoped that August would eventually realise how writing was not a means of making a decent living, she did nothing but encourage him to write the love story, as the publishers had advised.

"Winter will soon be upon us again, son," she constantly reminded him. "Why not give this winter one last stab at completing your masterpiece...I know how your heart is overflowing with emotions, capture them on the pages afore they hideaway, just like *you've* been doing of late!"

August looked lovingly across the breakfast table at his ma, oddly disturbed by a flashback of the previous winter when she'd been taken so ill. In that instant, he decided to honour his mother's wish and put his mind to the last attempt of writing his book, during the impending winter.

"As always, Ma, you're *quite* right; I will pour out my heart onto the pages, of what will become a bestselling book and if I don't succeed, then come next year, I will work the land and make you proud of me!"

"I'm always proud of you, August Miller, no matter what you choose to do with your life!"

"Then, I will go into the City and return home with supplies for the winter and a ream or two of paper!"

"Buy a little extra, son for dear Prudence."

A bond had since formed between Prudence and Winifred; they often shared an afternoon pot of tea and conversation. Prudence now smiled more and was thankful for the gentle companionship she'd found in Winifred.

"*Tilly*, please remind me of what it's like to feel warm!" whispered Eleanor, through her chattering teeth, as they lay side by side in the freezing dormitory. Tilly thought for a moment,

"Do you remember when the sweat just pours out from your skin and your hair sticks to your head, beneath your bonnet? When your mouth is so dry that your tongue sticks to its roof and all you want to do is to stick your entire body under the pump. *Oh yes*, another memory, when you desire nothing more than cool water to drink and the pump only dribbles out a warm and murky coloured, liquid!

"I'm not sure which season I prefer, Tilly, but I can't stand feeling so desperately cold, with my hands and feet numb!"

"Spring is my favourite season; it's as though the entire world has been born again, as though it's been given another opportunity. It's neither too hot nor too cold!" uttered Tilly, as she took off her shawl and gently placed it on to Eleanor's frail body. It had taken a long time, for Eleanor to recover from her spell in solitary confinement; with the lack of decent food in the workhouse, once anyone became ill and lost weight, it never seemed to return to their bodies again. But at least her spirits had recovered and she was now much calmer after Mr and Mrs Killigrew had been forced to leave the workhouse, during the summer.

Mr Killigrew had become gravely ill, after the episode of the stabbing with the scissors into his thigh. His leg had become infected and gangrenous and Mrs Killigrew had taken so long before calling the Doctor out to him, that there was no other option than to amputate his leg. Afterwards, his health deteriorated at such an alarming speed, that the board of workhouse officials soon advertised for a replacement master and mistress, for the Cowley Road workhouse. Mrs Wolf and her brother had applied for the position, but we're not found to be suitable, on account of their age and the fact that they were siblings, not husband and wife. However, Mr and Mrs Barnet were proving to be well suited to their new positions. Both in their forties, they were strict but not mean and thankfully, Mr Barnet only had eyes for his devoted wife. They had immediately taken a strong liking to Tilly which at first struck Tilly and Eleanor as being quite peculiar and worrying, but one day, Mrs Barnet let it slip that Tilly could be the twin sister of her dear daughter, who she had lost during a cholera outbreak some twenty years ago. It was uncanny, she had told Tilly, of how similar she was to her dear little, Rosie.

"Do you feel a little warmer now?" whispered Tilly as she rubbed Ellie's back, soothingly.

"Yes, thank you, Tilly. Where would I be without you? You're like my very own guardian angel!"

Tilly suppressed her giggles, not wanting to wake any of the other women.

"Hardly! But I do love you, Ellie!"

"I love you too, Tilly."

"This time next year, we will have made our *big escape* and we will be free!"

"Where will we go? How will we survive? We have no money, no family...at least we are safe in the workhouse."

Tilly sat up, surprised by Ellie's sentiments.

"That's not, *'Ellie talk'*...whatever happened to your dreams...what about that lad you love too...*August Miller*...surely you've not stopped yearning for him after the many nights I've listened to you talking about nothing else and what about your grandmother? Don't you intend to search for her, once you are free?"

"August Miller is probably married to another by now...besides I don't know if his feelings for me were anything more than that of passing acquaintances. As for my grandmother, I have no idea of where she lives or if she is even still alive and if she is, whether she wants me showing up in her life!"

"Supposing, your grandma is desperate to be united with you? Supposing August Miller dreams about you every night and has sworn that no other will ever take your place in his heart!"

"I'm tired, Tilly, too tired to talk or think any more!"

Tilly kept up her whispering in Eleanor's ear, knowing that her friend was still awake,

"Well, I'm going to dream of that handsome man, who can't keep his eyes off me in church every Sunday. I'm sure he has fallen in love with me...he's so exceptionally handsome! Maybe he's an angel, sent to save me...I don't believe such a lad has ever passed my eyes before! And I'm going to plead with Mrs Barnet for you to be permitted to attend church...that stupid cow, Killigrew had no right to insist that you were never to leave the workhouse, on account that you were a danger and had a madness about you...I'm going to beg Mrs Barnet to erase it from the book! She and Mr Barnet know that you're perfectly normal... Those *bloody* Killigrews, they were both bloody mad!"

"*Shuss*...for heaven's sake...some of us are trying to sleep!" voiced a couple of vexed women. Tilly hadn't realised how her voice had gradually amplified, with her anger.

"*Sorry!*"

CHAPTER TWENTY-FIVE
July 1877.

It was a pleasantly warm morning, as Eleanor
and Tilly worked the modest patch of land
they'd been allocated. Under a new and much-
welcomed innovation, by Mr and Mrs Barnet, a
Rota had been set up, where six women at a time
from the sewing room, were given a week's
break to tend to the workhouse gardens. Since
the men attended to all the heavy work
involved, the women's work during July was
mostly to keep the weeds at bay and harvest the
ripe peas, runner beans and redcurrants. Shortly
after his arrival, Mr Barnet had also insisted that
a large overgrown section of land behind the
workhouse, should be cleared and made good
use of. It was now a blossoming potato field. The
new master and mistress of Cowley workhouse
were as eager and hard-working as the
Killigrews had been unconcerned and lazy, they
also possessed a far kinder nature and shared
the fruit of the inmate's labour, rather than keep
them solely for their benefit or sell them and
keep the profits, which was common
practice during the days when Mr Killigrew had
taken charge.
 "When will these marrows be ready for picking
then, Tilly?" enquired Eleanor, as she gently
turned the soil with her hoe, pulling out any

undesirable weeds.

"Maybe in September, that's when most vegetables are at their best and tastiest; we might be eating marrow stew come September!"

"It's coming up to August," declared Eleanor, wistfully, as she ceased her work to look up at the clear blue sky. "Almost two years since I first met, August Miller...he has forgotten me, I am certain, but he will stay in my heart until I die!"

"Say his name!" insisted Tilly.

Eleanor looked baffled, *"What? August Miller?"*

"Keep repeating it over and over, out loud and then your heart will always remember him, even if one day, you forget...*go on,*" she urged. "It's true, believe me!"

"People will definitely think me mad if I do that!" giggled Eleanor.

"You won't be heard, out here....go on, Ellie...*please*...it will make you feel happy too!" implored Tilly.

"Oh...all right then...just to please you, my dear friend! August Miller, August Miller, August Miller, August Miller...."

The loud clanging of the chain on the front gate caused Ellie to stop her chanting, they both watched as Mr Wolf hurried as fast as his old age would allow him, with his bunch of keys at the ready. On the other side of the lofty black iron gates stood a pair of delivery men, who were impatiently rattling the heavy chain against the gate, even though they could see Mr

Wolf approaching. As Mr Wolf slowly dragged the gates open, the delivery men jumped on to their wagon and proceeded through them and up the driveway towards the workhouse entrance. The huge wagon was piled high, but whatever was on it was concealed beneath a precautionary rain cover.

"Just look at Wolf's face!" Tilly cried out. "I don't think I've ever seen such a wide grin on his wrinkled old face!"

"Perhaps Mr Barnet has bought him a grand, new bed...one for his sister too...they deserve a few comforts in their old age and on account of how loyal they've been over the years! Can you believe that they have lived in a workhouse since they were young tots! It's the only life they know or will know...it's positively heartbreaking!"

Tilly and Eleanor looked to each other before simultaneously turning their heads to face the open gate. In his haste and excitement, Mr Wolf had broken one of the strictest workhouse rules, that the main gate must be chained and locked at all times. He'd been so overwhelmed by the huge delivery that it had slipped his mind to secure the gates again.

"I don't want to end up like Wolf and his sister...I don't want to be here in five decades still dreaming of the life which I never had!" said Eleanor, in a small voice.

"Me too...I've got plans and I intend to live

them, come what may!"

"We'll have to go now if we're to seize this chance of a lifetime, Tilly; before someone alerts old Wolf that he's forgotten to lock up!"

"The delivery wagon will be leaving soon!"
Hesitating for a brief second, they looked at each other, both knowing what each other was thinking. Then dropping the hoes onto the ground, hand in hand, they ran faster than they'd ever run in their lives.

"*Keep going!*" yelled Tilly, "don't look back...we have to find somewhere to hide out until we can rid ourselves of this workhouse garb!"

Puffing out of breath, Eleanor could feel every beat of her heart and was not able to speak, but she obeyed Tilly's instructions and kept running. Through the ominous gates and out onto the bustling main thoroughfare, where it became impossible to conceal their escape. Nobody, however, seemed too bothered or made any attempt to stop them.

"Better stop running now, Ellie, we're attracting too much attention," puffed Tilly, clutching her chest.

"What if Mr Barnet comes after us...we need to get far away from this area...somewhere where they'll never find us!"

"We're not prisoners, *Ellie*, being held by the law...and if we can find work and board, no one will have any right to take us back to the workhouse! Calm down, Ellie, try and act natural."

"Sorry, Tilly, I'm just getting horrid flashbacks of solitary and it's sending shivers through my body!"

Tilly stopped in her tracks and spontaneously hugged Eleanor, "Don't think about those awful days, Ellie, you will *never* go in that dreadful place again...think of the workhouse as your past...like sawdust blowing in the wind!"

"It might be a little easier if we could find some decent clothes to wear...I hate these drab and conspicuous workhouse dresses!"

"Do you have any money in your bloomers?" asked Tilly.

"I have thruppence, how about you?"

"Only a couple of pennies and a farthing! I dropped my coins last night and that old witch, Ivy swore blind that my sixpence had fallen through the floorboards; reckon she snapped it up like a bird catching the early morning worm!"

"Never mind," consoled Eleanor, "I'm sure we'll have enough to buy a few items of clothing from the pawnbroker's."

"Have you ever been to a pawnbroker's before, Ellie?"

"I sold a few of my mother's gowns after she died. When I was hiding in my old garden shed!"

"Supposing the pawnbroker recognises our workhouse dresses and becomes suspicious, though?"

"Tilly! Didn't you just tell me how we're not prisoners on the run!"

"That was before the sight of so many affluent folk made me feel out of place...I've never seen so many finely dressed people in one town!"

After they'd crossed over Magdalen Bridge, they advanced along the busy High Street, where the grand university buildings took precedence. As impressive carriages and general delivery carts rattled through the street, Tilly couldn't take her eyes off the hideous stone gargoyles which seemed to be watching her every step and threatening to swoop down upon her at any minute, sending an eerie feeling through her bones.

Eleanor laughed, "Have you never been to Oxford City before, Tilly?"

"I came from Bicester workhouse soon after the Cowley Road one was built, Bicester is a quiet little village...I came here once, but I was too young to remember much, apart from going to the fair! Maybe we should go to Bicester to find work...there's plenty of farms always in need of dairy hands and milkmaids!"

Eleanor froze on the spot and glared crossly at Tilly, "Farm work! *Absolutely not!* That is positively back-breaking work...and a couple of pretty girls like us will have all the farmhands chasing after us...*no thank you.* I think we should smarten ourselves up and look for something far more respectable and refined."

Keeping her thoughts to herself, Tilly didn't respond but just kept walking, she knew that Ellie had led a privileged life before her tragedies had taken place and sensed that she was simply forgetting her new and much-reduced status in life since she'd stepped outside of the workhouse and was once again treading on familiar ground. Eleanor caught up with her friend and fell into line beside her, realising how snobbish she must have sounded; she felt as though she'd stolen her harsh speech straight from her late mother's mouth. She must remember who she was now, she warned herself.

"Do we keep walking straight!" asked Tilly.

"Yes, just for a little bit longer. I'm sorry, Tilly, I didn't mean to sound like a snob, it was a good idea, but I think there will be more opportunities for us here, in the City."

"And perhaps more chance of you running into your, *August Miller*!"

Just the very mention of his name never failed to put a smile upon Eleanor's face.

"And when we have secured work and board, we can go to St Mary and St John Church every Sunday! You will turn that young man's head when he sees you dressed like a proper lady and I can at last talk to my poor ma and tend to her grave."

"I don't even know his name. Maybe I just

imagined him to be admiring me, when all along he was probably thinking how terrible it was that the vicar allowed us lowly workhouse folk to even step over the threshold of God's Holy house!"

"Well, we'll soon find out, once we have ourselves fixed up, Tilly!"

"I wish I felt as optimistic as you, Ellie."

"It's usually the other way round...what a pair we are!"

They soon reached the water pump on the corner of Turl Street, a narrow alley which took them into Market Street, behind the covered market, where the stench of raw meat and dung was ever prevalent. Eleanor quickly surveyed the surroundings before, discreetly, lifting her dress slightly to retrieve her coins.

"Shall I get my coins out too?"

"No, we will need to buy some food, besides I'm sure I can make an excellent transaction with my money. Let's hurry, it stinks down this way!" Both girls wrinkled their noses as they increased their pace.

Just before they reached Cornmarket Street, Eleanor pointed to the dreary-looking pawnbroker's, a single fronted shop with its paintwork dull and faded, it was squashed in between a shoemaker's shop and an apothecary and set back a little as though it were hiding in shame.

Tilly looked sceptical, "Are you sure we'll find something in there! *For both of us?*"
Eleanor wasn't too confident but she tried to sound positive, wanting to keep Tilly's hopes up. "I'm sure we will leave here with a new and elegant ensemble, Tilly!"

There was no fooling the canny old pawnbroker, who immediately recognised the workhouse garb.
 "What have we got here then? Two workhouse escapees...hope you haven't run off with the Master's gold watch!" chuckled the plump pawnbroker.
 Posing a look of shock, Eleanor dabbed her eyes with the cuff of her dress,
 "Oh, Sir...if that were *only* the case! I have left my poor mother and three young siblings down by the river's edge, while I come a begging to your charitable nature..." Eleanor gave a little whimper as she continued to dab the tears, which were now genuine and rolling down her flushed cheeks.
The pawnbroker suddenly lost his jovial disposition, concentrating seriously on Eleanor... "What, in God's name, has happened?" he pleaded.
 The stuffy odour from inside the shop no longer bothered Tilly, as she watched in fascination as her friend's dramatic performance continued.
 "It was the most fearsome of fires which swept

through our cottage, my pappa is burnt from head to toe after rescuing the little ones, who were sleeping up in the loft and my mother is beside herself. We have lost everything and on top of that, we fear that my poor, pappa will never work again. These clothes you see my sister and me dressed in are simply old rags which a kindly neighbour so generously donated, to cover our modesty. You see, we were all in our nightwear when the fire broke out! My poor sister has since lost her tongue...it was the shock, you see!" Eleanor wrapped her arm around Tilly, in a show of affection, before bursting into loud sobs.

"I'm so sorry sir, my mother warned me not to become over-emotional, in your presence, she said it would look as though I was begging, which I'm not because my mother gave me thruppence for the purchase of some of your much older, threadbare dresses; that being, of course, if you happen to have such items in your lovely shop."

The pawnbroker was visibly upset by Eleanor's story, his jaw had dropped and he stood rubbing his brow as he looked around at the mountainous piles of unorganized clothing, which filled his shelves.

"That's strange, I never heard nothing about no fire.."

"Oh, that's because we come from Farringham, it's a small hamlet about six miles north of

Oxford, but my pa insisted that we came into the City, he said that my ma and me might find some work here too..."

"You are a courageous young lass...your poor family...May The Almighty take pity on you all and ease your suffering. I will certainly be praying for you!"

"Thank you, Sir, you are too kind, isn't he, sister?" Tilly nodded her head and copied Eleanor by dabbing her dry eyes, hoping the pawnbroker wouldn't notice her lack of tears.

"Tell you what!" exclaimed the pawnbroker, suddenly, "You young ladies come around this side of the counter and have a jolly good rummage around...find an outfit for the young uns, your ma and yourselves and we'll call it thruppence for the lot."

"Is there any particular pile of clothing you wish us to look through, Sir?" Eleanor enquired, timidly.

"*No, no, no*, you just pick whatever takes your fancy, while I go and make us a cup of tea and in my experience, a spoonful of honey goes down a treat when you've been inhaling smoke...maybe your sister just has a burnt throat from the hot fumes! I'm sure she'll be talking again very soon!"

Trying to hide her excitement, Eleanor replied, in a small and pitiful voice, "I do hope your right, Sir, I'm already missing her conversation."

CHAPTER TWENTY-SIX

An hour later and with a loaf of bread between them, Tilly and Eleanor were sat on the riverbank, relaxing in the warm afternoon sunshine. Their thruppence had bought them six adequate dresses from the generous pawnbroker and three attractive bonnets. Telling him that there were no dresses to fit her three younger sisters, Eleanor had suggested that if she took another woman's gown, her mother could make two dresses out of it. The pawnbroker had insisted they should take three dresses, so that each child would then have two dresses each, expressing his awareness of how quickly little uns soiled or tore their clothes.

"I still can't get over your theatrical performance, Ellie!" repeated Tilly, for the umpteenth time.

"Neither can I...I did quite enjoy it, though...I hope it isn't a sin to tell such lies!"

"They were simply little white lies to get us out of a pickle!" consoled Tilly, as she chewed hungrily on the bread crust.

"I've suddenly realised that the older I get, the more I'm becoming like my dear, mamma! She could give the most outrageous performances; in fact, she practically spent her entire life acting, making out she was somebody she was not....a wealthy, socially privileged lady, mingling with the better folk of Oxford...but, sadly, she had very few friends, just men who were besotted by her flirtatious behaviour and her stunning beauty!"

"That's quite a confession, Ellie. Your late ma was obviously a woman who knew what she wanted!"

"Maybe," uttered Eleanor as flashbacks of Beatrice clouded her thoughts.

"As soon as we have fixed ourselves up with work and a roof above our heads, we will stroll along Cowley Road of a Sunday and attend Church. We can both spend some time at our dear mamma's gravesides!"

"Oh, Tilly, *dearest Tilly*, please forgive me! You must think me heartless and uncaring. I forgot that you too have lost your dear parents and that your mamma is buried in the same cemetery as mine!"

"I *never* think of you as such, Ellie, you are like a true sister to me and your heart is as soft as pure silk. It is twelve years since I lost my mother, may God rest her soul and she was very sick too. I was only seven years old; your loss was far more recent and you spent more years with her than I did with mine. If my mother was still alive she would be living a horrible life in the workhouse and I would never have even thought about escaping, so you see, dear Ellie, everything works out for a reason. We must make the most of our lives and make every day count! And as soon as we attend church, I will work on getting that handsome young man to say a few words to me!"

"And how exactly do you propose to do that, dearest, Tilly?"

Tilly was deep in thought, as she threw a handful of crumbs to a nearby gathering of hungry Eider ducks.

"I think you may have to teach me some of your acting techniques, Ellie; I might do or say something clumsy and scare him off for good!"

"Tilly! You are older than me by two years, you should be teaching *me* about such matters...I have no idea about the etiquette of courtship, otherwise, I'd not have spent nearly two years in the workhouse and I'd be safe in the arms of, August Miller! And by the way Tilly, I too regard you as my dear sister; I hope we will share our sisterly bond for the rest of our lives."

Sharing a quick embrace, both Tilly and Ellie were glad of each other's caring sisterhood.

"Well, anyway, first things first, dearest sister, we must find somewhere to live, or we will be taken back to the workhouse!"

"Please don't even mention that place, Tilly...I'd rather die than go back there!"

"How do you actually go about finding a place to work?" quizzed Tilly, "and a place to live?"

"I haven't a clue...maybe if we visit a few shops and casually ask if they have, or know of, any jobs? I do know that the estate and land agency can help with finding lodgings, but of course, we need money before we can enquire there and if it's the same agent who I had the misfortune of meeting two years ago, I doubt he will give us the time of day" stated Eleanor.

"Hmm, sounds a bit vague to me, but I suppose anything is worth a try or we might end up sleeping with the ducks for the night. But first, we must change out of these awful workhouse dresses!"

"We could change beneath the bridge over there, but best if we wait until folk have gone home for their supper."

"Then it will be too late to visit the shops, Ellie and we won't have any choice but to sleep here!"

"Well, it won't be as bad as the dormitory on a winter's night...I'm sure it won't become much cooler, overnight!"

With a heavy sigh, Tilly tended to agree to Eleanor's plan, concluding that at least they would have the entire following day in which to make their search.

They slept far better than they could have imagined possible upon the grassy riverbank and were only woken by the noisy quacking of half a dozen ducks, still convinced that they had more bread to offer them. The bright morning sun was out in full and felt warm against Eleanor's face. She felt happy for the first time in a long while and overwhelmed by the huge relief that she'd not be consuming a bowl of watery gruel and spending the day in the sewing room or weeding the vegetable garden. She viewed her new summer dress, wishing that the floral print wasn't quite as faded, but it was a hundred times prettier than the dull grey workhouse dresses, which she and Tilly had now rolled up to use as pillows. Her mind drifted back to the time when she and August had viewed the lodging room, in Bullingdon Road; how wonderful it would be if she and Tilly could find such a place...if only she had a pot of gold...she daydreamed, life would become so much easier...

"Come on Ellie, we can't sit here all day, besides I'm starving!" declared Tilly, disturbing Eleanor's reverie. "How about you take me to that place you went with, August...what was it called again? I can't possibly have forgotten, since you must have mentioned it at least five hundred times, or more!"

Giving Tilly a playful nudge, Eleanor laughed shyly. "*The Copper Kettle* and I might have mentioned it only half a dozen times! Shouldn't we just buy a couple of bread rolls from the bakery, though, we need to be extra careful with what little money we have and I caught sight of an apple tree further along the road; ripe, juicy-looking apples as red as ladybirds, just hanging in abundance and waiting to be picked!"

"Very well, then, I suppose the Copper Kettle

will have to wait until we become wealthy Oxfordshire ladies!"

After they'd both consumed a couple of apples, they began their walk into the City, complimenting each other on how pretty they both looked, as they strolled along.

"You have such dainty features, Tilly, I'm quite jealous; you appear so light and nimble whereas my bones are somewhat large and clumsy in comparison!"

Tilly burst out into a fit of laughter, "Oh, Ellie, you do say the funniest of things! In my opinion, you have the figure of a woman, curvy and mature...I'm like a scrawny school girl and just look at those golden ringlets poking out from beneath your bonnet, my mousey hair just hangs, like a frayed cotton cloth!"

"Well I think you are quite the beauty, Tilly, your hair is soft and silky and has a shine to it, my curls have a mind of their own, they're quite impossible to tame! I'm so glad, though, that Mr and Mrs Barnet changed the rules about having our hair hacked off, as soon as it grew!"

"I think we should go to Queens Street first, if I remember correctly, there's a large clothing shop with its sewing room above it, maybe there might be a job for us there," suggested Eleanor.

"*Sewing!* I thought we could work in a grocery perhaps, or even a bakery...anything would be better than sewing all day long again!"

"I quite agree, Tilly, but to begin with we must

find a job that we can at least boast on having experience in. We urgently need work and lodgings, otherwise, we'll end up back in the workhouse!"

"I suppose so," voiced Tilly, a little reluctantly. "Where is Queen Street, anyway...I was only six on my last visit to Oxford. It was the last happy adventure with my parents that I can remember, we went to the fair...It will always be one of my *best* childhood memories! Did you ever go to the fair, Ellie?"

"I did, but not with my mamma...with Peggy...my late father's mother in law, but it was still fun and back then, I wasn't aware as to who she really was...just our lovely housekeeper!"

"Oh, yes, *her!*" said Tilly, remembering Eleanor's anecdotes about her family.

"Queens Street is the one which branches left at the crossroads, at the top of this street, by St Martin's Church."

The bustling streets were filled with the rattling sound of copious carriages and delivery wagons, as it was approaching mid-morning. The continued clement weather had brought many shoppers out and with everyone seeming relaxed and cock a hoop, there was an ambience of joy throughout the City. Trim figured ladies paraded in their latest pastel-hued ensembles, trimmed with the finest Chantilly lace which matched their elegant lace parasols.

"This is the place," declared Eleanor, as she

suddenly came to a halt, grabbing hold of Tilly's arm. She looked up at the impressive, Italian styled facade of honey-coloured, Bath stone. It stood four storeys tall, with the ground floor shop open to gentlemen wishing to purchase quick and almost ready to wear suits. They both peered in through the small glass panes, hoping for a kind looking person, who they might dare approach.

"Look, Tilly! At the rear of the shop, there's a woman...I think she works here too!"

"Where? I can't see a female, only stuffy looking gentlemen!"

Tilly was right, there was no woman to be seen, causing Eleanor to think she'd imagined the presence of a female in what appeared to be a male-dominated, establishment. Eleanor almost touched her forehead upon the glass in trying to survey every inch of the shop floor, she noticed one gentleman, he was admiring his new suit in front of the long looking glass, as another man tilted its frame, at various angles. Eleanor couldn't help laughing to herself, the man had squeezed his huge, overhanging belly into a waistcoat, which looked as though it would soon explode. His face was quite pink, as he concentrated on exhaling at a minimum.

Then, Eleanor suddenly caught sight of the woman as she approached the salesman and handed him a tape measure. She smiled at the customer, who in return only managed a nod of his head, as he slowly undid the buttons on the waistcoat.

"Shall we go in?" suggested Eleanor, wanting to act quickly before she lost her nerve.

"Oh, I'm not sure, Ellie, it doesn't look like the type of place where we'd fit in!"

"That's not the way to think, Tilly, we are young and full of energy, we are experts with a needle and thread and our eyes are sharp! And anyway, I heard it from a very reliable source that, they employ seamstresses to work upstairs, where all the suits are tailored."

Looking dubious, Tilly wrung her hands whilst thinking.

"Who was your reliable source then?"

"Mrs Thompson, the Doctor's wife, she was always well informed as to what was going on in Oxford!"

"Why don't we call on her then, maybe she might help us," suggested Tilly.

"Oh, I couldn't do that now, it's been too long since I've seen her and I'd rather wait until I can present myself in a less desperate state. I don't trust anyone enough. She might even send us back to the workhouse...no, as much as I would love to see her and the Doctor again, I think it wiser to establish ourselves first."

Tilly sighed, "Well if *I* knew any folk in Oxford, I'd be knocking on their doors and asking for their help!"

Eleanor had already put one foot over the

threshold of, Hyde & son's shop floor, leaving Tilly with no choice, but to follow behind, quickly.

CHAPTER TWENTY-SEVEN

The mixed aroma of brand new fabric and beeswax polish overwhelmed the spacious tailor's shop. Rows of duplicate suits hung on shinning brass rails, hats in every size and shape were displayed behind lofty, glass-doored cupboards and rows of small, brass handled, drawers housed an assortment of men's gloves, handkerchiefs, cravats and all manner of accessories which made up the gentleman's striking ensemble. Hyde & Son credited themselves as being one of the first modern tailors of the nineteenth century, where instead of waiting a week or two and having to endure endless fitting appointments, a gentleman could walk in off the street and leave after half an hour kitted out in a fashionable outfit of the highest quality.

Wilma Hyde was the steering force behind her somewhat bashful, husband; an accomplished seamstress herself, in the early days, she had worked every given hour, cutting sewing and producing the fine men's wear. Although she would have preferred to be creating elegant ladies fashions, she was determined to work alongside her beloved, Austin and knew how he took pleasure in fine gentleman's attire and would welcome the chance to be the renowned tailor behind the best dressed Oxfordshire menfolk. Nowadays, Wilma employed only the best seamstresses to work upstairs, in what she referred to as 'the engine room', while she took on a more gentle role in the office and kept an eye on Austin, always at the ready to give her advice. She was also in sole charge of the accounts and nothing was more pleasing to her than when a client handed her a payment, together with a satisfied smile.

Eleanor and Tilly stood gingerly, just inside the doorway. The man with the protruding belly glanced at them, immediately feeling uncomfortable by their presence. Austin Hyde cleared his throat and as if by magic, Wilma shot out of the office and glided across the gleaming wooden floor towards Eleanor and Tilly, where, with pursed lips and raised eyebrows, inspected them from bonnet to boot as though they were an item of furniture, which she was contemplating purchasing.

"This is a gentleman's establishment!" she finally declared.

By now, Eleanor and Tilly were both feeling awkward and blushing significantly.

Eleanor already sensed that Tilly would stand in silence, leaving the conversation up to her, which in a way she was glad of since Tilly was less eloquent than her and would likely ruin any chances of employment, they might have.

"Oh yes, we are aware of that, Ma'am, we are here to offer our expert needlework skills in your employ, should there be such a vacancy, of course!"

Wilma stared hard at Eleanor as she spoke.

"Where have you come from?"

"Come from?" quizzed Eleanor, sounding surprised. "We are local girls, looking for work...that is all...we haven't come from *anywhere*!"

Austin Hyde cleared his throat again, causing his wife to immediately leave Eleanor and Tilly's side as she hastened to him. He spoke in whispers, occasionally glancing at Eleanor and Tilly.

Wilma returned and ushered the girls to the rear of the shop. There wasn't enough room in her tiny office for them all, so with Wilma standing in its doorway and Tilly and Eleanor just outside of it, the conversation continued.

"Where do your families live?"

"We are both orphans, Ma'am."

Wilma Hyde's expression didn't soften at all on hearing this, in fact, she suddenly appeared more suspicious as her sharp nose seemed to flare and she licked her thin lips with the tip of her tongue. Eleanor was beginning to wish that she'd not been so truthful.

"So where do you reside...er...what are your names, by the way?"

"I'm Eleanor, although Tilly always calls me Ellie! We live in Bullingdon Road...it's just off Henley Road. We have lodgings there!"

"Hmmm....do you have any references?"

Eleanor shook her head, "We've been doing casual work."

"I will, of course, need to see a sample of your needlework and assess your capabilities...come back after luncheon and be prepared to sew...and depending on your, so-called, expertise, we will take it from there."

Both girls couldn't believe their luck. They thanked Wilma Hyde and left the shop with a spring in their step, trying to conceal their excitement until they reached the street.

"Can we really afford to take on more staff, Wilma, darling?" moaned Austin, as he hung up the closed sign.

"Come and eat, my love, I've made us some tasty beef sandwiches!"

"Not from yesterday's beef I hope...I've been suffering all day after consuming that leathery meat! I dread to think how my teeth will ever cut through it, now that it's cold!"

"I thought it was fine and so did Charles...your teeth are becoming weak with age, I fear!"

"They most certainly are not...all my family have good strong bones *and* teeth, nobody has lost a tooth yet!" exclaimed Austin, defensively.

"Can we discuss the young women, who I'm thinking of employing if they prove as good as their word? Do you know, there was something very familiar about that Eleanor, she reminded me of Beatrice Jackson...do you remember her, darling?"

Austin's eyes lit up and his jaw suddenly seemed to chew a little faster,

"Vaguely," he lied, as his memory recalled the most attractive and charismatic female he'd ever come upon, who could change a dreary dinner party into the jolliest and most entertaining of evenings. He had indulged in many a conversation with her, which had always taken place whilst Wilma was either out of the room or engrossed in conversation and oblivious to the flirtatious mannerisms of Beatrice Jackson. She had insisted he called her Bea as she'd go out of her way to stoke one of his dishevelled hairs back into place, or straighten his necktie. She would gaze deep into his soul throughout the conversation, making him feel as though he was the only man in the entire room. She could wipe away his shyness in an instant and he never failed to melt beneath her spell. He remembered how his heart would plummet, leaving him quite melancholy, should he arrive at a function to discover that Beatrice Jackson wasn't there.

"She was a very attractive woman, wasn't she Austin...the life of the party if I recall!"
"Was she dear, can't say I ever took much notice of the woman! Hmm, I must say; these sandwiches are quite delicious...the beef must have tenderized overnight!"

"Don't be ridiculous, Austin...you don't need to

prove that you have strong teeth, especially not to me!... I wonder what happened to her!"

"Who?"

"*Beatrice Jackson,* of course! Aren't you paying attention to anything I'm saying, Austin!"

"Oh, *her*...maybe she moved out of town...did she even have children?"

"I don't know...come to think of it...I don't know much about her at all. She was the type of woman who was just always there; she had such a presence about her, but it would seem that nobody knew a thing about her private life...I don't even know which part of Oxford she came from!"

"Perhaps she was a dinner party, ghost..." laughed Austin, his thoughts still firmly lodged in the past.

Wilma sighed heavily, "Perhaps I will take them on temporarily, maybe just for repair and alteration work..."

"You are simply being nosey, Wilma!"

"Not nosey! Austin...*curious*....female curiosity, that's what it is!"

"If you say so, dear!"

"Did you pay any attention to me yesterday, when I mentioned that I'd been to the book shop?"

"My dear, I never fail in paying attention to you!"

"It's quite ironic, don't you think?"

"What is?" questioned Austin, appearing quite

puzzled.

"You see I was right, you weren't paying attention!"

"Wilma, please get to the point of this conversation...our luncheon break is nearly over!"

"It's ironic that the book I purchased, just yesterday should have the title, *Searching for Eleanor*!"

"Purely a coincidence, darling...don't allow your overactive female mind to make something of nothing, there must be scores of Eleanors, it's hardly a rare name!"

"You can be very *boring* sometimes, Austin. You lack imagination!"

Austin sighed, wishing for a moment's peace to return to his daydream of when Beatrice Jackson was part of his social life, "I suppose it's another soppy romance! Who wrote it?"

"August Miller...his debut work, apparently and yes, it *is* a love story, Austin!"

"Must have been written by a woman then and I was correct about that beef, it's given me a ghastly toothache!"

Wilma hurriedly cleared away the crumbs and returned the muslin sandwich cloths to the empty tin before pouring out two glasses of lemonade, which had become warm from the heat of the day.

"You probably have a bit of sinew stuck between them, that's all. Drink this, it might wash it away!"

Austin grunted as he took the glass.

"There was something important I had intended to tell you this luncheon, my darling. Should I save it for later?"

Austin's eyes opened wide above the glass beaker, "No, my dear...if there is important news of any kind, I wish to hear it immediately...it might slip your mind later, especially once you get your head stuck into your new book!"

"Very well, my darling; I'm with child!"

Austin spluttered and choked before jumping up from his stool with a wide beaming smile upon his face, "My darling...*what wonderful news!*" he declared taking both her hands in his. "Why didn't you tell me earlier, we could have gone out for luncheon and celebrated in style!"

"Austin, it was worrying enough when I gave birth to little Charles seven years ago, when I was already considered too old for such activities, at thirty-two. Do you realise, I will be forty when my time of confinement arrives...I will be the laughing stock...people will say such awful things about me!"

"Nobody will dare to utter a vindictive word about you, every one of our friends and associates will be delighted for us, my darling...besides, you look more like a woman in her late twenties; there isn't a wrinkle upon your beautiful face or a grey hair amongst your crowning glory. We must take extra care of your health, though and you *must* sit down at all times from now on *and* no more lifting bolts of heavy fabric! You have made me a very happy man, my darling…when will our new son arrive?"

Already wishing that she'd waited another few weeks before announcing her news, Wilma was longing for a daughter and Austin's immediate assumption that she was growing another son in her belly only annoyed her further.

"In the new year, my love, mid-January, 1878 to be precise!"

" Splendid…splendid. I suggest you sit down for the remainder of the afternoon and relax with your new book."

"Don't be so silly, Austin, I'm expecting those young ladies this afternoon and I've yet to prepare any tasks for them. I was aiming to appear professional!"

"Another son….a brother for Charles… wonderful…I never thought to be a father again, *old girl*! What a wonderful day it's turned out to be! "

"Please don't refer to me as, *Old girl*…have a little sensitivity, Austin!"

CHAPTER TWENTY-EIGHT

After hearing his wife's wonderful news, all thoughts and images of the beguiling, Beatrice Jackson disappeared from Austin's mind and were replaced by future visions of himself, surrounded by his two strapping, young men in their famous clothing empire. That was until curiosity forced him to personally open the door when Eleanor and Tilly arrived, shortly before two o'clock and he witnessed for himself that his wife was correct in her analysis of the fairer of the two. Although most of Eleanor's hair was concealed beneath a bonnet, which, in Austin's opinion, had seen better days; the tiny golden ringlets, which had found a way to escape were the exact colour as that of Beatrice's hair.

"Good afternoon, ladies," he joyfully greeted, with his eyes fixed only on Eleanor. "My good wife will be down very soon if you would care to wait at the rear of the shop floor." He devoured her sparkling blue eyes with his and for a split second, considered, he was standing in front of that extraordinary woman, who he had once been infatuated with.

"Thank you, Sir," they replied, in unison as they hastened over the threshold and were once again hit by the strong aroma of beeswax polish. With his sudden assumption that Beatrice Jackson may have a sister who resembled her,

Austin found it impossible to hold his tongue, "Are you young ladies sisters, by any chance?"

"No," replied Eleanor, since his question seemed to be directed more towards her than Tilly. "But we are as good as and are lifelong companions!" Before they'd returned to the shop, Eleanor had already discussed with Tilly how she intended to pretend she'd been an orphan for the same length of time as her, she believed it would prevent any uncomfortable questions and they could both pretend they had very limited memories of any family.

"Do you have any sisters, by chance?" he questioned, to which both Eleanor and Tilly shook their heads and hurried towards the rear of the shop. Thankfully a customer arrived, requiring Austin Hyde's attention.

"Strange man...with odd questions!" whispered Tilly.

"Not really, Tilly, he is probably just nervous in the presence of females!"

"Well, he couldn't take his eyes off you, Ellie! You certainly seem to attract and captivate the men!" she giggled under her breath.

"Oh, don't say that Tilly, I don't want another, *Killigrew* on my hands!"

"I'm only teasing, Ellie!"

"You don't think he's been talking to that pawnbroker, do you? Maybe that's why he was so concerned whether or not we have sisters!"

"*Good afternoon girls!*" sounded the sudden, high

pitched voice of Wilma Hyde, as she burst through a small door adjacent to where they were stood.

"Good afternoon, Mrs Hyde."

"I presume my husband has been talking to you since I don't recall disclosing my name to you this morning!" she smiled, but Tilly and Eleanor could only share furtive glances.

"Follow me, I'll take you upstairs where my ladies are arduously at work. I have a couple of alterations I'd like you to attend to and I'd also like an example of your finest running and backstitching, which I will also be roughly timing and then, if you impress me enough, I'd like to see how accurate you are at laying and cutting some of Hyde & Son's finest quality cloth...don't look so worried, girls, I'll only be permitting you to work on remnants, when it comes to the cutting!"

By the time she'd finished her speech, they'd reached the top of the three flights of stairs. They followed her through another door and were met by the sound of the noisy treadle sewing machines. There were four of them in total, behind which sat four mature women, all fully focussed on the cloth they held as the needle and thread moved so quickly, that it was hardly visible. Nobody lifted an eyebrow as they entered the overly warm and stuffy room. Wilma led them straight passed the workers to the side of the room and to a large wooden table, which was surrounded by an odd collection of half a dozen chairs and stools.

"I do hope they haven't been using the work table to put their greasy luncheon on," she muttered, as she glided her hand across its surface.

"Take a seat, girls and make yourselves comfortable, before you begin!" she instructed. Tilly and Eleanor took the nearest chairs and sat down, both feeling far from comfortable. Eleanor's hands felt sticky, she worried how she'd ever manage to hold a needle let alone work with it. Wilma marched across the room and returned with a bundle of fabric and a gentleman's suit in her arms.

"Just imagine you're back in the sewing room, working on mailbags!" whispered Tilly.

"Right! I want the sleeves on this jacket shortened by one and three-quarter inches. These trouser legs have to be let down by one inch and the pocket, which is ripped, has to be repaired. There is also a square of calico for each of you, on which I would like to see an example of straight and I emphasise, *straight,* lines of your neatest stitching. You have forty-five minutes until I return. You will find scissors, thread and needles in the labelled drawers, which are situated in each corner of the room! Good luck girls!"

She turned around and had already vanished through the door before Tilly and Eleanor had fully acknowledged her list of instructions.

"Did she say the sleeves had to be shortened or let down?" mumbled Eleanor, under her breath.

"We could simply walk out of here and find work on a dairy farm! She sounds just as strict, if not worse, than old, Wishbone!"

"No, Tilly, we mustn't give up so quickly, we can do this, we are both excellent needle workers!"

Thirty minutes later, Tilly and Eleanor had completed all the tasks and were sat waiting for Mrs Hyde's return. Fascinated by the speed at which the women working the sewing machines were able to stitch their cloth, Eleanor wondered why the workhouse had never thought to purchase such incredible machines. Mrs Hyde was punctual to the minute and as the wall clock reached the forty-five minutes they'd been given, she glided across the room and was quickly picking up the items they'd been working on, scrutinizing every single stitch. She blinked rapidly and Eleanor noticed how pale and tired she appeared, compared to when they'd met that morning. With little expression evident upon her face, she appeared neither pleased nor unpleased with their work, but gave no indication and offered no compliments or words of disapproval.

Wilma Hyde *was* impressed with the sewing and although she kept her opinions close to her heart, she could tell that these girls were no strangers to a needle and thread; their needlework was of a neat and exceptionally high standard. Already clandestinely deciding to employ Eleanor and Tilly, Wilma was feeling too exhausted to supervise any further trials and longed for a quiet afternoon, with her feet up and her head in her new book. She hoped there wouldn't be any difficult clients in the shop that afternoon, which Austin would require her assistance with.

"I won't beat about the bush, girls…you've done very well and I would like to offer you both employment at Hyde & Son. I'm afraid I have an urgent appointment, which has suddenly arisen, so we won't have time to proceed with the remaining tests, but anyway, to begin with, you will only be working on alterations and repairs."

"When will we be able to use the sewing machines?" stressed Tilly, sounding disappointed. Eleanor gave her a sharp tap with her foot, under the table, fearful that Tilly might give cause for Mrs Hyde to change her mind.

Wilma Hyde stared coldly at Tilly, "Those very costly machines are only to be used by fully trained machinist and it takes six months to learn how to handle them. They can be extremely dangerous and if I should hear that you've been anywhere near them your employment will be immediately terminated…is that understood?"

Tilly and Eleanor nodded, feeling like naughty school children in front of their teacher. Tilly had already made up her mind that she disliked Mrs Hyde.

"Good, then I will see you both at eight o'clock prompt in the morning and I detest tardiness too. Let us begin as we mean to carry on Eleanor and Tilly and I assure you we will all be happy. In the morning, I will register all your details and go through the list of Hyde & Son rules and regulations with you. You will be paid one shilling and sixpence a week, to begin with. Now, let me show you out and make haste to my appointment."

Feeling as though they'd been rudely thrown out onto the pavement, Tilly and Eleanor meandered speechless through Cornmarket Street, both deep in their thoughts about the afternoon's events. The sight of a tray of bright red jam tarts in the window of the bakery stopped them in their tracks.

"Can we afford a jam tart, Ellie...I'm ravishing!"

"Me too! Oh come on, we deserve a treat, especially after that gruelling episode with Mrs Hyde!"

"Are you sure you wouldn't prefer to find work on a farm, Ellie, we would probably be given lodgings too?"

"I don't call sleeping in a draughty hayloft, lodgings, Tilly. Besides, we will soon be earning

three shillings a week between us! That will be
enough to rent a modest house, just for
ourselves...imagine that, a proper house where
we will go home to every evening. We will
decorate it with beautiful paintings and
ornaments and sew pretty cushions and
curtains...It will be wonderful, Tilly, just you
wait and see!"

Ellie's ideas did sound appealing, thought Tilly,
but unlike her, she had become so used to the
workhouse over the years that it sounded more
like a dream than an idea which could actually
become reality.

"We have to earn those three shillings first, Ellie.
Where will we sleep until then?"

For the first time, Eleanor was becoming
annoyed by Tilly's childish moaning and
ingratitude.

"We should be grateful that the weather is so
accommodating, Tilly...I see no reason why we
can't sleep down by the river for a few more
nights. Maybe I can persuade Mrs Hyde to pay
us in advance!"

"*I doubt that!* She certainly doesn't look like the
trusting type; you should ask her husband, I
caught him staring after you again, this
afternoon!"

"That would certainly be a move in the wrong
direction, Tilly...I don't want to risk giving him
the wrong idea, especially as he seems to have
his eye on me! That will probably be the only

reason why I'd leave this job...if he gives me any trouble!"

Tilly laughed out loud... "We haven't even started yet Ellie and I imagine we will be treated worse than in the workhouse, sewing room!"

"If either of us feels too unhappy there, we will look for work elsewhere," assured Eleanor. "We must also go over our story before the morning, we don't want to look like liars on our first day when Mrs Hyde takes our details."

"We can hardly give our address as '*the river bank*' neither!" joked Tilly.

The appearance of an irate looking woman from inside the bakery suddenly put an end to their discussion, "My boss wants to know if you intend to purchase anything because while you're stood there, blocking the display and making such a ruckus, no other customers can get a glimpse of these delicious cakes and loaves!"

"Oh, we're so sorry," exclaimed Eleanor and Tilly, in harmony. "We were just finding it so difficult to make our choice!"

The shop assistant gave them a dubious look. To make up for their annoying behaviour, Eleanor and Tilly spent nearly all of their remaining finances on jam tarts, tea cakes and a loaf of bread, with just enough left to purchase two cups of tea from a friendly old, costermonger, who was a permanent fixture in Cornmarket Street. It had been a long time since they'd drunk anything other than water from the roadside fountains and they gulped down the tea, thirstily. After returning their cups to the street vendor, they strolled past the many shops until reaching a small grassy area in St Giles, where they rested and consumed a share of the bread and Jam tarts.

"I really don't like the thought of sleeping on the river bank for another week," complained Tilly. "We're bound to have thunderstorms soon...and suppose someone is watching us...it's not safe, Ellie! You must know *somebody* in Oxford who could help us...what about your mother's friends...didn't you tell me that she spent most of her time socialising?"

Eleanor chewed her jam tart slowly, it had strangely lost its sweetness all of a sudden and as much as she hated to admit it, Tilly was right, it wouldn't be safe to sleep on the riverbank until they'd found somewhere to live, but the nagging threat of the workhouse was ever-present in her mind.

"I've never told anyone this before, but after my pappa died, not one of my mother's, so-called, friends took the bother to enquire after her and then, when she died shortly afterwards, still nobody showed their face. I don't think that my mother had any *real* friends. She was obsessed with socialising with the rich folk of Oxford, especially when I became older. She used to host the occasional dinner party, but I'm sure those guests weren't the same people with who she spent her later years mingling with."

"I'm sorry, Ellie," said Tilly in a tiny voice, noticing how grief-stricken her dear friend looked. "Was your poor mother very ill before she passed away?"

Tears fell from Eleanor's sad blue eyes as she remembered that day. For as long as she lived, she knew the memory and image of how she'd discovered her poor mother would never leave her. Tilly wrapped her arms around her, wiping away Eleanor's tears with her fingertips.

"Oh, Ellie, I should never have asked...I do so hate to see you upset."

"It's not your fault, Tilly, but I *will* tell you the truth about my mother now. You are like my sister and we shouldn't have secrets...not that it is a secret, really, simply a fact which I prefer to keep to myself. You see, Tilly, my mother took her own life and I was the one who discovered her...She hung herself."

Tilly gasped loudly as her hand spontaneously shot up and covered her gaping mouth.

"Oh, Ellie, that's dreadful...you poor, poor girl...how awful it must have been for you...you must have felt *so* lonely...I'm so sorry, Ellie!" With her arms still encircled around her shoulders, Tilly squeezed her closely, as she felt her own tears well up and overflow.

CHAPTER TWENTY-NINE

After the continued persistence from Mr Levi,
Peggy and Rayne took him up on his kind offer
and moved into the spare room above his shop.
It took two days to clear the largest room they
were to share from its copious piles of unsold
and mostly unsellable stock, which Mr Levi had
accumulated over the years, especially after the
passing away of his wife, more than fifteen years
since. Before accepting his offer, Peggy aimed to
make it abundantly clear and repeated herself
countless times, that it was to be a strictly
business arrangement; she and Rayne would pay
him a weekly rent for their lodgings and he, in
return, would set down any house rules that he
wished them to conform to. He made none and
was simply delighted that his empty home was
now filled with chatter and laughter and he
could keep company with his favourite two
females in the East End. He also took great
pleasure in Peggy's exquisite cooking skills and
by how tidy and spotless his small scullery was
now looking. Peggy cooked a meal every
evening when she'd finished her work in the
grocery; it was as easy to cook for two as it was
for three, she'd insisted. Rayne was now playing
her violin in various pitches, in and around the
market hall of Covent Garden and although it
was a good half an hour's walk away, the

increased income, which she was now making, most days, made the walk worth it. Tommy Kettle would go out of his way to escort Rayne home, giving Peggy some peace of mind. With Elizabeth Jackson, refusing to put one foot in the East End ever again, Rayne would meet up with her in Regents Park, most Sunday afternoons. But with every week which passed, their relationship was becoming more and more strained and awkward. They failed to see eye to eye on any subject and as Rayne was slowly becoming more at home in her new community and loving the caring and down to earth ways of most of its inhabitants, she no longer yearned to be part of her mother's social circle, attending formal dinner parties, where the protocol was to turn a blind eye to the scandalous money and food which were wasted amongst the so-called well-bred, wealthy upper class. In Rayne's eyes, those type of people were shallow and completely blind to the real world, where there was far more poverty than wealth. She had taken on a new ethos since living amongst the East Enders and saw no reason why every man and woman shouldn't be given the same opportunities. Finding her daughter's changed views quite disturbing, Elizabeth now stayed clear of any conversation regarding such subjects, leaving very little left to speak about during their Sunday rendezvous. She could not even trust Rayne to keep her opinions to herself and for that reason, never invited Rayne back to where she shared a home with her widowed companion.

During the harsh winter months, it wasn't worth the long trek across London to sit in the freezing park, so now, after two years since Elizabeth had deserted her daughter and mother, they only met on the odd occasion, which would be officially arranged in advance, by correspondence.

Peggy was used to spending years away from her daughter and was furtively glad that Rayne was not following in her mother's snobbish footsteps. Originally an Eastender herself, she had first-hand experience of poverty and had also experienced the ways of the rich folk; although there were always advantages to having enough money, food and firewood it didn't always make for a sincere heart. She had met some lovely wealthy people during her years in Oxford, but she was also aware that there were many extremely rich folk who considered themselves a rank above everyone else, simply because they were born with a silver spoon in their mouths and it was those folk who she despised.

Knowing that they couldn't impose themselves on Mr Levi indefinitely, Rayne and Peggy were saving as much as they could, with the intention of one day starting their own business in the East end. Peggy had a dream of running a grocery shop with her and Rayne living in the accommodation above and transforming it into their perfect cosy home. Ideally, she would rather purchase such a property rather than lease one; at least it would guarantee a secure future for Rayne, she considered. But for the time being, all three of them were quite happy to continue with the present arrangements.

It was a sweltering hot day in July and much to the disappointment of the huge crowd which had gathered, Rayne had to constantly take breaks from playing her music to wipe away the sweat from her sticky hands. Amongst the old and young alike, she had become a much-adored and prominent figure around Covent Garden, also delighting the costermongers who were convinced that Rayne's catchy tunes not only put the customers in a joyful mood, it also encouraged them to spend more freely. Stood in the crowd that day was August Miller, a regular visitor to the East End, he'd never lost hope of discovering a lead to Eleanor. It was coming up to two years since he'd first been mesmerized by her and with his determination to find her seeming to increase, he knew he would find no tranquillity in his heart until she was part of his life again. He wondered if she'd noticed his book, which was, according to his publisher, selling like penny licks on a hot summer's day. Coming to London regularly also allowed him to walk past many of the bookshops and make note of those which were displaying his book in their windows. Bound in deep scarlet, buckram with gold embossed lettering; it never failed to put a smile on his face when he witnessed an arrangement of his work behind the glass panes, for every passer-by to see. He had read the book to his mother; she'd insisted that it would have more meaning coming from his voice and was left with an even stronger sense and knowing that her son was bewitched by, Eleanor and that his life would be in limbo until he discovered her whereabouts.

August took out his pocket watch, it was getting late and he'd promised his mother that he would be returning that evening. His foot tapped to the pretty tune as he once more viewed every face in the crowd, praying for a miracle.

"I see yer can't keep yer feet still, neither," sounded a friendly voice, from over his shoulder. As August immediately turned around, Tommy Kettle beamed a proud smile at him.

"Yes, she's a talented, violinist," replied August, glad of someone to chat to. "Is she a relative of yours?"

"I 'ope she will be; one fine day," he replied, barely taking his eyes off the young musician. "I'm 'oping that she might wed me!"

"Have you proposed to her yet?" enquired August, squinting from the bright sun as he looked up at the tall stranger.

"Not yet...I ain't plucked up enough courage an' I knows that if I ask 'er an' she turns me down, our friendship will be over!"

"Take some advice from a man with a broken heart and don't let her slip away. Maybe she is simply waiting to be asked...females are difficult to fathom out; most of the time they say one thing but mean another. They become quickly annoyed when you express too much affection and disappointed when they think they are being ignored. It's all about getting the right balance!"

Tommy mulled over August's advice, still not diverting his focus from Rayne.

"Yer sounds like a bit ov an expert on the womenfolk!"

August sighed, "I wish I could boast that I was; I'm just telling you what I wished somebody had told me two years ago, that's all."

The tune came to an end and seeing that Rayne was returning her fiddle and bow into its leather case, the crowd began to disperse, with some folk complaining that she had finished too soon and some calling out, begging for an encore. Rayne smiled and made hand gestures to the crowd to emphasise how overheated she felt. Having already noticed Tommy in the crowd, she was curious to find out who the handsome man he was chatting to was and hurried towards him.

"Hello, Tommy!" She smiled; displaying her perfectly aligned white teeth. She was a pretty girl, thought August, but not beautiful like his beloved, Eleanor. She was light footed and moved gracefully, like a delicate butterfly flitting from one flower to another, in tune with the pretty little melodies she played.

"Another successful day?" enquired Tommy.

"But of course...apart from the pong from the river, it's the perfect weather for folk to hang about and enjoy a tune!" She glanced bashfully at August as she spoke, wishing that Tommy might introduce him to her, but without a word from Tommy, August didn't hesitate to speak,

"I most certainly enjoyed your music, you are most talented, Miss..."

"Rayne, you may call me Rayne and in case he hasn't introduced himself to you yet, this is my good friend Tommy!" she announced, knowing how Tommy could be a bit slow and backwards when it came to matters of social etiquette. August gave a little nod of his head as he placed his right hand upon his chest and declared, "I am, August Miller and I am delighted to meet you, Rayne!" Feeling awkward and annoyed by how Rayne could so easily mimic the better folk when it suited her, Tommy butted in, rudely.

"We best get goin' Rayne, yer know 'ow yer grandma, worries if yer late fer supper!"

"Tommy! I'm no baby, you know! It is late afternoon, a fine summer's day and the streets are still bustling with folk...anyone would think it was approaching the midnight hour, to hear you speak!"

"Well actually, I must be on my way too, I'm travelling back to Oxford tonight and should be boarding the stagecoach by now!"

Rayne didn't try to conceal her disappointment, "Oh, that's such a shame; my grandmother would love to discuss Oxford with you, I'm sure! Can't I persuade you to come for some supper before your travels...I'm quite certain there will be a later stagecoach!"

August knew that the next stagecoach would be departing on the following day, but part of him saw this as a golden opportunity to, perhaps, have a permanent pair of eyes and ears in Whitechapel. If he enlightened Rayne and her family about his quest, to find Eleanor, they might by chance discover some information one day and send news to him.

"You are most kind, Rayne and if you are sure it won't be any inconvenience to your grandmother, I would love to accept your generous invitation!"

"Of course it won't be an inconvenience, August, Grandmamma always cooks far too much supper, doesn't she Tommy?"

Tommy nodded, with a heavy heart; he was already feeling jealous as he witnessed Rayne's enthusiasm and over-familiar, interaction with August Miller!

"Do you often travel to Whitechapel, Mr Miller?" asked Rayne.

"*Please*, call me August...and yes, I am a regular visitor here!"

"What an extraordinary coincidence that you should come from Oxfordshire! Grandmother spent many years there...and to be honest, I do believe she secretly pines for the beautiful City!"

CHAPTER THIRTY

It came as quite a surprise to August when he discovered that Rayne and her grandmother lived above the pawnbroker's shop. He took an immediate liking to Mr Levi, who recognised his name, declaring how he'd seen his book displayed in the window of the book shop when he'd taken an afternoon stroll, a couple of days ago. Rayne was delighted that she could now boast how she knew a famous author, although August repeatedly maintained that he was far from famous, yet. Tommy had declined Rayne's invitation to supper, already riled in the way she was flirting with the handsome stranger, he knew he'd lose control of his jealous temper and likely end up severing all ties with Rayne and her family. As much as he'd instantly taken to August, and appreciated his advice, he secretly prayed that he'd make a speedy return to Oxford and not show his face in the East End again.

"Well, I never!" declared Peggy as she sat opposite August at the dinner table, pleased by his handsome appearance and his impressive good manners. "We have an Author from Oxford, seated at our supper table! How extraordinary! Did you tell Mr Miller that I lived in Oxford for near on fifteen years, Rayne!"

"Please, call me, August!" he implored.

"Only if you call me, Peggy!"

"What is *your* name, Uncle Levi?" quizzed Rayne.

"Rayne!" Peggy, admonished, "Where are your manners? Mr Levi is the oldest one seated at the table and deserves some respect, especially from you, *young lady!"*

"Ahh! It is no bother to me!" expressed Mr Levi, with a twinkle in his watery eyes, "My given name is, *Levi!* You see, my last name contains every single letter of the alphabet...at least twice! Nobody can pronounce it...in fact...I can barely pronounce it myself!"

Mr Levi amused everyone with his witty declaration. "I have been Mr Levi for so many years, that just plain, Levi, no longer sounds familiar to me, even though it was my dear mother's favourite word to holler out morning noon and night!"

Peggy proudly cut into the meat pie she'd baked, placing a slice on everyone's plate. "So what brings you to this part of London, August? I wouldn't have thought that Whitechapel was the place for a young, up and coming, author!"

"Huh!" protested Mr Levi, "I'd say it is the *perfect* place...we are surrounded by a mixed bag of characters here; best place in the world to inspire this literary gent!"

"What is your book about, August?" asked Rayne, dreamily. "Oh, I do wish I'd have seen it too. I will take a detour in the morning...which book store did you see it in, Uncle Levi?"

"Enough questions, Rayne!" ordered Peggy, not wanting her pie to lose its heat.

"I tell you, it's a love story, *Looking for Eleanor*...I remember the title because it's a familiar name, which these two women are always mentioning!" stated Mr Levi, before filling his mouth with a forkful of pie.

"It's actually called, *Searching for Eleanor!*" corrected August, who was now more interested in knowing why Eleanor was a familiar name, rather than devouring the delicious-looking golden pastry, meat and gravy on his plate.

"Ahh! Looking, searching...all the same...but it *is* a love story, I know that for certain!"

"This pie is simply delectable, Peggy...you are an excellent cook!" declared August.

"Yes, Grandmamma, I couldn't agree more, it's one of your best...I didn't realise I was so hungry. It has been far too hot to eat anything all day. I pray it will be a little cooler tomorrow."

"Your granddaughter is a most proficient musician; she captures the hearts of all the folk, out there!"

"Tomorrow it will be sticky and hotter and the Thames will stink like a thousand putrid chamber pots, but we will have a thunderstorm come evening!"

"Mr Levi! That is hardly the conversation for the dinner table!" cried Peggy crossly.

Rayne quickly changed the subject, "Why did

you choose 'Searching for Eleanor' as the title, August?"

"Let the man eat his victuals!" voiced, Mr Levi. "Why do women always want to talk when there is good food waiting to be eaten!" For the next five minutes, the only sound was that of cutlery upon plates and Mr Levi's rather loud chewing. As soon as the plates were empty, Peggy and Rayne cleared the table and swiftly returned, with a large pot of tea.

"Now is a far more fitting time to ask our guest your questions, Rayne," announced Peggy as she poured out the tea, "but don't be too persistent; it's not right that you should interrogate August on his first visit!" she smiled cordially at August.

"Actually, my book isn't simply a love story; it's my way of calling out to a young woman who has taken the firmest of holds on my heart. I fell in love with her two years ago; she haunts my soul and I know I will never find happiness until I find her. Stories of love are not my usual genre, but I could write about nothing else since Eleanor came into my life."

Rayne melted as she listened to August's fervent declaration of love, she wished someone as handsome as he would feel so passionately about her one day. "Oh, that's so romantic, isn't it Grandmamma..."

"She must be an extra special young woman to push you to such extremes to win her heart!" uttered Peggy, her thoughts momentarily reminiscing on the only Eleanor she'd ever known, throughout her life. She wondered what had become of her now. She had left it too long and should have gone to support her after discovering that Beatrice had died. A feeling of guilt flooded through her, stealing away her smile.

"What's wrong Grandmamma, you look quite unwell...is it the heat? You shouldn't have cooked today...."

"Don't fuss, Rayne, I'm perfectly well; young August here has just set my thoughts to *our* Eleanor...and when all is said and done, there is no taking away the fact that I love her as I love you, Rayne and I pray that The Almighty will forgive me for my negligence of her."

"Oh, Grandmamma, you worry needlessly, she is likely living the life of a princess, otherwise she would be sure to have turned up, begging on our doorstep!"

Forgetting the presence of their supper guest, Peggy slammed her teacup onto its saucer, causing Mr Levi to choke as he instantly eyed his best and most expensive china.

"How can you be so uncaring of your half-sister, Rayne...where is your heart and where is your respect for me? I spent years of my life with Eleanor! She grew up before my very eyes and no matter how much you protest or make snide and bitter remarks and insinuations about that poor child, know that I love her as much as I love you!" Peggy had left the seat of her chair and was leaning over Rayne, her hand ready to strike her granddaughter's face. Mr Levi followed suit and stood up too, *"Peggy! Peggy! She is young and speaks in haste! Of course, she loves her half-sister...don't you, young one?"* he focussed his last words on Rayne, willing her to issue the right response and calm her distraught grandmother.

Rayne was quick to calm the embarrassing situation, she couldn't believe her grandmamma was actually about to hit her, in front of August Miller.

"Of course I love my half-sister and long to meet her one day, Grandmamma...it's not my fault that she hasn't come to see us, is it?"

August wasn't sure where to look, but with everything he'd heard he was becoming convinced that Rayne was the half-sister which The Reverend Doyle and Doctor Thompson had spoken of. He felt his heart pulsating noisily in his chest, he wanted to stare at Rayne to see if he could detect any similarities between her and his beloved Eleanor. The name, Peggy suddenly sounded familiar too and he was sure it was the name which Eleanor had mentioned when she'd spoken of her housekeeper. If only he'd paid more attention to her words instead of losing his senses whilst drowning in her entrancing sapphire eyes. Love seemed to have the power to dissolve one's mind and send it into oblivion, he considered as he stared into his teacup.

"I do apologise, August!" expressed Rayne, just as soon as Mr Levi had poured Peggy another cup of tea, joking about how his heart might not be able to withstand losing one of his best teacups.

"There is nothing to apologise for, Rayne, this heat is enough to make the coolest of heads explode! But on hearing your conversation, it has me wondering if, perhaps, my Eleanor and your half-sister are, by some extraordinary miracle, the same young woman!"

It was a statement which had the most sobering effect in the small parlour, of Mr Levi's home. Shocked by August's announcement, nobody could find any suitable words to say and as Peggy considered that Eleanor would have been far too young, two years ago, to have fallen in love with August, Rayne felt a stab of jealousy and silently prayed that her half-sister was not who this handsome stranger was searching for and also that he would never find her.

Peggy sipped her tea, not quite knowing what to say on the matter. She still felt embarrassed about her little outburst and Eleanor was on her mind now more than she'd been, since leaving Oxford. Mr Levi was the first to speak and using his clam and sensible way to discover a few facts, like an experienced detective, he began his questions. It took but one question, in which he asked August if he knew of Eleanor's last place of residence. As August uttered, Henley Road; this time, the teacup fell from Peggy's grasp as her tears began to spill from her downcast eyes. Mr Levi released a long sigh as he viewed the two halves of the cup, with its dainty handle abandoned some distance from it. He glanced at Peggy and was deeply touched by her sorrowful look. "There's no need to cry over broken crockery, even if it is one so fine and expensive!" he teased, hoping to bring back Peggy's smile. August went on to explain everything he could about when and where he'd last seen, Eleanor and how he'd not discovered, until long after she was supposed to move in the lodgings, in Bullingdon Road, that her mother had passed away. Peggy couldn't believe how she could have simply disappeared and was riddled with guilt that she'd been so selfish in abandoning her, especially knowing how self-centred and uncaring Beatrice could be. At the root of every problem was that loathsome, Edward Jackson and if she'd not been so intent on guiding her daughter into his arms all those years ago, none of this would ever have happened.

"It's all my fault!" she sobbed into her hands, "I should never have left them, I caused Beatrice to take her own life and it's all my fault that poor Eleanor is nowhere to be found...Oh, Dear God, please let her be safe...don't let there be another death on my conscience!"

With Rayne trying desperately to console her

distraught grandmother, Mr Levi and August discussed ideas of where she could have gone, with the obvious one being the workhouse. He suggested that August should check on all the local workhouses again, just in case she had been admitted since his last inquiries.

"Perhaps she might see your book in a shop window; that would surely lead her to you!" voiced Rayne, trying to sound sympathetic to August's problem.

"If only," he stated, grimly, "I'm afraid, Eleanor has no idea of where I live, but I *have* left instruction with the Oxford book shops which are selling my book, for them to give Eleanor my address, should she, by chance, inquire after me. I know it might appear as though I'm grasping at straws, but anything is worth trying!"

"I suppose it is, August, but are you quite sure that Eleanor didn't have another love in her life? If she is anything like I've heard her mother was like...well, you might be in for a huge disappointment," whispered Rayne, hoping her grandmother wouldn't hear her spiteful comments.

The hurt which Rayne's painful remark caused, showed on August's sombre face, as his brow deeply furrowed.

"I don't think Eleanor had anyone else...I'm sure I would have sensed it. Surely you would realise if your Tommy had another love in his life, wouldn't you?"

"*My Tommy!* Goodness!" cried Rayne, "Tommy is nothing more to me than a harmless, lap dog. He's useful to have around and will do literally anything that I ask of him, but he's more like a brother. I certainly don't harbour any romantic affection for him!"

Immediately feeling sorry for poor Tommy, who had struck him as a fine young man, August wondered if perhaps he had been merely living in a dream world, where Eleanor was concerned. Was it possible that she had no feelings for him? Could she have completely forgotten that he even existed? Maybe she did have another, maybe she was in his arms at this very moment, perhaps even married. A lot could have happened over the past two years, while he had been nurturing his broken heart and allowing the world to slip by him, without much care for anything, apart from his beloved, Eleanor.

"More tea, August?" offered Peggy, breaking into his reverie.

"Er, no thank you, Peggy, I really *have* taken up too much of your time and it's getting late...thank you for your kind hospitality, but I will take my leave of you now."

"Oh, but you must stay the night, mustn't he Uncle Levi? It's *far* too late to travel to Oxford!" cried Rayne.

"Humm, I never knew you were the transport expert all of a sudden, young Rayne. August is a free man and if he wishes to leave then so be it, but of course, he is welcome to stay the night...I would never turn anyone out onto the street at this hour!"

There was a moment of awkwardness.

"Perhaps Grandmamma and I might visit Oxford very soon, isn't that true, Grandmamma? I know how much you miss it!" declared Rayne, her eyes open wide, showing no sign of tiredness.

Taking out a notebook from his jacket pocket, August quickly scribbled down his address and ripped out the page, "Please, if you do happen to hear anything about Eleanor's whereabouts, I would appreciate it if you would write to me at this, address and I too, will inform you if I have any news of your half-sister, Rayne." His voice was strained and weary and from feeling so euphoric a few hours earlier, he felt as though his heart had rapidly plummeted into darkness again, leaving his thoughts tangled and in knots.

"You must call on us again, when you visit Whitechapel, August! We would love to hear your news...wouldn't we Grandmamma?" expressed Rayne, insensitive to August's downcast mood. He nodded with a small smile as he said his goodbyes.

Relieved to be out on the street and alone, the sound of distance thunder had a calming effect on August and reminded him that he was just one insignificant human being in the colossal universe and not the only man to have had his heart broken. Poor Tommy, he mused; women could be quite heartless.

As Mr Levi cleared away the dishes, not trusting them in Peggy's hands after the eventful evening, Rayne's thoughts were solely on August Miller; he was handsome, well mannered and well-spoken. He was artistic, an author and probably a poet too. What a perfect match for her, she considered; if only she could win his heart.

"Don't think I didn't hear that nasty remark you made, about Eleanor, to Mr Miller, *Rayne Jackson!* You should be ashamed of yourself *and* of the terrible way you spoke of poor Tommy, who has stood by your side so devoutly! Don't get ideas on August Miller, he is clearly head over heels in love with your half-sister! It wouldn't hurt you to remember that you *have* a half-sister too. Eleanor is a lovely girl, who was fortunate enough to only inherit her mother's beauty; her nature is not at all like that of her mother's. Now I'm going to bed and in the morning we will discuss how we can go about looking for that poor, girl!"

CHAPTER THIRTY-ONE

Eleanor and Tilly had been left with no choice, other than to continue sleeping on the riverbank every night until they received their first week's pay. Without as much as a farthing between them and only a mouldy crust left, they were living off the fruits from overhanging apple and pear trees, which they went in search of most days, after a gruelling day's work in Hyde's stifling sewing room. Referred to as, *those orphan girls* by the four, self-righteous women who operated the sewing machines and who looked down their noses at Eleanor and Tilly, life was now feeling even more like a continuous struggle. Mrs Hyde seemed to spend her days cooped up in her tiny office with her head stuck inside a book, taking little notice of the strained atmosphere between her workers. She would show her face in the sewing room twice a day when delivering a box full of repairs and alterations for Tilly and Eleanor, all of which were precisely labelled with instructions. Mrs Hyde would collect them shortly before five o'clock, at the end of the working day. Each time she entered the sewing room, she never failed to inquire with the four women as to how '*the new girls*' were settling in and every time they would be as sweet as pie in their replies, leaving Mrs Hyde with the impression that they were like one happy family.

With no other option than to bathe, fully dressed in the river Cherwell every day, leaving their clothes on their bodies to dry off in the balmy afternoon sunshine, with the lack of soap and their clothes often damp, Eleanor and Tilly had become aware of their somewhat unpleasant aroma, which gave way for the women to make snide remarks and insults. Eleanor would often reminisce on her earlier life, when she could have a sweet-smelling hot bath every day if she so wished and when she would often dab some of her mother's perfume behind her ear; she could still remember its intoxicating aroma and likened it to an entire summer bed of full blooms, squeezed into a pretty crystal bottle.

"We stink like river rats and our second-hand dresses look a disgrace!" declared Eleanor as she and Tilly rested on the river bank to dry off.

"I'm starving!" replied Tilly. "I've eaten so many of these sour apples that the inside of my belly is as sore as my fingers are, from all that sewing! It was a whole lot easier sewing mail and flour sacks!"

"My stomach hurts too and it's only Wednesday, as well!"

"Oh Ellie, I don't think I can manage three more days without proper food, I swear my nose can detect cooking from five miles away now! What I'd give for a meat pie and a cup of tea...hmmm!"
Eleanor wasn't feeling hungry, her stomach hurt

too much and hearing Tilly's mention of meat pies only reminded her of the time just after her pappa had died and she'd been a regular customer at the pie shop in Cowley Road and of the day when August had been waiting outside for her.

"When we get paid, we'll be able to afford some new, second-hand clothes...and a meal...*won't we, Ellie?* Or does *every* penny have to go towards our lodgings?"

"Well, we definitely won't be able to go back to the same pawnbroker from who we got these clothes, that's for sure."

"There must be another one somewhere, surely?"

"Oh, Tilly, we'll worry about that when we have some coins in our hands, my stomach hurts too much...I don't remember feeling such pain, even when I was in solitary, these are far worse than hunger pains! I never want to see another apple again! I just want to try and sleep!"

"But it's not even sunset yet, Ellie!"

Eleanor didn't answer but curled up into a ball, in the hope that sleep would soon wipe away her pains.

"Shall we take a stroll to the Wednesday market, there might be some leftovers going free!" suggested Tilly.

"Probably more apples knowing our luck!"Eleanor groaned. "My belly hurts too much for me to even *think* about walking there, but, I don't mind if you want to go by yourself...I might feel better after a nap."

Tilly jokingly told the nearby ducks to take good care of her dear friend, promising them a few mouthfuls of bread if she struck lucky at the market.

"Oh, very funny, Tilly...I always knew that you and that flock shared a mutual understanding!"

"Are you sure you won't come with me...you sound a bit more cheerful now!"

No sooner had Tilly finished her sentence than Eleanor suddenly grabbed hold of her stomach, crying out in pain.

"Maybe I should stay with you, after all!" voiced Tilly, becoming increasingly worried about Eleanor's health.

"No, Tilly, you go, I'll be fine and besides maybe my stomach will improve if I eat something else, other than sour fruit!"

"I'll be as quick as I can, and even flirt outrageously with the costermongers if it means returning with something wholesome for your supper!"

"Don't get into trouble, Tilly," warned Eleanor in a small voice, as she watched Tilly hurry through the field of tall purple cornflowers, chicory and wild teasels before disappearing onto the roadside and out of view.

After a long and sweltering day beneath the scorching sun, most of the costermongers had already left their pitches and the few which remained were in the process of packing up. A couple, who Tilly presumed were husband and wife, were sitting on small wooden stools behind a large copper urn and a few dried up fruit cakes. As Tilly approached the table, most of what she'd presumed was fruit, suddenly flew away.

"Oh, my Dear Lord!" she exclaimed. "All your fruit has just flown away, before my eyes!"

The middle-aged couple, who had been engrossed in conversation, gazed up at Tilly.

"Are you *simple*, girl! Those are me wife's best fruit buns. They beats them Banbury cakes any day of the blooming week, I tell you!"

"That might have been the case when they came out of the oven, but they've been sitting here beneath the baking sun, feeding the flies...they are likely as dry as a stone by now and would give you a toothache *and* an ache in your belly; enough to ruin your day and keep you glued to the chamber pot!"

"How dare you insult me wife's fruit buns...who d'you think you are, little madam!"

"Oh, I'm not insulting your wife's fine fruit buns, in fact, I've had the pleasure of eating them before and you are right, they are simply divine!"

The couple was dumbstruck as they sat listening to Tilly.

"I'm actually protecting the excellent reputation which your cakes have justly earned. Supposing someone should purchase one now...I think I can safely say, they'd not complement them, in fact, quite the opposite...it would do your future business no good at all...in fact..."

"That will do, thank you very much! I don't know who you think you are, but me and the wife have been serving the good folk of Oxford since you were naught but a pip!"

"Oh, my dear, don't waste your breath...it's too blooming hot to get yourself in a state...it's high time we were on our way home, anyway! Can't wait to put me feet in a bucket of cold water!"

"I know a lovely family of ducks, down by the river, who would be absolutely delighted to take these stale buns off your hands!" declared Tilly, causing the couple's mood to instantly change as they roared with laughter.

"Ducks...ducks!" exclaimed the woman, with tears in her eyes. "You're either soft in the head, girl or you've spent too many hours under the sun! But your duck friends are welcome to these old buns...you've certainly put a smile on our faces and there ain't been much else to smile about all day!"

"Thank you, so much; you don't happen to have any leftover tea in that urn that I could take off your hands I suppose?" she asked, timidly.

"Does that blooming duck family like a cup of tea too?" chuckled the woman, as she placed all the fruit buns into a bag. Her husband had laughed so much that he was now coughing and spluttering. The woman slapped him vigorously on his back with one hand and he immediately ceased. She then retrieved an old ale bottle, from under the table and filled it with the overly brewed warm tea. "There ain't no milk, lass, that went sour by midday, but I will put some sugar in it for you, or your blooming duck family, if they do happen to be partial to a sup of tea!"

Tilly couldn't wait to tell Eleanor about her success and see her face light up when she handed her tea and fruit buns; she had even surprised herself by being so confident in apprehending the costermongers, concluding that she was learning some of Ellie's skills. With eight fruit buns and a bottle of sweet black tea, they would surely sleep on a full belly tonight. A huge raindrop suddenly landed on the back of her hand and the sound of thunder rumbled like a warning in the distance, Tilly now had an ominous feeling that she and Ellie were in for a tougher than usual night ahead.

The streets were nearly empty. Most folk would be relaxing after the oppressive heat of the day, maybe eating a light supper in their garden, mused Tilly. A few horse carts rattled along at a snail's pace through the streets, with even the horses feeling overheated and lethargic. As she diverted from the road, down to her and Eleanor's spot on the riverbank, a young boy with his cap in hand came sprinting up to greet her,

"Are you Tilly?" he puffed, out of breath. His cheeks were bright red and his sweaty hair was stuck to his forehead. Before giving him her full attention, Tilly peered over the top of his head in search of Ellie. She was nowhere in sight, causing Tilly to instantly sense that something had happened to her.

"Yes, I'm Tilly...did my friend tell you my name? Do you know where she is?" she blurted out, in a muddled tongue.

The boy gazed up at her, his huge circular eyes appearing alarmed as he spoke, "Me pa has just carted her off to hospital!"

"*Carted her off?* **Hospital!**" repeated Tilly, taken by complete shock. "She's not a sack of flour, to be carted off!"

"Well, me pa works at the flour mill, so she might as well be! I hope your friend doesn't pass away like me ma did when she were carted off to hospital."

"Where *is* the hospital, can you take me to it, please!" begged Tilly, now even more distraught by the boy's fearful statement.

"I can't, Miss, me pa told me to stay put 'til he comes back for me."

Feeling quite numb, Tilly had no idea as to where the hospital in Oxford was.

"Can you tell me where it is then...you see I'm not familiar with the City?"

"Do you know where the Ashmolean Museum

is, Miss...In Beaumont Street?"
Tilly shook her head in slow-motion, as she
racked her brains, trying to remember where the
hospital was situated; she vaguely remembered
going there with her mother many years ago.
  "D'you know where the fair is, then? Everybody
knows where the fair is!"
  "*Oh, yes, I do...*"
  "Then you just keep walking along that street
and you'll soon find it!"
  "Thank you, thank you," she cried as she
hurried away.

  By the time she'd reached the main entrance of
the Radcliffe Infirmary, the rain was falling
heavily in huge drops, the like of which Tilly
had never before witnessed. A foreboding
darkness had descended upon Oxford making it
feel more like midnight than early evening.
Thankful that she'd just missed the sudden
downfall and remained dry, Tilly met with a
stern-faced porter in the spacious stone
vestibule. He pulled the sliding window of his
tiny niche open and peered over the top of his
wire-rimmed spectacles, waiting for Tilly to
speak. Her tongue seemed to be moving faster
than her brain was thinking. Having already
decided to say that she was Ellie's sister, the
appearance of two men, one with only one leg,
leaving the hospital, seemed to muddle her
thoughts more than ever as she forced the

unwilling words out of her mouth.

"I'm looking for…*Ellie*…she's my s..s..sister …she's very sick, I fear…and…Oh, dear…did she come past you at all, Sir…please!…is sh..sh..she here!"

The porter continued to stare at Tilly, wondering if she'd yet finished her sentence. Seeing how distressed the young woman was, he was convinced she was related to the earlier and only admission of the evening. He peered down at his admissions book.

"I do believe you're inquiring after a Miss Eleanor Whitlock…"

"Oh yes, *yes I am*…how is she, which room is she in?…can I go to her …"

"Steady on now Miss, I'm afraid she's not been in here long enough for me to answer any of your questions. Take a seat and in due course, I will find Matron and make some enquiries after your sister."

Still clutching the bag of fruit buns, Tilly had completely lost her appetite. She sat nervously, praying silently that Ellie's stomach pain was down to the number of apples she'd consumed over the week. Two nurses entered through the arched doorway, they marched in step with one another, looking quite smart and regimental in their immaculate uniforms.

"Good evening, Mr Dunkley!" the nurses chirped, merrily.

The porter smiled instantly and returned a

greeting as the nurses proceeded past Tilly, as though she were invisible.

The coolness of the stone vestibule, together with the sudden drop in temperature caused Tilly to shiver. Her shawl and the rest of her and Eleanor's spare set of clothes were hidden beneath a small bushy shrub by the riverside, but Tilly already knew she would not be returning to sleep their again, that night. Ellie was ill, the pelting rain showed no sign of easing off and suddenly everything in the world seemed overly depressing to Tilly.

CHAPTER THIRTY-TWO

After wandering the streets of London in a circle since leaving the company of Rayne, her grandmother and Mr Levi, August took comfort in the sound of the rumbling thunder which was gradually becoming louder. Huge jagged cracks of lightning intermittently illuminated the gunmetal grey sky as August felt the first drops of rain upon his face as he looked up in admiration of the dramatic night sky. He cared not if he became soaked, in fact, he welcomed the prospect. With nowhere to go, although he wasn't short of funds, he didn't wish to spend the night in an unfamiliar hotel room. Maybe he was simply being an over-emotional romantic, but in a strange way, he suddenly felt closer to Eleanor than he'd felt in many months. Perhaps the evening spent with her housekeeper and her rather mean, half-sister, had brought about such feelings, was the thought which passed through his deep thinking, but he quickly dismissed such thoughts, sensing that wherever Eleanor might be at this moment in time, she had not forgotten him.

Two hours had passed before Tilly heard any news of Eleanor. She had sat shivering, feeling quite alone as she viewed the few people who entered and left the hospital. The porter was submerged in reading every single word of the newspaper, which was folded discreetly underneath his admissions ledger, but he had been kind enough to make Tilly a cup of tea after she'd been sat there for over an hour and in return, she offered him one of the fruit buns, which she'd been clinging on to all evening. He took a quick peek into the bag and politely declined her offer, saying how the fruit would only give him indigestion at such a late hour.

A middle-aged man entered the vestibule; dressed in a smart well-tailored suit and carrying a Gladstone bag, Tilly's odd, but first thoughts, were that it was not one of Hyde's convenient suits. He unexpectedly came to a halt in front of Tilly and gazed down at her.

"I presume you are, Miss Whitlock...Eleanor Whitlock's sister?"

"Oh, yes!" exclaimed Tilly, taken by surprise and a little slow to recognise the mention of Ellie's full name.

"I'm Doctor Hawthorn," he stated, with little facial expression. He hurriedly continued,"Your sister, has been most fortunate to have been brought here, just in time. We have had to remove her appendix and although it has left her gravely ill, I am optimistic that with having youth on her side, she will make a full recovery, but she will be spending the next few weeks here, in hospital. From the limited information we have, am I correct in believing that you and she have been orphans for many years?"

There were a handful of questions that Tilly wished to ask him, but he seemed in a hurry to leave the hospital.

"Yes, Doctor Hawthorn...can I see her...what is an appendix? I've never heard that word before ....was it because of the apples she ate?"

Doctor Hawthorn's eyebrows rose slightly, as he continued to gaze at Tilly. "One of the nurses will be along shortly to speak to you, Miss Whitlock, but I can confidently say that you will not be able to see your sister tonight. Good evening."

Before Tilly had time to draw breath, he was marching through the doors.

Having listened in on the entire conversation, Mr Dunkley came out from his kiosk with some kind words of comfort. Exhausted and deeply troubled by the Doctor's news, there was nothing Tilly could do to hold back her fountain of tears, which had been on the brink of overflowing all evening.

"There now, Miss Whitlock, you heard what Doctor Hawthorn said...God willing, your sister will soon be fully recovered." He passed her his large, starched handkerchief. "Nurse will soon be here to give you some comfort, no doubt. Would you like another cup of tea?"

Tilly nodded as she dabbed her wet face. She would accept a dozen cups of tea if it meant that she didn't have to step out of the hospital and into the dark lonely night by herself. She looked up at the wall clock, it was nearly midnight and she could still hear the heavy rain against the high windows of the vestibule. In eight hours she was supposed to commence her working day at Hyde's...how would she cope without Ellie...where would she sleep of a night? She had no idea of what to do except to pray for a miracle. Mr Dunkley soon returned with the tea and was closely followed by the nurse. She was younger than Tilly had expected and although she looked tired, she wore a kind and cheery face and was sympathetic. She enlightened Tilly about the operation, which Eleanor had undergone, and ensured her that it had nothing to do with the fact that she'd consumed so many apples. She also repeated the Doctor's instructions that Eleanor was not to have any visitors until the following day. But since she'd informed Tilly that her sister was still sleeping and would likely spend most of the next twenty-four hours drifting in and out of sleep, there would be little point in visiting her. The nurse assured Tilly that she'd let Eleanor know how her sister was eager to visit and had been waiting in the hospital all evening.

With no reason to keep Tilly in the hospital and with Mr Dunkley not offering any more refreshments, Tilly felt obliged to leave.

"Good night, Sir," she said, in a small voice on passing by his window, "I expect I will see you again tomorrow."

Mr Dunkley eyed the clock, "You mean later on today, I think! I will be finished in six hours and won't be returning until six O'clock evening time, so if you arrive in the afternoon, you'll find Mr Cooper in my place! You have a good night's sleep and don't go worrying too much...your sister is being well looked after; we have the *most caring* nurses and *best* doctors here at the Radcliffe Infirmary!"

Tilly stepped outside, immediately putting her foot into a deep puddle. Heavily veiled by the dense rain clouds, there was no sign of the moon or a single, shining star in the night sky. The amber street lamps popped and fizzled as drops of rain managed to seep through their coverings. It took but five minutes before Tilly was soaked through to her skin. Wrapping her arms around herself gave little comfort as she shivered uncontrollably. She hadn't a clue as to where she was heading, the streets were virtually empty, although, in the distance, she could hear the unruly sounds of drunkards and prayed that they were heading in the opposite direction to her. She soon reached the first shop front; it had a recess to its entrance and offered the first opportunity to shelter from the rain. The recess was deep and Tilly sank down into its furthest corner, away from the pavement, relieved to be out of the rain. She removed her thin summer bonnet and squeezed out the excess water, her soaked and grubby dress was in a dreadful state and Tilly knew she must look even worse than how she was feeling. She nibbled on the remaining fruit buns, now soft from the rainwater, but surprisingly tastier than earlier. She closed her tired eyes, wishing she was in a warm and cosy bed and wishing that she and Ellie hadn't been so hasty to run away from the workhouse, especially after the arrival of Mr and Mrs Barnet.

Suddenly aware of a looming shadow, Tilly immediately opened her eyes to the disturbing sight of an old and bedraggled looking man, who was staring down at her in the oddest of ways. He was soaked through and his overgrown beard and hair dripped upon his bare and filthy toes, which poked out from his worn-out boots. Tilly felt her bowels contract as he stepped into the shop's recess. He was heavily built and the pungent aroma of his unwashed clothes and body soon overtook the damp air. His wide frame took up the entire width of the entrance and Tilly knew that if she made a sudden run, he could easily grab hold of her. His presence had awakened her and on this day, if anything else could go wrong, she was sure it would be her being savaged by the wild-looking man in front of her. Slowly sliding her back up the shop door, Tilly stood on her feet realising that the stranger was much taller than she'd thought.

"I don't have any money, you know!" she announced, nervously.

He didn't reply but licked his lips as he stared at the half-eaten, fruit bun in Tilly's hand.

"You can have this if you like...."

He quickly shot out his hand from his torn pocket, causing Tilly to jump. The bun fell from her grasp and on to the floor. They both stood motionless, with Tilly silently praying that he would bend over to retrieve it so she could dash to safety. He appeared reluctant to move but, kept his focus on the bun. Suddenly, the tramp opened his mouth wide and emitted a loud and terrifying howl, like a wolf howling at the full moon. Tilly's spontaneous reaction was to run and keep running until she was so out of breath, but hampered by a painful stitch in her side, she could run no more. Expecting to see the wild man on her trail, she dared to glance over her shoulder, but thankfully, he was nowhere to be seen. The display of beautiful gowns in the next shop caught her attention. A Peach, silk gown, trimmed with cream lace and a dainty rows of mother of pearl buttons, immediately caught her eye, but the outfit which appealed to Tilly the most was an emerald green velvet two-piece suit over an elegantly frilled cream, silk blouse. She stood dreaming of what it would be like to own such clothing, but with one eye constantly looking over her shoulder her dreams were cut short. She ambled from one shop to another, completely unaware that the rain had now ceased. The sound of footsteps infused her with a renewed sense of fear. She darted into the recess of the next shop, hoping to remain out of sight to whoever was marching along the path. The display in this shop was dull and boring in comparison to the colourful dress shop; books balanced on top of one another, some closed, some half-open. The footsteps faded away and Tilly let out a sigh of relief, noticing that it had, at last, stopped raining and on the horizon she could just see the hazy sun, as it began to rise. Resting her head against the window, as she yawned wearily, Tilly took an interest in the shiny gold lettering of one of the books...reading it twice and rubbing her eyes, a buzz of excitement suddenly took away her tiredness as she recognised the author's name...."*August Miller!*" she uttered, "*August Miller! Oh, Ellie, it's your sweetheart, the man of your dreams! August Miller!*" She felt sad that Ellie wasn't standing by her side, knowing how elated she would be. Her eyes then read the rest of the gold lettering; she wanted to remember the name of the book so she could tell Ellie the good news as soon as she was allowed to visit her. Her heart skipped a beat as she read the title..."*Oh, Good Lord!*" she cried out, louder than she would have wished in such a quiet and deserted place, "*Searching for Eleanor*...Oh, how romantic!" she declared. A middle-aged man passed by, followed by his obedient hound, he viewed Tilly suspiciously, but unable to suppress her smiling face, she greeted him warmly. He politely doffed his hat and returned the greeting before increasing his pace. Tilly giggled. After such a terrible night, there was news which would fill poor Ellie with joy; it was abundantly clear that August Miller did feel the same way for Ellie, as she did for him, mused Tilly, in awe of such romantic notions...if only she had some money, it would make the perfect gift for Ellie and maybe help speed her recovery.

Wilma and Austin Hyde approached their shop, warily, wondering why an unkempt girl was loitering outside at such an early hour. From the moment Tilly came into their sight, they passed comment on how mortifying it was to have such waifs and strays hanging around the streets of Oxford when there were adequate workhouses in the county. It wasn't until they'd almost reached the entrance of Hyde & Son, that Austin was the first to realised it was young, Tilly Vine.
"Isn't that one of our new workers?" he questioned, in a low voice.
"What on earth has happened to her?" exclaimed Wilma. "She looks dreadful! I hope she's not caught the plague...and where is Eleanor...Oh my word, Austin, we should tread carefully, think of the baby I'm carrying and of our precious boy at home!"

"You're quite right, as always, my dearest; you wait here while I talk to her and see what's been going on."

"Don't get too close to her, my love."

Wilma took her hand from the crook of Austin's arm and stood on the spot whilst watching her husband.

Tilly was so glad to see a familiar face that she immediately hurried towards him, eager to explain the night's events; she would tell him how she'd been sat outside the hospital all night, petrified to walk home alone at such a late hour.

"Er...Miss...Tilly...Miss Vine...." Austin found his tongue quite twisted as the girl neared him at such speed. *"Keep your distance!* Are you unwell?" he suddenly bellowed, on hearing Wilma shouting her instructions, from a few yards away.

"It's not me who's sick, Sir, but Ellie..."

" Oh, Good Lord...is it the plague...*Cholera? Typhoid?*...highly contagious you know...and Mrs Hyde is in a very delicate disposition, with child!"

"A baby!...that's wonderful news, Mr Hyde, but you don't need to worry, Ellie is in the hospital, she had to have her app...her intestines removed...well, a bit of them, anyway. She is *so* sick... I'm afraid she might die! I've been at the hospital all night, I was that afraid to go home by myself!" Tilly could speak no more, her throat became constricted and her face turned a bright

shade of scarlet, as she broke down into an overdue outburst of tears. While Mr Hyde applied a gentle tap on her back and offered few words of comfort, Wilma stood aghast, holding her hand over her gaping mouth, as she witnessed her husband's proximity to the ailing girl.

"Come along, Mrs Hyde!" he beckoned, "Miss Vine is only plagued by lack of sleep and you can't catch that!"

CHAPTER THIRTY-THREE

By the time morning break arrived, it was evident, that despite her doggedness to continue working, Tilly was far too overtired to carry on. Mr and Mrs Hyde were concerned for her health and that of Eleanor's; they also had the good name of their shop to consider and couldn't risk a scandal being spread by one of the machinists.

"She appears quite reluctant to return to her lodgings, Austin," confirmed Wilma, shortly after break time. "She's adamant that with her intention to return to the hospital to visit Eleanor, it's not worth her going home!"

"Doesn't she wish to wash and change her clothing!" quizzed Austin. "She looks in a dreadful way and as much as I'd prefer not to mention it, she does have a rather unpleasant odour about her."

"Maybe I should go with her to the hospital...I do sympathise with those poor orphans, especially when such an unfortunate event like this should arise!"

"You're probably correct, as usual, my darling and I've noticed you're looking rather tired yourself, are you feeling quite well?"

"Please don't fuss, Austin, I feel absolutely fine, but it might be a good idea if I take her home and perhaps find an old gown of mine which she can wear."

"*Jolly good idea*...just sort the women upstairs out before you leave, my love. I doubt we will be busy today, Thursday is usually a quiet one!" Tilly was glad of Mrs Hyde's suggestion that she should accompany her to her home at luncheon break, but not so pleased that she also intended to visit Ellie in the hospital. It meant that she'd have to be careful of every word she uttered. Paradise Street was only a short walk from the shop and they soon reached the smart-looking house, which was adjacent to a narrow stretch of the river. There was no front garden, just two, pristine, white stone steps in front of the deep red, front door. Tilly was mesmerised by the loud, gushing sound as she gazed at the torrents of water, surge beneath a small stone bridge.

"It becomes far noisier and rises quite alarmingly high in the winter months," stated Wilma Hyde, as she unlocked the front door. Tilly followed her in; the sound of a piano filled the orderly home and there was a sweet smell of freshly cut flowers and baked pastry emitting a comforting, homely feel. Tilly felt her heart contract, as the ambience of Mrs Hyde's home reminded her of the cottage she once lived in with her dear parents, many years ago. The sound of a deep, male voice and female giggling immediately put a frown upon Mrs Hyde's face. She made a hand gesture for Tilly to remain in the hall, while she crept on tiptoes towards the back of the house. She'd just past the first doorway when a young boy came running out, crashing into Mrs Hyde, "*Mamma, Mamma!*" he exclaimed merrily, "You came home early...I thought I could smell your perfume!" He wrapped his arms around his mother, his shoulder-length head of light brown curls, covering his face. Tilly watched with a tear in her eye... more than anything, she missed, being part of a family and for the second time, that day, she was reminded of her brief childhood. Mrs Hyde gently prised off her son's hold on her skirts, lifting his face in line with hers as she bent down to him.

"Does Emma have a guest, poppet?" she whispered, still hearing male laughter coming from the dining room, at the rear of the house.

"It's just her brother, Mamma, he's a very likeable sort!"

"*Brother?*" mumbled Mrs Hyde, wondering why Charles' governess had never mentioned having a brother to her when she'd spoken of her family.

"Does he often visit?"

Charles tilted his head from side to side in slow-motion, nervously chewing on his bottom lip. He could sense that his mother was not pleased.

"Hmm, sometimes," he replied, dubiously. Suddenly, Wilma Hyde marched noisily across the polished floor and stormed into the dining room. Emma immediately jumped out of the tall man's arms, her usually fair complexion turning the same shade as the red roses in the centre of the dining table.

"Would you care to introduce me to your **brother**, Emma!" she raged, glaring at the young woman and completely ignoring the dishevelled man, standing as cool as an icicle by her side. Emma was lost for words and could only stand and stare; her senses already informing her that she was about to lose her position in the Hyde's household.

I pay your wages to teach my son, not to cavort with men and entertain them under my roof!" cried Mrs Hyde. "Charles informs me that this is not the first time either! I want you out of my home this instant and you will not be receiving a reference from me...you are an irresponsible, young woman and you have taken advantage of the trust which I placed in you!"

"Don't worry, my little rosebud, you will always have a place in my heart!" declared the young man in a jaunty manner.

"Oh, *be quiet Huxley*, I always knew something like this would happen before long...wait outside while I pack my bag and don't you dare to disappear on me!"

Meanwhile, Charles took position a few feet away from Tilly. He stared curiously at her for a while before speaking,

"Are you going to be my new governess?"

"No, I work for your parent's...I sew jackets and trousers."

"That sounds awfully boring...would you like to be my new governess?"

Charles Hyde was an amusing boy, thought Tilly as she smiled at him.

"Did you fall in the river?" he then asked, bluntly, as he edged closer to her and appeared to be inspecting her.

"I got caught in last night's heavy rainstorm."

"Oh, were you frightened?"

Before Tilly could answer him a young man suddenly hastened through the hallway, causing a gust of wind as he passed by Charles and Tilly.

"Goodbye, Huxley," Charles called out. He was ignored as the furious man slammed the front door with all his strength, sending a shock wave through the house.

A cacophony of heavy feet traipsing up and down the stairs, together with doors being opened and slammed was shortly followed by Emma, as she preceded her beau out through the front door. Mrs Hyde was in a state of near collapse as she sat down on the bottom stair, causing Charles to dash to her side.

"Oh, Mamma, are you going to swoon again...shall I fetch your smelling salts?" Not waiting around for her to reply, he sped off, shortly returning with a small bottle, which he'd already opened and was waving under his mother's nose. She took him in her arms.

"My sweet, darling boy, Mamma has had a most upsetting day and now you are left without a governess."

"Please don't make me go to school again, Mamma, *please!"*

"Oh my precious, I would *never* send my sweet lamb to those packs of hungry wolves...you are *too* dear to me!" Charles left his mother's side, happy by her assurance.

"Now let me go upstairs and find some dry clothing for poor, Miss Vine, who has also had a ghastly morning!"

"Can't Tilly be my governess, Mamma, I like her very much and she does have a kind face!"

"I can see you've already made yourself acquainted with her, but you must call her Miss Vine, for the time being, let's not allow our manners to slip."

"Alright, Mamma!"

The Hyde's cook arrived at her usual time of three O'clock, she had her own front door key and made her way straight to the kitchen, where she promptly hung up her jacket and bonnet and replaced it with an apron and mop cap before conducting a quick check that the house was in a tidy state and that Charles had eaten his luncheon, which was one of Emma's jobs to prepare. Rosa was an attractive woman of thirty-three; she had turned her back on the prospect of ever getting married after losing her betrothed in a tragic riding accident, some eleven years previously. She had vowed that no man could

ever take his place and being the youngest
sibling of four, with her sister and two brothers
already married, she felt that it was her destiny
to take care of her doting parents as they reached
their twilight years. She spent about five hours
every day working in the Hyde's home, insisting
that she not only cooked for them but clean and
generally keep house too. She was gifted with an
overwhelming abundance of energy, never
seeming to tire and during the five years that
she'd been employed by the Hydes she had
become more like one of the family.

Now wearing a pretty pastel lemon and green
striped, dress, Tilly sat in the front parlour with
Mrs Hyde and Charles, sipping tea from
delicately hand-painted, china teacups. Mrs
Hyde had insisted that Tilly ate a thick wedge of
bread spread with calves foot jelly followed by a
large petticoat tail of shortbread. Tilly nibbled
slowly while Charles observed her and Mrs
Hyde continuously claimed how tired the ordeal
with Emma had left her feeling and how she
now had the added burden and extra stress of
having to find a suitable new governess for
young Charles, not to mention the worrying
news of Eleanor. It had been a day she wished
not to have to live through ever again, she
declared. Tilly thought she was being rather
dramatic; considering her wealthy status, a
replacement could easily and quickly be found,
but she remembered Mr Hyde's comment about

her being with child and presumed it was the major reason behind her emotional state.

"Mamma! Who will give me my piano lesson this afternoon?"

"Oh, my sweet poppet, don't fret, Mamma will soon find you a new governess and your lessons will resume!"

"Charles does so love to play the piano, it's his favourite pastime; I'm sure he is destined for the grand music halls of London, or even Paris!" Mrs Hyde proudly announced. *"Do you play, Tilly?"*

"Oh, no, I'm afraid I don't have a musical bone in my body, Mrs Hyde!"

Finding her statement hilarious, Charles couldn't contain his childish giggles and proceeded to roll around like a floppy rag doll, repeating Tilly's words.

"Charles! That's quite enough!" his mother admonished. "Go and see if Rosa has made any lemonade yet and then, perhaps, you might amuse yourself in the garden for a while, Miss Vine and I require some peace and quiet."

Charles unquestioningly, listened to his mother and headed for the door, but stopped before leaving, *"Please* let, Miss Vine be my new governess, Mamma..." he begged.

"Run along child!"

"It isn't always easy to find a governess who is an accomplished pianist," complained Wilma Hyde.

"Ellie can play...she told me that she used to

take part in recitals, here in Oxford!"

Mrs Hyde's thin eyebrows lifted, "How fascinating...so, how well does she play?"

"Oh, I've never heard her myself, we didn't have a pianoforte in the workhouse..." Tilly immediately buttoned her mouth, hoping that by some miracle, Mrs Hyde had not paid much attention to her, but already there was a mixed look of horror and confusion upon her face.

"**Workhouse!**" she cried out loudly. "*You* and *Miss Whitlock* are from the *workhouse!*"

Tilly nodded her head slowly.

"Is today the day in which I discover that I can trust nobody!" voiced Mrs Hyde, despairingly?

"Perhaps if you let me explain, it won't seem so bad...Ellie and me are still humans, you know, with the same emotions as you and any other ...we didn't *choose* to live in the workhouse, but now we choose *not to* and are determined to make a success of our lives! Is that so wrong and terrible?"

"Well, Miss Vine, I don't consider myself an unreasonable woman, so I will give you the next hour to explain your story, with no lies, before I decide whether or not to keep you in my employ at Hyde & Son. You may speak on behalf of Miss Whitlock too since you seem to be as thick as thieves and she is unable to state her case at present!"

In the strained atmosphere of the pristine parlour, part of Tilly had the impulsive urge to issue Mrs Hyde with a few choice words and walk out, but in the back of her mind, she knew that acting on impulse would likely see her back in the workhouse again so she kept firmly seated and counted to ten in her head. Her thoughts went to Ellie, dear Ellie; she prayed she was recovering from her surgery and in the next few minutes of silence, she asked herself what Ellie would do if she was here in her place. The shock of the events seemed to have taken away her tiredness, she took in a deep breath, knowing that what she was about to disclose to the stony-faced, Mrs Hyde would make a huge difference to the next few months of hers and Ellie's life.

"Very well, Mrs Hyde, I promise to tell you everything and to be as honest as possible, but I cannot tell you everything about Ellie, because her story is much more sensitive than mine and she might never forgive me if I say too much...but I will tell you enough. This morning, your husband told me that you are with child and I believe your son must be about seven or eight, that was how old I was when my dear pa died, my mother became too ill to carry on and we were sent to the workhouse!"

Mrs Hyde shook her head in annoyance, "He had no business to tell you that, but yes it is true!" She spontaneously placed her hand on her stomach as she spoke. "Please continue, Miss Vine."

Just as the grandfather clock struck four, Tilly

had told Mrs Hyde almost everything which had taken place since Ellie arrived at the workhouse. All of a sudden, Charles ran into the room clutching a posy of flowers which he and Rosa had cut from the garden. Rosa followed behind,

"Would you care for some fresh tea, Mrs Hyde?" Wilma Hyde had tears in her eyes and a dozen or more questions that she wished to ask of Tilly. She now knew that Eleanor Whitlock was the daughter of the eccentric, Beatrice Jackson and the many puzzles she'd harboured were now falling into place. She had sensed that Eleanor had been brought up in a superior class than Tilly and with her uncanny similarity to the beautiful Beatrice; it didn't come as a huge shock to discover their close relationship. Tilly had only disclosed that Ellie's parents had both passed away, sparing the tragic details about her mamma.

"Mamma, why are you crying?" Charles cuddled his mother, his small hand stroking her back affectionately.

"Look, I picked you some flowers! Do you like them? Can I go and pick some for Miss Vine, now?"

"My darling, Charles, they are divine and smell so fragrant. Yes, you may pick Miss Vine a posy and could you also pick a bouquet for Miss Whitlock, who is very ill and in hospital."

"*Miss Whitlock?*" questioned Charles, looking confused. "Do I know her, Mamma?"

"Not yet my darling, but I'm sure you will, very soon."

CHAPTER THIRTY-FOUR

There wasn't a single cloud in the soft, blue September sky as Mrs Hyde and Tilly arrived outside the Radcliffe Infirmary in the impressive carriage, which had been hired especially to bring Eleanor back to her new home, in Paradise Street. It had been a harrowing time during the first week after Eleanor's operation and there were many times when Tilly had cried into her pillow at night, terrified that she would lose her beloved and only friend in the entire world, Tilly couldn't bear the thought of being alone again. Now, just over four weeks later, Eleanor was well enough to leave the hospital and it was to be a huge surprise for her that she was going to share a lovely, new bedroom with Tilly in Mr and Mrs Hyde's home.

Wilma Hyde had been left heartbroken after hearing Tilly's explanation of everything that had happened to Eleanor, since the sudden passing of her father. Tilly had omitted little detail from her account and recalled how Eleanor had nearly been burnt alive when she'd taken refuge in her garden shed and how the evil Mr Killigrew had made her life in the workhouse a living hell with his infatuation of her and also of how she'd nearly died after being left in solitary for weeks on end. Tilly had spoken passionately about her beloved friend, wiping away her tears as she recalled how she'd nursed her back to health when she'd been on the brink of death.

Understanding how Tilly had formed a close, sisterly bond with her dear friend, Wilma was sure it was the same for Eleanor; they were two young women both with a trail of tragedies behind them, but with the determination to make good for themselves. Wilma admired that fighting spirit in them, in a way it reminded her of her own youth when she had stood up to her rights in refusing to marry the wealthy landowner, who her parents had insisted upon. She had already fallen in love with Austin Hyde, a young city tailor, who she set out to win and after three long years of trying to persuade her parents to bless the relationship and agree to their marriage, she was successful and the marriage, finally, went ahead. Using every ounce of energy they could muster, Wilma and Austin spent their early years of marriage working long hours and saving every penny, which eventually paid off when they had accumulated enough funds to open, *Hyde & Son*.

After discussing their plight, Austin and Wilma were unanimously decided that they wished to help the young women as much as they could and with Emma having left so suddenly and with a new baby on the way, it seemed like a marvellous idea to have them both living and helping out in their home. Eleanor was to become Charles' new governess when she was fully recovered, but in the meantime, much to Charles' delight, Tilly would take on that role until, in the future, she could assist Rosa with her chores, which also came as good news to Rosa; glad that her heavy responsibilities were to be lightened. Emma's old room, with the addition of an extra bed, was large enough for both of them to share. For Tilly, who had never in her life had a bedroom of her own or lived in such a fine home, it was as though all her dreams had suddenly come true. On her daily hospital visits, Tilly hadn't mentioned a word about the new arrangements and continued to pretend that she was working in the sewing room at Hyde & Son, but now, since she'd been paid, could afford a cheap, rundown lodging house. Making sure that she always wore her old dress from the pawnbroker's on every visit, even though a fine collection of clothes had been donated to her by Rosa and Mrs Hyde, Eleanor only made one comment, just a few days before she was due to be discharged when she'd stressed that surely by now Tilly could afford a new, second-hand dress from one of the market stalls in oxford. Tilly had been quick to reply, saying how she was saving every spare penny to go towards the rent of their future home.

Being the same build and height as Eleanor, Rosa had hung three practical, day dresses which she no longer wore, in Tilly's wardrobe for when Eleanor came home; some of the clothes, which had once belonged to her older sister, who was of a smaller frame, were given to Tilly. Rosa had said how her sister had married a wealthy man, who'd insisted she had a complete new wardrobe of fashionable and stylish outfits made for her as soon as they were married, so her old clothes were left abandoned in an old wooden trunk.

It came as a huge shock to Wilma when Tilly had enlightened her that the book she was reading was written by Eleanor's sweetheart. She continued to explain how they had lost contact with one another shortly after meeting and how Eleanor feared that he had since forgotten her. Having almost read his book, Wilma assured Tilly that it was clearly evident that, August Miller was as in love with Eleanor as any man could be with his true love and she believed that August had written the book with the intention that it might lead her back to him. But as much as Tilly was bursting to tell Eleanor about how she'd discovered his book in the shop window, Wilma's advice was that she should wait until Eleanor was strong again and able to cope with such sensitive news, after all, she had reminded Tilly, she still doesn't know where he lives and vice versa, so it might add even more unwanted stress for Eleanor to cope with, in her fragile condition.

"Good morning, Mr Dunkley!" chirped Tilly, as she stepped into the cool vestibule.

"Good morning, Miss Whitlock...whoops, sorry, Miss Vine...just can't get used to your new name!"

During the second week of her daily hospital visits, Tilly had confessed to the kind, Mr Dunkley that she had lied about being Eleanor's sister, although she did stress to him that they were as good as sisters and shared a love and strong bond which only two orphans could understand.

"Today's the day then!" he announced in high spirits. "I hope you'll pop back in here one day and tell me all your news. I'm certainly going to miss our little chats!"

"Of course I will, Mr Dunkley, you've been so kind to me over the weeks, I can't thank you enough...maybe I'll treat you to a fruit bun when I do pop in..." They both laughed, remembering the stale buns which she'd offered him all those weeks ago.

"Well, I might not turn down a fresh one!"

"I will make sure that it is hot from the baker's oven, Mr Dunkley!"

Eleanor was stood by her bed wearing her faded dress, which the nurse had kindly washed for her. Looking underweight, she had a wide welcoming smile upon her gaunt face.

"*Tilly!*" she proclaimed, "I can't believe I'm

actually leaving the hospital...I'm so happy!"

"Me too, Ellie!" They hugged each other affectionately, both unable to hold back their tears of joy.

"I've got a surprise for you, Ellie!"

Eleanor held on to Tilly's arm, her legs not used to holding her weight. Two cordial nurses waved her off, wishing her well and saying how they would miss her after the many weeks she'd spent on their ward.

"I love surprises, Tilly...I'm already so excited to be leaving here that I feel I might burst!"

"Don't do that, Ellie, otherwise you'll be back in your hospital bed again!" teased Tilly.

"Is it far to your new lodgings, Tilly?"

"Not *my* new lodgings, Ellie! *Our* new lodgings...and yes, it is quite a long walk, but we are travelling in style today!"

"Thank the Good Lord, I'm already exhausted and we've not even left the hospital!"

"It will take you some time to become strong again, Ellie, but just like when you came out of solitary, you *will* make a speedy recovery and soon be back to your old self!"

"I hope so and I hope Mrs Hyde will still keep my job open for me, it isn't right that you should have to support me."

"That's what true sisters do; Ellie and I don't want to hear another word spoken on such matters!"

"Ooh, you're beginning to sound like a very

bossy sister!"

Outside, Eleanor relished in the warm September sun as it touched her skin, "Oh, Tilly, it smells so fresh out here! I'd forgotten what the outside smelt like! It is such a delight not to have that pungent hum of carbolic acid in my nostrils anymore!"

"I couldn't agree more, it always made me gag when I first entered your ward!"

Eleanor suddenly caught sight of Mrs Hyde who was waving from inside the carriage,

"Look, Tilly, Look who's here...what a coincidence!"

"That's part of the surprise!" beamed Tilly. "Mrs Hyde hired this carriage to take you home in!"

"Oh, Tilly, everyone has been so kind to me!" she choked, trying to blink away her tears.

"Dear, Eleanor!" exclaimed Mrs Hyde, as she pushed the carriage door open. "How wonderful it is to see you up and about at long last!"

Mrs Hyde had visited Eleanor on a couple of occasions, but nothing was mentioned about the new arrangement or that Tilly was now residing in her home. Tilly assisted Eleanor into the carriage and they were soon on their way, leaving the hospital behind them.

"I thought perhaps you might like to take some refreshments at my home first, Eleanor?"

Eleanor glanced furtively to Tilly, trying to read her thoughts, regarding Mrs Hyde's offer. Tilly's wide smile gave her the answer.

"That's awfully kind of you, Mrs Hyde and thank you so much for hiring this lovely carriage, I honestly don't think I could have walked another step...my time in hospital has left me feeling extremely weak!"

"My dear, you have been through a horrendous ordeal and undergone a huge and dangerous operation, it will take time and patience before you feel your old self again and you mustn't worry about your position at Hyde & Son, simply worry about getting yourself fighting fit again and at a gentle pace!"

"Thank you, Mrs Hyde, you have reassured me and lifted the worry from my mind."

The carriage soon drew up outside the Hyde's residence, in Paradise Street, where Tilly and Mrs Hyde carefully helped Eleanor step down safely on to the narrow strip of pavement. No sooner had the horse begun to trot away than the front door was pulled wide open by Rosa who greeted them warmly, allowing Tilly to introduce Eleanor to her. Immediately sensing that Tilly had become quite well acquainted with the Hyde family during her absence, she thought it odd that Tilly should introduce Rosa to her and not Mrs Hyde.

"Charles will be so happy to meet you, at last, Ellie...ooh, you don't mind if I call you Ellie, do you? Only Tilly has spoken so much about you that I already feel as though I know you!"

"Of course not," confirmed Eleanor, baffled by

how at ease Tilly appeared with Mrs Hyde and her staff.

The sound of footsteps hurrying along the hallway caught everyone's attention, as Charles raced to greet them. He stopped suddenly as soon as he noticed Eleanor, feeling a little shy and in awe of how pretty she was. He remembered how his mother had told him that it was still a secret that Miss Whitlock was to be his governess and chewed his bottom lip, a little nervous that he might say something he shouldn't and ruin Tilly's and his mother's surprise.

"Goodness, what a gathering!" declared Wilma Hyde, as she removed her hatpin. "Why don't you show our special guest into the front parlour, Charles, I'm sure poor, Miss Whitlock would prefer to rest on the couch!"

Charles' face lit up by his mother's suggestion.

"Would you care to rest in our parlour, Miss Whitlock, you will be more comfortable, I'm sure," he announced, in his best, grown-up manner.

Already quite taken by the adorable Charles Hyde, Eleanor allowed the young boy to hold her hand as he gently guided her into the front parlour.

"I do believe that Rosa is going to bring us a glass of lemonade and sandwiches...do you like lemonade, Miss Whitlock?"

Wilma and Tilly tried hard to conceal their

laughter as they watched Charles entertaining Eleanor, like a proper little gentleman.

"He already adores her after five minutes!" whispered Wilma to Tilly. "Do you think, she has a clue about our little surprise yet?"

"I don't think so, but I have a feeling that Charles might let something slip from his mouth before long!"

"Hmmm," agreed Wilma, "my thoughts exactly and we have so much to tell her too...let's try and wait until we've had afternoon tea."

Rosa soon arrived with tea and an assortment of sandwiches, dainty sponge bites and miniature jam tartlets, reminding Eleanor of the day when she'd accompanied August to the Copper Kettle. Charles squeezed himself in between Tilly and Eleanor on the couch, while Wilma Hyde sat opposite them in a rigid looking armchair, issuing Charles with an occasional glare of warning, to which he merely smiled cheekily at his mother.

"Can I call you, Ellie too?" he requested, as he sat listening to the conversation about Eleanor's stay in the Radcliffe Infirmary and the prolonged summer weather.

"Certainly not, young man!" Wilma immediately intervened.

Charles looked downhearted, "But I don't call Tilly, Miss Vine anymore, do I, Mamma?"

"I don't mind if it is alright with you, Mrs Hyde," assured Eleanor.

"It wouldn't be proper, Eleanor...Charles is becoming far too informal with the ladies, these days and I worry it might be seen as quite inappropriate, Eleanor."

Eleanor smiled as Charles munched on his third cake, now avoiding his mother's glaring eyes. The conversation continued for a little longer; Rosa brought in a jug of boiling water and more cups of tea were enjoyed.

"May I ask Miss Whitlock a question, Mamma?" said Charles politely, after his long silence, in which he'd eaten far more than anyone else.

Wilma sighed, "Very well, my darling, but afterwards I think you should go and play in the garden for a while."

"I will, Mamma!"

Turning his head to face Eleanor, he asserted his question, "How many names *do* you have? Is your name, Eleanor or Ellie?"

Eleanor smiled; she felt a sudden urge to cuddle this sweet boy in her arms but knew it wouldn't be appropriate on their first meeting and with Charles being her employer's son.

Sensing that Eleanor was perhaps tiring and feeling a little embarrassed by her son's curiosity, Wilma hastily answered him, "Charles, my darling, it's similar to when Rosa sometimes calls you, *Charlie*, it's what is known as an informal name, which is only used by those who are closely connected and familiar; do you understand?"

"Why do you never call me Charlie, Mamma?"
"Charles! Garden! Good boy!"
Charles always knew when his Mamma was serious and this was one of those times; he jumped up from the couch and skipped to the door, "Miss Whitlock!" he said before leaving. "You have a famous name! Did you know that Mamma has a b…"

"That will do, Charles…" cried Wilma."Go and have some fresh air!"

"May I pick Miss Whitlock some flowers, Mamma?"

Wilma nodded abruptly, her entire face now tense and of a scarlet hue.

"Sometimes, *that boy* can be as demanding *and* as difficult as his father!" she exclaimed, with the back of her hand resting across her forehead.

CHAPTER THIRTY-FIVE

"Why don't you take Eleanor upstairs to freshen up, this September warmth is always far stickier than the previous months, don't you find?"

Tilly knew that this was her cue to explain the new arrangement, in the privacy of her room.

"Can you manage the stairs, Ellie?"

"I think so; maybe I could hold your arm, Tilly?"

"Of course you can, come along let's go and splash out faces!"

Climbing the flight of stairs took Eleanor longer than anticipated and Tilly insisted that she sat in the pink velvet, reading chair to regain her breath.

"Is this Rosa's room? It's beautiful!" she uttered as her eyes travelled around the spacious bedroom. She glanced at the two, cosy-looking, beds along each wall; they were adorned with the prettiest floral coverlets she'd ever seen, the walls were hung with luxurious wallpaper covered with pink and cream lilies and minute hummingbirds. There was a well-equipped washstand in one corner, where Tilly was splashing her face with water from the patterned porcelain, washbowl. There was also a matching chest of drawers and wardrobe in the room and two deep pile rugs next to each bed. The view from the window looked out onto a well-stocked garden and she counted a row of five apple trees as she viewed, the adorable, Charles attempting to clamber up one of them. Eleanor loved the room, it reminded her of when she and her dear mother lived in Henley Road and as she wondered what state Tilly's knew lodgings would be in, she knew it would be a far cry from the luxury that now surrounded her.

"Are you feeling quite well, Ellie?" Tilly was concerned that her dear friend was looking much paler now than a couple of hours ago.

"I'm fine, Tilly, just tired...is it far to our lodgings, only I'd rather set off quite soon if you don't mind. I'm sure I'll feel much better in the morning, after a good night's sleep."

Unable to keep it a secret for a second longer, Tilly, knelt next to Eleanor, "You wanted to know whose room this is, Ellie, well, this is *our room* and we will be living here from now on and *not* working in Mr and Mrs Hyde's sewing room! When you are fully recovered and *not a day before*, you will be Charles' new governess and I will be a housemaid and help Rosa out a little in the kitchen, too. Mrs Hyde is expecting a baby next year and Emma, the previous governess was dismissed rather suddenly, but that is another story for later and so you see, everything has turned out just perfectly!"

After so many surprises already that day, Eleanor was finding Tilly's disclosure quite difficult to believe; it was a far cry from sleeping on the riverbank and being penniless, which had been the situation before her hospital admission.

She gazed around the beautiful room again, words somehow failing to roll off her tongue.

"Say something! Ellie!" laughed Tilly.

There was a gentle tap on the door and Mrs Hyde poked her head in,

"Have you told her!" she asked, smiling excitedly.

"Could one of you pinch me...I feel as though I'm in the midst of a wonderful dream!"

Wilma and Tilly giggled and Tilly gave her dearest friend the gentlest of pinches on her arm, "There now, I promise you this is not a dream, Ellie!"

"How do you feel about being Charles' governess, Eleanor?" enquired Mrs Hyde. "I must confess to you, my dear that my husband and I knew your mother and were very sad when Tilly informed us how you lost both your parent's so suddenly. We socialised in many a function alongside your dear mother and from the first time I saw you, I had my suspicions that you were Beatrice Jackson's daughter; you have her beauty. Your mother was a most popular woman, but sadly there wasn't anyone who knew her address, so when she ceased to show up at every function, it was presumed that she'd perhaps, moved away."

Wilma didn't mention how nobody was aware that Beatrice had a daughter or that she was a shocking flirt.

"I would be delighted and honoured to be your

adorable son's governess, Mrs Hyde, but how can you be sure that I'm suitable for such a responsible position?"

"I have heard that you are a most accomplished pianist and I presume you received a decent education...am I correct?" Eleanor nodded, still in a daze and quite unable to take everything in.

"Well, there we go then, but there is one condition and it's that you must make a full recovery before you commence...Charles can be a handful and I don't want him wearing you out before you have fully recuperated! But feel free to make use of our pianoforte in the meantime, I'm sure Charles will be delighted. Now I'll leave Tilly to fill you in on everything else while I take a little nap and we will all enjoy a celebratory meal together this evening when Mr Hyde returns."

"Thank you so much, Mrs Hyde, you have been kindness itself and congratulations; Tilly told me about your joyful news!"

Mrs Hyde impulsively ran the flat of her hand across her stomach, "Thank you dear!" she said in a small voice, before making her exit.

The remainder of the afternoon was spent with Tilly talking none stop, enlightening Eleanor about everything which had taken place since the evening when she'd been rushed to the hospital. She also put on a fashion parade, presenting Eleanor with the copious ensembles which filled their wardrobe, delighting Eleanor even more. Eleanor didn't imagine that she could be any happier and doubted she'd ever be able to thank Tilly, the Hyde family and Rosa enough. Tilly insisted that if it wasn't for the fact that Eleanor was the daughter of Beatrice Jackson and a skilled pianist with a good educated, the situation would be very different and they would both, most likely, be back in the workhouse. But as Eleanor cuddled her dearest friend, she reminded her of the pledge they'd made and how they vowed to always look out for one another, just like real sisters.

No matter how much Tilly nagged Eleanor to take a nap before the evening's celebrations, in all the excitement, her tiredness seemed to have disappeared. Eleanor couldn't wait to try on one of her new gowns and to meet Mr Hyde again. Life was a strange affair, she pondered as she rested upon her new bed; she would never in a million years have thought that after five weeks of meeting Mr and Mrs Hyde, she and Tilly would be living and working in their home. She hadn't much liked them to begin with, but now, even after just a few hours of leaving hospital, she felt as though she was home and for once in a long time the future was looking rosy.

Shortly before dinner, Rosa came to their room which allowed Eleanor the chance to thank her for the collection of clothes she'd given her. Rosa was lovely, thought Eleanor and it was clear that she and Tilly already got on well together and had formed a trusting friendship.

"Mrs Hyde has told the young master that you are to be his new governess," informed Rosa. "He's that excited, I doubt he will manage to sit still at the dinner table! Be prepared for a hundred or more questions, Eleanor!"

"Oh, dear, he's such a sweet-natured boy, I'm really looking forward to the day I can start my new position...feel free to call me Ellie, Rosa. Eleanor can be a bit of a mouthful. When my dear mother was alive, she loathed hearing anyone shorten it to Ellie; our housekeeper often called me Ellie, though!"

"My full name is Rosalind, but even my parents never call me that!"

"And mine is Matilda, but I only remember my ma call me by it once...when she was cross with me!"

Eleanor laughed, "You must have been a very well behaved child then, Tilly, if she only had to use it once!"

"Isn't it strange how parents must spend months thinking up names for their children, which they then shorten!" stated Rosa.

"I wonder what Mr and Mrs Hyde will name their baby?" puzzled Tilly.

"I expect a name from the royal household, past or present!" suggested Rosa. "Ooh, gosh, I must hurry back to the kitchen...the chickens need basting!"

Rosa hurried out leaving Eleanor and Tilly in

agreement with what a lovely woman she was.

Dinner was a formal affair, in honour of Eleanor's recovery and an official welcome to both the young women into the Hyde's home, even though Tilly already felt quite at home. After this day, they would take their meals in the kitchen and Tilly would be serving the family and cleaning up after Rosa had left, which was usually at eight o'clock. There was barely sight of the snow-white, tablecloth beneath the huge spread of tantalizing food which filled every dish and platter. Three plump and golden chickens took centre place, surrounded by crisply roasted potatoes and dishes piled high with vegetables, freshly picked from Mr Hyde's, lovingly tended vegetable garden. Although feeling ravenous, Eleanor worried that after a month of eating like a sparrow, she would be full up within two mouthfuls; she didn't want to appear rude. Charles insisted he sat next to Eleanor, causing Rosa the inconvenience of having to switch the table settings. Turned out in a fetching, forget-me-not blue gown and with her fair curls arranged to frame her beautiful face, Eleanor's similarity to Beatrice Jackson was uncanny, causing Mr Hyde to find it quite impossible to divert his eyes from her. He was glad, though, that she didn't appear to have inherited Beatrice's flirtatious and daring nature; Eleanor was as coy as Beatrice was brazen, he reflected gratifyingly and she would make a jolly good governess for his son, he considered. Thankfully, Wilma was already aware that it would be a struggle for Eleanor to consume a large portion and assured her, several times, that she was to eat only what she felt comfortable with and that at any time throughout the day or night, she could help herself to anything in the kitchen. Overhearing his wife's softly spoken words, Austin Hyde, said eagerly,

"Please *do* feel free to help yourself, Miss Whitlock, otherwise I fear my luncheon will be chicken sandwiches for the rest of the month!"

"It won't, Pappa, because chicken is my most favourite food in the entire world!"

Everyone laughed at Charles' statement, as Austin added another slice of succulent chicken breast onto his plate. "Do you mean to tell me that you prefer chicken over those delicious cakes and pastries which Rosa, so expertly makes?" teased Austin.

Charles gazed wide-eyed up at the ceiling as he made his decision, "Pappa, that's not a fair question, because they aren't in the same cagatory!"

"I think you mean category," whispered Eleanor, as Mr and Mrs Hyde tried to keep a straight face.

When everyone had finished eating, a tray of coffee was placed in the drawing-room and while Rosa cleared the table and Charles asked if he could spend the last half an hour of daylight in the garden, Mr and Mrs Hyde, Eleanor and Tilly found the ideal opportunity to discuss certain issues about the new arrangements and payment. Mrs Hyde also stressed how she wished Charles to address Eleanor formally and properly since she was to be his governess. Little time had elapsed before Charles returned and the minute he stepped into the drawing-room, Wilma's heart did a somersault beneath her rib cage as she suddenly spotted what he was holding under his arm. Not taking any notice of his mother's searing looks and infused with excitement, Charles skipped merrily toward Eleanor and held August Miller's book in front of her face,

"I thought you might like to see Mamma's new book; is that how you write *your* name too?"

A silence swept through the room as all eyes were focussed on Eleanor who was staring hard at the book, reading its title and author's name, as though she was in the midst of a dream. She ran her fingers over the gold embossed lettering as her bottom jaw dropped slightly,

"Yes...that is exactly how I write my name," she muttered, in shock.

"Why didn't you tell me? How long have you known about this book, Tilly?"

All of a sudden Tilly felt a surge of guilt rush through her. She sat uneasily, feeling as though she had betrayed her dearest friend, even though she was merely looking after her.

"You mustn't blame Tilly," uttered Mrs Hyde. "If anyone is at fault, it is me! I felt you weren't strong enough for the dizzy heights of love and romance just yet; you've been through an emotional storm and as I said to Tilly, you need time to regain your strength and to be fully in control of your emotions. I know that you've harboured feelings for this young, *August Miller* for a lengthy period and it is obvious that his heart aches for you too, Eleanor! Love of such strength can never be dissolved. The book is a beautiful story of love and it is clearly written with you in mind. August Miller is a talented, young author and I have a strong premonition that we will all soon become quite well acquainted with him. I suggest you read the book, my dear; it may be that he has written a clue within the lines as to how you can contact him, one which is only recognisable to you. If your future is meant to be with him, Eleanor, then mark my words that it will be!"

Tilly had moved closer to Eleanor as tears trickled down her face; taking hold of her hand, she prayed that Eleanor wouldn't think that to keep the book a secret from her was an act of selfishness, on her part. Eleanor suddenly felt the need to retire for the day; it had been a long and eventful one and its grand finale had felt like salt being rubbed into her raw wounds. She furtively wondered how long this news would have been kept from her if young Charles hadn't disclosed it and why it was proving to be so difficult for her and August to cross paths again...was their union not meant to be, she questioned?

CHAPTER THIRTY-SIX

Winifred Miller cut the thread of the last pair of bloomers, adding it to the modest pile to be sold in Oxford. According to August, it was to be her final piece of work. Wiping the condensation away with the corner of her shawl she gazed out of the tiny cottage window, August was late, she mused, as she looked up at the ominous, white sky. A few intermittent snowflakes floated down softly and there was a ghostly silence about the hamlet. The first winter snow had arrived, it was four days until Christmas and it looked as though they were set for a whiteout. The sudden sound of rattling wheels upon the dirt track alerted her as she stretched her neck and squinted her eyes to see who, if anyone was entering the hamlet; she prayed it was August. Experience had taught her how suddenly and quickly the skies could empty their load of snow, making it treacherous for horse and cart. Recognising, Duke, the massive hamlet Shire horse, she let out a sigh of relief, her tense mood instantly lifting. She was looking forward to a cosy winter with August at home for the festivities, knowing that he would be with her until the weather eased up again.

 "We're going to celebrate in real style this year, Ma!" declared August, as he put down the first load of wooden crates. A gust of wind blew straight through the open door causing the candle flames to dance erratically. "Stay inside, Ma, it's bitter out here and we don't want a repeat of last winter, with your ill health!"

It took another four trips from the hamlet stable to the cottage door before August had unloaded the cart. The tiny parlour was now stacked with a tower of supplies.

"I bought twenty-five bundles of firewood too, but I've left those in the stable, I thought the neighbours could help themselves if they get short!"

"That was very thoughtful of you, August. Now get yourself out of those wet clothes afore you catch a cold, son, I'll put the water on to boil...looks as though we're in for a heavy snowstorm and that wind is getting up too!" August smiled to himself, his ma was so stuck in her ways that it still hadn't sunk in that her son was now an author and his debut book was selling fast, up and down the country. His publisher had informed him that, *'Searching for Eleanor'* had become this year's most popular Christmas gift from every beau to his sweetheart. But the only person he prayed had read it was his darling, Eleanor, he hoped she knew how much he loved her and how his life was frozen in time, waiting for their reunion.

Winifred began emptying the crates, "Did you fetch me any more material, August?" she called up the stairs. It was a habit of his mother's which always put him in a panic, her voice was low and immediately thinking she was in some kind of trouble, he quickly pulled his braces over his shoulders and within two strides he was standing next to her.

"*Material!*" she repeated, "I finished that last bolt earlier today...how am I going to keep my hands busy through the winter months?"

August took a large parcel from one of the crates, "Here you are, Ma, this should keep your hands busy."

Her eyes opened wide when she discovered the length of fine woollen cloth, in an attractive shade of plum, and ten skeins of soft lilac wool.

"It's for you so that you can sew a new dress for the winter *and* knit a new shawl!" August announced, proudly, before she had the chance to speak.

"Oh, son, this must have cost you a small fortune...you should look after that money of yours, money has a nasty habit of drying up like pond water, beneath the summer sun!"

"I *am* looking after it Ma, trust me and buying a present for my dear mother is money well spent! I was thinking I might buy you a sewing machine too, but..."

"*Ooh!*" cried Winifred, in alarm, "I wouldn't dare to go near one of those dangerous machines, they've got the devil in them, I reckon, from all the stories I've heard...they're for the factories, not the home! Besides, how would I keep me hands busy with one of them, more likely it would chew them off or put stitches through them!"

August couldn't suppress his laughter, "So I take it you like the material, then?"

"Of course I do, son, I'd be a fool not to, but you mustn't waste your money...I got plenty of old dresses tucked away in me bedroom."

"Exactly! *Old* and *tucked away*, so it's about time you had a smart new one!"

"Well, I can't see it would make no difference since I barely see anyone these days, apart from Prudence and she wouldn't notice if I'd sewn a couple of flour sacks together...she's a right troubled soul is that poor woman, which reminds me that we should invite her here on Christmas day."

"I quite agree, Ma, you two should spend more time together, save you both from being so lonesome, especially when I'm away in London or Oxford."

"It breaks my heart when I remember how different this hamlet was when you were a lad, I knew everyone then, but all my old friends and neighbours have either moved out or passed on and as much as the young families bring a boost of vitality and a buzz about the place, they don't have much time for a couple of old fashioned women like me and Prudence!"

August placed a box of Turkish delight before her, sensing her sorrow. He knew how difficult it must be at this time of year when she reminisced on the days of her youth. Life was quite similar to a book, he mused and even if the ending was a happy one, reaching the end of it was always a sad affair.

"I wanted to talk to you about that, Ma...I've had an idea!"

Winifred wasn't listening any more, she suddenly seemed more intrigued with trying to prise the lid off the wooden box before her.

"Pour the tea, son and pass me a knife so I can open this box!"

"Look at the snow, Ma! It's falling thick and heavy!"

"Thank God you came back from Oxford in time!"

"Here, pass me that box before you do yourself an injury, Ma!"

Winifred poured two cups of tea while August eased off the lid and relished in watching his ma chew on the extra sweet delights.

"I know what you want to talk to me about!" she stated, after swallowing her mouthful. "You've got plans for us to move to Oxford...to the busy City!"

Completely shocked by his mother's astute perception, August was in awe of what a remarkable woman his mother was.

"How on earth did you know?" he eventually asked.

"I'm your mother; I know everything and that is

something which is often overlooked. Young men and women strut around with their fancy airs and graces, forgetting that there is someone who knows them better than they know themselves! Mothers are the ones who make the world tick along like a clock, not the men of this world...they're nothing but overgrown boys!"

"That's a bit mean! Are you saying that I'm still a boy, disguised in a man's body!" joked August, as he helped himself to a lump of Turkish delight.

"Maybe I am, but you don't need a mother so much now, it's the woman who dances in your heart and keeps you awake at night! She is the answer to all of your problems and dragging me to live in Oxford won't solve anything!"

"I know that Ma, but it will make life easier for you and you will meet new folk and be able to shop in town when you fancy it; life will be more exciting!"

"I'm too long in the tooth to be looking for excitement and I'm not too keen on those townies; I'm happy here with my memories, son. I just want to see you happy and contented and with this 'Eleanor girl'. I often wonder if your overactive imagination didn't simply invent this young woman!"

"Heavens above, Mother! Anyone listening to your talk might get the impression that I'm a mad man! Of course, Eleanor exists, I sat down to tea with her half-sister, do you remember?

Nobody knows where she is...*nobody!* How can someone just vanish into thin air like that?" Feeling she'd been a little unkind by her accusations, Winifred went to August's side and hugged him, "If the Good Lord wants her to cross your path again, believe me, she will, son. Perhaps 1878 will be the year of your union, now let's get these provisions put away and *thank you,* August, you've made your mother a very happy old woman. I will start work on my new dress tonight...I might even be wearing it on Christmas day!"

"Well, as long as you don't go overdoing it, I want you to take life at a slower pace, Ma, I'm making enough money now with the sale of my book and I intend to continue. If this snow doesn't let up, I might have another book ready come springtime!"

"I'm proud of you son! You deserve all the happiness in the world and I pray every night that my future daughter in law will be called Eleanor *and* that she is the right girl for you." Feeling a tightness in his throat, August merely smiled at his ma as he began to empty the crates, which were taking up most of their living space. Winifred helped, amazed by the luxurious items which August had purchased; they were definitely going to have a Christmas to remember.

It was long after midnight, the following night

when August was sat with pen to paper. He could hear his ma's gentle breathing coming from upstairs as he struggled to find the right words to start the first chapter of his new book. Words had a habit of teasing him, they would be as clear as the icicles which now hung from every cottage window in the hamlet, but whenever he prepared his ink, the words seemed to melt away inside his head, leaving him staring at the blank paper. A sudden orange glow from outside, shone brightly through the curtains; August glanced at the clock on the mantlepiece, it was two-thirty and too early for sunrise. The sound of shrill voices together with the heavy pummelling upon his cottage door soon alerted him that a fire had broken out in East Hanwell. Leaving his chair in a hurry to rush outside, the strong odour of smoke soon filled his nostrils and had already created a huge dark cloud, in the snow-laden night sky. Prudence's cottage was burning so fiercely, that it would be impossible to extinguish it with the hamlet's limited resources.

"We must try and rescue the old dear!" hollered a young man, who was stood back from the burning cottage, reluctant to act on his advice. Bits of burning debris blew away into the night sky like shooting stars and the crackle of wooden beams burning and then crashing to the ground was an indication of how rampant the unforgiving fire had now taken hold of the antiquated structure.

As the men, women and older children discarded their futile buckets, August made a brave and spontaneous dash through the back door of the cottage.

As gasps and pessimistic words tumbled out of the mouths of the on looking crowd, everyone stood back from the intense heat waiting and watched intently.

The fire which had started at the front of the house had yet to take its angry hold on the tiny scullery and the narrow, wooden ladder which led up to the bedroom. August screamed out to Prudence as he raced up the ladder, but plumes of smoke hit the back of his throat, immediately choking him. Knowing that it would only be minutes before the aggressive flames burnt their way through the thin partition wall and took hold of the entire cottage, August was racing against time. A huge crash sounded; sparks flew everywhere like dancing fireflies and August viewed the gaping hole in the roof of Prudence's bedroom, where the beam had collapsed and the thatch was now burning out of control like a tinder box.

Through the thick smoke, August caught a glimpse of Prudence; she was sat up in bed, her terrified face just visible beneath her overhanging woollen hat and scarf. August sensed that the terrible shock had rendered the poor old women immobile.

"Mrs Prudence! He yelled, "I'm going to get you out of here!"

There wasn't a twitch or a sound from Prudence, making August's mission all the more difficult. He couldn't be sure that the wooden floorboards would take his weight and if they gave way while he was carrying Prudence, they would both fall to their death and be roasted alive.

"Mrs Prudence, you must get out of bed and make your way towards me! *Please hurry!* We don't have much time left!"

The first sound to come from her was a deep-rooted wail, but she still refused to move.

"Mrs Prudence! Make your way to me and I will carry you to safety!"

Being forced to inhale the thick, black smoke, August began choking again. His eyes stung and watered from the heat, as he coughed into his shirt opening hoping for a respite from the crippling irritant. When he lifted his head, to his delight, Prudence was crouched in front of him by the top of the ladder.

"There's nothing left for me here lad, just leave me to die. Save yourself...you're young and have a life to live yo...." cut short as the dense smoke choked her, August grabbed hold of her and carried her precariously down the ladder, grateful that she was as light as a feather.

As the sound of the neighbour's cheering filled the hamlet, Prudence's cottage came crashing to the ground and now resembled a bonfire, all signs of it ever being a dwelling, now vanished. Having been woken up by all the commotion, Winifred was the first to push her way through the crowd, with her hand on her heart and prayers of thanks and gratitude upon her lips.

CHAPTER THIRTY-SEVEN

They had feasted on the chicken and duck which August had bought for Christmas dinner and spent the afternoon nibbling on dainty sweet treats, delicious roasted nuts and fresh fruit, all washed down with a special brand of tea, for the occasion. As the limited light of the day drew to an end, Winifred and Prudence relaxed on the wooden settle next to the burning stove while August sat at the table, gazing wistfully out of the cottage window. His paper, pen and ink were positioned in front of him, but merely posing as a decoy, for on this day he had no intention of writing, but was simply enjoying the peace; he knew that the women would omit him from their conversation if they thought him to be preoccupied. His ears were overflowing with the compliments which his mother and Prudence continuously praised him with and he'd had more than enough of being called, *a hero*. He didn't consider himself a hero at all; he'd merely followed his instincts and rescued an old woman from a burning cottage.

The snowy sky was still sifting tiny remnants of snow dust to add to the two-foot deep, white carpet, which froze solid every night. August's thoughts were fixed on his darling Eleanor as he wondered how she was spending the day. He'd posted a Christmas card to Mr Levi, Peggy and

Rayne; having heard nothing from them he presumed they'd not made any discoveries about Eleanor's whereabouts, neither. His thoughts went to poor, Tommy Kettle? He wondered if he'd yet enlightened Rayne of his true feelings towards her and what her response had been. She had a nasty selfish streak to her, he reminisced, which could be forgiven, since she'd been through an upheaval just as Eleanor had *and* she was a year younger too!

"What was the name of those fancy tea leaves, again?" Winifred called out, breaking into his reverie. August sighed heavily.

"Grey's Bergamot oil tea, ma, or just Grey's for short!"

"Oh yes, you were quite correct, Prudence; your memory is sharper than mine, it would seem!"

"Must have been all that smoke I breathed in! It probably did more good than harm!"

"Well, I doubt that!" laughed Winifred.

"It's a poignant time of year," said Prudence in a small voice..."I'm so glad that August rescued me, now. Did he mention that I ordered him to leave me to burn with my cottage?"

Winifred gasped, loudly, catching August's attention.

"*No! He never did*...but *why,* Prudence? What made you say that? Why would you wish for such a dreadful end?"

"This has been the best Christmas I've had in decades, Winifred. I usually feel so lonely at this time of year, especially when the weather is bad and keeps you confined in your home. I tell you, the devil himself takes hold of those with idle hands and idle minds!"

"You should count your blessings, Prudence, there's many a woman in your situation who would have found herself in the workhouse by now; you're fortunate that our Squire only asks a few hours of your time during harvest...I do believe he prefers our older generation to the flighty younger ones!"

"There's also the fact that my cottage is the worst one in the hamlet and hasn't had any repair work in over fifteen years!

"You mean, it *was* the worst cottage!" Winifred reminded her.

"Ah! Don't remind me, I doubt the Squire has even heard about the fire yet with it being Christmas time; he's likely gone away for the festivities."

August picked up his pen, feeling a sudden urge to write a poem, but he kept one ear listening in on the conversation.

Prudence continued in a low voice, "Once a woman has brought life into this world, there isn't a single day which passes when her thoughts don't ponder on her child or children. Do you know what I mean, Winifred? When a baby is born, *nothing* is ever the same again!"

"Ah, I know that *all too well*, my dear, there isn't a single day when I don't remember my little,

Gideon, August's twin. But I take comfort that he's now in heaven and not suffering the trials of life and one day, God willing, we will be united again."

"Oh I'm sorry, Winifred, it had completely slipped my mind...*me and my mouth!* I doubt there is anyone alive who doesn't have a heartbreaking story to tell and who hasn't suffered the loss of a loved one!"

"Don't feel bad, Prudence, I don't expect you to remember my sorrows, it was many years ago too."

"I think of my daughter every day and night; she haunts me. I wonder sometimes if I was too harsh to judge and condemn her. We have both been living separate lives. Does she think of me as I of her? And then there was the baby...the one she had with *him*. I used to blame him for all of my troubles, but life has taught me that everyone is usually accountable for their own actions. My daughter chose him, knowing he was a married man and likely knowing that he intended to remain married and that she was just his plaything. Beautiful she was...everyone said how beautiful she was and I would feel so proud to be her mother, but thinking back, if her looks had been plain, she might still be my daughter to this day, might have even married a local lad and be living in the hamlet and sharing this Christmas day with us. Beauty can be a curse, don't you think, Winifred?"

Becoming intrigued by Prudence's open-heartedness, Winifred wanted to hear more about her past years.

"Well, I suppose the menfolk are always after the best looking amongst the women, it's how the Good Lord created them but there is many a beauty living in this very hamlet, take Iris Fielding, she's a pretty lass if ever I saw one and one day soon, some lucky young man is going to claim her as his bride!"

August pretended not to hear his mother's mention of the girl she wished to become her daughter in law, but he was intrigued by Prudence's life story and hoped she'd continue; it might make for some interesting chapter ideas in his new book, he mused.

"So what exactly happened to your daughter, Prudence...when did you last have any contact with her? It's never too late, you know; fences can always be mended!"

Prudence pulled her shawl around her shoulders as Winifred added some more wood to the fire. "That northerly wind blows right through these haystacks!" she grumbled.

She waited for Winifred to sit down again before continuing, "It was just a week after her baby was born, my granddaughter who I've not seen since...." Prudence began to count on her fingers, "She must be seventeen, nearly eighteen by now...no, I tell a lie, may the Good Lord forgive me, she was born just after the harvest so she will be eighteen in about nine or ten months if my memory serves me right. Just a few weeks old she was...I didn't want to cradle her, but Beatrice insisted and put the tot in my arms without warning. I thought that if I didn't hold her I'd form no attachment to her...*how very wrong I was.* Beatrice wanted to make amends, she wanted me to be part of her life again, but I couldn't. You see, she'd born that baby out of wedlock. *He* was still married to his first wife and Beatrice didn't seem to care, she said that everyone thought she *was* married, she'd even taken his name so it didn't matter, she claimed. But it mattered an awful lot to me, she was living in sin and my granddaughter was illegitimate!"

As August listened carefully to her every word, he couldn't believe his ears. Was this a coincidence or could Prudence actually be Eleanor's grandmother, he considered. He silently prayed that his mother would keep up the conversation on the same subject. Fortunately, Winifred was becoming more and more intrigued and was desperate to hear the rest of Prudence's story.

"Didn't your daughter ever try and contact you after that day?" she asked, in a gentle tone.

Prudence wetted her lips with the last drop of cold tea from her cup and although Winifred knew she should refill the pot, she didn't want to risk Prudence cutting short her intriguing story.

"Why would she? She knew how I felt about her circumstances, she begged me to stay and I know she wanted to include me in her life, but she'd let me down badly and I was ashamed of her, ashamed of what folk would say too. I knew where to find her, so I believe Beatrice thought it was up to me to make the next move!"

Prudence stopped briefly to dab her watery eyes, "Do you know, Winifred, I remember that sweet baby's face looking up at me as though it happened yesterday, *my little Eleanor*...She was like the prettiest star, shining in the sky on a cloudless night...and she was innocent, it wasn't her fault she was illegitimate and yet I've been punishing her for all these years...maybe that makes *me* the bad person! Is it any wonder the Creator wanted to see me burnt alive...reckon I deserve to!"

August was speechless as every piece of the puzzle slowly came into place. He was sat in the same cottage as Eleanor's grandmother, he mused, but the saddest fact was that *he* knew of Beatrice's fate and he was still no closer to finding his darling Eleanor.

"You mustn't talk like that Prudence!" admonished, Winifred as she took hold of Prudence's hands in hers. "The Good Lord didn't allow you to lose your life in the fire, but maybe it was a way of making you see your errors; maybe this will spur you on to seek out your daughter and granddaughter and become a happy family once more...look for the positives in every problem, Prudence, my dear, not the negatives!"

August left his chair, "I'm going to make a fresh pot of tea!" he declared.

"Your lad is a real treasure, Winifred, as well as being a brave hero too! Is it that fancy new tea, August? What is it called again? I must admit that I've become quite partial to its taste!"

August smiled, "It's Grey's tea, Mrs Prudence!"

"Oh, yes, I remember now!"

CHAPTER THIRTY-EIGHT

Finding the right opportunity after Prudence had retired for the night, August informed his ma of the bad news that she would have to break to Prudence, come morning.

"*My, my, my*, what a small world it is after all!" declared a baffled Winifred, shaking her head in disbelief. "*That poor woman*; she was hoping for a happy reunion, not a journey to the cemetery to mourn her only child! And to think that all this time, your sweetheart's grandmother has been under our very noses! It's uncanny!"

"I have just realised something, Ma...and why I didn't I think of it earlier I'll never know! I could kick myself for being so stupid!" expressed August, as he paced urgently across the tiny space in the cottage, mumbling under his breath.

"Oh, August! For the love of The Dear Lord! You're making me feel quite giddy! What's come over you? Too much rich food in one day, I'd say...a plate of cabbage and potato, that's what we will feast on tomorrow! It seems as though we've all lost our rational thoughts!"

"*Ma*, the answer to where I will find Eleanor has been staring me in the face and I've been a fool not to have thought of it earlier! She will surely visit her mother's graveside and I know which cemetery she rests in! I simply need to be there when she is! Most probably on a Sunday, I'd suspect...Oh, when will this infuriating snow melt!"

"Don't raise your hopes too high, son, it breaks me heart to watch you suffer disappointment after disappointment! It could be that the young girl has left this area all together! She could be anywhere in the country by now, perhaps even in service in some grand Estate north of the country!"

Not liking his mother's negative suggestions, August said no more on the subject but had already decided where his first journey would be, after the thaw set in.

Prudence cried out loud when Winifred broke the sad news to her; it was as though her heart had been stabbed, with the sudden and devastating news ripping through her aged body.

"*My little Beatrice*! Life was so short for you, my darling and I let you down...Oh, Beatrice, please forgive me, my darling child, please forgive me!" she sobbed repeatedly as she curled up on the settle, as though there was no one else in the room with her. Winifred did all she could to comfort her and later that day, August told her everything he could remember about her beautiful, kind-hearted granddaughter. He also spoke of his love for her and how he was going to find her if it took the rest of his life. Prudence took comfort in his declaration, knowing how impossible it would be for her to leave the hamlet in search of her. She was glad that August was in love with her, he was a decent and honourable young man *and* he had saved her life to which she would always be grateful for and even more so if he should find her little Eleanor.

Having lost everything in the fire and with the landlord not willing to rebuild the cottage in a hurry, just for one person, it was decided that Prudence would move in with Winifred and August, for the time being; August was hopeful that this might persuade his mother to move into the City with him come the spring. Winifred donated a few items of clothing to her and they spent the remaining winter days busily, knitting and sewing. Prudence also asked if she could read his book since she now knew it was centred on her granddaughter.

"I have a feeling that 1878 is going to be a year which will see many changes to our lives!" she declared, optimistically.

With Whitechapel swathed in a blanket of snow and the freezing temperatures proving too cold for folk to stand around listening to her music, Rayne was forced to spend her days inside. She felt bored and trapped and was finding life very dull in the continuous company of her grandmother and Uncle Levi, who seemed quite content to lounge around all day long. Tommy was spending a few days with his family in Ludgate Hill and she presumed that it was the bad weather keeping him away, for such a long period. She picked up the card which they'd received from August Miller and ran her hands over it, letting out a long sigh; she knew it would be a while until he travelled to Whitechapel again. She held the card against her chest, "Oh, my dearest, August, you have held this card and now it feels as though you have placed your hand upon my heart!" she declared, theatrically. Peggy suddenly burst into the room, causing Rayne to jump, "Hello, Grandmamma!" she uttered, sounding a little guilty.

Peggy huffed loudly, appearing to be in a bit of a fluster, "Since you seem to have nothing better to do than to sit idle, staring out of the window, you might like to come down to the shop, Uncle Levi has decided to have a good clean up since there's barely any trade at the moment!"

"Of course I will, Grandmamma, you only had to ask!"

Clandestinely tucking the card into her pocket, she followed Peggy back downstairs where Mr Levi was perched on a low stool, surrounded by small hills of merchandise. There was one for the pocket watches, one of assorted necklaces and bracelets and another of rings; then there were the huge mountains of clothing and another of shoes and boots. Mr Levi looked up as they entered the shop, a happy grin lighting up his wrinkled face.

"Ah, my favourite ladies have come to my rescue! This is my *undercover* stock and all these items have not been reclaimed, so I am going to make this New Year the year where I make my fortune and become a man of riches, *huh?* What do you think? It's been sat doing nothing for decades! What you think, Rayne? Is your Uncle Levi a wise old owl? What you say, Rayne?"

Rayne cast her eyes over the mess, the sight made her feel miserable just knowing how long it would take to organise, what looked like a load of old junk and the choking odour of unwashed clothing and old worn-out boots made her gag.

"*Uncle Levi*, I doubt you'll get rich with those old clothes, *they stink* and are, in all probability, infested with fleas; plus, they are *twenty* years out of date by the look of them. I suggest you burn them before your good stock becomes infested too!"

"Don't be so rude, Rayne, this is Uncle Levi's lifetime's work...it's not for you to voice your opinion, just to help organise things and since you have youth on your side you will likely not tire for a long while, *unlike us!*"

"She might be right, Peggy, look at me arms, already covered in bites; I'm itching like a filthy hound!"

Both Peggy and Rayne immediately felt their skin crawl, with an instant desire to scratch themselves.

"I fetch the yard broom an' sweep 'em outside, we'll have ourselves a cosy bonfire later! Good idea, huh?"

Rayne quickly opted for the task of sorting through the heap of tangled bracelets, already deciding to feign sickness after an hour had passed. Mr Levi set to sweeping out the old clothes into the back yard and Peggy sat polishing the assortment of rings, placing each one in an individual box ready to go on display. Keeping one eye on the clock, time passed by at a snail's pace for Rayne and she'd already had enough after ten minutes. A silver bangle caught her eye, it was the only bracelet which wasn't tangled and it appeared less tarnished than everything else in the pile. As she carefully studied it she noticed an inscription on its inside, *'my darling angel, I will hold you in my heart until you are mine'*, she read it a couple of times. Love was beautiful, she mused, with August's handsome face in mind; how her heart would sing for joy if such a gift had been given to her, especially if it was from the artistic, August Miller, who had a flair for expressing his love. She slipped the bangle into her skirt pocket, along with the Christmas card and with her head full of romantic notions, set to sorting through the rest of her pile.

By early January, the cold spell snapped and as

temperatures rose slightly, the snow was replaced by icy, cold rain which slowly washed away the snow. In the City's streets where it had mixed with soot and horse dung, its pure whiteness had now formed the most unpleasant discoloured sight, making the torrential rain a most welcome arrival amongst the inhabitants.

Charles watched with sadness as patches of green grass began to poke through the enchanting, white garden as the snow melted away. He'd enjoyed himself so much, throwing snowballs with Tilly and Miss Whitlock, but now, with Christmas over and the snow disappearing, Charles felt as though there would be little fun anymore. His mamma was now spending much of the day resting, while she and the entire household held their breath, waiting for the arrival of the new baby. Still undecided on his feelings of welcoming a new baby into the house, he had yet to make up his mind as to whether he'd prefer a brother or sister. With everyone constantly reminding him that once the baby arrived, he would have to be much quieter about the house, the prospects of any fun in the foreseeable future was also looking bleak; he just hoped that he would still be allowed to play the piano. Miss Whitlock had taught him so much since she'd been his new governess, she could play so well and he adored listening to her.

"Young master Charles, don't you have any

learning to be getting on with, instead of wasting your time staring at the melting snow?" declared Tilly, as she hurried around the room, armed with a feather duster.

"Miss Whitlock said that I could have a piano lesson this morning, so I'm just waiting for her to arrive. Where is she, Tilly?"

"She'll be here in one shake of a lamb's tail, young man!" said Tilly as she brushed her feather duster over Charles' bare knees."

Tilly and Eleanor had adjusted quickly to their new roles in the Hyde's household. Eleanor had made a swift recovery, which had been aided by the kind treatment she'd received from Mr and Mrs Hyde, not to mention Rosa and Tilly and it was only a couple of weeks after she'd arrived when she'd begun teaching Charles. He adored Eleanor and worked extra hard to please her and to prove that he was a clever and quick learning pupil.

Eleanor gracefully entered the modest front parlour, where Charles took most of his lessons and where the piano was situated.

"Miss Ellie!" declared Charles, excited as ever by her arrival. "I've been waiting all morning for you!"

Tilly and Eleanor shared an amused smile,

"Well, Master Charles, I do apologise for keeping you waiting but it is only just, eight-thirty!"

"I rose early this morning as I'd planned to play

out in the snow, before lessons, but Tilly wouldn't unlock the door *and* she hid the key!"

"And I told you why, didn't I, Charlie! The snow is melting fast and you would have become soaked to the skin and caught a nasty cold too! Your poor mamma has enough to worry about, without the added concern of a sick boy!"

Charles glance at Eleanor for some support, but was disappointed by her words,

"Tilly was absolutely right in keeping you in, Charles...I certainly don't want a coughing, sneezing boy spluttering over me all day!"

"May I have my piano lesson this morning then, since I've already had one disappointed today!"

"I'm sorry, Charles, your mamma is still in bed and needs her rest. We don't want to wake her up now, do we?"

"I suppose!" he sighed, "Mamma is always tired...will she be tired once the baby has arrived?"

"She will be," affirmed Tilly, "but only to begin with, but won't it be fun to have a little brother or sister?"

"Hmm, maybe," muttered Charles, looking even more downcast.

"Right then! Let us start this new day with some mathematics...I trust you've been learning your multiplication tables, Master Charles!"

With the snow melting rapidly, Eleanor persuaded Tilly that they should make the journey to Cowley Road come the following Sunday before the next bout of winter weather should arrive and render them housebound again. With Mrs Hyde's baby due in a week or so, reminded Eleanor, there might not be another opportunity to visit their mother's resting places for a while too.

When Sunday morning arrived, they set off early on the four-mile walk to St Mary and St John Church. The air was crisp and dry but extremely cold and a biting wind seemed to penetrate through their winter clothing. They marched quickly, in a bid to keep warm and by the time they'd walked through the City and arrived at The Plain, where both Cowley Road and Henley Road branched off from, both girls were adorned with bright red cheeks and noses which matched the berries on the holly wreaths they'd made to lay at their mother's resting places. They giggled at the appearance of each other, but we're both feeling apprehensive at the prospect of walking up Cowley Road and past the workhouse.
 "There are bound to be some of the workhouse inmates in church, Ellie, especially since Mr and Mrs Barnet are a compassionate couple!"
"Do you think they will be angry with us, for running off as we did, they might have got into trouble, old Mr Wolf could have lost his job since it was him who left the gates open!"
"Oh, I don't know, Ellie, I'm sure they won't be

too hostile towards us, after all, we've done well for ourselves, haven't we?"

"I feel as though there's an entire flutter of butterflies inside my stomach!" admitted Eleanor.

Tilly linked her arm through the crook of Eleanor's, "Come on now, Ellie, we can face *any* problem together; you and I are a formidable team, remember!"

"Well, I just wish I shared your confidence at this moment in time!"

"Nobody mightn't recognise us dressed in these fine clothes and with our amusing red faces!" teased Tilly, as they proceeded on the final leg of their journey.

All conversation was silenced as they approached the workhouse, each one with their memories weighing heavy on their thoughts; they had been the darkest of days for Eleanor, days she associated with both mental and physical agony and even though it was only two and a half years ago, she felt she'd grown up so much since losing her parents. The workhouse was a chapter in her life that she wished to blot out, it sent shivers down her spine and the only good to come of it was that it was where she'd met Tilly.

Tilly was also bombarded with the sad memories of her mother and a lonely, tough and often terrifying existence. The workhouse had stolen her childhood, made her a tougher person and forced her to grow up quickly, but she had met the best sister anyone could wish for and she knew that if it hadn't been for Ellie, she would not be where she was today and might have even lived her entire life in the foreboding institution.

The street was becoming busier, all of a sudden, with smartly attired local folk making their way to church. Families walked in an orderly fashion as though already contemplating the spirituality of the day and preparing themselves for a morning of prayer and hymns. Some folk arrived in freshly washed gigs and had even tied a ribbon in their horse's mane.

Tilly and Eleanor prepared to enter the cemetery and lay their wreaths of holly, which Rosa had taught them how to make, at their beloved mother's gravesides. For Eleanor, it was the first time in more than two years that she'd been able to visit the grave and she was already feeling an uncomfortable lump in her throat as flashbacks of the day she'd found her poor mamma came to life, in her mind's eye.

CHAPTER THIRTY-NINE

With their mother's graves situated on opposite sides of the church, by the time Eleanor and Tilly reached its arched stone entrance, some fifteen minutes later, the local flock had almost filled every row of pews, leaving only a few places to the rear of the church vacant. Emotionally choked and with watery eyes, the young women linked arms in support as they stepped over the church's threshold. Since they were the last to arrive and sat at the rear, behind all the prying eyes, nobody took any notice of them. Eleanor immediately recognised Mr and Mrs Barnet who were standing with a row of workhouse women and Mrs Wolf and Mrs Wishbone who took up another row, with a few of the elderly men from the workhouse. Disappointed that the young man who used to pay her so much attention was nowhere in sight, Tilly consoled herself that it was probably for the best and she was enduring a far better life now, to be interested in the first man who gave her any attention. As they sat through the Reverend Doyle's sermon, Eleanor worried about the reaction they'd receive from the Barnets when it was time to leave; should she and Tilly make a hasty exit she pondered or simply act normally? Forty-five minutes later as the final prayer was being read, she decided the latter would be more suitable. After all, she considered, why should she and Tilly spend the rest of their life hiding when they had done nothing wrong.

"*I don't believe my eyes*!" Eleanor suddenly heard a woman exclaim, as they were slowly making their way out of the church. "Is that you, *Petal*? Young, Eleanor Jackson?"

Eying each other warily, Eleanor suddenly realised that there was only one woman in Oxford who called her '*Petal*,' and as she turned around she came face to face with Doctor Thompson and his wife, both with glowing smiles across their faces.

"Miss Jackson! If only you knew how delighted I am to encounter your presence at long last...I feel as though I've unearthed a casket of gold!" declared Doctor Thompson, joyfully.

From the corner of her eye, Eleanor watched with relief as the workhouse group chatted briefly with Reverend Doyle by the entrance before leaving the church.

"Oh, Doctor Thompson, Mrs Thompson, I can't express how it pleases me to see you again after such a long period!" replied Eleanor, thrilled to see their kind and familiar faces. "This is my *dearest* friend, Tilly."

Tilly greeted them with a smile, "I'm so pleased to meet you, at last, Ellie has spoken so much about you that I feel I know you well already!"

Mrs Thompson was radiant, "You must join us for Sunday luncheon...mustn't they Albert?"

"I can't think of a more appropriate way to celebrate our joyous reunion, Cynthia, but perhaps these young ladies have prior arrangements?"

"What do you say, Petal?" persisted Mrs Thompson, eager to disclose the news they had for Eleanor in the privacy of her home.

"We would simply love to, wouldn't we, Tilly?"

Tilly was elated that Eleanor had accepted the invitation, "Oh, yes! Indeed, this cold weather and the long walk to arrive here have given me a fearful hunger!"

Everyone laughed at Tilly's animated reply.

"Miss Jackson! Is it really you?" voiced the Reverend, as he finished saying his farewells to the last of his flock.

Eleanor giggled as she viewed the shock on his and Mrs Doyle's faces.

"And I do believe I recognise this young lady as well?" he said, focussing on Tilly. "Didn't you used to reside across the road, in the workhouse?"

"We both did, Reverend Doyle!" announced Eleanor. Her declaration was met with gasps from both couples who couldn't believe what Eleanor was telling them.

"We have such news for you, Miss Jackson!" uttered Mrs Doyle, joyfully, "We had the pleasure of meeting your young beau!"

As Eleanor stood astonished, from what she was hearing, Mrs Thompson was quick to intervene.

"Miss Jackson and her dear friend have accepted our invitation to luncheon, so we will tell her *all* the news over a relaxing meal and in the warmth of our humble home. *I must say*, Reverend Doyle, your church is extremely chilly this morning!"

"I'm actually called Miss Whitlock now!" Eleanor affirmed, but with little attention given whilst the elders busily discussed luncheon arrangements.

"We had better make haste, Doctor Thompson, we don't want the luncheon to spoil now do we?" nagged Mrs Thompson.

"Would you and Mrs Doyle care to join us too?" invited Doctor Thompson, out of politeness, which to the huge relief of Mrs Thompson was declined just as politely?

The Doctor and his wife had arrived on foot to church that morning, making the short ten-minute return journey a chance for gentle and polite conversation and for Doctor and Mrs Thompson to become more acquainted with Tilly. Taking the quickest route, it had slipped Doctor Thompson's mind that they would pass by Eleanor's old home. Eleanor suddenly froze and stood staring up at the townhouse, a tidal wave of memories gushing through her mind. She shivered and Mrs Thompson suggested they hurried home where, she assured them, there was a blazing fire waiting to warm them all.

"Is this where you used to live, Ellie?" asked Tilly, in a small and barely audible voice as though she was back in the cemetery.

Eleanor blinked away her unshed tears and linked her arm through Tilly's, "Yes, Tilly," she sighed, "but that seems like another lifetime ago now; I've grown up an awful lot from those old days and I know more of who I am now, which is a blessing."

The evocative memories of Beatrice Jackson never failed to waylay Doctor Thompson every time he passed by the house, which was more often than he cared to. He often wondered how many other men were haunted by her everlasting impression.

"Mrs Thompson is quite right, there are little benefits to be had from standing around on this bitterly cold day! And I'm starving as I'm sure you all are!"

The delicious aroma of roast lamb accosted them the second they stepped over the threshold. The cosy house was warm and inviting. Eleanor and Tilly felt most welcome as Mrs Thompson offered them a sweet sherry, but since they'd never tasted anything so powerful before they declined the offer and Mrs Thompson made a pot of tea instead.

It wasn't until after the delicious meal had been consumed and they were all relaxing by the fireside sipping more tea that the conversation took on a more serious note. The Thompsons were taken by shock to hear how Eleanor had spent the past couple of years, compelling Cynthia Thompson to repeatedly reach for her pocket-handkerchief. Tilly explained how Eleanor had been left near to death after the cruel treatment she'd received from Mr Killigrew and been locked away in solitary confinement for weeks on end. Eleanor was swift to passionately voice how Tilly had gently nurtured her back to health and went on to tell them how Tilly had also taken such care of her when she'd had yet another close call to death's door and had undergone drastic surgery. Together they explained how a happy ending had come about from Eleanor's hospital admission and how they were at last settled and enjoying life in the Hyde's household. Mrs Thompson had become quite thrilled, declaring how Doctor Thompson had purchased his newest suit from Hyde & Son, last springtime; she was curious as to whether it was when they had been employed there.

"Isn't it a small world!" she stated, feeling much cheered by the more joyful conclusion to Eleanor's account.

"And are you fully recovered from your emergency appendectomy, Eleanor...you're no longer in any pain and you *do* feel quite strong again, I trust? No sudden attacks of queasiness, I presume?" Feeling, partly responsible for the late Beatrice Jackson's daughter, Doctor Thompson was thorough in his medical inquiries.

"I'm quite fit and well, thank you, Doctor Thompson," Eleanor politely replied with a little giggle.

Doctor Thompson rubbed his hands together and straightened his back, there was a broad smile upon his face and a faint twinkle in his eye,

"Well, in that case, I have some exciting news for you, Eleanor!"

Mrs Thompson couldn't keep quiet for a second longer; she felt it her business to speak of such delicate matters,

"*Oh! Petal!*" she cried, "We entertained your young man! Didn't we Albert? Here! In this very room! Such a handsome man and clearly besotted with you! Have you two love birds been united again? Did he manage to trace you?"

"He wrote a whole book!" announced Tilly. "It was about a man who was losing his mind because of his overpowering love for a woman called Eleanor, who he'd lost contact with! It is such a beautifully written story!"

"*Oh how romantic*!" declared Mrs Thompson. "Does that mean that he *still* hasn't found you?" she continued. "I take it you harbour the same feelings for this young man too, Petal?"

Tilly quickly responded, "Oh yes, Mrs Thompson, it's all I've heard since the day Ellie came to the workhouse...*August Miller*! It is a name which I will remember for the rest of my life!"

Eleanor and Doctor Thompson shared a smile as Tilly and Mrs Thompson were now deep in conversation speculating the romance between Eleanor and August.

"Am I permitted to speak, ladies?" interrupted Doctor Thompson, his domineering voice causing an instant silence in the room.

"I have August's address, Eleanor, should you wish to write to him and put the poor young man out of his misery. He will be absolutely delighted to know that you are safe and well; the rest of course is up to you and your tender heart! I also have some more news for you, Eleanor. It has transpired that you have a half-sister. She is about a year younger than you and as far as I know, resides in Whitechapel, London with none other than *Peggy*, who happens to be her grandmother!"

Eleanor sat numb from the news, it was a lot to take in. A half-sister, she mused, not sure if this was good news or not, but knowing she could at last write to August excited her far more than the news of a half-sister who had been kept a secret from her all these years; she wondered if her mother had known about her too.

"Eleanor also has a grandmother, don't you?" Tilly disclosed with excitement.

"Yes!" uttered Doctor Thompson, "if my memory serves me correctly, I do believe I met her just after you arrived into the world,

Eleanor!"

"Have another cup of tea, Petal!" voiced Mrs Thompson. "I'll add an extra spoonful of sugar, it always helps with shock and you've certainly had one shock after another this afternoon, *you poor girl!*"

"Thank you, Mrs Thompson. I do feel a little numb from all the dramatic news, but I do love August and have carried a torch for him since our very first meeting, which was just after my pappa passed away. I can't wait to write to him!"

"Sounds like true love to me, with no mistake, Petal; he will be jumping up and down with joy when he receives your correspondence!"

The afternoon had left Eleanor with a lot to think about and after declining Doctor Thompson's offer of a ride home in his gig, not wanting to put him out anymore, Eleanor insisted that they were perfectly happy to walk and with August's address safely secured in her reticule, they expressed their thanks and bid Doctor and Mrs Thompson farewell, assuring them that they'd keep in touch. Mrs Thompson had also taken their address, intending to correspond with Eleanor.

"We'd better hasten Tilly, we've been away for almost seven hours, Mr and Mrs Hyde will be worried about us; I only said that we were going to church for the morning!"

"This is the fastest my legs are prepared to move

after all that food and cups of tea!"

"You'll soon quicken your pace when this icy wind touches your bones!"

"Maybe, but at present, I still feel pleasantly warm. I do like your friends, the Doctor and his wife and it's clear they were very fond of your dear ma, too! Fancy finding out that you have a half-sister! If that were me I'd not be able to sleep a wink until I'd met her!"

"Nothing in my family is straightforward, Tilly! I have an ominous feeling about Rayne Jackson, and I'm in no hurry to meet her. I expect she was thoroughly spoilt by my pappa and will most likely look down her snooty nose at me, viewing me as the worthless, illegitimate daughter of her father's lover!"

"You never know, Ellie, at least not until you've met her!"

"Well if I'm going to search for anyone after August, it will be my grandmother...Doctor Thompson spoke highly of her. He seemed to think that she'd no idea that my mother had birthed me until she'd arrived on the doorstep! Oh, why is my family so unconventional!"

Tilly linked her arm through Eleanor's as a gust of wind gave them both a slight push along the street. The lamplighters were already out doing their job and the sun was quickly setting amid a glorious violet and crimson sky.

"Come along, *Petal*!" she teased, "let's walk a little faster!"

Half an hour later they turned into Paradise Street, immediately noticing how the house appeared to be in darkness.

"I can't believe that Mr and Mrs Hyde haven't bothered to light the lamps!" moaned Tilly.

"Well, it is Rosa's day off! They've probably become so used to us lighting the lamps and fires of a Sunday that they forgot!"

"I pray they've lit the fires! I'm freezing and there's nothing worse than going into a freezing house!"

Eleanor laughed, "Ooh, listen to you! Would never have thought we once slept in the ice-cold dormitory of the workhouse or down on the riverbank!"

"Well, I'm used to some of life's luxuries now, Ellie and I try my hardest to forget about all those nights when I shivered myself to sleep, especially when I was a child and too scared to sleep in my clothes or snuggle in with another poor shivering soul."

Eleanor sometimes forgot how Tilly had spent a decade in the workhouse and had missed out on so many years of her childhood.

"There is nobody in the world who deserves a few luxuries in their life more than you, my sweet, sister!"

Giggling together they stepped over the threshold into a dark and very cold house.

CHAPTER FORTY

They hurried to light the lamps and Tilly set to kindling the fires in the three downstairs rooms, the kitchen was the only lit room where the short wick of the lantern emitted an insignificant glow. The sound of footsteps hurrying down the stairs immediately told Tilly and Eleanor that it was young Charles, stampeding to greet them. "*Tilly! Miss Ellie!*" he cried out excitedly, after rushing from room to room until finding them in the drawing-room, where Tilly was crouched lighting the fire and Eleanor drawing the curtains. His face was bright red and his hair and clothes in a dishevelled state.

"Oh, it *is* you! You've been gone for *ages*!"

"Is everything quite alright, my dear boy?" asked Eleanor.

Immediately running towards her, Charles wrapped his arms around her waist, burying his head into her thick shawl. Tilly ceased trying to kindle the fire and got back on her feet.

"What is it, Charlie? What's wrong?"

Embarrassed that he was crying, Charles kept his face hidden as he spoke, brokenheartedly, "I thought you had left forever...I thought you weren't coming back!"

As Tilly and Eleanor hugged and kissed him, assuring him that they would never simply walk out on him in such a cruel way and explaining how they had gone to dinner with Eleanor's old friends, Charles, at last, eased his face from hiding and looked up at them, his watery eyes wide and alert and a beaming smile upon his face.

"*Mamma has had the baby!*" he proclaimed.

Thrown by the shock and left tongue-tied, Eleanor and Tilly looked in astonishment at each other.

"I have a little sister," continued Charles, casually.

"Is the doctor still here?" were the first words which came out of Eleanor's mouth.

"Oh, no, he left *ages* ago! Would you like to come upstairs and see her? She's very small and quite pink, but Mamma said she will soon grow to be quite beautiful!"

Excitement permeated both girls who were thrilled to hear the good news.

"You go up first, Ellie while I make a tray of tea and sandwiches, I'm sure Mrs Hyde must be starving!"

"Pappa made some tea already, but we didn't have any dinner today, though. Mamma was too tired to cook."

Eleanor hugged the innocent child, as she and Tilly giggled at his announcement.

"Then I will fry you a plate of sausages! How does that sound, young man?"

Already licking his lips in anticipation, Charles jumped up and down on the spot, "Good! That sounds very good! Can I stay downstairs with you Tilly? I've already seen my new sister and she's quite a boring baby!"

Wilma Hyde was sat up in bed looking well and smiling happily as she greeted Eleanor. Mr Hyde was slouched in the window seat and on reflection, appeared more exhausted and traumatised from the birth than his wife. A tiny pink-faced baby, swaddled in a finely knitted, white shawl, laid aside the bed in her lavish crib, adorned with a white lacey canopy and scalloped, cream lace trimmings.
 "Congratulations, Mr and Mrs Hyde!" expressed Eleanor as she gingerly neared the bed.
"Oh thank the Good Lord for your return!" expressed Mrs Hyde. "I don't know which was worse, the pain of childbirth or having to put up with a fretful Charles, who was convinced that you and Tilly had eloped!"
 "I'm so sorry, Mrs Hyde, we accepted an invitation to dinner with my family's doctor and his wife."
"There is no need to apologise, Eleanor, Sunday is your day off and you may do as you please...I will have to install a little more self-restraint into that boy's emotions though! I doubt he would have fretted after Emma in the same way. He does so adore you, you know!"
"As I do him, Mrs Hyde, he is a remarkable young boy! But how are you? Are you not in

need of a long sleep?"

"Twenty minutes she slept for and look at her, she looks a sight fresher than me!" complained Mr Hyde, wearily. "But I am now a proud father of the most beautiful daughter! Take a peek at her, Miss Whitlock, isn't she just the prettiest baby you've ever seen?"

"Oh, Austin, *really!* All babies are the prettiest in their parent's eyes!"

Eleanor peered into the crib, "You are quite correct, Mr Hyde, she most definitely is the prettiest baby I've ever seen, *she is beautiful*! Have you given her a name yet?"

"Felicity, Florence Hyde." voiced Mrs Hyde, proudly.

"Oh, that's such a pretty name too!"

Tilly soon arrived with a pot of tea, sandwiches and cakes, which prompted Mr Hyde to leave the bedroom and join Charles, downstairs, to devour the sausages, leaving the women to coo over the new baby and for Eleanor to tell Mrs Hyde about the news she'd received from Doctor Thompson.

Mrs Hyde listened intently, gasping in shock when she heard about Eleanor's half-sister. She was delighted to hear that, at long last, Eleanor was in possession of August Miller's address and encouraged her to contact him as soon as possible.

"I hope you're not going to marry this young man in haste and desert us, though!" she uttered.

"We couldn't possibly manage without you, not now, and it would surely break Charles', young heart. He is so fond of you, but then again, I see no reason why you and your husband couldn't move in here! I'm sure we'd all get along splendidly and what a bonus for Charles, having an author to influence him! Oh, Eleanor, 1878 is looking to be an eventful year indeed!"

"Mrs Hyde!" objected Eleanor, "I haven't seen August for over two years and prior to that we had the briefest of encounters...it might be different between us now and as for marriage, I can't envisage me becoming, Mrs Miller for quite some time, even if we do still feel the same about each other."

"Oh, Eleanor, *I have read his book*, the man is besotted with you and I know you are merely being cautious when you speak of your feelings. I happen to be a woman who has loved and still loves, passionately. I hear the sound of your heart, beating like that of an orchestra's kettle drum every time August Miller is mentioned. Don't risk losing him after all this time, for true love seldom finds its way into our lives more than once, my dear."

The subject was immediately dropped as Felicity's engaging cries rang out from her crib.

"*The baby is awake!*" exclaimed Tilly, as she and Eleanor stretched their necks to peer into the crib.

"Oh just look at her! She is *so* beautiful! May I

cradle her, Mrs Hyde?"

"Of course you may, Eleanor, I hope you'll both become quite accustomed to the dear little soul since I plan to return to the shop as soon as possible. Mr Hyde is struggling by himself, especially with the formidable machinists, but please don't breathe a word of my plan to him, girls. I don't wish to employ a nanny but if you, Tilly, would be willing to take on the lion's share of such a role, with Rosa and Eleanor helping you out a little, should Felicity proves too much of a handful, well, I think we will all muddle along quite successfully. What do you say, Tilly?"

Tilly didn't need any time to consider the offer, she was euphoric and accepted immediately, delighted that she would have her own proper position in the Hyde's household, rather than feeling like a spare part in the finely run house. Wilma Hyde was also delighted by Tilly's instant response and promptly informed her that she was hoping to return to her husband's side by early springtime.

Felicity was passed between Tilly and Eleanor, arousing their maternal feelings. She was the sweetest gift to cherish at the end of such a perfect day and as the warm room and the eventful and tiring day caused everyone to yawn, baby Felicity gave her audience a sample of her most audible voice as she cried for her mother's sustenance.

"I think it is bedtime for everyone!" yawned Mrs Hyde, as she cradled the baby, close to her breast.

Tilly hastily stacked the empty crockery on to the tray and Eleanor placed some more coals onto the fire.

"Goodnight Mrs Hyde and Miss Felicity!" they whispered in unison, before leaving the bedroom.

"God Bless, girls!" said Mrs Hyde, in a small voice and with an affectionate smile across her weary face.

It was pitch black and unbearably cold when Eleanor first woke. With so many thoughts swimming around inside her head she lay in the darkness with the blanket pulled up to her chin as she mentally composed a letter to August. She wondered how long it would take for a letter to arrive in East Hanwell, especially if the snow had yet to thaw in that part of Oxfordshire. Mrs Hyde had informed her that it was about eight to ten miles away; she'd passed by on a few occasions, she had also said that there were, as far as she could see, only a dozen small thatched cottages within the hamlet. Eleanor had never imagined August to reside outside of the City, he seemed too at home when she'd been with him and just didn't look the type of man to live in a sleepy hamlet far from the hustle and bustle of city life. With a sudden feeling that she didn't know him at all, she wondered if perhaps she'd spent the previous two years simply chasing a dream and had merely persuaded herself that she was in love with August. With a muddled mind and the unfamiliar sound of a crying baby coming from the opposite end of the house, Eleanor fell back to sleep again, telling herself that everything would look clearer in the light of day.

Five weeks had passed since the birth of Felicity and as the first signs of spring began to appear, Eleanor had yet to compose and post a letter to August, confiding in Tilly, late one night that she believed it would appear too forward on her part.

"*After all this time!*" protested, Tilly. "You've always been so eager to find him and contact him! August Miller has provided you with the hope that's kept you strong and determined to succeed since you lost your parents. If I were in your boots..."

"*What Tilly?* If you were in my boots would you really have simply thrown yourself into his arms without thinking, without even a second thought? I'm scared, Tilly! I fear that we might both have been clinging on to a dream and absence has clouded it over so much that we have both been mistaken and both been chasing after something which might not even exist. Suppose one of us feels different after all this passing time? Is it fair to break the heart of the other, all over again? Might it not be better to allow us both to carry on with the taste of such a sweet dream in our hearts?"

Tilly jumped out of her bed, all plans of an early night now abandoned; she had to get through to her dear sister and would make it her business to install some rational thinking into Ellie's head. She perched herself at the end of Eleanor's bed.

"You can't be serious Ellie! That is the silliest statement you've ever said since the day I met you! So supposing you carry on with this dream in your heart and August does the same...both of you living half a life, waiting and wondering? Years will slip you by, you know, and you'll find yourself an old woman, still wondering, *what if*? And I, as your devoted sister will not allow that to happen!"

Eleanor already had tears rolling off her cheeks. She knew that Tilly was speaking wisely, but *she* wasn't the one madly in love with, August Miller and about to initiate a possible termination to the bliss she held in her heart. She had become accustomed to the dull ache, but to endure another broken heart when August discovered that she wasn't the girl he'd imagined her to be was unbearable.

"I simply hoped that he would find me, Tilly. In my mind I pictured him writing to me or waiting at the end of the street for me when he knew I'd be passing; a romantic assignation, perhaps, which would spark a fire in both of us!" Tilly let out a long sigh, "For goodness sake, Ellie, you heard what the Doctor's wife said; August hasn't stopped searching for you, he inquired with the Reverend Doyle after you, he visited the Doctor in the hope of finding where you had vanished to, he even took a journey to London, thinking that you might have gone there! He wrote a book in honour of you! August Miller loves you and that is a fact. In my opinion, the fires in both of your hearts are well and truly alight! You *must* write to him, Ellie. Suppose he calls on Doctor Thompson again, who informs him that you have had his address for weeks! The first thought to pass through his mind will be that you no longer love him! He will be left heartbroken! Who knows? That could have already happened! *Don't risk losing him, Ellie*! It's as clear as the stars in the night sky that you love him and that you were destined for each other!"

Tilly's words sent alarm bells ringing, Eleanor immediately bolted out of her bed, wrapped her shawl around her shoulders and once again sat down at the writing bureau. What if August *had* already called on Doctor Thompson, she panicked, he would definitely presume she wanted nothing to do with him.

"*Oh, Tilly!*" she burst out, sobbing dramatically, "I have wasted every single sheet of paper and envelope!"

"Stop that crying, *Petal*! I'll get some from Mr Hyde's desk, I'm sure he won't mind!"
Eleanor laughed at Tilly's imitation of Cynthia Thompson. She felt as though she was bordering on hysteria as her tears and laughter merged. Tilly was right, she mused, the sooner she wrote this letter the calmer she would feel! Dear Tilly, she was the best friend and sister she could ever wish for.

Winifred Miller studied the quality envelope which was embossed with the name, Hyde&Son next to the penny red stamp. Annoyed that August had left home early that morning, she showed it to Prudence, before securely placing it on the mantlepiece, behind the vase of snowdrops.
"I've never heard of Hyde&Son," confessed Prudence. "Sounds like it could be a lawyer to me; they always have fancy envelopes like that!"
 "*A lawyer*!" gasped Winifred, with her hand on her heart. "My August has never done anything wrong in his entire life...it must be from a book publisher...*yes*...that must be it…a book publisher, he *is* an author after all!"
"So when did he say he was coming home, then? The suspense is too much for me to bear!"
 "I don't even know where he went to...he set off early, but I know he took Duke with him...maybe he went to buy some provisions since the larder is looking empty!"

"You couldn't wish for a more loyal son than your August, Winifred, he's worth ten of some of the young rascals who've grown up in this hamlet over the years!"

"Ah, yes, I've been very fortunate. Thank the Good Lord!"

Deciding to spend the afternoon turning over the soil in the small cottage garden, their patience was soon rewarded when August suddenly appeared with a spade in hand, offering his help.

"We were just about to stop for the day son: time for a, well-earned pot of tea, I think, don't you Prudence?"

CHAPTER FORTY-ONE

The fine drizzle hadn't ceased all morning and as Eleanor marched from the back door to the front, stopping every so often to glance at her reflection in the looking glass, the entire household in Paradise Street was feeling her anxiety. Even little Felicity, who was now six weeks old, was affected by the atmosphere and Tilly and Charles daren't speak a single word to Eleanor. Her rendezvous with August was set for two o'clock and after three days of trying on every outfit in her wardrobe, Eleanor was yet to be convinced that she appeared at her best. A warm, turquoise jacket over a navy plaid dress with a plain, but matching flowerpot hat to top the ensemble had been the winning attire for the extra special day. With her hair pinned up beneath the hat, there was just a glimpse of her golden curls on display. She had prayed all morning for the drizzle to stop, not wanting to arrive at the Copper Kettle wet through and with the hem of her skirt soaked from the filth of the pavements. As the hands on every clock in the house neared one-thirty, by some miracle the sun was slowly pushing her way through the pale sky and the drizzle had, at last, died down. It was a good omen, thought Eleanor as she peered out of the window. After hurriedly saying her goodbyes to everyone, hardly hearing their wishes of good luck, Eleanor picked up her reticule from the vestibule table and ambled along Paradise Street, feeling every beat of her nervous heart, which seemed to be in tune with her footsteps. It was only a fifteen minute walk to the Copper Kettle, but since she had to pass by Hyde&Son, Eleanor decided to call in on Mr Hyde; he always had a calming effect on her. He spoke his mind, always saying the appropriate words and she desperately needed his moral support to help calm her nerves.

"Dear Eleanor, you look as pretty as a picture and if you don't mind me saying, you are the image of how I remember your dear, mamma!" Declared Austin Hyde, the minute Eleanor stepped into the empty shop.

"Thank you, Mr Hyde; I feel so very nervous and fear I might not even be able to hold a teacup steady without spilling it!"

"Remember, my dear, Mr Miller will no doubt be feeling as anxious as you, if not more. This is a meeting which both of you will embrace in your hearts for the rest of your lives, make sure it is one which you both thoroughly enjoy. It will be a story to tell your children and your grandchildren and in my opinion, it is a beautiful love story!"

Eleanor felt her cheeks burning and knew they'd turned crimson, "Oh, Mr Hyde, you have succeeded in embarrassing me, that's for sure! August will see my pink face and run a mile, I fear!"

"August will take one look at your enchanting face and fall helplessly in love with you all over again, only this time he will make a vow, never to lose you!"

"Thank you, Mr Hyde, I'd better be on my way now!"

"God be with you, Miss Eleanor Whitlock!"

Eleanor smiled to herself as she stepped out of the shop; Mr Hyde had certainly calmed her nerves and given some meaningful thoughts to focus on. With still another ten minutes until she was due at the Copper Kettle, she stopped outside the bakery in Cornmarket Street where memories of the time when she and Tilly had escaped the workhouse and were sleeping on the riverbank came flooding back; she would purchase some jam tarts before returning home, she decided.

"We really must stop bumping into each other like this, Miss Whitlock!"

Eleanor felt her heart melt. She immediately recognised August's alluring voice as though it had only been days since last hearing him. Overcome with butterflies in her stomach, she felt her legs tremble as she turned to face him. With her voice becoming trapped in her throat she could only smile at his handsome face as he too appeared to have been struck dumb all of a sudden. As their eyes met and held each other,

Eleanor knew immediately that nothing had altered between them; they were as much in love as they'd ever been, but with the difference that they now both knew how strong their feeling were for each other. August positioned his arm, encouraging Eleanor to take a hold of it as they walked silently on a floating cloud, towards the Copper Kettle. He took the longest route and just before they reached the tea room, he unexpectedly came to a halt,

"It's no good Eleanor, I have to take you in my arms, if only for a second to prove to myself that I'm not dreaming!"

She turned to him, careless of what people would think as he wrapped his strong, protecting arms around her slender body. She breathed in the sweet aroma of him as the side of her face rested upon his chest. The beat of his heart sounded strong and fast as he gazed down lovingly at her. Their eyes met once more, but this time their closeness blurred all vision as their lips finally touched and the gentle soft kiss which they both feared would never transpire, took their breath away.

"I love you, Eleanor Whitlock; you are my world and have made me feel alive again!"

"I love you too, August," she replied coyly, feeling her cheeks overheat.

They sat in the same concealed alcove as they'd done over two years ago, but this time the roaring fire and the low burning lanterns created a cosy, romantic ambience. Hardly taking his eyes off Eleanor, August requested the same order as they'd had on their first visit, though both of them were neither hungry nor thirsty on this occasion.

"I feel as though you've been with me for every second of every day since the moment I first met you!" declared August, as he reached out to place his hand on top of hers. She felt a warm tingle pulsating through her body and yearned to be in his embrace again.

"I should have asked you where you lived, back then. I have never once ceased thinking of you and waiting for you, August Miller and I have found myself in some very dark and gloomy places, where at times I thought I would never even live to share this moment in time with you!"

"We will never be parted like that again, my beautiful Eleanor, I promise you and our hearts will beat as one until the stars fade away!"

Eleanor relished in his sweetly worded sentiments, knowing that they came with sincerity, straight from his heart.

She smiled affectionately at him, wishing for time to stand still while she was in his company. As though he had read her very thoughts, he uttered, seriously, "I have no idea how I will be able to say goodbye to you when this day comes to an end, but I suppose I will have to become accustomed to torture until you agree in becoming my wife."

The suddenness of his marriage proposal rendered Eleanor speechless; she had never expected it on their first encounter.

"Forgive me my sweet Eleanor, but being a *pensmith*, sometimes causes my heart to speak out loud! I wish not to pressure you into anything impulsive, but there you have it; I want to marry you, Eleanor Whitlock. I want to wake up every morning and look at your beautiful face upon the pillow next to mine and I want to grow old and grey whilst your hand is in mine! You must expect an official and more romantic proposal of marriage in due course, but I just needed to let you know how seriously I feel about you!"

"Nothing could be more romantic than your spontaneous heartfelt words; you have lifted my spirits so high that they have reached the stars, *Mr Penpusher!*"

They both laughed, as they remembered the small dispute they'd had about August's title.

"Well, Miss Whitlock, I hope your spirits will soon fall from the stars because I couldn't possibly spend my life with a maiden who has lost her spirits!"

The refreshments were slowly consumed as Eleanor recalled the many events which had taken place in her life over the past years, shocking August many times and engulfing his heart with sadness. The news of her position as governess to Master Charles Hyde impressed him, he could sense that she had, at last, found some real happiness in her sorrowful life and had a good and sincere friend in Tilly, who she spoke of with such affection.

The terrible plight of her mother would always cause a searing pain in her heart, but August hoped that with time the painful memory and tragic loss would become a little easier for her to bear, especially when he took her on his planned surprise journey to East Hanwell so she could be united with her grandmother, who he'd not and didn't intend mentioning to her just yet. August spoke about the success of his book, delighted to hear that it had reached its one and only intended audience. He also gave a brief account of Eleanor's half-sister, but since he'd concluded quite a low opinion of her didn't wish to elaborate too much, merely describing her as *'pleasant enough'*. Eleanor was shocked to hear how her father's other family had also fallen into the ugly void of poverty, although without wanting to feel too spiteful felt she would have been annoyed if they were wealthy and living a life of luxury. Strangely though, she still felt no urgency to come face to face with Rayne Jackson.

As the afternoon, all too quickly, merged into early evening and they had outstayed their welcome in the warmth of the Copper Kettle,

August accompanied Eleanor back to Paradise Street. With her arm linked through his, they both clandestinely wished the walk could last for hours. A raw wind was increasing, bringing small splatterings of sleet and rain but neither of them were undeterred by the weather as their love burnt like a warm glowing flame in their hearts.

"This is a lovely house, Eleanor, it comforts me and eases my mind that you've found such a kind family and loyal friends to live with."

"Yes, I have indeed been blessed. Why don't you come in, I know everyone will be more than delighted to meet you, at long last, especially poor Tilly who has had to put up with me fretting about you since the day I entered the workhouse!"

August shuddered,

"What is it? What's wrong?"

"It's the harrowing thought of you suffering so much in that workhouse; I should have been more thorough in my search for you...I feel so guilty and I will spend my life making it up to you, my sweet, darling!"

Nothing could prevent them from locking into each other's arms as Eleanor turned to face him and set his mind at rest.

"You have nothing to be guilty about, August Miller, what happened was meant to be and it will make us stronger for our new life together! I love you and we are together, at long last, and that is all that matters!"

"I love you too my beautiful, Eleanor."

As they stood in the chilling February wind, Eleanor felt the warmest glow burning from within her; she knew for certain that from this day forth, August Miller would be included in her life; she felt truly happy and had a powerful sense that her real-life was only just beginning and the dark memories from the past were soon to be submerged forever.

Eleanor stepped over the threshold still feeling as though she was floating on a cloud. August had declined to join her since he had to collect Duke from the High Street stables and wanted to return home before the weather worsened, but he'd arranged to collect Eleanor on Sunday afternoon and take her to East Hanwell to meet his mother and give her the surprise which he'd bitten his tongue copious times throughout the afternoon to keep secret. Winifred and Prudence were both under the impression that the letter, which August had received, was from a book publisher who wished to meet him in private on Sunday. He would tell his mother as soon as he found a moment alone with her, but wished to keep the surprise about Eleanor from Prudence until they came face to face. The only obstacle which might prove disruptive to his plan was the weather, which was already making him nervous as old Duke plodded along unhappily in the chilling wind.

Eleanor was bombarded with a barrage of questions from everyone the minute she walked into the house; even Rosa had popped in on her day off, claiming that she'd not sleep a wink until she'd heard the good news about the long-awaited meeting, which she'd deemed to be the romance of the decade. Mrs Hyde had declared how Eleanor was a changed girl, due to her beau. The worry which she always detected Eleanor had carried around with her, had been miraculously lifted. August had removed the worries and stress from Eleanor, leaving her as light as feather, swirling in the summer breeze. With tears in her eyes, Tilly hugged her dearest friend and Eleanor reassured her that whatever the future was about to deliver, nothing would change the unconditional vow which they'd made and they would remain as sisters forever. The only long face in the Hyde's household was that of young Charles, who had been furtively hoping that Eleanor would not even meet her long lost beau, let alone return home so elated. He couldn't bear the thought of losing the best governess he'd ever had. He loved Eleanor, almost as much as he loved his mamma, although he had kept his feelings close to his heart, but would now have to nag and convince his mamma to do everything in her power to keep Eleanor from marrying, August Miller so that she wouldn't leave. As he sat sulking in the corner of the room, Eleanor was the only one to notice how withdrawn he'd become. As the evening drew to an end and Mr Hyde escorted Rosa home and Tilly was busy tidying the kitchen while Mrs Hyde was settling Felicity down for the night, Eleanor sat next to Charles,

"Why the long face, Master Charles?" she questioned as she stroked his overhanging curls from out of his eyes.

Charles rested his chin in his hand, looking downcast at the ground and refusing to make eye contact with Eleanor. She tickled his sides with both hands, but he just wriggled annoyingly.

"Oh Charles, who has upset you, my sweet boy?"

There was a long silence before he finally found his tongue, "*You have!* You're going to marry Mr Miller and leave and..." He burst into tears as he wrapped his arms tightly around Eleanor's neck. "Please don't leave, Miss Ellie, I don't want another governess, I only want you…please don't marry Mr Miller. Can't you wait until I'm twelve and have gone to study at Winchester College!"

"*My goodness!*" exclaimed Eleanor. "You *are* thinking ahead! What if I promise not to do anything to upset you? Will you be happy with that? And I won't be getting married for a while, you know and even when I do become Mrs Miller, I might *still* be your governess. Who knows, by then, you might be *wishing* for a new one!"

"No, I won't! I would never wish for any other governess! *Never!"*

"Well, in that case, I will do everything in my power to continue to be your governess, Master Charles!"

"So you're not getting married on Sunday, then?"

Eleanor burst into laughter, realising how Charles had been listening in on the conversation and completely muddled what he'd heard.

"Certainly not! Oh, Charles, I hope that one day I have a son who's just as sweet and loving as you! Now, how about a quiet duet before bedtime?"

"Oh yes please, can we play that new one, the Chop Waltz?"

"We can indeed; that jolly tune will be sure to put a smile on your sour little face before bedtime!"

CHAPTER FORTY-TWO

Sunday seemed to take a month to arrive, with both August and Eleanor living the few days with their heads immersed in dreamy clouds. The weather had been considerate and Sunday morning began cold but sunny with a promising blue sky. Once again, Eleanor's wardrobe had been turned upside down as she changed her mind time and time again in a bid to satisfy her eye when she looked into the looking glass. Not only did she want to impress August, but she wanted a suitable outfit which would give off all the right signals to his mother. By how August had spoken of her, Eleanor sensed that she was a typical, old fashioned countrywoman, wishing for her son to marry a hamlet girl and considering any young woman from the City to be flighty and too demanding to bring her son any long-lasting happiness.

"I'm not sure if I enjoy watching you try on every item of clothing twice or detest it!" Tilly joked, as she sat on her bed offering her opinion.

"Oh, Tilly, I'm really not sure what pleases the older, hamlet generation, especially when it is to be your future mother in law...I don't want anything to go wrong today. I must make a good impression on Mrs Miller, they do say that it's the first impressions which count!"

"Mrs Miller will be so taken by your innocent

sweetness, that whatever you wear won't make a ha'penny's difference. Don't get yourself into such a nervous state, Ellie, just enjoy the day as it comes. I suppose every mother in the world is entitled to be a little picky when she's inspecting her future daughter in law!"

"*Tilly!* That's not funny, you're just making this knot in my belly tighten even more!" she stressed, playfully throwing a lace glove at Tilly.

"That's because you insisted I tied your corset up so painfully tight! You're more likely to pass out at Mrs Miller's feet at this rate and she'll think you're a feeble sort!"

Half dressed, Eleanor threw herself down onto her bed with a huge sigh, "I give up, Tilly...I'm exhausted from all this changing ...*you* choose me a suitable outfit!"

"Only if you promise to wear it and not change your mind again!"

There was a light knock on their bedroom door, "May I come in?"

"Of course you can, Rosa!" they replied in harmony, surprised that she was even present on her day off.

Rosa stood with a wide smile stretched across her attractive face, "Look, I have the perfect winter dress for you to wear this afternoon, I suddenly remembered making it last year, but I didn't like the colour next to my skin, it makes me look jaundice! You are welcome to have it, Ellie, it will suit your fair complexion perfectly!"

Eleanor leapt up from her bed, "Oh Rosa! It's beautiful, I love this shade!" In her sheer delight, she wrapped her arms around Rosa and kissed her cheek. "You went out of your way on your day off to bring me such a beautiful, duck egg dress! How can I ever thank you enough!"

Rosa couldn't stop smiling, she loved Eleanor and after witnessing how in love she was with August, it reminded her of herself, many years ago, and she wished for everything in Eleanor's path to run smoothly.

"Thank you Rosa!" cried Tilly, "You've saved me from a morning of torture!"

As laughter filled the untidy bedroom, Eleanor tried on the woollen dress which fitted like a glove and gave her sapphire, blue eyes a tinge of duck egg to them. There was also a matching jacket, smartly trimmed with black satin.

"You are a *skilled* seamstress to have made such a beautiful garment, Rosa!" gasped Eleanor as she twirled in front of the looking glass, thrilled with her reflection. Both Rosa and Tilly were in full agreement of how striking Eleanor looked.

"Oh, my goodness! Just look at the time! August will be waiting for me very soon...Oh, Tilly..."

"Don't worry, I know, You don't have time to hang up the dozen gowns strewn across the room...It will be my pleasure and I'm looking forward to a relaxing afternoon, so hurry along, my dear sister and enjoy your day!"

Eleanor planted a loving kiss on Tilly's cheek

and another on Rosa's, "Oh I'm such a fortunate girl to have such lovely sisters!" she declared, before pulling on her boots and racing down the stairs like a whirlwind on a calm day.

Seated up high upon the old and battered horse cart, Eleanor felt her heart skipping beats from the moment her eyes caught sight of him. Dressed in a warm, light brown suit, he had a fine, strong-looking figure and Eleanor just yearned to be in his arms again. August was mesmerized as he watched her walking towards him, so much so that he left it until the last minute before jumping down from the cart to greet her.

"Oh my sweet Eleanor, you look more beautiful than ever...I have missed you so much and thought of nothing other than this day since I was last by your side!" Although the streets were busy with afternoon strollers, there was no power in the world which could prevent August from briefly taking her into his embrace.

Ten minutes later they had left the City behind them and were surrounded by the barren, winter countryside. Earthy fields neatly divided by brown hedges and dry stone walls. Huge skeletal trees loomed on the horizon and sweet-smelling smoke wafted from the chimneys of isolated farmhouses and cottages. Duke seemed to know his way along the narrow track, allowing August and Eleanor to chat nonstop throughout the journey. Eleanor knew it was partly her nerves which were making her so talkative, even the cold air had failed to keep her hands free from a nervous sweat. They spoke a lot about Mrs Miller, with August reassuring Eleanor that she had nothing to be nervous about. He told her repeatedly, though, that there was a surprise waiting for her in East Hanwell, which was setting Eleanor's nerves on edge even more. As they turned around a tight bend, about fifty minutes into the journey, a small gathering of cottages came into sight and could be viewed from over the hedge as they rode past.

"That's East Hanwell!" announced August.

Eleanor stretched her neck and slightly lifted her body from off the cart's seat. Smoke was coming from every chimney and a few children could be seen playing outside. Her eyes suddenly caught sight of the remains of Prudence's burnt out cottage which instantly returned the upsetting memories of the garden shed fire.

"I hope nobody was injured in the fire!" she spontaneously declared. It was not the response August was expecting, but then he was used to seeing the sorry sight every time he arrived at the hamlet and had forgotten how it stuck out like a sore thumb against the pretty clump of thatched dwellings.

Duke carried on past the hamlet, leaving Eleanor staring over her shoulder.

"I'm afraid Duke and the wagon won't squeeze through the gap in the hedge, so we'll have to go as far as the opening up ahead and return on t'other side!" he explained. "And nobody was hurt in the fire, thank The Lord. There was only one, very sweet old woman who lived there and it was, in fact, me who rescued her!"

"*August Miller!* An author and a valiant hero too!"

"Hmm, I have since been named '*the hero*', which I continue to point out to all that I am not! I merely did what came naturally and acted on impulse to rescue my neighbour!"

"Well, I am proud of you August, many a selfish man would have turned his back and left the task to another. What happened to the poor old woman...I hope she has family living in the hamlet...it must have been awful for her and I can speak from experience at being trapped in a burning home, although I suppose a shed doesn't actually categorise as a home!"

"A fire is a fire, no matter if you live in a castle or a wooden pen; the thick blinding smoke and the ferocious heat are always just as deadly!" expressed August, passionately, as Duke took the bend widely, leading them into the heart of East Hanwell.

"You will meet the sweet old dear very soon, Eleanor, because she's been living with us since she lost her home!"

"Oh, dear! I hope that doesn't mean I'm to be

inspected by two older women now! Was that the surprise, by any chance?" she said, jokingly. August appeared very serious all of a sudden as he helped her down from the cart. He kept hold of her hands longer than was needed for her safe footing and looked into her eyes, sending a, now familiar, tingle through her body, "Yes, my sweet darling, that *is* the surprise! Now, are you ready? I dare say my ma has boiled the water five times by now!"

A Robin suddenly flew down and perched on the wagon just a couple of feet from Eleanor, he tilted his head and chirped, "Oh, look, August, he's flown down to wish me good luck!"

"No! He's flown down to tell you that you have nothing to worry about!"

The tiny cottage parlour seemed suddenly overcrowded as they stepped over the threshold. Both Winifred and Prudence were stood to attention, prompting August into giving them a peculiar look.

"*At ease ladies, at ease,*" teased August, "Eleanor is no different from a hamlet girl and you wouldn't stand like a couple of regimental captains if one of them was to call on you!"

Eleanor smiled warmly at them, already knowing that the younger-looking of the two was Mrs Miller.

"I can't tell you how it warms my heart to meet you, at last, Miss Whitlock!" expressed Winifred.

"As it warms my heart too, Mrs Miller, but please, call me Eleanor or Ellie if you prefer; my friends call me Ellie, they insist it rolls off the tongue easier!"

Before there was a chance for Winifred to continue the conversation, Prudence suddenly hastened towards, Eleanor; her spontaneous reaction not completely shocking Winifred and August as they held their breath and watched with intrigue.

"*Eleanor...my darling, Eleanor...*" Prudence wrapped her arms around Eleanor as her tears dampened her wrinkled face. Taken by surprise, Eleanor presumed that the old woman, who August had rescued from the burning cottage, was not quite in control of her wits; she returned the embrace, feeling sorry for her.

"Nearly two decades I've waited for this moment; eighteen years ago, I held you in my arms...you are the image of my Beatrice, as beautiful as a summer meadow!"

Eleanor took a step back, the reality of the old women's words suddenly making sense.

"*Grandmamma?* Oh my goodness! Grandmamma! Is it really you?"

As she stared hard into her face, Eleanor *could* detect a slight similarity to her late mother. The reality of the surprise overwhelmed her, she felt light-headed as the tiny warm room spun around before her eyes and the women's voices became muffled. August rushed to catch her in his arms and escort her to the settle while Winifred quickly poured the tea!"

"Isn't that uncanny!" stated Prudence, "that's the exact effect it had on me when I heard the news that Beatrice had born her!"

From then on the afternoon passed by too fast. Amazed by how quickly Eleanor appeared so at home in the cosy cottage as she chatted with Winifred and Prudence, August was quite content to sit back and take in the comforting scene. It warmed August's heart to witness the instant bond between Eleanor and her grandmother. After all that Eleanor had been through, the picture unravelling before his eyes was that of a united and loving family and he knew that he was to be part of Eleanor's life for the rest of his days. It took less than the time it took to drink a cup of tea, for Winifred to understand why her son was so in love with the beautiful and warm-hearted Eleanor and it looked as though she would be a most prominent figure in their lives from this day forth.

Eleanor's entire body was buzzing with excitement as she and August made the journey back into Oxford; she snuggled up close to him as the cold evening air descended. A vibrant sunset of deep plum, pink and ginger illumination the vast horizon and as Eleanor looked up at August's handsome face she couldn't stop herself from placing a hurried kiss upon his cheek.

"I'm so happy, August! *So happy*...I just pray that it will last!"

August pulled on the reins, bringing Duke to a standstill as he turned to face Eleanor, his expression serious,

"Of course it will last, my love, why wouldn't it? We have found each other now *and* you have been united with your grandmother, who clearly loves you. Marry me my beautiful Eleanor, I love you so much, be safe in my arms forever...what's there to wait for?"

As their lips met and they held each other, closely, both wishing for the moment to last forever, Eleanor knew that there was nothing in the world she wished for more, than to become August's wife.

****

Printed in Great Britain
by Amazon